DELTA WEDDING

By Eudora Welty

A Curtain of Green and Other Stories
The Robber Bridegroom
The Wide Net and Other Stories
Delta Wedding
The Golden Apples
The Ponder Heart
The Bride of the Innisfallen and Other Stories
Thirteen Stories
Losing Battles
One Time, One Place
The Optimist's Daughter
The Eye of the Story: Selected Essays and Reviews
The Collected Stories of Eudora Welty
Selected Stories
One Writer's Beginnings
Photographs

DELTA WEDDING

EUDORA WELTY

A HARVEST BOOK
HARCOURT BRACE & COMPANY
San Diego New York London

Library of Congress Cataloging-in-Publication Data
Welty, Eudora, 1909–
Delta wedding: a novel/by Eudora Welty.
p. cm.
ISBN 0-15-124774-9
ISBN 0-15-625280-5 (pbk.)
I. Title. II. Series.
PS3545.E6D4 1991
813'.52—dc20 90-22030

Printed in the United States of America
L M N O P Q

To
John Robinson

DELTA WEDDING

I

The nickname of the train was the Yellow Dog. Its real name was the Yazoo-Delta. It was a mixed train. The day was the 10th of September, 1923—afternoon. Laura McRaven, who was nine years old, was on her first journey alone. She was going up from Jackson to visit her mother's people, the Fairchilds, at their plantation named Shellmound, at Fairchilds, Mississippi. When she got there, "Poor Laura little motherless girl," they would all run out and say, for her mother had died in the winter and they had not seen Laura since the funeral. Her father had come as far as Yazoo City with her and put her on the Dog. Her cousin Dabney Fairchild, who was seventeen, was going to be married, but Laura could not be in the wedding for the reason that her mother was dead. Of these facts the one most persistent in Laura's mind was the most intimate one: that her age was nine.

In the passenger car every window was propped open with a stick of kindling wood. A breeze blew through, hot and then cool, fragrant of the woods and yellow flowers and of the train. The yellow butterflies flew in at any window, out at any other, and outdoors one of them could keep up with the train, which then seemed to be racing with a butterfly. Overhead a black lamp in which a circle of flowers had been cut out swung round and round on a chain as the car rocked from side to side, sending down dainty drifts of kerosene smell. The Dog was almost sure to reach Fairchilds before the lamp would be lighted by Mr. Terry Black, the conductor, who had promised her father to watch out for her. Laura had the seat facing the stove, but of course no fire was burning in it now. She sat leaning at the window, the light and the sooty air trying to make her close her eyes. Her ticket to Fairchilds was stuck up in her Madge Evans straw hat, in imitation of the drummer across the aisle. Once the Dog stopped in the open fields and Laura saw the engineer, Mr. Doolittle, go out and pick some specially fine goldenrod there—for whom, she could not know. Then the long September cry rang from the thousand unseen locusts, urgent at the open windows of the train.

Then at one place a white foxy farm dog ran beside the Yellow Dog for a distance just under Laura's window, barking sharply, and then they left him behind, or he turned back. And then, as if a hand reached along the green ridge and all of a sudden pulled down with a sweep, like a scoop in the bin, the hill and every tree in the world and left cotton fields, the Delta began. The drummer with a groan sank into sleep. Mr. Terry Black walked by and took the tickets out of their hats. Laura brought up her saved banana, peeled it down, and bit into it.

Thoughts went out of her head and the landscape filled it. In the Delta, most of the world seemed sky. The clouds were large—larger than horses or houses, larger than boats or churches or gins, larger than anything except the fields the Fairchilds planted. Her nose in the banana skin as in the cup of a lily, she watched the Delta. The land was perfectly flat and level but it shimmered like the wing of a lighted dragonfly. It seemed strummed, as though it were an instrument and something had touched it. Sometimes in the cotton were trees with one, two, or three arms—she could draw better trees than those were. Sometimes like a fuzzy caterpillar looking in the cotton was a winding line of thick green willows and cypresses, and when the train crossed this green, running on a loud iron bridge, down its center like a golden mark on the caterpillar's back would be a bayou.

When the day lengthened, a rosy light lay over the cotton. Laura stretched her arm out the window and let the soot sprinkle it. There went a black mule—in the diamond light of far distance, going into the light, a child drove a black mule home, and all behind, the hidden track through the fields was marked by the lifted fading train of dust. The Delta buzzards, that seemed to wheel as wide and high as the sun, with evening were going down too, settling into far-away violet tree stumps for the night.

In the Delta the sunsets were reddest light. The sun went down lopsided and wide as a rose on a stem in the west, and the west was a milk-white edge, like the foam of the sea. The sky, the field, the little track, and the bayou, over and over—all that had been bright or dark was now one color. From the warm window sill the endless fields glowed like a hearth in firelight, and Laura, looking out, leaning on her elbows with her head between her hands, felt what an arriver in a land feels—that slow hard pounding in the breast.

"Fairchilds, Fairchilds!"

Mr. Terry Black lifted down the suitcase Laura's father had put up in the rack. The Dog ran through an iron bridge over James's Bayou, and past a long twilighted gin, its tin side looking first like a blue lake, and a platform where cotton bales were so close they seemed to lean out to the train. Behind it, dark gold and shadowy, was the river, the Yazoo. They came to the station, the dark-yellow color of goldenrod, and stopped. Through the windows Laura could see five or six cousins at once, all jumping up and down at different moments. Each mane of light hair waved like a holiday banner, so that you could see the Fairchilds everywhere, even with everybody meeting the train and asking Mr. Terry how he had been since the day before. When Mr. Terry set her on the little iron steps, holding her square doll's suitcase (in which her doll Marmion was horizontally suspended), and gave her a spank, she staggered, and was lifted down among flying arms to the earth.

"Kiss Bluet!" The baby was put in her face.

She was kissed and laughed at and her hat would have been snatched away but for the new elastic that pulled it back, and then she was half-carried along like a drunken reveler at a festival, not quite recognizing who anyone was. India hadn't come—"We couldn't find her"—and Dabney hadn't come, she was going to be married. They piled her into the Studebaker, into the little folding seat, with Ranny reaching sections of an orange into her mouth from where he stood behind her. Where were her suitcases? They drove rattling across the Yazoo bridge and whirled through the shady, river-smelling street where the town, Fairchild's Store and all, looked like a row of dark barns, while the boys sang "Abdul the Bulbul Amir" or shouted "Let Bluet drive!" and the baby was handed over Laura's head and stood between Orrin's knees, proudly. Orrin was fourteen—a wonderful driver. They went up and down the street three times, backing into cotton fields to turn around, before they went across the bridge again, homeward.

"That's to Marmion," said Orrin to Laura kindly. He waved at an old track that did not cross the river but followed it, two purple ruts in the strip of wood shadow.

"Marmion's my dolly," she said.

"It's not, it's where I was born," said Orrin.

There was no use in Laura and Orrin talking any more about what anything was. On this side of the river were the gin and compress, the railroad track, the forest-filled cemetery where her mother was buried in the Fairchild lot, the Old Methodist Church with the steamboat bell glinting pink in the light, and Brunswicktown where the Negroes were, smoking now on every doorstep. Then the car traveled in its cloud of dust like a blind being through the fields one after the other, like all one field but Laura knew they had names—the Mound Field, and Moon Field after Moon Lake. When they were as far as the overseer's house, Laura saw all the cousins lean out and spit, and she did too.

"I thought you all liked Mr. Bascom," she said, after they got by.

"It's not Mr. Bascom now, crazy," they said. "Is it, Bluet? Not Mr. Bascom now."

Then the car crossed the little bayou bridge, whose rackety rhythm she remembered, and there was Shellmound.

Facing James's Bayou, back under the planted pecan grove, it was gently glowing in the late summer light, the brightest thing in the evening—the tall, white, wide frame house with a porch all around, its bayed tower on one side, its tinted windows open and its curtains stirring, and even from here plainly to be heard a song coming out of the music room, played on the piano by a stranger to Laura. They curved in at the gate. All the way up the drive the boy cousins with a shout would jump and spill out, and pick up a ball from the ground and throw it, rocketlike. By the carriage block in front of the house Laura was pulled out of the car and held by the hand. Shelley had hold of her—the oldest girl. Laura did not know if she had been in the car with her or not. Shelley had her hair still done up long, parted in the middle, and a ribbon around it low across her brow and knotted behind, like a chariot racer. She wore a fountain pen on a chain now, and had her initials done in runny ink on her tennis shoes, over the ankle bones. Inside the house, the "piece" all at once ended.

"Shelley!" somebody called, imploringly.

"Dabney is an example of madness on earth," said Shelley now, and then she ran off, trailed by Bluet beating plaintively on a drum found in the grass, with a little stick. The boys were scattered like magic. Laura was deserted.

Grass softly touched her legs and her garter rosettes, growing sweet and springy for this was the country. On the narrow little walk along the front of the house, hung over with closing lemon lilies, there was a quieting and vanishing of sound. It was not yet dark. The sky was the color of violets, and the snow-white moon in the sky had not yet begun to shine. Where it hung above the water tank, back of the house, the swallows were circling busy as the spinning of a top. By the flaky front steps a thrush was singing waterlike notes from the sweet-olive tree, which was in flower; it was not too dark to see the breast of the thrush or the little white blooms either. Laura remembered everything, with the fragrance and the song. She looked up the steps through the porch, where there was a wooden scroll on the screen door that her finger knew how to trace, and lifted her eyes to an old fanlight, now reflecting a skyey light as of a past summer, that she had been dared—oh, by Maureen!—to throw a stone through, and had not.

She dropped her suitcase in the grass and ran to the back yard and jumped up with two of the boys on the joggling board. In between Roy and Little Battle she jumped, and the delights of anticipation seemed to shake her up and down.

She remembered (as one remembers first the eyes of a loved person) the old blue water cooler on the back porch—how thirsty she always was here!—among the round and square wooden tables always piled with snap beans, turnip greens, and onions from the day's trip to Greenwood; and while you drank your eyes were on this green place here in the back yard, the joggling board, the neglected greenhouse, Aunt Ellen's guineas in the old buggy, the stable wall elbow-deep in a vine. And in the parlor she knew was a clover-shaped footstool covered with rose velvet where she would sit, and sliding doors to the music room that she could open and shut. In the halls would be the rising smell of girls' fudge cooking, the sound of the phone by the roll-top desk going unanswered. She could remember mostly the dining room, the paintings by Great-Aunt Mashula that was dead, of full-blown yellow roses and a watermelon split to the heart by a jackknife, and every ornamental plate around the rail different because painted by a different aunt at a different time; the big table never quite cleared; the innumerable packs of old, old playing cards. She could remember India's paper dolls coming out flatter from the law books than hers from a shoe box, and smelling as if they were scorched from it. She remembered the Negroes, Bitsy, Roxie, Little Uncle, and Vi'let. She put out her arms like wings and knew in her fingers the thready pattern of red roses in the carpet on the stairs, and she could hear the high-pitched calls and answers going up the stairs and down. She thought of the upstairs hall where it was twilight all the time from the green shadow of an awning, and where an old lopsided baseball lay all summer in a silver dish on the lid of the paper-crammed plantation desk, and how away at either end of the hall was a balcony and the little square butterflies that flew so high were going by, and the June bugs knocking. She remembered the sleeping porches full of late sleepers, some strangers to her always among them when India led her through and showed them to her. She remembered well the cotton lint on ceilings and lampshades, fresh every morning like a present from the fairies, that made Vi'let moan.

Little Battle crowded her a little as he jumped, and she had to move down the board a few inches. They could play an endless game of hide-and-seek in so many rooms and up and down the halls that intersected and turned into dead-end porches and rooms full of wax begonias and elephant's-ears, or rooms full of trunks. She remembered the nights—the moon vine, the ever-blooming Cape jessamines, the verbena smelling under running feet, the lateness of dancers. A dizziness rose in Laura's head, and Roy crowded her now, but she jumped on, keeping in with their rhythm. She remembered life in the undeterminate number of other rooms going on around her and India, where they lay in bed—life not stopping for a moment in deference to children going to sleep, but filling with later and later laughter, with Uncle Battle reciting "Break! Break! Break!," the phone ringing its two longs and a short for the Fairchilds, Aunt Mac reading the Bible aloud (was she dead yet?), the visiting planters arguing with Uncle Battle and her other uncle, Uncle George, from dining room to library to porch, Aunt Ellen slipping by in the hall looking for something or someone, the distant silvery creak of the porch swing by night, like a frog's voice. There would be little Ranny crying out in his dream, and the winding of the Victrola and then a song called "I Wish I Could Shimmy like my Sister Kate" or Uncle Pinck's favorite (where was he?), Sir Harry Lauder singing "Stop Yer Ticklin', Jock." The girls that were old enough, dressed in colors called jade and flamingo, danced with each other around the dining-room table until the boys came to get them, and could be watched from the upper landing cavorting below, like marvelous mermaids down a transparent sea.

In bed Laura and India would slap mosquitoes and tell each other things. Last summer India had told Laura the showboat that came on the high water and the same old Rabbit's Foot Minstrel as always, and Laura told India "Babes in the Wood," Thurston the Magician, Annette Kellerman in "Daughter of the Gods," and Clara Kimball Young in "Drums of Jeopardy," and if Laura went off to sleep, India would choke her. She remembered the baying of the dogs at night; and how Roy believed when you heard dogs bay, a convict had got out of Parchman and they were after him in the swamp; every night of the world the dogs would bay, and Roy would lie somewhere in the house shaking in his bed.

Just then, with a last move down the joggling board, Roy edged Laura off. She ran back to the steps and picked up her suitcase again. Then her heart pounded: India came abruptly around the house, bathed and dressed, busily watering the verbena in the flower bed out of a doll's cream pitcher, one drop to each plant. India too was nine. Her hair was all spun out down her back, and she had a blue ribbon in it; Laura touched her own Buster Brown hair, tangled now beyond anyone's help. Their white dresses (Laura's in the suitcase, folded by her father, and for a man to fold anything suddenly nearly killed her) were still identical, India had blue insertion run in the waist now and Laura had white, but the same little interlocking three hoops were briar-stitched in the yokes, and their identical gold lockets still banged there against their chests.

"My mother is dead!" said Laura.

India looked around at her, and said "Greenie!"

Laura took a step back.

"We never did unjoin," said India. "Greenie!"

"All right," Laura said. "Owe you something." She stooped and put a pinch of grass in her shoe.

"You have to wash now," said India. She added, looking in her pitcher, "Here's you a drop of water."

All of a sudden Maureen ran out from under the pecan trees—the cousin who was funny in her head, though it was not her fault. Besides her own fine clothes, she got India's dresses that she wanted and India's ribbons, and India said she would get them till she died. She had never talked plain; every word was two words to her and had an "l" in it. Now she ran in front of Laura and straddled the walk at the foot of the steps. She danced from side to side with her arms spread, chanting, "Coulin Lau-la can-na get-la by-y!" She was nine too.

Roy and Little Battle ran up blandly as if they had never let Laura joggle with them at all, giving no recognition. Orrin walked tall as a man up from the bayou with a live fish he must have just caught, jumping on a string. He waved it at little Ranny, who at that moment rode out the front door and down the steps standing on the back of his tricycle, like Ben Hur, a towel tied around his neck and flying behind him. The dinner bell was ringing inside, over and over, the way Roxie rang—like an insistence against disbelief. Laura, avoiding sight of the fish, avoiding India's little drop, and Ranny and Maureen, made her way up the steps. Just as she reached the top, she threw up. There she waited, like a little dog.

But Aunt Ellen, though she was late for everything, was now running out the screen door with open arms. She was the mother of them all. Something fell behind her, her apron, as she came, and she was as breathless as any of her children. Now she knelt and held Laura very firmly. "Laura—poor little motherless girl," she said. When Laura lifted her head, she kissed her. She sent India for a wringing-wet cloth.

Laura put her head on Aunt Ellen's shoulder and sank her teeth in the thick Irish lace on the collar of her white voile dress which smelled like sweet peas. She hugged her, and touched her forehead, the steady head held so near to hers with its flying soft hair and its erect bearing of gentle, explicit, but unfathomed alarm. With the cool on her face, she could see clearer and clearer, though it was almost dark now, the pearl-edged side comb so hazardously bringing up the strands of Aunt Ellen's dark hair. She let her go, and if she could she would have smoothed and patted her aunt's hair and cleared the part with her own fingers, and said, "Aunt Ellen, *you* must never mind!" But of course she couldn't.

Then she jumped up and ran after Orrin into the house, beating India to the table.

"Where's Uncle George?" Laura asked, looking from Uncle Battle around to everybody at the long, broad table. At suppertime, since she had come, she was expecting to see everybody gathered; but Uncle George and his wife, Aunt Robbie, would not drive in from Memphis until tomorrow; Aunt Tempe and her husband Uncle Pinck Summers and their daughter Mary Denis's little girl, Lady Clare Buchanan, were not driving over from Inverness until Mary Denis had her baby; and the two aunts from the Grove, Aunt Primrose and Aunt Jim Allen, had not come up to supper tonight. There was just Uncle Battle's and Aunt Ellen's family of children at the table—besides of course the two great-aunts, Great-Aunt Shannon and Great-Aunt Mac, and Cousin

Maureen who lived here with them, and only one visitor, Dabney's best friend, Mary Lamar Mackey of Lookback Plantation—it was she who played the piano.

"Skeeta! Next!" called Uncle Battle resoundingly, fixing his eye on Laura. She passed her plate up to him. Uncle Battle, her mother's brother, with his corrugated brow, his planter's boots creaking under the table when he stood to carve the turkeys, was so tremendous that he always called children "Skeeta." His thick fair hair over his bulging brow had been combed with water before he came to the table, exactly like Orrin's, Roy's, Little Battle's, and Ranny's. As his eye roved over them, Laura remembered that he had broken every child at the table now from being left-handed. Laura was ever hopeful that she would see Uncle Battle the Fire-eater take up some fire and eat it, and thought it would be some night at supper.

"How Annie Laurie would have loved this very plate!" Uncle Battle said softly just now, holding up Laura's serving. "Breast, gizzard, and wing! Pass it, boy."

Even cutting up the turkeys at the head of his table, he was a rushing, mysterious, very laughing man to have had so many children coming up busy too, and he could put on a tender, irresponsible air, as if he were asking ladies and little girls, "Look at me! What can I do? Such a thing it all is!", and he meant Life—although he could also mention death and people's absence in an ordinary way. It was his habit to drive quickly off from the house at any time of the day or night—in a buggy or a car now. Automobiles had come in just as Uncle Battle got too heavy to ride his horse. He rode out to see work done or "trouble" helped; sometimes "trouble" came at night. When Negroes clear to Greenwood cut each other up, it was well known that it took Uncle Battle to protect them from the sheriff or prevail on a bad one to come out and surrender.

"Now eat it all!" Uncle Battle called to her as the plate reached her. But it was a joke, his giving her the gizzard, she saw, for it was her mother that loved it and she could not stand that piece of turkey. She did not dare tell him what he knew.

"Where is Dabney?" she asked, for it was Dabney they had been talking about ever since they sat down to the table, and her place by her father was empty.

"She'll be down directly," said Aunt Ellen. "She's going to be married, you know, Laura."

"Tonight?" asked Laura.

"Oh!" groaned Uncle Battle. "Oh! Oh!" He always groaned three times.

"Where is her husband now?" Laura asked.

"Now don't, Battle," said Aunt Ellen anxiously. "Laura naturally wants to know how soon Dabney will marry Troy. Not till Saturday, dear."

"This is only Monday," Laura told her uncle consolingly.

"Oh, Papa's really *proud* of Dabney, no matter how he groans, because she won't wait till cotton picking's over," said Shelley. She was sitting beside Laura, and looked so seriously even at her, that the black grosgrain ribbon crossing her forehead almost indented it.

"I am, am I?" said Battle. "Suppose you help your mother serve the pickled peaches at your end."

When Laura looked at her plate, the gizzard was gone. She almost jumped to her feet—she almost cried to think of all that had happened to her. Next she was afraid she had eaten that bite without thinking. But then she saw Great-Aunt Shannon calmly eating the gizzard, on the other side of her. She had stolen it—Great-Aunt Shannon, who would talk conversationally with Uncle Denis and Aunt Rowena and Great-Uncle George, who had all died no telling how long ago, that she thought were at the table with her. But just now, after eating a little bit of something, the gizzard and a biscuit or so—"No more than a bird!" they protested—she was escorted, by Orrin, up to bed without saying a word. Great-Aunt Mac glared after her; Great-Aunt Mac was not dead at all. "Now be ashamed of yourself!" she called after her. "For starving yourself!"

The boys all looked at each other, and even unwillingly, they let smiles break out on their faces. The four boys were all ages—Orrin older than Laura, Roy, Little Battle, and Ranny younger—and constantly seeking one another, even at the table with their eyes, seeking the girls only for their audience when they hadn't one another. They were always rushing, chasing, flying, getting hurt—only eating and the knot of their napkins could keep them in chairs. All their knickerbockers, and Ranny's rompers, had fresh holes for Aunt Ellen in both knees every evening. They ate turkey until they bit their fingers and cried "Ouch!" They were so filled with their energy that once when Laura saw some old map on the wall, with the blowing winds in the corners, mischievous-eyed and round-cheeked, blowing the ships and dolphins around Scotland, Laura had asked her mother if they were India's four brothers. She loved them dearly. It was strange that it was India who had to be Laura's favorite cousin, since she would have given anything if the boy cousins would let her love them most. Of course she expected them to fly from her side like birds, and light on the joggling board, as they had done when she arrived, and to edge her off when she climbed up with them. That changed nothing.

The boys were only like all the Fairchilds, but it was the boys and the men that defined that family always. All the girls knew it. When she looked at the boys and the men Laura was without words but she knew that company like a dream that comes back again and again, each aspect familiar and longing not to be forgotten. Great-Great-Uncle George on his horse, in his portrait in the parlor—the one who had been murdered by the robbers on the Natchez Trace and buried, horse, bridle, himself, and all, on his way to the wilderness to be near Great-Great-Grandfather—even he, she had learned by looking up at him, had the family trait of quick, upturning smiles, instant comprehension of the smallest eddy of life in the current of the day, which would surely be entered in a kind of reckless pleasure. This pleasure either the young men copied from the older ones or the older ones always kept. The grown people, like the children, looked with kindling eyes at all turmoil, expecting delight for themselves and for you. They were shocked only at disappointment.

But boys and men, girls and ladies all, the old and the young of the Delta kin—even the dead and the living, for Aunt Shannon—were alike—no gap opened between them. Laura sat among them with her eyes wide. At any moment she might expose her ignorance—at any moment she might learn everything.

All the Fairchilds in the Delta looked alike—Little Battle, now, pushing his bobbed hair behind his ears before he took up a fresh drumstick, looked exactly like Dabney the way she would think at the window. They all had a fleetness about them, though they were tall, solid people with "Scotch legs"—a neatness that was actually a readiness for gaieties and departures, a distraction that was endearing as a lack of burdens. Laura felt their quality, their being, in the degree that they were portentous to her. For Laura found them all portentous—all except Aunt Ellen, who had only married into the family—Uncle George more than Uncle Battle for some reason, Dabney more than Shelley.

Without a primary beauty, with only a fairness of color (a thin-skinnedness, really) and an ease in the body, they had a demurring, gray-eyed way about them that turned out to be halfway mocking—for these cousins were the sensations of life and they knew it. (Why didn't Uncle George come on tonight—the best loved? Why wasn't Dabney on time to supper—the bride?) Things waited for them to appear, laughing to one another and amazed, in order to happen. They were forever, by luck or intuition, opening doors, discovering things, little or cherished things, running pell-mell down the stairs to meet people, ready to depart for vague and spontaneous occasions. Though everything came to Shellmound to them. All the girls got serenaded in the summertime—though Shelley last summer had said it pained her for Dabney to listen *that way.* They were never too busy for anything, they were generously and almost seriously of the moment: the past (even Laura's arrival today was past now) was a private, dull matter that would be forgotten except by aunts.

Laura from her earliest memory had heard how they "never seemed to change at all." That was the way her mother, who had been away from them down in Jackson where they would be hard to believe, could brag on them without seeming to. And yet Laura could see that they changed every moment. The outside did not change but the inside did; an iridescent life was busy within and under each alikeness. Laughter at something went over the table; Laura found herself with a picture in her mind of a great bowerlike cage full of tropical birds her father had shown her in a zoo in a city—the sparkle of motion was like a rainbow, while it was the very thing that broke your heart, for the birds that flew were caged all the time and could not fly out. The Fairchilds' movements were quick and on the instant, and that made you wonder, are they free? Laura was certain that they were *compelled*—their favorite word. Flying against the bad things happening, they kissed you in rushes of tenderness. Maybe their delight was part of their beauty, its flicker as it went by, and their kissing of not only you but everybody in a room was a kind of spectacle, an outward thing. But when they looked at you with their lighted eyes, picked you out in a room for a glance, waiting for you to say something in admiration or "conceit," to ask the smallest favor, of any of them you chose, and so to commit yourself forever—you could never question them again, you trusted them, that nothing more inward preoccupied them, for you adored them, and only wanted to be here with them, to be let run toward them. They are all as sweet as Ranny, she thought—all sweet right down to Ranny—Ranny being four and the youngest she could see at her end of the table, now angelically asleep in his chair with a little wishbone in his fist.

Just as Roxie was about to clear the table, Dabney

gently but distractedly came in—dressed in blue, drying tears from her eyes, and murmuring to her mother as she passed her chair, "Oh, Mama, *that* was just because my brain isn't working; why did you bring up your children with faulty brains?"

"She ought to have drowned you when you were little," said Uncle Battle, and this was their extravagant way of talk. "Sit down, I saved you a wishbone and a heart besides what poor pickings is left."

"Run some more biscuit in the oven, Roxie," Ellen said. "I think too you'd better bring Miss Dabney a little ham, there's such a dearth of turkey to tempt her."

"Say it again, Mama," said Ranny, opening his eyes. Then he smiled at Dabney.

"What were you crying about—the worry you're bringing down on your father?" Battle said.

Holding out her plate for her father to serve (she sat close by him, at his right), Dabney smiled too, and waited. How beautiful she was—all flushed and knowing. Now they would tease her. An only child, Laura found teasing the thing she kept forgetting about the Delta cousins from one summer to the next. Uncle Battle might put the heart on Dabney's plate yet, knowing she could not bear to look at the heart; though Dabney would know what to do. Was it possible that it was because they loved one another so, that it made them set little traps to catch one another? They looked with shining eyes upon their kin, and all their abundance of love, as if it were a devilment, was made reckless and inspired or was belittled in fun, though never, so far, was it said out. They had never told Laura they loved her.

She sighed. "Where's Aunt Primrose and Aunt Jim Allen?"

"Why don't you ask any questions about who's here?" said India.

"They said I had to come see them and *tell* them first," said Dabney, beginning to eat hungrily. "Touchy, touchy."

"I'm touchy too," said Uncle Battle.

"Oh, *Laura*!" cried Dabney delightedly. "I didn't know you'd got here! Why, honey!" She flew around the table and kissed her.

"I came to your wedding," said Laura, casting pleased, shy glances all around.

"Oh, Laura, *you* want me to marry Troy, don't you? You approve, don't you?"

"Yes," said Laura. "I approve, Dabney!"

"You be in my wedding! You be a flower girl!"

"I can't," said Laura helplessly. "My mother died."

"Oh," cried Dabney, as if Laura had slapped her, running away from her and back to her place at the table, hiding her face. "It's just so *hard*, everything's just so *hard*. . . ."

"Here's your little ham, Miss Dab," said Roxie, coming in. "Do you good."

"Oh, Roxie, even you. No one will ever believe me, that I just can't swallow until Saturday. There's no use trying any more."

"You can bring the ice cream and cake then, Roxie," Aunt Ellen said. "It's Georgie's favorite cake, I do wish they could be here a day sooner!"

They sat sighing, eating cake, drinking coffee. The throb of the compress had never stopped. Laura could feel it now in the handle of her cup, the noiseless vibration that trembled in the best china, was within it.

It was hard to ever quite leave the dining room after supper. It would be still faintly day, and not much cooler. They all still sat, until the baby, who had hung teasing crumbs and coffee out of them from her high-chair ("Mama, let Bluet eat at the table!") wilted over like a little flower in her kimono with the butterfly sleeves and was kissed all around and carried up in flushed sleep in Dabney's overeager arms.

The table was in the middle of the large room, and there was little tendency to leave even that. But besides the old walnut-and-cane chairs (Great-Grandfather made them) there were easy chairs covered with cotton in a faded peony pattern, and rockers for the two great-aunts, sewing stands and fire shields beside them, all near the watery-green tile hearth. A spready fern stood in front of the grate in summertime, with a cricket in it now, that nobody could do anything about. Along the wall the china closets reflected the windows, except for one visible shelf where some shell-pattern candlesticks shone, and the Port Gibson epergne, a fan of Apostle spoons, and the silver sugar basket with the pierce-work in it and its old cracked purplish glass lining. At the other end of the room the Victrola stood like a big morning-glory and there, laid with somebody's game, was the card table Great-Grandfather also made out of his walnut trees when he cut his way in to the Yazoo wilderness. A long ornate rattan settee, upslanting at the ends, with a steep scrolled back, was in the bay alcove. In the half-moon of space behind it were marble pedestals and wicker stands each holding a fern of advanced size or a little rooted cutting, sometimes in bloom. Overhead, over the loaded plate rails, were square oil paintings of splitmelons and cut flowers by Aunt Mashula as a young girl.

This evening there was nobody but Uncle Battle to take cherry bounce, and hating anything alone he would not have it but with a groan sat down and took Bluet's doll out of his chair onto his knee. Dabney wandered in, Aunt Ellen wandered out, Mary Lamar Mackey wandered across the hall into the music room and began to play softly to herself, but nobody else, Great-Aunt Mac or anybody, could be persuaded to stir. Maureen, gentle now, sat on a stool and listened, listened for the cricket. In a little while Dabney and Shelley and Mary Lamar would have to go dress for a dance in Glen Alan, but now the two sisters stretched on the settee, each with her head at an elevated end and her stockinged feet in her sister's hair. Catching the light like drops of a waterfall the fronds of a maidenhair fern hung from a dark tub over them.

"Fan us, fan us, India," said Dabney, though the big overhead fan turned too.

"Ranny will fan you, before he goes to bed," India said, and Ranny came radiantly forward with Great-Aunt Shannon's palmetto.

"Ho hum," said Dabney. "You'd think I had nothing to do. I wonder if Troy is in from the fields."

"There's one speck of light left," said Shelley.

"Cousin Laura," said Orrin kindly, looking up from his book at her. He leaned on the table. "You weren't here, but Uncle George and Maureen nearly got killed."

"Uncle George?" Laura alone had not reclined; she stood looking into the big mirror over the sideboard which reflected the whole roomful of cousins.

"Ranny, you fan too hard. They nearly let the Yellow Dog run over them on the Dry Creek trestle." Dabney softly laughed from her prone position.

India moaned from the chair she was leaning over to read a book on the floor.

"It was almost a tragedy," said Shelley. She lifted up her head, then let it fall back.

"Why did they let the Yellow Dog almost run over them?" Laura made her way to the table and leaned on it to ask Orrin, who answered her gravely, with his finger in his place in the book. "Here's the way it was—" For all of them told happenings like narrations, chronological and careful, as if the ear of the world listened and wished to know surely.

"The whole family but Papa and Mama, and ten or twenty Negroes with us, went fishing in Drowning Lake. It will be two weeks ago Sunday. And so coming home we walked the track. We were tired—we were singing. On the trestle Maureen danced and caught her foot. I've done that, but I know how to get loose. Uncle George kneeled down and went to work on Maureen's foot, and the train came. He hadn't got Maureen's foot loose, so he didn't jump either. The rest of us did jump, and the Dog stopped just before it hit them and ground them all to pieces."

Uncle Battle looked at Dabney with a kind of outraged puffing of his sunburned cheeks, a glare in her direction like some fatherly malediction; whether it was meant for Dabney herself in front of his eyes, or for what he had heard, Laura could not tell. And as if glaring itself made him nervous he dandled the ragged doll heavily on his knee.

Dabney gave a half-smile. "The engineer looked out the window—he said he was sorry."

Laura looked at her gravely. "I'm glad I wasn't there," she told her.

Then Aunt Ellen came in, meditatively, as the hall clock finished striking two which meant it was eight. She had a feather on her skirt—had she been out for her precious guinea eggs? She was a slight, almost delicate lady, seeming exactly strong enough for what was needed of her life. She was scarcely taller than Orrin, and Dabney and Shelley had been both taller and bigger than their mother for two years. She walked into the roomful of family without immediately telling them anything. She was more restful than the Fairchilds. Her brown hair and her dark-blue eyes seemed part of her quietness—like the colors of water, reflective. Her Virginia voice, while no softer or lighter than theirs, was a less questioning, a never teasing one. It was a voice to speak to the one child or the one man her eyes would go to. They all watched her with soft eyes, but distractedly.

She was one of those little mothers that the wind seems almost to hurt, and they knew they needed to look after her. She held very straight in her back, like a little boy who can do right in dancing class. And while she meditated, she hurried—how she hurried! She was never slow—she was either still or darting. They said she had no need for hurry with a houseful of Negroes to do the first thing she told them. But she did not wait for them or anybody to wait on her. "Your mother is killing herself," Battle's sisters told the children. "But you can't do a thing in the world with her," they answered. "We're going to have to whip her or kill her before she'll lie down in the afternoons, even." They spoke of killing and whipping in the exasperation and helplessness of much love. Laura could see as far as that she was the opposite of a Fairchild, and that was a stopping point. Aunt Ellen would be seen busy in a room, where Aunt Tempe for instance was never seen except proceeding down halls, or seated. She never cared how she dressed any more than a child. Aunt Tempe said to India last summer, in the voice in which she always spoke to little girls, as if everything were a severe revelation, "When your mother goes to Greenwood she simply goes to the closet and says, 'Clothes, I'm going to Greenwood, anything that wants to go along, get on my back.' She has never learned what is reprehensible and what is not, in the Delta." She was often a little confused about her keys, and sometimes would ask Dabney, "What was I going for?" "Why am I here?" When she threw her head back dramatically, it meant she was listening for a baby. Her small sweetly shaped nose was sparingly freckled like a little girl's, like India's in summer. Sometimes, as when now she stood still for a moment in the room full of talking people, an unaccountable rosiness would jump into her cheeks and a look of merriment would make her eyes grow wide. Down low over the dinner table hung a lamp with a rectangular shade of tinted glass, like a lighted shoe-box toy, a "choo-choo boat" with its colored paper windows. In its light she would look over the room, at the youngest ones intertwining on the rug and hating so the approach of night, the older ones leaning across the cleared table, chasing each other in a circle, or reading, or lost to themselves on the flimsy settee; Battle pondering in his way or fuming, while from time to time the voices of the girls called out to the telephone would sound somewhere in the air like the twittering of birds—and it would be as if she had never before seen anything at all of this room with the big breasting china closets and the fruit and cake plates around the rail, had never watered the plants in the window, or encountered till now these absorbed, intent people—ever before in her life, Laura thought. At that moment a whisper might have said Look! to her, and the dining-room curtains might have traveled back on their rings, and there *they* were. Even some unused love seemed to Laura to be in Aunt Ellen's eyes when she gazed, after supper, at her own family. Could she get it? Laura's heart pounded. But the baby had dreams and soon she would cry out on the upper floor, and Aunt Ellen listening would run straight to her, calling to her on the way, and forgetting everything in this room.

II

How Ellen loved their wide and towering foreheads, their hairlines on the fresh skin silver as the edge of a peach, clean as a pencil line, dipping to a perfect widow's peak in every child she had. Their cheeks were wide and their chins narrow but pressed a little forward—lips caught, then parted, as if in constant expectation—so that their faces looked sturdy and resolute, unrevealing, from the side, but tender and heart-shaped from the front. Their coloring—their fair hair and their soot-dark, high eyebrows and shadowy lashes, the long eyes, of gray that seemed more luminous, more observant and more passionate than blue—moved her deeply and freshly in each child. Dear Orrin, talking so seriously now, the dignity in his look! And little Ranny with his burning cheeks and the silver bleach of summer on his hair, so deliberately wielding the fan over his sisters! She had never had a child to take after herself and would be as astonished as Battle now to see her own ways or looks dominant, a blue-eyed, dark-haired, small-boned baby lying in her arms. All the mystery of looks moved her, for she was with child once more.

In the men grown, in Battle and George, it was a paradoxical thing, the fineness and tenderness with the bulk and weight of their big bodies. All the Fairchild men (the old-maid sister, Jim Allen, would recite that like a bit of catechism) were six feet tall by the time they were sixteen and weighed two hundred pounds by the time they were forty. But Battle weighed two hundred and fifty, and groaned to be gentle as he was; and George, though he was not himself fat, was markedly bigger and fairer than any of them in the early portraits, as if he were not a throwback to the type (which had faltered but little, after all, through marriages with little women like her, like Laura Allen and Mary Shannon before her) but a new original—a sport of the tree itself. She guessed she apprehended everything through the way they looked and felt—George sometimes more than Battle. Battle wore the glower of fatherhood or its little undermask of helplessness, that George had not put on. And George had remained left-handed, the thing they all inherited, as was somehow visibly apparent not just momently but always—perhaps by such a thing as the part in his hair. Her secret tremor at Battle's determined breaking of her children's left-handedness made her cherish it like a failing in George.

The fineness in her men called to mind their unwieldiness, and the other way round, in a way infinitely endearing to her. The fineness could so soon look delicate—nobody could get tireder, fall sicker and more quickly so, than her men. She thought yet of the other brother Denis who was dead in France as holding this look; from the grave he gave her that look, partly of hurt: "How could I have been brought like this?" as Battle cried in the Far Field when his horse, unaccountably terrified at the old Yellow Dog one day, threw him and left him unable to raise himself from the ditch.

"Oh, it was cloudy, or we would have remembered it was time for the Dog," Orrin was saying, looking up from his book. "We wouldn't have made that mistake another day, when we could see the sun."

"The Dog was most likely running an hour late, and it wouldn't have done us any good." Dabney smiled. She twisted her foot in Shelley's hair, where they were lying together on the settee. "I'm making a hole in your net with my big toe."

"I won't lie here with you any longer," Shelley said languidly. But she did not move, or close her eyes fully. She looked rather dreamily down the slope of her own body, middy blouse, skirt, dark-blue stockings, and up Dabney's, light-blue stockings, light-blue swiss dress with one lace panel momently floating in Ranny's breeze, and Dabney's just-washed hair flying on her clasped hands behind her head. Dabney's face was suffused and soft now as Bluet's when she was waked from her nap. Her eyes seemed to swim in some essence not tears, but as bright—an essence that made the pupils large. The sisters looked now into each other's eyes, and as if there was no help for it, a flare leaped between them. . . .

There was a lusty cry from Maureen.

"She's caught the cricket. She's pulling his wings off—she'll kill the cricket." Roy was on his feet.

"Don't stop her, don't stop her. Let her have her way," Battle said, his voice rumbling in Ellen's ears.

"The cricket minded, I think," Ranny said, holding the fan still.

"Come help me make a cake before bedtime, Laura," said Ellen; now she saw Laura with forgetful eyes fastened on her. She's the poor little old thing, she thought. When a man alone has to look after a little girl, how in even eight months she will get long-legged and skinny. She will as like as not need to have glasses when school starts. He doesn't cut her hair, or he will cut it too short. How sharp her elbows are—Maureen looks like a cherub beside her—the difference just in their elbows!

"I'll be glad to, Aunt Ellen," Laura said, and put her hand in hers as if she were Ranny's age. She came along in a toiling little walk.

"Get out of the kitchen, Roxie. We want to make Mr. George and Miss Robbie a cake. They're coming tomorrow."

"You loves *them*," said Roxie. "You're fixin' to ask me to grate you a coconut, not get out."

"Yes, I am. Grate me the coconut." Ellen smiled. "I got fourteen guinea eggs this evening, and that's a sign I ought to make it, Roxie."

"Take 'em all: guineas," said Roxie belittlingly.

"Well, you get the oven hot." Ellen tied her apron back on. "You can grate me the coconut, and a lemon while you're at it, and blanch me the almonds. I'm going to let Laura pound me the almonds in the mortar and pestle."

"Is that very hard?" asked Laura, running out for a drink at the water cooler.

Ellen was breaking and separating the fourteen eggs. "Yes, I do want coconut," she murmured. For Ellen's hope for Dabney, that had to lie in something, some secret nest, lay in George's happiness. He had married "beneath" him too, in Tempe's unvarying word. When he got home from the war he married, in the middle of one spring night, little Robbie Reid, Old Man Swanson's granddaughter, who had grown up in the town of Fairchilds to work in Fairchild's Store.

She beat the egg whites and began creaming the sugar and butter, and saying a word from time to time to Laura who hung on the table and watched her, she felt busily consoled for the loss of Dabney to Troy Flavin by the happiness of George lost to Robbie. She remembered, as if she vigorously worked the memory up out of the mixture, a picnic at the Grove—the old place—an exuberant night in the spring before—it was not long after the death of Annie Laurie down in Jackson. Robbie had tantalizingly let herself be chased and had jumped in the river with George in after her, everybody screaming from where they lay. Dalliance, pure play, George was after that night—he was enchanted with his wife, he made it plain then. They were in moonlight. With great splashing he took her dress and petticoat off in the water, flung them out on the willow bushes, and carried her up screaming in her very teddies, her lost ribbon in his teeth, and the shining water running down her kicking legs and flying off her heels as she screamed and buried her face in his chest, laughing too, proud too.

The sisters'—Jim Allen's and Primrose's—garden ran right down to the water there—how could they have known their brother George would some day carry a dripping girl out of the river and fling her down thrashing and laughing on a bed of their darling sweet peas, pulling vines and all down on her? George flung himself down by her too and threw his wet arm out and drew her onto his fast-breathing chest. They lay there smiling and worn out, but twined together—appealing, shining in moonlight, and almost—somehow—threatening, Ellen felt. They were so boldly happy, with Dabney and Shelley there, with Primrose and Jim Allen trembling for their sweet peas if not daring to think of George's life risked, and India seizing the opportunity of running up and sprinkling them with pomegranate flowers and handfuls of grass to tickle them. Dabney had brought young Dickie Boy Featherstone along that night; they had sat timidly holding hands on the river bank, Dabney with a clover chain circling and festooning her like a net. They had chided Robbie, she had endangered George—he could not swim well for a wound of war. But no one can stare back more languorously and alluringly than a rescued woman, Ellen believed, from the memory of Robbie's slumbrous eyes and surfeited little smile as she lay on George's wet arm. George was delighted as by some passing transformation in her, speaking some word to her and making her look away toward them overcome with merriment—as if she had beguiled him in some obvious way he found absurd and endearing—as if she had tried to arouse his jealousy, for instance, by flirting with another man.

As Ellen put in the nutmeg and the grated lemon rind she diligently assumed George's happiness, seeing it in the Fairchild aspects of exuberance and satiety; if it was unabashed, it was the best part true. But—adding the milk, the egg whites, the flour, carefully and alternately as Mashula's recipe said—she could be diligent and still not wholly sure—never wholly. She loved George too dearly herself to seek her knowledge of him through the family attitude, keen and subtle as that was—just as she loved Dabney too much to see her prospect without its risk, now family-deplored, around it, the happiness covered with danger. "Look who Robbie Reid is!" they had said once, and now, "Who is Troy Flavin?" Indeed, who was Troy Flavin, beyond being the Fairchild overseer? Nobody knew. Only that he had a little mother in the hills. It was killing Battle; she heard him now, calling, "Dabney, Dabney! Dickie Boy Featherstone's blowing his horn!" and at the telephone Dabney was talking softly to Troy, "I'm with Dickie Boy Featherstone, gone to Glen Alan. . . . Good night. . . . Good night. . . ." It seemed to Ellen that it was for every one of them that added care pressed her heart on these late summer nights ("Now you can taste, Laura," she said), care that stirred in her and that she herself shielded, like the child she carried.

"Now, Laura. Go get that little bottle of rose water off the top shelf in the pantry. Climb where Roy climbs for the cooky jar and you'll reach it. . . . Now be putting in a little rose water as you go. Pound good."

She poured her cake out in four layer pans and set the first two in the oven, gently shutting the door. "Be ready, Laura, when I call you. Oh, save me twenty-four perfect halves—to go on top. . . ."

She began with the rest of the eggs to make the filling; she would just trust that Laura's paste would do, and make the icing thick on top with the perfect almonds over it close enough to touch.

"Smell my cake?" she challenged, as Dabney appeared radiant at the pantry door, then coming through, spreading her pink dress to let her mother see her. Ellen turned a little dizzily. Was the cake going to turn out all right? She was always nervous about her cakes. And for George she did want it to be nice—he was so appreciative. "*Don't* pound your poor finger, Laura."

"I wasn't going to, Aunt Ellen."

"Oh, Mother, am I beautiful—tonight?" Dabney asked urgently, almost painfully, as though she would run if she heard the answer.

Laura laid down the noisy pestle. Her lips parted. Dabney rushed across the kitchen and threw her arms tightly around her mother and clung to her.

Roxie, waiting on the porch, could be heard laughing, two high gentle notes out in the dark.

From an upper window India's voice came out on the soft air, chanting,

> *Star light,*
> *Star bright,*
> *First star I've seen tonight,*
> *I wish I may, I wish I might*
> *Have the wish I wish tonight.*

For a moment longer they all held still; India was wishing.

2

It was the next afternoon. Dabney came down the stairs vaguely in time to the song Mary Lamar Mackey was rippling out in the music room—"Drink to Me Only with Thine Eyes." "Oh, I'm a wreck," she sighed absently.

"Did you have your breakfast? Then run on to your aunts," said her mother, pausing in the hall below, pointing a silver dinner knife at her. "You're a girl engaged to be married and your aunts want to see you." "Your aunts" always referred to the two old-maid sisters of her father's who lived at the Grove, the old place on the river, Aunt Primrose and Aunt Jim Allen, and not to Aunt Tempe who had married Uncle Pinck, or Aunt Rowena or Aunt Annie Laurie who were dead. "I've got all the Negroes your papa could spare me up here on the silver and those miserable chandelier prisms—I don't want you underfoot, even."

"They saw me that Sunday they came up to dinner," said Dabney, still on the stairs.

"But you weren't engaged that Sunday—or you hadn't told."

A veil came over Dabney's eyes—a sort of pleased mournfulness.

"They'll ask me ten thousand questions."

"Let me go!" said India quickly. She was sitting on the bottom step finishing a leaf hat. "I'm not really busy."

"Come on, then," said Dabney. She ran down and leaned over her little sister and smiled at her for what seemed the first time in years.

"I can come! I'll hop!" Bluet instantly came hopping up with one shoe off, her sunny hair flying. In the corner Roxie's little Sudie, who was "watching" her, stretched meek on the floor with chin in hand. Little Battle tore through the house but didn't stop a minute, except to spank Dabney hard. Mary Lamar Mackey dreamily called, "Where are you all going?"

"Now get away from Dabney *everybody*, and let her go," said Ellen. "No, Dabney, not Ranny either, this time. You'll dawdle and let him fall off the horse—and Primrose and Jim Allen'll have to invite you to supper."

"Will they have spoon bread?" cried India.

"That's enough, India. You can carry that bucket of molasses if you're going, and I think I'll send a taste more of that blackberry wine—wait till I pour it off."

"You can wear this, Dabney." On her two forefingers India offered up the leaf hat to her sister, who had on a new dress.

"Oh, I couldn't! Never mind, you wear it," said Dabney. She herself fixed it on India's hair. Dabney had gotten awfully fixy, said the calm stare in India's eyes at that moment. The little girl set her jaw, Dabney frowned, and one of the rose thorns did scratch.

"Be sure that sack on the front porch gets to Jim Allen!" called their mother from the back porch. "Oh, where's my wine!"

"Vi'let! Vi'let!"

"Take Aunt Primrose my plaid wool and my cape pattern!" called Shelley from right under their feet. She was under the house looking for the key to the clock which she insisted had fallen through the floor. "In Mama's room! Vi'let!"

Dabney drew her brows together for a moment—Shelley was a year older than she was, and now that Dabney was the one getting married, she seemed to spend her time in the oddest places. She ought to be getting ready for Europe. She had to go in a month. She said she "simply couldn't" go to any of the bridge parties, that they were "just sixty girls from all over the Delta come to giggle in one house." She would hardly go to the dances, some nights. "Shelley, come out! . . . Mama, do you think they want *all* those hyacinth bulbs?" she called.

"They're onions! India, did you call Little Uncle to bring up Junie and Rob?"

"Little Uncle!"

"Wait a second, India," said Dabney. She caught at her sticking-out skirt. "You look plenty tacky, India—you're just the age where you look tacky and that's all there is to it." She sighed again, and ran lightly down the steps. "You ride with the onions, I'm going to see Troy tonight."

"Well, my golly," said India.

"We ought to send them back that candy dish—but can't send it back empty!" called Ellen in a falling voice.

Little Uncle and Vi'let got them loaded up on the horses and fixed all the buckets and sacks so they weren't very likely to fall open. "I don't know why we didn't take the car," Dabney said dreamily. They rode out the gate.

India said, "Haven't I got to see Troy, and the whole family got to see Troy, Troy, Troy, every single night the rest of our lives, besides the day? Does Troy hate onions? Does he declare he hates them? Does he hate peaches? Figs? Black-eyed peas?"

"We'll be further away than that," said Dabney, still dreamily.

It was a soft day, brimming with the light of afternoon. It was the fifth beautiful week, with only that one threatening day. The gold mass of the distant shade trees seemed to dance, to sway, under the plum-colored sky. On either side of their horses' feet the cotton twinkled like stars. Then a red-pop flew up from her nest in the cotton. Above in an unbroken circle, all around the wheel of the level world, lay silvery-blue clouds whose edges melted and changed into the pink and blue of sky. Girls and horses lifted their heads like swimmers. Here and there and far away the cotton wagons, of hand-painted green, stood up to their wheel tops in the white and were loaded with white, like cloud wagons. All along, the Negroes would lift up and smile glaringly and pump their arms—they knew Miss Dabney was going to step off Saturday with Mr. Troy.

A man on a black horse rode across their path at right angles, down Mound Field. He waved, his arm like a gun against the sky—it was Troy on Isabelle. A long stream of dust followed him, pink in the light. Dabney lifted her hand. "Wave, India," she said.

There was the distance where he still charmed her most—it was strange. Just here, coming now to the Indian mound, was where she really noticed him first—last summer, riding like this with India on Junie and Rob. (Though later, they would go clear to Marmion to sit in the moonlight by the old house and by the river, teasing and playing, when it was fall.) And she looked with joy, as if it marked the pre-eminent place, at the Indian mound topped with trees like a masted green boat on the cottony sea. That he was at this distance obviously not a Fairchild still filled her with an awe that had grown most easily from idle condescension—that made it hard to think of him as he would come closer. Troy, a slow talker, had been the object of little stories and ridicule at the table—then suddenly he was real. She shut her eyes. She saw a blinding light, or else was it a dark cloud—that intensity under her flickering lids? She rode with her eyes shut. Troy Flavin was the overseer. The Fairchilds would die, everybody said, if this happened. But now everybody seemed to be just too busy to die or not.

He was twice as old as she was now, but that was just a funny accident, thirty-four being twice seventeen, it wouldn't be so later on. When she was as much as twenty-five, he wouldn't be fifty! "Things will probably go on about as they do now," she would hear her mother say. "It isn't as if Dabney was going out of the Delta—like Mary Denis Summers." They would have Marmion, and Troy could manage the two places. "Marmion can't belong to Maureen!" she had cried, when she first asked.

"Yes—not legally, but really," her father said; he thought it was complicated. So Dabney had said to Maureen, "Look, honey—will you give your house to me?" They had been lying half-asleep together in the hammock after dinner. And Maureen, hanging over her to look at her, her face close above hers, had chosen to smile radiantly. "Yes," she said, "you can have my house-la, and a bite-la of my apple too." Oh, everything *could* be so easy! Virgie Lee, Maureen's mother, was not of sound mind and would have none of Marmion. It might have been more fun to ask George for the Grove, and see . . . but too late now, and the Grove was not the grandest place. Troy had simply slapped his hand on his saddle when she told him, at the way she could have Marmion with a little airy remark! She had blushed—surely that was flattery! Troy was slow on words.

"I don't hear anything but nice things about Troy," everybody was telling her. As though he were invisible, and only she had seen him! She thought of him proudly (he was right back of the mound now, she knew), a dark thundercloud, his slowness rumbling and his laugh flickering through in bright flashes; any "nice thing" would sound absurd—as if you were talking about a cousin, or a friend. Later they would laugh together about this. Uncle George would be on her side. He would treat it as if it wasn't any side, which would make it better—make it perfect . . . unless he got on Troy's side. He liked Troy. . . .

"There goes Pinchy, trying to come through," said India, to make Dabney open her eyes. Sure enough, there went Pinchy wandering in the cotton rows, Roxie's helper, not speaking to them at all but giving up every moment to seeking.

"I hope she comes through soon." Dabney frowned.

"I forgot the onions, too."

"Hyacinths, you mean."

"Onions. You're crazy as a June bug now, Dabney," said India thoughtfully. "Will I be like you?"

"You're crazy the way you forget things, onions or hyacinths either."

Troy was far to the right now—they had turned. They rode around the blue shadow of the Indian mound, and he was behind her. Faintly she could hear his busy shout, "Sylvanus! Sylvanus!"

"All the Fairchilds forget things," said India, beginning to gallop joyfully, making the wine splash.

They rode through the Far Field and into the pasture where three mules were looking out together from a green glade. The sedge was glowing, the round meadow had a bloom like fruit, and the sweet gums were like a soft curtain beyond, fading into the pink of the near sky. Here the season showed. Queen Anne's lace brushed their feet as they rode, and the tight green goldenrod knocked at them. She seemed to hear the rustle of the partridgy shadows.

Sometimes, Dabney was not so sure she was a Fairchild—sometimes she did not care, that was it. There were moments of life when it did not matter who she was—even where. Something, happiness—with Troy, but not necessarily, even the happiness of a fine day—seemed to leap away from identity as if it were an old skin, and that she was one of the Fairchilds was of no more need to her than the locust shells now hanging to the trees everywhere were to the singing locusts. What she felt, nobody knew! It would kill her father—of course for her to be a Fairchild was an inescapable thing, to him. And she would not take anything for the relentless way he was acting, not wanting to let her go. The caprices of his restraining power over his daughters filled her with delight now that she had declared what she could do. She felt a double pride between them now—it tied them closer than ever as they laughed, bragged, reproached each other and flaunted themselves. While her mother, who had never spoken the first word against her sudden decision to marry or questioned her wildness for Troy or her defiance of her father's wishes, in the whole two weeks, somehow defeated her. Dabney and her mother had gone into shells of mutual contemplation—like two shy young girls meeting in a country of a strange language. Perhaps it was only her mother's condition, thought Dabney, shaking her head a little. Only when she forgot herself, flashed out in the old way, shed tears, and begged her pardon, did Dabney feel again in her mother's quick kiss, like a peck, her watchfulness, the kind of pity for children that mothers might feel always until they were dead, reassuring to the mother and the little girl together.

Troy treated her like a Fairchild—he still did; he wouldn't stop work when she rode by even today. Sometimes he was so standoffish, gentle like, other times he laughed and mocked her, and shook her, and played like fighting—once he had really hurt her. How sorry it made him! She took a deep breath. Sometimes Troy was really ever so much like a Fairchild. Nobody guessed that, just seeing him go by on Isabelle! He had not revealed very much to her yet. He would—that dark shouting rider would throw back the skin of this very time, of this moment. . . . There would be a whole other world, with other cotton, even.

It was actually Uncle George who had shown her that there was another way to be—something else. . . . Uncle George, the youngest of the older ones, who stood in—who was—the very heart of the family, who was like them, looked like them (only by far, she thought, seeing at once his picnic smile, handsomer)—he was different, somehow. Perhaps the heart always was made of different stuff and had a different life from the rest of the body. She saw Uncle George lying on his arm on a picnic, smiling to hear what someone was telling, with a butterfly going across his gaze, a way to make her imagine all at once that in that moment he erected an entire, complicated house for the butterfly inside his sleepy body. It was very strange, but she had felt it. She had then known something he knew all along, it seemed then—that when you felt, touched, heard, looked at things in the world, and found their fragrances, they themselves made a sort of house within you, which filled with life to hold them, filled with knowledge all by itself, and all else, the other ways to know, seemed calculation and tyranny.

Blindly and proudly Dabney rode, her eyes shut against what was too bright. Uncle George would be coming some time today—she would be glad. He would be sweet to her, sweet to Troy. In a way, their same old way, the family were leaving any sweetness, any celebration and good wishing, to Uncle George. They had said nothing very tender or final to her yet; hardly anything at all excited, even, about the marriage—beyond her father's carrying on, that went without saying. They had put it off, she guessed, sighing. This was too much in cotton-picking time, that was all—or else they still had hope that she would not do this to them. Dabney smiled again—she smiled as often as tears, once started, would fall—her flickering eyes on India shaking her switch like a wand at a scampering rabbit. Uncle George would come and say something just right—or rather he would come and not say any special thing at all, just show them the champagne he brought for the wedding night, while Shelley, perhaps, was coaxed to cry—and they would not fret or worry or hold back any longer. Dabney herself would then be entirely happy.

"Has James's Bayou really got a whirlpool in the middle of it?" cried India intensely.

"No, India, always no, but *you* stay out of it." They rode into the tarnished light of a swampy place.

"But has it really got a ghost? Everybody knows it has."

"Then don't ask me every time. Just so she won't cry for my wedding, that's all *I* ask!" Dabney sighed.

"I'd love her to cry for me," India said luringly. "Cry and cry."

Just then, directly in front of them, Man-Son, one of the Negroes, raised his hat. How strange—he should be picking cotton, thought Dabney. But everything seemed to be happening strangely, some special way, now. Nodding sternly to Man-Son, she remembered perfectly a certain morning away back; of course, it was then she had discovered in Uncle George one first point where he differed from the other Fairchilds, and learned that one human being can differ, very excitingly, from another. As if everything had waited for her to be about to marry, for her to fall in love, it seemed to her that all, even memories and dreams, grew clear. . . .

It was a day in childhood, they were living at the Grove. She had wandered off—no older than India now—and had seen George come on a small scuffle, a scuffle with a knife, out in the woods—right here. George, thin, lanky, exultant, "wild," they said smilingly, had been down at the Grove from school that summer. Two of their little Negroes had flown at each other with extraordinary intensity here on the bank of the bayou. It was in the bright sun, in front of the cypress shadows. At the jerk-back of a little wrist, suddenly a knife let loose and seemed to fling itself in the air. Uncle George and Uncle Denis (who was killed the next year in the war) had just come out of the bayou, naked, so wet they shone in the sun, wet light hair hanging over their foreheads just alike, and they were stamping their feet, flinging out their arms, starting to wrestle and play, and Uncle George reached up and caught the knife. "I'll be damned," he said (at that she thought he was wounded) and turning, rushed in among the thrashing legs and arms. Uncle Denis walked off, slipping into his long-tailed shirt, just melted away into the light, laughing. Uncle George grabbed the little Negro that wanted to run, and pinned down the little Negro that was hollering. Somehow he held one, said "Hand me that," and tied up the other, tearing up his own shirt. He used his teeth and the Negroes' knife, and the young fighters were both as still as mice, though he said something to himself now and then.

It was a big knife—she was sure it was as big as the one Troy could pull out now. There was blood on the sunny ground. Uncle George cussed the little Negro for being cut like that. The other little Negro sat up all quiet and leaned over and looked at all Uncle George was doing, and in the middle of it his face crumpled—with a loud squall he went with arms straight out to Uncle George, who stopped and let him cry a minute. And then the other little Negro sat up off the ground, the small black pole of his chest striped with the shirt bandage, and climbed up to him too and began to holler, and he knelt low there holding to him the two little black boys who cried together melodiously like singers, and saying, still worriedly, "Damn you! Damn you both!" Then what did he do to them? He asked them their names and let them go. They had gone flying off together like conspirators. Dabney had never forgotten which two boys those were, and could tell them from the rest—Man-Son worked for them yet and was a good Negro, but his brother, the one with the scar on his neck, had given trouble, so Troy had got his way when he came, and her father had let him go.

When George turned around on the bayou, his face looked white and his sunburn a mask, and he stood there still and attentive. There was blood on his hands and both legs. He stood looking not like a boy close kin to them, but out by himself, like a man who had stepped outside—done something. But it had not been anything Dabney wanted to see him do. She almost ran away. He seemed to meditate—to refuse to smile. She gave a loud scream and he saw her there in the field, and caught her when she ran at him. He hugged her tight against his chest, where sweat and bayou water pressed her mouth, and tickled her a minute, and told her how sorry he was to have scared her like that. Everything was all right then. But all the Fairchild in her had screamed at his interfering—at his taking part—*caring* about anything in the world but them.

What things did he know of? There were surprising things in the world which did not surprise him. Wonderfully, he had reached up and caught the knife in the air. Disgracefully, he had taken two little black devils against his side. When he had not even laughed with them all about it afterwards, or told it like a story after supper, she was astonished, and sure then of a curious division between George and the rest. It was all something that the other Fairchilds would have passed by and scorned to notice—hadn't Denis, even?—that yet went to a law of his being, that came to it, like the butterfly to his sight. He could have lifted a finger and touched, held the butterfly, but he did not. The butterfly he loved, the knife not. The other Fairchilds never said but one thing about George and Denis, who were always thought of together—that George and Denis were born sweet, and that they were not born sweet. Sweetness then could be the visible surface of profound depths—the surface of all the darkness that might frighten her. Now Denis was dead. And George loved the *world*, something told her suddenly. Not them! Not them in particular.

"Man-Son, what do you mean? You go get to picking!" she cried. She trembled all over, having to speak to him in such a way.

"Yes'm, Miss Dabney. Wishin' you'n Mr. Troy find you happiness."

They rode across the railroad track and on. The fields shone and seemed to tremble like a veil in the light. The song of distant pickers started up like the agitation of birds.

"Look pretty. Here we are," said India.

They were riding by the row of Negro houses and the manager's house. The horses lifted their noses, smelling the river. Little Matthew saw them and opened the back gate, swinging on it, and ran after them to help them off Junie and Rob. He put his little flat nose against the horses' long noses and spoke to them. Dabney and India loaded him up. Great-Grandmother's magnolia, its lower branches taken root, spread over them. Only bits of sunlight, bright as butterflies, came through the dark tree.

The house at the Grove, a dove-gray box with its deep porch turned to the river breeze, stood under shade trees with its back to the Shellmound road. It was a cypress house on brick pillars now painted green and latticed over, and its double chimneys at either end were green too. There was an open deck, never walked any more, on its roof; it was Denis's place—he had loved to read poetry there. The garden, sun-faded, went down to the dusty moat in which the big cypresses stood like towers with doors at their roots. The bank of the river was willowy and bright, wild and unraked, and the shadowy Yazoo went softly colored and lying narrow and low in the time of year.

Aunt Primrose caught sight of them through the window of the kitchen ell, and agitatedly signaled to them that they must go round to the front door and not on any account come in at the back, and that she was caught in her boudoir cap and was ashamed.

They waded through the side yard of mint and nodding pink and white cosmos, the two pale bird dogs licking them. Lethe flew out to help and fuss at Matthew, while Aunt Primrose—they could hear her—spread the screen doors wide. "Bless your hearts! Mercy! What all have you got there, always come loaded!" she cried. A brown thrush, nesting once again in September, flew out of the crape-myrtle tree at them and made Dabney nearly drop the wine she was carrying herself, to catch at her hair. Aunt Primrose, as if she should have known that thrush would do that, ran out with little cries—for she was the most tender-headed of the Fairchilds and could not bear for anyone to have her hair caught or endangered.

India was allowed to go find Aunt Jim Allen, who was the deaf aunt. She was in the first place India looked, the pantry, tenderly writing out in her beautiful script the watermelon-rind-preserve labels and singing in perfect tune, "Where Have You Been, Billy Boy?" India tickled her neck with a piece of verbena.

"Why, you monkey!" She was embraced.

Then, "Dabney!" and both aunts at last clutched the bride, their voices stricken over her name.

"We'll sit in the parlor and Lethe will bring us some good banana ice cream, that's what we'll do. (*Oh*, I was sorry when the figs left!)" said Aunt Jim Allen.

"Then you'll have to turn straight around and start back," said Aunt Primrose.

They went on. "You're looking mighty pretty. I declare, Dabney, if Sister Rowena had lived, I don't know what she would have said. I don't believe she could have realized it. Did you feel this way about Mary Denis

Summers, Jim Allen? I didn't." In their pinks and blues they looked like two plump hydrangea bushes side by side. "She's having a baby right this minute," India put in, while Dabney was saying, "It's some of Mama's wine, and she apologizes if it's not as good as last year, and Shelley's cape—she says please don't work too hard on it and put out your eyes, but she could wear it on the *Berengaria* and wrap up. And I'm afraid we forgot the hyacinths, but we can send them by Little Uncle in the morning."

Matthew, just now making his way in from the back, put everything down on the carpet in one heap. Both aunts immediately ran and extracted all away, with soft cries.

"Neither Dabney nor me is scared to stay out after dark by ourselves, Aunt Primrose," India said.

"Nonsense."

Dabney felt as if she had not been at the Grove with her aunts since she was a little girl—all in two weeks they had gone backward in time for her. She looked at them tenderly.

"I started you a cutting of the Seven-Sister rose the minute I heard you were going to be married," said Aunt Primrose, pointing her finger at her.

Aunt Primrose was the youngest aunt, she was next to George, and Jim Allen had been next to Denis. They were both pretty for old maids. Aunt Primrose had almost golden hair, which she washed in camomile tea and waved on pale steel curlers which after twenty years still snapped harshly and fastened tightly, because her hair was so fine. Her skin was fine and tender as Bluet's, and it had never had the midday sun to touch it, or any sun without a hat or a parasol between her and it. Her eyes were weak, but she could not be prevailed on to wear ugly glasses. Her tiny ears, fine-lined and delicate, had been pierced when she was seven years old (the last thing her mother had done for her before the day she fell dead) and she wore little straws through the holes until she was big enough for diamonds. Her throat was full, with a mole like a tiny cameo in its hollow, which sometimes struggled with the beat of her heart, and her voice might have come out of such a throat like a singer's, but it did not, being too soft and timid; Aunt Jim Allen's came out strong. She was growing plumper in the last few years, but she was always delicate and was thought of as the little sister of the family. Her hands (with her mother Laura Allen's rings) most naturally clasped, and then suddenly flew apart—as if she were always eager to hear your story, and then let it surprise her. She could not tolerate a speck of dust in her house, and every room was ready for the inspection of the Queen, Aunt Mac said belittlingly. Her dresses, and Aunt Jim Allen's, were all dainty, with "touches," and they wore little sachets tied and tucked here and there underneath, smelling of clove pinks or violets, nothing "artificial." Aunt Primrose was sweet to Aunt Jim Allen and never said a cross word all day to her or to Lethe or any of the men or her manager. She loved everybody but there was one living man she adored and that was her brother George. "As well I might," she said. She was not scared to live in the house alone with Jim Allen, because she simply had faith nothing would happen to her.

Both of them would tell you that Jim Allen was the better cake maker, but Primrose was better with preserves and pickles and candy, and knew just the minute any named thing ought to be taken off the fire. They swore by Mashula Hines's cook book, and at other times read Mary Shannon's diary she kept when this was a wilderness, and it was full of things to make and the ways to set out cuttings and the proper times, along with all her troubles and provocations.

It was eternally cool in summer in this house; like the air of a dense little velvet-green wood it touched your forehead with stillness. Even the phone had a ring like a tiny silver bell. The Grove was really Uncle George's place now; but he had put his two unmarried sisters in the house and given them Little Joe to manage it, and gone to Memphis to practice law when he married that Robbie Reid. Matting lay along the halls, and the silver doorknobs were not quite round but the shape of little muffins, not perfect. Dabney went into the parlor. How softly all the doors shut, in this house by the river—a soft wind always pressed very gently against your closing. How quiet it was, without the loud driving noise of a big fan in every corner as there was at home, even when at moments *people* sighed and fell silent.

The parlor furniture was exactly like theirs, there were once double parlors here at the Grove, furnished identically in Mashula Hines's day, but how differently everything looked here. Grandmother's and Great-Grandmother's cherished things were so carefully kept here, and the Irish lace curtains were still good except for one little new place of Aunt Primrose's that shone out. Once a cyclone had come and drawn one pair of the curtains out the window and hung them in the top of a tall tree in the swamp, and Laura Allen had had Negroes in the tree all one day instructed to get them down without tearing a thread, while her husband kept begging her to let them come help with the cows bellowing everywhere in the ditches, and then she had mended what could not help but be torn, so that no one could tell now which curtains they were.

There were two portraits of Mary Shannon in this room, on the dark wall the one Audubon painted down in Feliciana, where she visited home, which nobody liked, and over the mantelpiece the one Great-Grandfather did. It showed the Mary Shannon for whom he had cleared away and built the Grove—it had hung in the first little mud house; he had painted it one wintertime, showing her in a dark dress with arms folded and an expression of pure dream in the almost shyly drawn lips. There was a white Christmas rose from the new doorstep in her severely dressed hair. There were circles under her eyes—he had not been reticent there, for that was the year the yellow fever was worst and she had nursed so many of her people, besides her family and neighbors; and two hunters, strangers, had died in her arms. Shelley always thought, for some reason nobody understood, that this was why Great-Grandfather made her fold her arms and hide her hands, but India thought he could not draw hands, because she couldn't, and had not needed to try by giving her a good defiant pose. Dabney thought that Mary folded her arms because she would soon have her first child. Great-Grandfather only painted twice in his life, the romantic picture of his brother, in the library at home, and the realistic one of his wife—the two people he had in the world.

Mary seemed to look down at her and at the dear parlor, with the foolish, breakable little things in it. How sure and how alone she looked, the eyes so tired. What if you lived in a house all alone and away from everybody with no one but your husband?

"Dabney, where were you?" The aunts, with India holding their hands and swinging between them, came in. "Mary Denis Summers Buchanan has come through her ordeal—very well," said Aunt Jim Allen. "Tempe just telephoned from Inverness—didn't you hear us calling you? She wanted us to tell you it was a boy."

"I think Dabney's been eating green apples, but I feel all right," India said. Dabney stood watching them with her arms folded across herself, looking lost in wonder.

"Dabney! Do you feel a little . . . ? Run put back the spread and lie down on my bed." Aunt Primrose pulled her little bottle of smelling salts out of her pocket. "There's too much excitement in the world altogether," she said, with a kind of consoling, gentle fury that came on her sometimes.

"Why, India! I feel perfect!" laughed Dabney, feeling them all looking at her. And all the little parlor things she had a moment ago cherished she suddenly wanted to break. She had once seen Uncle George, without saying a word, clench his fist in the dining room at home—the sweetest man in the Delta. It is because people are mostly layers of violence and tenderness—wrapped like bulbs, she thought soberly; I don't know what makes them onions or hyacinths. She looked up and smiled back at the gay little knowing nods of her aunts. They all sat down on the two facing sofas and had a plate of banana ice cream and some hot fresh cake and felt better.

"Now hurry and start back," said Aunt Primrose. "Oh, you never do come, and when you do you never stay a minute! Oh—growing up, and marrying. India, you're still my little girl!" Aunt Primrose without warning kissed India rambunctiously and pulled her into her sacheted skirt.

Aunt Jim Allen took up her needle-point and the green-threaded needle. "I'm going to give you this stool cover with the calla lily, of *course*, Dabney. I'll have it ready by the time Battle can get Marmion ready, I dare say."

"Dabney will have to have some kind of little old wedding present from us to take home," said Aunt Primrose. "Jump up and pick you out something, honey. You take whatever you like. Don't want to see you hesitate."

"Oh—everything's so soon now," said Dabney, jumping up. "Papa said any kind of wedding I wanted I could have, if I had to get married at all, so I'm going to have shepherdess crooks and horsehair ruffled hats."

"Can anybody put their feet on the stool?" asked India. "Troy?"

"Hush, dear," said Aunt Primrose softly. "We *hope* not."

"I'm going to be coming down the stairs while Mary Lamar Mackey plays—plays something—but you'll see it all," and Dabney was walking, rather gliding, around on the terribly slick parlor floor among all the little tables full of treasures. Some old friends of hers—two little china dogs—seemed to be going around with her.

"I'm a flower girl," said India, following her. "Cousin Laura McRaven's not one, because Aunt Annie Laurie is dead. Cousin Maureen and Cousin Lady Clare are flower girls. Bluet's wild to be the ring-bearer but she can't be—she's not a boy. That's Ranny."

"I'm going to have my bridesmaids start off in American Beauty and fade on out," said Dabney, turning about. "Two bridesmaids of each color, getting paler and paler, and then Shelley in flesh. She's my maid of honor."

"Of course," sighed Aunt Primrose.

"The Hipless Wonder," said India. "Her sweater belts go lower than anybody in *Virginia's.*"

"Why, India."

"Then me in pure white," Dabney said. "Everything's from Memphis, but nothing's come."

"But if it does come, it will all be exquisite, honey," said Aunt Primrose a little dimly.

"Everything's from Memphis but me. I have Mama's veil and Mashula's train—I could hold a little flower from your yard, couldn't I?"

But both aunts looked a little gravely into her swaying glance.

"Who are the bridesmaids, Dabney, dear?" Aunt Jim Allen called out.

"Those fast girls I run with," said Dabney irresistibly. "The ones that dance all night barefooted . . ."

"Child!"

"She was just teasing," India said.

"Won't she take our present?" Aunt Primrose began to fan herself a little with the palmetto fan she had bound in black velvet so that when anyone wanted to pull it apart it couldn't be done.

"I hate to—I hate to take something you love!"

"Fiddlesticks!"

"We've never really *seen* Troy," Aunt Jim Allen said faintly. She did sound actually frightened of Troy. "Not close *to*—you know." She indicated the walls of the green-lit parlor with her little ringed finger.

"You'll *have* to see him at the wedding," India told her loudly. "He has red hair and cat eyes and a *mus*-tache."

"I'm going to have him trim that off, when we are married," said Dabney gravely.

"It's not as if you were going out of the Delta, of course," Aunt Jim Allen said, looking bemused from her little deaf perch on the sofa. "Now it's time you chose something."

Dabney stopped, and her hand reached out and touched a round flower bowl on the table in front of her. It was there between the two china retrievers—was it the little bunny in one mouth that looked like Aunt Jim Allen, and the little partridge in the other that was Aunt Primrose? "I'd love a flower bowl," she said.

"You didn't take the prettiest," warned India.

Both aunts rose to see.

"No, no! No, indeed, you'll not take that trifling little thing! It's nothing but plain glass!"

"It came from Fairchild's Store!"

"Now you'll take something better than that, missy, something *we'd* want you to have," declared Aunt Primrose. She marched almost stiffly around the room, frowning at all precious possessions. Then she gave a low croon.

"The night light! She must have the little night light!" She stood still, pointing.

It was what they had all come to see when they were little—the bribe.

"Oh, I couldn't." Dabney drew back, holding the flower bowl in front of her.

"Put that down, child. She must have the night light, Jim Allen," said Aunt Primrose, raising her small voice a clear octave. "Dabney shall have it. It's company. That's what it is. That little light, it was company as early as I can remember—when Papa and Mama died."

"As early as *I* can remember," said Aunt Jim Allen, making her little joke about being the older sister.

"Dabney, Dabney, they're giving you the night light," whispered India, pulling at her sister's hand in a kind of anguish.

"I love it." Dabney ran up and kissed them both and gave them both a big hug to make up for waiting like that.

"And Aunt Mashula loved it—that waited for Uncle George, waited for him to come home from the Civil War till the lightning one early morning stamped her picture on the windowpane. *You've* seen it, India, it's *her* ghost you hear when you spend the night, breaking the window and crying up the bayou, and it's not an Indian maid, for what would she be doing, breaking our window to get out? The Indian maid would be crying nearer your place, where the mound is, if *she* cried."

"Jim Allen wants all the ghosts kept straight," said Aunt Primrose, flicking a bit of thread from her sister's dress.

"When did that Uncle George come back?" asked India.

"He never came back," said Aunt Primrose. "Nobody ever heard a single word. His brother Battle was killed and his brother Gordon was killed, and Aunt Shannon's husband Lucian Miles killed and Aunt Maureen's husband Duncan Laws, and yet she hoped. Our father and the children all gave up seeing him again in life. Aunt Mashula never did but she was never the same. She put her dulcimer away, you know. I remember her face.

Only this little night light comforted her, she said. We little children would be envious to see her burn it every dark night."

"Who's Aunt Maureen?" asked India desultorily.

"Aunt Mac Laws, sitting in your house right now," said Aunt Primrose rapidly. It made her nervous for people not to keep their kinfolks and their tragedies straight.

"Oh, it'll be company to you," Aunt Jim Allen said, while India, just to look at the little night light, began jumping up and down, rattling and jingling everything in the room. "There's nobody we'd rather have it, is there, Primrose, having no chick nor child at the Grove to leave it to?"

"I should say there isn't!" called Aunt Primrose to her. "Though George loved it, for a man. Where would that little Robbie put it, in Memphis? What would she *set* it on?" And taking a match from the mantelpiece she walked over to the little clay-colored object they all gazed at, sitting alone on its table, the pretty one with the sword scars on it. It was a tiny porcelain lamp with a cylinder chimney decorated with a fine brush, and an amazing little teapot, perfect spout and all, resting on its top.

"Shall we light it?"

India gave a single clap of the hands.

Aunt Primrose lighted the candle inside and stepped back, and first the clay-colored chimney grew a clear blush pink. The picture on it was a little town. Next, in the translucence, over the little town with trees, towers, people, windowed houses, and a bridge, over the clouds and stars and moon and sun, you saw a redness glow and the little town was all on fire, even to the motion of fire, which came from the candle flame drawing. In two high-pitched trebles the aunts laughed together to see, each accompanying and taunting the other a little with her delight, like the song and laughter of young children.

"Your tea would be nice and warm now if you had tea in the pot," said Aunt Primrose in an airy voice, and gave a dainty sound—almost a smack.

"Oh," said India gravely, "it's precious, isn't it?"

"You'll find it a friendly little thing," said Aunt Jim Allen, "if you're ever by yourself. Look! Only to light it, and you see the Great Fire of London, in the dark. Pretty—pretty—" She put it in Dabney's hand, still lighted, with its small teapot trembling. Aunt Primrose, with a respectful kind of look at Dabney, lifted the pot away and blew out the light.

Dabney held it, smiling. Then the aunts both drew back from the night light, as though Dabney had transformed it.

"Are you going to take it with you when you go on your honeymoon with Troy?" cried India.

"India Primrose Fairchild," said Aunt Primrose, looking at her own sister.

"Little girls don't talk about honeymoons," said Aunt Jim Allen. "They don't ask their sisters questions, it's not a bit nice."

"It's just that she loves the night light too," said Dabney. India took her around the waist and they went out together.

"Uncle George's coming from Memphis today. He's bringing champagne!" said Dabney over her shoulder.

"Mercy!" said both aunts. They smiled, looking faintly pink as they came to the door in the late sun. "I declare!" "George—wait till I get hold of him!" "He'll bring all the champagne in Memphis! We'll be tipsy, Primrose! He'll make this little family wedding into a Saturnalian feast! *That* will show people," Aunt Jim Allen said without hearing herself.

"Bless his heart," said Aunt Primrose. "When's he coming to see us? Tell him we expect him to noon dinner day *after* tomorrow. Ellen can have him first."

"You'll be coming up to dinner," said Dabney. "Aunt Tempe and Lady Clare and Uncle Pinck will be there and dying to see you."

"Mercy! Lady Clare!" said Aunt Primrose. "Don't let her do your mother the way she did at Annie Laurie's funeral, stamp her foot and get anything she wants."

"She's grown up more and been taking music," said Dabney, "and I've made her a flower girl."

She kissed them, with both hands around her present. Now that she was so soon to be married, she could see her whole family being impelled to speak to her, to say one last thing before she waved good-bye. She would long to stretch out her arms to them, every one. But they simply never looked deeper than the flat surface of any tremendous thing, that was all there was to it. They didn't try to understand *her* at all, her love, which they were free, welcome to challenge and question. In fact, here these two old aunts were actually *forgiving* it. All the Fairchilds were indulgent—indulgence was what she couldn't stand! The night light! Uncle George they indulged too, but they could never hurt him as they could hurt her—she *was* a little like him, only far beneath, powerless, a girl. He had an incorruptible, and hence unchallenging, sweetness of heart, and all their tender blaming could beat safely upon it, that solid wall of too much love.

"I declare I don't know how you're going to get a wedding present home on horseback—breakable," said Aunt Primrose rather perkily.

"Of course she can, and run out and cut those roses too, Dabney. You've got India to help carry things."

"Dabney can carry her night light home," said India. "I'll tote the little old bunch of flowers."

The others sat in the porch rockers and watched Dabney cut the red and white roses. "That's not enough—cut them all now, or we'll be mad."

"It's not like you were going away, or out of the Delta. Things aren't going to be any different, are they?" called Aunt Jim Allen. "Put those in something, child, and carry 'em to your mother. Tell her not to kill herself."

"Yes'm."

Aunt Primrose lifted one rose out of Dabney's bouquet as she went by. "What rose is that?" she asked her sister loudly.

"Why, I don't recognize it," said Aunt Jim Allen, taking it from her. "Don't recognize it at all."

They're never going to ask Dabney the questions, India meditated. She went up to Aunt Jim Allen and worried her, clasped and unclasped her harvest-moon breastpin, watching the way her sister went just a little prissily down the hall, being sent after a vase.

They don't make me say if I love Troy or if I don't, Dabney was thinking, clicking her heels in the pantry. But by the time she came back to the porch, the flowers in a Mason jar of water, she knew she would never say anything about love after all, if they didn't want her to.

Suppose they were afraid to ask her, little old aunts. She thought of how they both drew back to see her holding their night light. They would give her anything, but they wouldn't touch it again now for the world. It was a wedding present.

But, "I hope I have a baby right away," she said loudly, just as she passed in front of them. India saw Dabney's jaw drop the moment it was out, just as her own did, though she herself felt a wonderful delight and terror that made her nearly smile.

"I bet you *do* have, Dabney," said India. She came up behind her and began to pull down on her and rub her and love her.

Aunt Primrose took a little sacheted handkerchief from her bosom and touched it to her lips, and a tear began to run down Aunt Jim Allen's dry, rice-powdered cheek. They looked at nothing, as ladies do in church.

"I've done enough," Dabney thought, frightened, not quite understanding things any longer. "I've done enough to them." They all kissed good-bye again, while the green and gold shadows burned from the river—the sun was going down.

Dabney's cheeks stung for a moment, while they were getting on their horses. The sisters rode away from the little house, and Dabney could not help it if she rode beautifully then and felt beautiful. Does happiness seek out, go to visit, the ones it can humble when it comes at last to show itself? The roses for their mother glimmered faintly on the steps of the aunts' house, left behind, and they couldn't go back.

They rode in silence. It was late, and the aunts might have been going to insist that they stay to supper, if

Dabney hadn't said something a little ugly, a little unbecoming for Battle's daughter.

"The thorns of my hat hurts," said India.

She looked over at Dabney riding beside her, but would Dabney hear a word she said any more? Through parted lips her engaged sister breathed the soft blue air of seven o'clock in the evening on the Delta. In one easy hand she held the night light, the most enchanting thing in the world, and in the other hand she lightly held Junie's reins. The river wind stirred her hair. Her clear profile looked penitent and triumphant all in one, as if she were picked out and were riding alone into the world. India made a circle with her fingers, imagining she held the little lamp. She held it very carefully. It seemed filled with the mysterious and flowing air of night.

II

Just at sunset at Shellmound, meanwhile, Roxie and the others heard the sound of stranger-hoofs over the bayou bridge. Then coming over the grass in the yard rode Mr. George Fairchild—in his white clothes and all—on a horse they had never seen before. It was a sorrel filly with flax mane and tail and pretty stockings. "She's lady broke. She's wedding present for Miss Dab." But just then the little filly kicked her heels. "Bitsy always think he knows." "Wouldn't it be a sight did Mr. George pull out and take a little swallow out of his flask made all of gold, sitting where he is—like he do take?" "Miss Ellen! Here come Mr. George!"

"Where's Robbie?" Ellen called, running down the

steps, lightfooted as always at the sight of George coming. "Little Uncle!" she called to both sides, and Little Uncle came running.

Ranny, barefooted, came flying over the grass, and George put out an arm. Ranny leaped up and was pulled on beside him. He rode up with him sideways, both bare feet extended gracefully together like a captured maiden's. The little red filly almost danced—oh, she was so wet and tired. George was bareheaded now and his Panama hat was on the head of the little filly and she tossed at it.

"I came on Dabney's wedding present—where's Dabney?" he called.

"A horse! Ranny, look at Dabney's horse! Oh, George, you shouldn't. —Ranny, I thought you were in bed asleep."

"She was up at auction—I got on her and rode down." George dismounted and Little Uncle led the horse around the house with Ranny riding. "Little Uncle!" George ran after, and gave some kind of special directions, Ellen supposed, and accepted his hat from Little Uncle who bowed.

"All the way from Memphis? How long did it take you?" Ellen took hold of him and kissed him as if he had confessed a dark indulgence. "Just feel your forehead, you'll have the sunstroke if you don't get right in the house. Roxie!"

"Where's Dabney?" he asked again at the front door, and suddenly smiled at her, as if she might have been whimsical or foolish. She told him but he did not half listen. He was looking at her intently as they went through the hall and into the dining room. Nobody was there. He threw his coat and hat down and fell with a groan on the settee, which trembled under him the way it always did. "Warm day," he said at last, and shut his eyes. Roxie brought him the pitcher of lemonade, and he lifted up to drink a glass politely, but he would not have any cake just then. "I'll stretch a minute," he told Ellen, and at once his eyes shut again. She took his shoes off and he thanked her with a distant groan. She pulled the blinds a little, but he seemed far gone already with that intensity with which all the Fairchilds slept. In the darkened room his hair and all looked dark—turbulent and dark, almost Spanish. Spanish! She looked at him tenderly to have thought of such a far-fetched thing, and went out. The melting ice made a sound, and suddenly George did sigh heavily, as if protesting in his sleep.

"Poor man, he rode so *far*," she thought.

"I'm in trouble, Ellen!" he called after her, his voice wide and awake and loud in the half-empty house. "Robbie's left me!"

She ran back to him. He still lay back with his eyes shut. The Spanish look was not exhaustion, it was misery.

"She left me four days and nights ago. I'm hoping she'll come on here—in time for the wedding." He opened his eyes, but looked at her unrevealingly. All the affront of Robbie Reid came in a downpour over Ellen, the affront she had all alone declared to be purely a little summer cloud.

"I never saw anybody get here as wrinkled up in my life." She kissed his cheek, and sat by him wordlessly for a little. "Why, Orrin's meeting the Southbound, just in case you all came that way," she said, still protesting.

"She took the car. —That's how I thought of a horse for Dabney." He grinned.

Bluet, barefooted, with a sore finger, and with her hair put up in rags, came into the dining room to be kissed. "Don't give me a lizard," she decided to beg him.

He asked for his coat and gave her some little thing wrapped up in paper which she took trustingly.

Shelley came in chasing Bluet, and listened stock-still. "She'd better not try to come here!" she cried, when she understood what Robbie had done. Her face was pale. "We wouldn't let her in. To do you like that—you, Uncle George!"

He groaned and sat up, rumpled and yawning.

Battle came in, groaning too, from the heat, and was told the news. He closed his eyes, and shouted for Roxie or anybody to bring him something cold to drink. Roxie came back with the lemonade. Then he fell into his chair, where he wagged the pitcher back and forth to cool it.

Ellen said, "Oh, don't tell Dabney—not yet—spoil her wedding—" She stopped in shame.

"Then don't tell India," said Shelley.

"And we can't let poor Tempe know—she just couldn't cope with this," said Battle in a soft voice. "Hard enough on Tempe to have Dabney marrying the way she is, and after Mary Denis married a Northern man and moved so far off. Can't tell Primrose and Jim Allen and hurt them."

"Of course don't tell any of the girls," George said, staring at Shelley unseeingly, his mouth an impatient line.

"Look, George," Battle said at length. "What's that sister of her's name? Rebel Reid! I bet you anything I've got Robbie's with Rebel."

"I've a very good notion she is," George said.

There were voices in the hall, Vi'let's and somebody's, a vaguely familiar voice.

"Troy's here. What's he doing here?" Ellen looked at Battle. "Oh—he's invited to supper."

"Man! Why don't you go get her, are you paralyzed? Then wring her neck. Did you go—are you going?" Battle turned his eyes from George to Ellen, Shelley, Bluet, and around to Troy—standing foxy-haired and high-shouldered in the door, his slow smile beginning —to invite indignation.

"What else is in your coat, Uncle George?" Ranny asked politely in the silence.

"No, I'm not going," George said. He watched Ranny and Bluet mildly as they went through his coat pulling everything out, and kept watching how Ranny squatted down opening a present with fingers careful enough to unlock some strange mystery in the world.

"Oh, George," Ellen was saying. "Oh, Battle." She looked from one to the other, then went to watch helplessly at the darkening window, where they could hear the horses coming. "Here's Dabney."

As Dabney and India rode in, Uncle George was coming down the front steps to meet them. He always met them like that, and they could tell him from anybody in the world. He called Dabney's name across the yard; his white shirt sleeve waved in the dark. He helped them down with the night light, and Dabney took it from him with a little predatory click of the tongue.

"Everything's fine with you, I hear," said George. "Troy's in the house," and Dabney brushed against him and kissed him.

India saw Troy—he was a black wedge in the lighted window.

"It's all right," Dabney said, coolly enough, and ran up the steps.

But they heard it—running, she dropped the little night light, and it broke and its pieces scattered. They heard that but no cry at all—only the opening and closing of the screen door as she went inside.

India ran up to Uncle George and flung herself against his knees and beat on his legs. She could not stop crying, through Uncle George himself stayed out there holding her and in a little began teasing her about a little old piece of glass that Dabney would never miss.

3

It was so hard to read at Shellmound. There was so much going on in real life. Laura had tried to read under the bed that morning, but Dabney had found her and pulled her out by the foot. Now with Volume I of *Saint Ronan's Well* inside her pinafore, next to her skin, she went tiptoeing in the direction of the library, where no one ever went at this hour. She could hear nothing, except the sounds of the Negroes, and the slow ceiling fan turning in the hall, and the submissive panting of the dogs just outside under the banana plants, lying up close to the house. Even Mary Lamar Mackey had gone to Greenwood.

Laura generally hesitated just a little in every doorway. Jackson was a big town, with twenty-five thousand people, and Fairchilds was just a store and a gin and a bridge and one big house, yet she was the one who felt like a little country cousin when she arrived, appreciating that she had come to where everything was dressy, splendid, and over her head. Demonically she tried to be part of it—she took a breath and whirled, went ahead of herself everywhere, then she would fall down a humiliated little girl whose grief people never seemed to remember. The very breath of preparation in the air, drawing in or letting out, hurried or deep and slow, made Dabney's wedding seem as fateful in the house as her mother's funeral had been, and she knew the serenity of this morning moment was only waiting for laughter or tears.

Even from the door, the library smelled of a tremendous dictionary that had come through high water and fire in Port Gibson and had now been left open on a stand, probably by Shelley. On the long wall, above the piles of bookcases and darker than the dark-stained books, was a painting of Great-Great-Uncle Battle, whose name was written on the flyleaf of the dictionary. It was done from memory by his brother, Great-Grandfather George Fairchild, a tall up-and-down picture on a slab of walnut, showing him on his horse with his saddlebags and pistols, pausing on a dark path between high banks, smiling not down at people but straight out into the room, his light hair gone dark as pressed wildflowers. His little black dogs, that he loved as a little boy, Great-Grandfather had put in too. Did he look as if he would be murdered? Certainly he did, and he was. Side by side with Old Battle's picture was one of the other brother, Denis, done by a real painter, changelessly sparkling and fair, though he had died in Mexico, "marching on a foreign land." Behind the glass in the bookcases hiding the books, and out on the tables, were the miniatures in velvet cases that opened like little square books themselves. Among them were Aunt Ellen's poor mother (who had married some Lord in England, or had died) and the three brothers and the husbands of Aunt Mac and Aunt Shannon, who could not be told apart from one another by the children; but no matter what hide-and-seek went on here, in this room where so many dead young Fairchilds, ruined people, were, there seemed to be always consciousness of their gazes, so courteous and meditative they were. Coming in, gratefully bringing out her book, Laura felt it wordlessly; the animation of the living generations in the house had not, even in forgetting identity, rebuked this gentleness, because the gentleness was still there in their own faces, part of the way they were made, the nervous, tender, pondering forehead, the offered cheek—the lonely body, broad shoulder, slender hand, the long pressing thigh of Old Battle Fairchild against his horse Florian.

She turned, and there by the mantel was Uncle George. Uncle George, every minute being welcomed and never alone, was alone now—except, that is, for Vi'let, leaning from a stepladder with one knee on a bookcase, very slowly taking down the velvet curtains. He was rearing tall by the mantel, the gold clock and the children's switches at his head, wearing his white city clothes, but coatless, and his finger moved along the open edge of a blue envelope, which, in his hand then, appeared an object from a star. He gave Laura a serious look as she stood in the middle of the room, unconsciously offering him her open book with both hands. Over his shoulder stared the small oval portrait of Aunt Ellen in Virginia, stating flatly her early beauty, her oval face in the melancholy mood of a very young girl, the full lips almost argumentative.

There was nothing at all abstract in Uncle George's

look, like the abstraction of painted people, of most interrupted real people. There was only penetration in his look, and it reached to her. So serious was it that she backed away, out of the library, into the hall, and backwards out the screen door. Outside, she picked up a striped kitten that was stalking through the grass-blades, and held him to her, pressing against the tumult in her fingers and in his body. The willful little face was like a question close to hers, and the small stems of its breath came up and tickled her nose like flowers. In front of her eyes the cardinals were flying hard at their reflections in the car, drawn up in the yard now (they had got back from Greenwood). A lady cardinal was in the rosebush, singing so hard that she throbbed between her shoulder blades. Laura could see herself in the car door too, holding the kitten whose little foot stretched out. She stood looking at herself reflected there—as if she had gotten along so far like an adventurer in an invisible coat, as magical as it was unsuspected by her. Now she felt visible to everything.

The screen door opened behind her and Uncle George came out on the porch. They were calling him somewhere. She could see him in the red door, his hands were in his pockets and the letter was not showing on him.

"Skeeta! Like Shelley's kitten?" he remarked.

"No," she said, dropping it in the sheer perversity of excitement, because she thought that whatever had happened, he hoped Laura still liked Shelley's kitten. Now it chased the cardinals, which darted and scolded, though the lady cardinal sang on.

"What do you like best of anything in the world?" he asked, lighting his pipe now.

"Riddles," she answered.

"Uncle George!" they cried, but he began asking her, "As I was going to St. Ives." One thing the Fairchilds could all do was to take an old riddle and make it sound like a new one, their own. "One," she said, "you. You were going to St. Ives, all by yourself."

"Out of all those? Only me?" Then Dabney came out and grabbed him, and he looked over her head at Laura pretending he could not believe what he heard, as if he expected anything in the world to happen—a new answer to the riddle, which she, Laura, had not given him.

While they were all still seated around the table drinking their last coffee, Mr. Dunstan Rondo, the Methodist preacher at Fairchilds, paid a noon call. They were all tired, trying to make Aunt Shannon eat.

"Eat, Aunt Shannon, you've had no more than a bird."

"How can I eat, child," Aunt Shannon would say mysteriously, "when there's nothing to eat?"

They did not expect Mr. Rondo, they hardly knew him, but plainly, Ellen saw, he considered his dropping in a nice thing, since he was to marry Dabney and Troy so soon. Aunt Mac and Aunt Shannon vanished. The children started to run.

"Come back here!" Battle shouted. "You stay right here. Mr. Rondo, there's a baby too, somewhere."

"I'm afraid I'm not much of a Sunday School girl," Dabney told Mr. Rondo demurely as he took her hand, "But I'm the bride."

"By all means!" said Mr. Rondo, his voice hearty but uncertain. He sat in Battle's chair. Battle sat down on a little needle-point-covered stool and gave Mr. Rondo a rather argumentative look.

"I suppose you've met at some time or other my brother George, though he never put foot in a church that I know of. Fooling with practicing law in Memphis now—we're hoping he'll give it up and move back. He did plant the Grove over on the river, before he went to war."

Mr. Rondo and George shook hands.

"Why, I believe I married him," said Mr. Rondo.

"Of course! You did—you did. They got you out of bed in the middle of the night—you knew about it before we did!" Battle laughed at Mr. Rondo as at some failing in him.

"Is your wife the former Miss Roberta Reid from Fairchilds City?"

"Yes, sir."

"Yes, sir. That's who she is," Battle answered, also.

"And have they children?" asked Mr. Rondo, of Battle, as if that would be more polite.

Bluet, who never carried less than two things with her, hobbled in burdened under a suitcase and a croquet mallet. She was wearing a pair of Shelley's gun-metal stockings around her neck like a fur. "I'm their little girl," she said.

"They have not," said Battle. "And he loves them—eats mine up. He loves children and they love him. Look at Bluet kiss him." He scowled at Mr. Rondo.

"They get along beautifully, George and Robbie," said Ellen in open anxiety, making her way around the table toward Mr. Rondo. "It's in their faces—I don't know if you pay much attention to that kind of thing, Mr. Rondo?"

"In their faces?" Dabney asked, looking at her mother in astonishment.

"I was thinking of one picnic night, particularly, dear." Ellen's voice suddenly trembled.

"You mean when they put on the Rape of the Sabines down at the Grove?" asked Battle.

"A family picnic." Ellen smiled at the preacher firmly. "You should have come to dinner." She offered her hand, seeming to reproach him for not being invited. But Battle had said when she spoke of inviting him to one meal before the rehearsal supper, "Who wants a preacher to *eat* with them?" Mr. Rondo was so nice and plump, he looked as if he would have enjoyed the turkey too.

"A good deal, yes, a great deal in people's faces," he said.

"Well, entertain Mr. Rondo. Tell him about George on the trestle—I bet he'd like that," said Battle. "You tell it, Shelley."

"Oh, Papa, not me!" Shelley cried.

"Not *you*?"

"Let me," cried India. "I can tell it good—make everybody cry."

"All right, India."

"Very simply, now, India," said Ellen calmly. She sat up straight and held Ranny's hand.

"It was late in the afternoon!" cried India, joining her hands. She came close to Mr. Rondo and stood in front of him. "Just before the thunderstorm!"

Immediately in Shelley's delicate face Ellen could see reflected, as if she felt a physical blow now, the dark, rather brutal colors of the thunderclouded August landscape. "Simply, India."

"Let her alone, Ellen."

"What we'd been doing was fishing all Sunday morning in Drowning Lake. It was everybody but Papa and Mama—they missed it. It was me, Dabney, and Shelley, Orrin and Roy, Little Battle and Ranny and Bluet, Uncle George and Aunt Robbie—Mama, when's she coming? Soon? And Maureen. And Bitsy and Howard and Big Baby and Pinchy before she started seeking, and Sue Ellen's boys and everybody in creation."

"And Troy," said Dabney.

"Troy too. And then we didn't catch nothing. Came home on the railroad track, came through the swamp. Came to the trestle.

"Everybody wanted to walk it but Aunt Robbie said No. No indeed, she had city heels, and would never go on the trestle. So she sat down plump, but we weren't going to carry her! We started across. Then Shelley couldn't walk it either. She's supposed to be such a tomboy! And she couldn't look down. Everybody knows there isn't any water in Dry Creek in the summertime. Did you know that, Mr. Rondo?"

"I believe that is the case," said Mr. Rondo, when India waited.

"Well, Shelley went down the bank and walked through it. I was singing a song I know. 'I'll measure my love to show you, I'll measure my love to show you—' "

"That's enough of the song," said Dabney tensely.

" '—For we have gained the day!' Then Shelley said, 'Look! Look! The Dog!' and she yelled like a banshee and the Yellow Dog was coming creep-creep down the track with a flag on it."

"A flag!" cried Dabney.

"I looked, if you didn't," said India. "We said, 'Wait,

wait! Go back! Stop! Don't run over us!' But *it* didn't care!"

"Mercy!" said Mr. Rondo. Bluet, who had never taken her eyes off him, laughed delightedly and circled round him. George watched her, a faint smile on his face.

"It couldn't stop, India, it wasn't that it didn't care." Dabney frowned. "Mr. Doolittle was asleep. The engineer, you know." She smiled at Mr. Rondo.

"Who's telling this? Creep, creep. Then it was time for Aunt Robbie to jump up in her high heels and call 'George! Come back!' But he didn't. 'All right, sweethearts, jump,' Uncle George says, and the first one to jump was me. I landed on my feet and seat in an old snaky place. I made a horrible noise when I was going through the air—like this. . . . I looked up and saw Dabney get Ranny in her arms and jump holding him, the craziest thing she ever did, but Ranny said 'Do it again!' Creep, creep. Of course Roy hung by his hands instead of jumping, and Little Battle had to climb back and do it too. Look how ashamed they look! They got cinders in their eyes, both of them. Uncle George threw Bluet off, and Shelley picked her up. I forgot to say all the Negroes had run to the four corners of the earth and we could hear Pinchy yelling like a banshee from way up in a tree. That was before she started coming through."

"Go faster," said Dabney. "Mr. Rondo will get bored."

"Oh, well: Maureen caught her foot. She was dancing up there, and that's what she did—caught her foot good. Uncle George said to hold still a minute and he'd get it loose, but he couldn't get her foot loose at all. So creep, creep."

"It was coming fast!" cried Dabney. "Mr. Rondo, the whistle was blowing like everything, by that time!"

Mr. Rondo nodded, in a pleasant, searching manner.

"The whistle was blowing," said India, "but the Dog was not coming very fast. Aunt Robbie was crying behind us and saying, 'Come back, George!' and Shelley said, 'Jump, jump!' but he just stayed on the trestle with Maureen."

"Path of least resistance." Battle beamed at Mr. Rondo fiercely. "Path George's taken all his life."

"Hurry up, India," said Dabney. "Hurry up, India," said Ranny and Bluet, banging dessert spoons on the back of the preacher's chair.

"Now be still, or I won't let India go any further," Ellen said, her hand on her breast. Then Bluet beat her spoon very softly.

"Oh, well, Maureen said, 'Litt-la train-ain can-na get-la by-y,' and stuck her arms out."

Battle gave a short laugh. "India, you're a sight—you ought to go on the stage."

"Creep, creep." India smiled.

"Hurry up, India."

"Well, Maureen and Uncle George kind of wrestled with each other and both of them fell off, and anyway the Dog stopped in plenty time, and we all went home and Robbie was mad at Uncle George. I expect they had a fight all right. And that's all."

Bluet whimpered.

"Yes, that's all, Bluet," said Ellen. "India, you tell what you know about and then stop, that's the way."

"Now wait. Tell what Robbie said when it was all

over, India," said Battle, turning the corners of his mouth down. "Listen, Mr. Rondo."

"Robbie said, 'George Fairchild, you didn't do this for *me*!' "

Battle roared with cross laughter from his stool.

Dabney cried, "You should have heard her!"

Shelley went white.

"Robbie said, 'George Fairchild, you didn't do this for *me*!' " India repeated. "Look, Shelley's upset."

"Shelley can't stand anything, it looks like, with all this Dabney excitement," said Battle. "Now don't let me see you cry."

"Leave me alone," Shelley said.

"She's crying," India said, with finality. "Look, Mr. Rondo: she's the oldest."

"Who is Maureen?" asked Mr. Rondo pleasantly. "Is she this little girl?" He pointed at Laura.

"Oh, no, I wasn't there," Laura said, a little fastidiously.

He was fully told, that Maureen had been dropped on her head as an infant, that her mother, Virgie Lee Fairchild, who had dropped her, ran away into Fairchilds and lived by herself, never came out, and that she wore her black hair hanging and matted to the waist, had not combed it since the day she let the child fall. "*You've* seen her!" Their two lives had stopped on that day, and so Maureen had been brought up at Shellmound.

"Why, she's Denis's child!" they all said.

"She's just as much Fairchild as you are," said Battle. "So don't ever let me catch you getting stuck up in your life." He gave Laura a look.

"Is Maureen *my* first cousin?" Laura cried.

"We're kin to Maureen the same as we're kin to each

other," Shelley told her. "On the Fairchild side. Her papa was Uncle Denis and he was killed in the war, don't you remember?"

"I forgot," said Laura. "When will she comb her hair?"

"We'll let you know when she does." Shelley and Dabney giggled, looking at each other.

"I guess I'd better be going," said Mr. Rondo. "Midday's a busy time to call."

"But I know she won't comb it for your wedding, Dabney," said Battle. And he gave a hearty and rather prolonged laugh. "You might think your marrying Troy Flavin would bring anything about, but it won't make your Aunt Virgie Lee take the tangles out of her hair!" And he laughed on, groaning, as if it hurt his side.

And Dabney suddenly left the table. She had to be called three times, but when she came down she looked rather softened at being teased about her love before everybody. Mr. Rondo had already taken his departure, promising to be back to the rehearsal and supper on Friday night; they said they would show him just what to do.

Ellen stood at the foot of the stairs holding a cup of broth. George came out of the dining room lighting his pipe and went to her.

"I know I should worry a little more about Aunt Shannon," she began, and he lifted the napkin and looked at the broth. "Have a taste," she said, sighing.

"She's stubborn too," George said.

"I sent Laura up with this—but she wouldn't even drink it for her. She sent the poor little thing back."

He nodded. Aunt Shannon never wept over Laura, as

if she could not do it over one motherless child, or give her any immediate notice. In her the Fairchild oblivion to the member of the family standing alone was most developed; just as in years past its opposite, the Fairchild sense of emergency, a dramatic instinct, was in its ascendancy, and she had torn herself to pieces over Denis's drinking and Denis's getting killed. Insistently a little messenger or reminder of death, Laura self-consciously struck her pose again and again, but she was a child too familiar, too like all her cousins, too much one of them (as they all were to one another a part of their very own continuousness at times) ever to get the attention she begged for. By Aunt Shannon in particular, the members of the family were always looked on with that general tenderness and love out of which the single personality does not come bolting and clamorous, but just as easily emerges gently, like a star when it is time, into the sky and by simply emerging drifts back into the general view and belongs to the multitudinous heavens. All were dear, all were unfathomable, all were constantly speaking, as the stars would ever twinkle, imploringly or not—so far, so far away.

"You take her the broth, George. I believe she would drink it for you."

"Maybe so. Some days she thinks I'm Grandfather—or Denis," he said without rancor.

She still held on to the bowl, not able to worry enough about Aunt Shannon. How in his family's eyes George could lie like a fallen tower as easily as he could be raised to extravagant heights! Now if he was fallen it was because of his ordinary wife, but once it had been because he gave away the Grove, and before that something else. The slightest pressure of his actions would modify the wonder, lower or raise it. Whereas even the daily presence of Maureen and the shadowy nearness of Virgie Lee had never taken anything away from the pure, unvarying glory of Denis.

"Tell her to drink it for you," she said, and held out the bowl to him very carefully. He took it with the touching helpfulness of her son Ranny.

She watched him carrying it upstairs. Not for the first time, she wondered whether, if it had never been for Denis, George might not have been completely the hero to his family—instead of sometimes almost its hero and sometimes almost its sacrificial beast. But she thought that she could tell (as George turned on the landing and gave her a look as sweet as a child's of not wanting her to be anxious) that he was more remarkable than either, and not owing to Denis's spectacular life or death, but to his being in himself all that Denis no longer was, a human being and a complex man.

Battle came down the hall with a hangdog look, and she met him and comforted him for his impatience.

"If I weren't tied down," he said. "If I weren't tied down! I'd go find little Upstart Reid myself, and kill her. No, I'd set her and Flavin together and feed 'em to each other."

"Mr. Rondo came at the wrong time," Ellen said, kissing him. "It just wasn't a good day for Mr. Rondo."

"Go to sleep, Bluet, go to sleep," said Ellen monotonously to her baby. The house was nearly still; from below came faint noises from the kitchen, and from somewhere one little theme over and over on the piano. Mary Lamar Mackey played all day, the whole of her visit—as if the summer must speak a yearning each day through, yet never enough could she bring it to speak. Nocturnes were her joy.

"Go to sleep, Bluet, and I'll tell you my dream."

"Dream?"

Bluet was a gentle little thing, inquiring more gently than India, filled with attention, quick to show admiration and innumerable kinds of small pleasures—she was younger. All day she worked, carrying on, like a busy housewife, her loves and hates without knowing her small life was an open window where they all looked in and smiled at her. Now she lay in one of the big white-painted iron sleeping-porch beds with the mosquito net folded back against its head; it was like a big baby buggy that, too, would carry her away somewhere against her will. "Do you hear the dove, Mama?" Outside the summer day shimmered and rustled, and the porch seemed to flow with light and shadow that traveled outwards.

In a low voice Ellen told her dream to put the child to sleep. With one hand she held down her little girl's leg, which wanted to kick like a dancer's. Gradually it gave up.

"Mama dreamed about a thing she lost long time ago before you were born. It was a little red breastpin, and she wanted to find it. Mama put on her beautiful gown and she went to see. She went to the woods by James's Bayou, and on and on. She came to a great big tree."

"Great big tree," breathed the child.

"Hundreds of years old, never chopped down, that great big tree. And under the tree was sure enough that little breastpin. It was shining in the leaves like fire. She went and knelt down and took her pin back, pinned it to her breast and wore it. Yes, she took her pin back—she pinned it to her breast—to her breast and wore it—away—away . . ."

Bluet's eyelids fell and her dancing leg was still. Her lips suddenly parted, but with a soft sigh and a rapid taking back of the lost breath she was past the moment when she could have protested. She was asleep for the afternoon.

The dream Ellen told Bluet was an actual one, for it would never have occurred to her to tell anything untrue to a child, even an untrue version of a dream. She often told dreams to Bluet at bedtime and nap time, for they were convenient—the only things she knew that were not real. Ellen herself had always rather trusted her dreams. It was her weakness, she knew, and it was right for the children as they grew up to deride her, and so she usually told them to the youngest. However, she dreamed the location of mistakes in the accounts and the payroll that her husband—not a born business man—had let pass, and discovered how Mr. Bascom had cheated them and stolen so much; and she dreamed whether any of the connection needed her in their various places, the Grove, Inverness, or the tenants down the river, and they always did when she got there. She dreamed of things the children and Negroes lost and of where they were, and often when she looked she did find them, or parts of them, in the dreamed-of places. She was too busy when she was awake to know if a thing was lost or not—she had to dream it.

It was the night before that she had the dream she lured Bluet to sleep with. Actually, it had been in the form of a warning; she had left that out, for Bluet's domestic but bloodthirsty little heart would have made her get up and dance on the bed to learn what a warning was. She was *warned* that her garnet brooch, a present in courting days from her husband, that had been lying around the house for years and then disappeared, lay in the leaves under a giant cypress tree on the other side of the bayou. She had certainly forgotten it during the confusion of the morning and of dinnertime, and since, when Dabney burst into tears and ran out crying, "Excuse me for *living*!" Now the feeling of being warned returned, rather pleasantly than not, to Ellen's bosom. She put a little sugared almond on Bluet's pillow, for her fairies' gift, and left the sleeping porch on tiptoe.

Then, while she was rubbing the silver and glass with a whole kitchen and back porch full of Negroes, Sylvanus, old Partheny's son, came to the door.

"Miss Ellen. Partheny send for you. Say please come."

"Has she had a spell?"

"She in one," said Sylvanus. "Say please Miss Ellen come. Not me stay with her, Mr. Troy git me."

"Run on back to the fields, Sylvanus, I'll go."

She took off her apron, after first filling a small pot with some of Aunt Shannon's broth, for she might as well stop at Little Uncle's, she thought, where his wife Sue Ellen was going to have another one and not doing well, and speak in person to Oneida too about helping to dress all the chickens.

She put her head in at the dining-room door. There were just the two old aunts awake and about; Aunt Shannon was downstairs now, calmly sewing a bit of stuff.

"I'm going out a little while," she said.

"The more fool you," said Aunt Mac.

Aunt Mac was three years younger than Aunt Shannon. She had dyed black hair that she pulled down, spreading its thin skein as far as it would go, about her tiny, rosy-lobed ears. Little black ringlets bounced across her forehead as if they alone were her hair and the rest were a cap, an old-fashioned winter toboggan with a small fuzzy ball at the peak, which was her impatient knot. She was little with age. Somewhere, in mastering her dignity over life, she had acquired the exaggerated walk of a small boy, under her long black skirt, and went around Shellmound with her old, wine-colored lip stuck out as if she invited a dare. Her cheekbones, like little gossamer-covered drums, stood out in her face, on which rice powder twinkled when she sat in her place under the brightest lamp. Her sharp, bright features looked out (though she was quite deaf now) as if she were indeed outdoors in her new cap, a bright boy or young soldier, stalking the territory of the wide world, looking for something to catch or maybe let get away, this time. She watched out; but very exactingly she dressed herself in mourning for her husband Duncan Laws, killed in the Battle of Corinth sixty years ago. A watch crusted with diamonds was always pinned to the little hollow of her breast, and she would make the children tell her the time by it, right or wrong. She whistled a tune sometimes, some vaguely militant or Presbyterian air that sounded archaic and perverse in a pantry, where she would sometimes fling open the cupboard doors to see how nearly starving they were. Her smile, when it came—often for India—was soft. She gave a trifling hobble sometimes now when she walked, but it seemed to be a flourish, just to look busy. Her eyes were remarkable, stone-blue now, and with all she had to do, she had read the Bible through nine times before she ever came to Shellmound and started it there. She and her sister Shannon had brought up all James's and Laura Allen's children, when they had been left, from Denis aged twelve to George aged three, after their dreadful trouble; were glad to do it—widows! And though Shannon drifted away sometimes in her mind and would forget where she was, and speak to Lucian as if he had not started out to war to be killed, or to her brother Battle the same way, or to her brother George as if he had been found and were home again, or to dead young Denis she had loved best—she, Mac, had never let go, never asked relenting from the present hour, and if anything should, God prevent it, happen to Ellen now, she was prepared to do it again, start in with young Battle's children, and bring them up. She would start by throwing Troy Flavin in the bayou in front of the house and letting the minnows chew him up.

But Aunt Shannon, when she would look around the room and know it, would catch her breath and ask for something—for a palmetto fan, anything; as if life were so piteous that all people had better content themselves with was to be waited on hand and foot; tend or be tended, the wave would fall, and it was better to be tended.

Ellen took one of the big black cotton umbrellas out of the stand and went out. The sun did press down, like a hot white stone. The whole front yard was dazzling; it was covered with all the lace curtains of the house drying on stretchers. Just then here came Roy, riding on his billy goat, in and out, just not touching all the curtains.

"Oh, Roy! I did think you were asleep! Are you being careful?"

"I'll never touch a curtain or make the tiniest hole, Mama. Want to watch me?"

"No, I trust you."

"Can I ride along behind you, Mama, where you're going?"

"Not this time," she said.

She crossed the bayou bridge, almost treading on the butterflies lighting and clinging on the blazing, fetid boards, and walked leisurely down the other side on the old Marmion path (when there had been a river bridge up this far) through the trees. She had been weary today until now. It seemed to her that Dabney's wedding had made everybody feel a little headstrong this week, the children flying out of the house without even pretending to ask permission and herself not being able as well as usual to keep up with any of it.

It was a clamorous family, Ellen knew, and for her, her daughter Dabney and her brother-in-law George were the most clamorous. She knew George was importunate—how much that man hoped for! Much more than Battle. They should all fairly shield their eyes against that hope. Dabney did not really know yet for how much she asked. But where George was importunate, Dabney was almost greedy. Dabney was actually, at moments, almost selfish, and he was not. That is, she thought, frowning, George had not Dabney's kind of unselfishness which is a dread of selfishness, but the thoughtless, hasty kind which is often cheated of even its flower, like a tender perennial that will disregard the winter earlier every year. . . . The umbrella was in her way now that she had come to the shade, and she could wish she had brought a little Negro along to carry it or the soup.

She noticed how many little paths crisscrossed and disappeared in here, the deeper she went. Who had made them? There had been more woods left standing here than she had remembered. The shade was nice. Moss from the cypresses hung deep overhead now, and by the water vines like pediments and arches reached from one tree to the next. She walked abstractedly, gently moving her extended hand with the closed umbrella in it from side to side, clearing the vines and mosquitoes from her path. There were trumpet vines and passion flowers. The cypress trunks four feet thick in the water's edge stood opened like doors of tents in Biblical engravings. How still the old woods were. Here the bayou banks were cinders; they said it was where the Indians burned their pottery, at the very last. The songs of the cotton pickers were far away, so were the hoofbeats of the horse the overseer rode (and once again, listening for them in spite of the quiet, she felt as if the cotton fields so solid to the sight had opened up and swallowed her daughter). Even inside this narrow but dense wood she found herself listening for sounds of the fields and house, walking along almost anxiously enough to look back over her shoulder—wondering if something needed her at home, if Bluet had waked up, if for some unaccountable reason Dabney had flown back from a party, calling her mother.

Then she heard a step, a starting up in the woods.

"Who's that?" she called sharply. "Come here to me."

There was no answer, but she saw, the way she moved in the woodsy light, it was a girl.

"Whose girl are you? Pinchy?" Pinchy, Roxie's helper, was coming through these days, and wandered around all day staring and moaning until she would see light. But Pinchy would answer Miss Ellen still.

"Are you one of our people? Girl, are you lost then?"

Still there was no answer, but no running away either. Ellen called, "Come here to me; I could tell, you are about the size of one of my daughters. And if you belong somewhere, I'm going to send you back unless they're mean to you, you can't hide with me, but if you don't belong anywhere, then I'll have to think. Now come out. My soup's getting cold here for an old woman."

Then since the girl remained motionless where she had been discovered, Ellen patiently made her way through the pulling vines and the old spider webs toward her. She was dimly aware of the chimney to the overseer's house stuck up through the trees, but in here it seemed an ancient place and for a moment the girl was not a trespasser but someone who lived in the woods, a dark creature not hiding, but waiting to be seen, careless on the pottery bank. Then she saw the corner of a little torn skirt poking out by the tree, almost of itself trembling.

"Come out, child. . . . It's luck I found you—I was just looking for a little pin I lost," she said.

"I haven't seen *no pin*," the girl said behind her tree.

When she heard the voice, Ellen stopped still. She peered. All at once she cried, "Aren't you a Negro?"

The girl still only waited behind a tree, but a quick, alert breath came from her that Ellen heard.

So she was white. A whole mystery of life opened up. Ellen waited by a tree herself, as if she could not go any farther through the woods. Almost bringing terror the thought of Robbie Reid crossed her mind. Then the girl seemed to become the more curious of the two; she looked around the tree. Ellen said calmly, "Come out here in the light."

She came out and showed herself, a beautiful girl, fair and nourished, round-armed. Not long ago she had been laughing or crying. She had been running. Her skin was white to transparency, her hazel eyes looking not downward at the state of her skirt but levelly into the woods around and the bayou.

"Stand still," said Ellen.

It was a thing she said habitually, often on her knees with pins in her mouth. She herself was sternly still, as if she expected presently to begin to speak—and speech at such a time would likely be stern questions that perhaps would find no answers. Yet at her side her arms slowly felt light and except for their burdens her hands would have gone out to the shadowy girl—she caught the motion back, feeling a cool breath as if a rabbit had run over her grave, or as if someone had seen her naked. She felt sometimes like a mother to the world, all that was on her! yet she had never felt a mother to a child this lovely.

The faint wind from the bayou blew in the girl's hair she had shaken out, marking somehow the time going by in the woods. None of her daughters stood this still in front of her, they tore from her side. Or even in the morning when she went to their beds to wake them, they never had a freshness like this, which the soiled cheek, the leafy hair, the wide-awake eyes made almost startling. None of her daughters, even Dabney, had a beauty which seemed to go out from them, as they stood still—

every time she had ever said "Stand still," had she hoped for this beauty? In Ellen's mind dimly was that poetic expression *to shed* beauty. Now she comprehended it, as if a key to all the poetry Denis once read had been given to her here in the bayou woods when this girl without pouting or curiosity waited when told.

"Way out here in the woods!" said Ellen. "You'll bring mistakes on yourself that way." She waited a moment. "You're no Fairchilds girl or Inverness girl or Round Bayou or Greenwood girl. You're a stranger to me." The girl did not give her any answer and she said, "I don't believe *you* even know who I am."

"I haven't seen *no pin*," said the girl.

"You're at the end of the world out here! You're purely and simply wandering in the woods. I ought to take a stick to you."

"Nobody can say I stole *no pin*."

Ellen dropped the old black umbrella and took hold of the young girl's hand. It was small, calloused, and warm. "I wasn't speaking about any little possession to you. I suppose I was speaking about good and bad, maybe. I was speaking about men—men, our lives. But you don't know who I am."

The warm, quiet hand was not attempting to withdraw and not holding to hers either. How beautiful the lost girl was.

"I'm not stopping you," Ellen said. "I ought to turn you around and send you back—or make you tell me where you're going or think you're going—but I'm not. Look at me, I'm not stopping you," she said comfortably.

"You couldn't stop me," the girl said, comfortably also, and a half-smile, sweet and incredibly maternal, passed over her face. It made what she said seem teasing and sad, final and familiar, like the advice a mother is bound to give her girls. Ellen let the little hand go.

In the stillness a muscadine fell from a high place into the leaves under their feet, burying itself, and like the falling grape the moment of comfort seemed visible to them and dividing them, and to be then, itself, lost.

They took a step apart.

"I reckon I was the scared one, not you," Ellen said. She gathered herself together. "I reckon you scared me—first coming, now going. In the beginning I did think I was seeing something in the woods—a spirit (my husband declares one haunts his bayou here)—then I thought it was Pinchy, an ignorant little Negro girl on our place. It was when I saw you were—were a stranger—my heart nearly failed me, for some reason."

The girl looked down at the red glass buttons on her dress as if she began to feel a kind of pleasure in causing confusion.

"Which way is the big road, please ma'am?" she asked.

"That way." Ellen pointed explicitly with her umbrella, then drew it back slowly. "Memphis," she said. When her voice trembled, the name seemed to recede from something else into its legendary form, the old Delta synonym for pleasure, trouble, and shame.

The girl made her way off through the trees, and Ellen could hear the fallen branches break softly under her foot. A fleeting resentment that she did not understand flushed her cheeks; she thought, I didn't give her this little soup. But still listening after her, she knew that the girl did not care what she thought or would have given, what Ellen might have cast away with her; that she never looked back.

III

" 'Go in and out the window, go in and out the window . . .' "

They held hands, high and then low, and Shelley, who was It because she was the big girl, ran stooping under their arms, in and out. They were playing in the shade of the pecan trees, after naps and a ride to Greenwood after the groceries, Shelley, India, Bluet, Maureen, Ranny, and Laura. Cousin Lady Clare was just now sent by Aunt Mac out to play with them too. She had come ahead of Aunt Tempe, her grandmother, to Shellmound, come by herself on the Yellow Dog, and now went around with her lower teeth biting her upper lip like William S. Hart. Little Uncle's little boys were up in the yard, crisscrossing with two lawn mowers cutting the grass for the wedding. Far in the back, Howard was beating the rugs with a very slow beat. The sound of the lawn mowers was pleading; they seemed to be saying "Please . . . please." The children were keeping out of mischief so that other people could get something done; Shelley was obeying her mother too, and this lowered her some in the eyes of them all, white and colored.

" ' . . . For we have gained the day.' "

Lady Clare said to Laura, "Ask Shelley can Troy French-kiss."

"I'm sure he can," Laura said loftily, for she had been here a day longer than Lady Clare, whatever French-kissing might be.

The song and the game were dreamlike to her. It was nice to have Shelley in the circle, but then it was lovely to have her out. It was funny how sometimes you wanted to be in a circle and then you wanted out of it in a rush.

Sometimes the circle was for you, sometimes against you, if you were It. Sometimes in the circle you longed for the lone outsider to come in—sometimes you couldn't wait to close her out. It was never a good circle unless you were in it, catching hands, and knowing the song. A circle was ugly without you. She knew how ugly it was from the face Maureen would make to see it, and to change this she would let her in. Even if she did not, Maureen would get in. Maureen was a circle breaker. She was very strong. Once she had hold of you, she was so gentle and good at first, she would surprise you. She looked around with a soft, pink look on her face—in a minute it was a daring look, and the next minute she would try to break your finger bones. She liked to change a circle into "Crack the Whip," and with a jerk of her arm she could throw ten cousins to the ground and make them roll over.

They played "Running Water, Still Pond," "Fox in the Morning, Geese in the Evening," and then "Hide-and-Seek." Once Lady Clare was It, because she was carrying a little Chinese paper fan that folded back on tiny sticks, then Shelley was It again. Laura ran to her best hiding place, down on the ground behind the woodpile in the back yard. She waited a long time crouched over and nobody came to find her. From where she hid she could see the back of the house, hear the Negroes, and upstairs on the long sleeping porch she could see Uncle George walking up and down, up and down, smoking his pipe. She listened to the dark, dense rustling of the fig trees, and once she put a straw down a doodlebug hole and said the incantation in a very low voice.

Then she saw Maureen running by, and Maureen saw her. With a leap Maureen was up on her woodpile. She did not say a word. She looked over from the top, and then after a strange pause, as if she could think, she pushed the whole of the piled logs down on Laura, upsetting herself too. "Choo choo," said Maureen, and then she ran away.

Laura at first was surprised, and then with great effort she began to extricate herself. The surprise, the heavy weight, and the uncertainty of getting out kept her so busy that at first she did not miss them coming to look for her. She had on her next-best white dress, and long tears showed in it, and long scratches marked up her legs and arms. She had the taste of bark in her mouth and kept spitting on the ground, though the taste was still there. Inside the house the light, tinkling sounds went on; Roxie's high laugh, like a dove cry, rose softly and hung over the yard. And from farther away the sigh of the compress reminded her of Dabney, who had gone somewhere.

Harm—that was what Maureen intended, that was what she meant by her speechless gaze. That was what made her stay so close to them all, what drove her flying over the house, over the fields that way, after the others. That was what put extra sounds in her mouth. It was the harm inside her.

"She likes to spoil things," India had explained matter-of-factly, and matter-of-factly Laura had accepted it. But the cousins were a clan. They all said things, and they all kissed one another, and yet they all had secret, despiting ways to happiness. At hide-and-seek a trick could be played on Laura, for she was still outside. She herself would never mean from the start to push down and overwhelm, or withhold any secret intention or hope in relish and delight.

Pushing the heavy logs from her, she felt shorn of pleasure in her cousins and angry in not having known that this was how the Fairchilds wanted things to be, and how they would make things be, when it pleased them. Uncle George was nowhere to be seen, and she thought she heard Shelley laughing and calling his name down in the house. A feeling of their unawareness of her came over Laura and crushed her more heavily than the harm of Maureen and the logs of wood, and she thought surely her mother would cry in Heaven to see her now, if she had not cried so far.

She licked the blood away clean from her arms, and looked at her knees to see if some old scabs had come off—yes. She was as black and ugly as a little Negro. She tied her sash tight around her hips. Without looking up she crept around the yard, with her locket in her mouth, around the cistern on her hands and knees, keeping low not to be seen, her feet dragging numbly. Under the snowball bush she hit both feet with her fists until she could feel the sting, and then, picking all the cinders one by one out of her elbows and skirt and out of her Roman sandals, she walked around the house and darted in to Home, which was the trunk of a tree, without being caught.

At that moment, touching Home, her finger to the tree, she was not happy, not unhappy. "Free!" she called, looking around, not seeing the others anywhere, but she had them every one separate in her head.

Then she saw Uncle George walk out of the house and stare out into the late day. She wanted to call out to him, but something would not let her. Something told her, ever since the look he gave her, that it was right for him to stand apart, and that when he opened an envelope in a room no one should enter. Now she felt matter-of-factly intimate with it, with his stand and his predicament. She thought of herself as growing up beside Uncle George, the way some little flowers and vines have picked their tree, and so she felt herself sure of being near him. She knew quite objectively that *he* would not disown her and uproot her, that he loved any little green vine leaf, and now she felt inner warnings that this was a miracle of safety, strange in any house, and in her this miracle was guarded from the contamination even of thinking.

As if by smell, by the smell of his pipe, she knew that he out of all the Delta Fairchilds had kindness and that it was more than an acting in kindness, it was a waiting, a withholding, as if he could see a fire or a light, when he saw a human being—regardless of who it was, kin or not, even Aunt Ellen, to whom he called and waved now—and had never done the first thing in his life to dim it. This made him seem young—as young as she. On the other hand, when all night she could hear coming up the dark stair well his voice soft and loud with Uncle Battle's bark after it, chasing, she gathered that he was hard to please in some things and therefore old. Uncle George and Uncle Battle would argue or talk until Uncle Battle hollered out the window for Roxie or Ernest to come up to the house and fix them their nightcaps.

She stored love for Uncle George fiercely in her heart, she wished Shellmound would burn down and she could run in and rescue him, she prayed for God to bless him—for she felt they all crowded him so, the cousins, rushed in on him so, they smiled at him too much, inviting too much, daring him not to be faultless, and she would have liked to clear them away, give him room, and then—what? She would let him be mean and horrible—horrible to the horrible world.

Would she? She leaned her forehead against the tree, with some shimmering design about him in her head coming like a dream, in which she was clinging, protecting, fighting all in one, a Fairchild flourishing and flailing her arms about. Of course it was all one thing—it was one feeling. It was need. Need pulled you out of bed in the morning, showed you the day with everything crowded into it, then sang you to sleep at night as your mother did, need sent you dreams. Need did all this—when would it explain? Oh, some day. She waited now, and then each night fell asleep in the vise of India's arms. She imagined that one day—maybe the next, in the Fairchild house—she would know the answer to the heart's pull, just as it would come to her in school why the apple was pulled down on Newton's head, and that it was the way for girls in the world that they should be put off, put off, put off—and told a little later; but told, surely.

Uncle George came down the steps and walked slowly over the fresh-cut grass, not seeing her for she was behind the big pecan tree. All his secret or his problem, or what was in the blue letter, though she did not know what it was, was sharp to her to see him go by, weighty and real and as cutting (and perhaps as filled with dreaded life) as a seashell she had once come on, on the seashore, and unwittingly seized.

"Don't cry out here, Laura," said a soft voice.

It was Little Battle, in his overalls. He poked a cold biscuit with a little ham in it into her mouth, and because she was startled stood by while she swallowed it. Then they ran into the house. "Oh, Little Battle!"

IV

Laura wanted so badly to be taken to their hearts (never wondering if she had not been, at any time before her own wish) that she almost knew what the Fairchilds were like, what to expect; but her wish was steadier than her vision and that itself kept her from knowing. Ellen saw it.

While she held supper for Dabney, late now at some bridesmaid's party, Ellen had walked out in the yard to feel the cool. It was first-dark, and the thrushes were singing tirelessly from the trees. She had walked through the yard where the children were playing and Vi'let was gathering in the curtains, past the flower beds, down toward the bayou. The evening was hot; it was the fragrance of the lemon lilies that was cool, like the breath from a mountain well. From the house came a momentary discord on the piano keys. That was Shelley passing through the music room, putting her hands down over Mary Lamar Mackey's. Then the slow, dwelling melody went on.

Ellen looked down the road for Dabney. Stretching away, the cotton fields, slowly emptying, were becoming the color of the sky, a deepening blue so intense that it was like darkness itself. There was a feeling in the infinity of the Delta that even the bounded things, waiting, for instance, could go on forever. Over and over from the bayou woods came the one high note, then the three low notes of the dove.

At her feet the bayou ran, low, long since cleared of trees here, and all but motionless. She thought it was like a mirror that was time-darkened, no longer reflecting very much, but an entity in itself. She remembered old, disparaging Partheny when she got to her, going so ill-advised on foot. In Partheny's house in Brunswicktown she had bent over the cot where the old woman lay out straight with her long toes pointing up and her eyes looking at the ceiling. "Partheny, do you hear me? Are you in a spell, Partheny?" Partheny was her nurse when her oldest children were little.

"Oh, I done had it," Partheny had said. "It over by this time. I were mindless, Miss Ellen. I were out of my house. I were looking in de river. I were standing on Yazoo bridge wid dis foot lifted. I were mindless, didn't know my name or name of my sons. Hand stop me. Mr. Troy Flavin he were by my side, gallopin' on de bridge. He laugh at me good—old Partheny! Don't you jump in dat river, make good white folks fish you out! No, sir, no, sir, I ain't goin' to do dat! Guides me home. You can go on back now, go on back, Miss Ellen, to your little girl puttin' on her weddin' veil. But don't set your heels down! Go real still."

She heard someone coming from the house, and saw from the glimmer of white clothes and the tall strolling walk of "company" that it was George—he waved briefly. He looked thin. Poor boy, he had not even eaten any to speak of, of the good coconut cake she tried to tempt him with. The noise of the children made him bite his lip, and he did not like Mary Lamar Mackey, this time.

She had not even taken her apron off; she clasped her hands before her. But he untied the apron when he came and threw it over the branches of a little dogwood tree. "Forget everything out here," he said, and stood looking out.

"I saw a runaway girl in the bayou woods, George,"

she said, "a white girl. Going just as fast to Memphis as she could go. Purely loitering. I saw her peeping out from behind a tree, the prettiest thing ever made. I very ill-advisedly went to Brunswick-town on foot, bý the short cut. There she was." She had never thought of mentioning the girl or seeing her. (Battle would say: "Ellen Fairchild, do you mean to tell me you've been out alone, a lone woman on foot, in these fields and woods? No gun either, I bet you all I've got.") But she was tired, and sometimes now the whole world seemed rampant, running away from her, and she would always be carrying another child to bring into it.

Now she saw by the dense evening light—for she always knew it when she saw it—a look on George's face that both endeared him to her and reminded her of all her anxiety for his comfort in life; the first source of the feeling, long ago, might have been that look—she did not know. It was only a tender change of countenance, a smile—but it looked like the vanishing of suspense. There was gratification and regret in it, at something you said. It was as if he had known life could not go on without this thing—now, like a crash, a fall, it had come. So you, having begun, without knowing it, some unfinished story to him, would then tell everything, perhaps. She never altogether understood George's abrupt, tender smile—yet without thinking she would often find herself telling the very thing that brought it to his face. It could not be amusement—for she had nothing funny about her, not a bone in her body. For instance, now—surely he could not be simply enjoying the idea of herself brought up against a wild runaway girl? For her heart still felt the strain. And certainly she knew he would not laugh at a girl that wanted to run away.

"Not far from here at all," she said. "She was asking the way to the public road."

He said at once, "Yes, I met her, as I was coming in."

Then she was speechless. It was a thing she had never learned in her life, to expect that what has come to you, come in dignity to yourself in loneliness, will yet be shared, the secret never intact. She gazed into the evening star, her lips unreasonably pressed together.

"And did she ask the way to the Memphis road?" she asked then.

"Yes, and I took her over to the old Argyle gin and slept with her, Ellen," said George.

She seemed to let go in her whole body, and stood languidly still under her star a moment, then pulled her apron where it still shone white in the dogwood tree and tried to tie it back on.

George made an impatient sound. Sometimes he, the kindest of them all, would say a deliberate wounding thing—as if in assurance that nothing further might then hurt you. It was always some fact—all true—about himself, just a part of the fact, which was the same as a wild, free kind of self-assertion—it was his pride, too, speaking out. Then impatiently, as if you were too close to a fire, he pulled you away from your pain.

"She's older than you thought," he said. His voice distressed her by sounding grateful to her—was it simply because she had neither flinched nor disbelieved him or said, "It amounts to nothing," like a Fairchild quick to comfort?

She glanced toward George, though she could no

longer see him. A feeling of uncontrollable melancholy came over her to see him in this half-light, which had so rested her before he came out. Dear George, whose every act could verge so closely on throwing himself away—what on earth would ever be worth that intensity with which he held it, the hurting intensity that was reflected back on him, from all passing things?

"Oh, George!" she cried, and then, "Sometimes I'm so afraid when Dabney marries she won't be happy in her life."

He patted her arm, yet not heavily or trying to turn her around. "Well, let's go in," she said. Yet she lingered, a little breeze seemed to stir over the bayou, and she was refreshed. George was the one person she knew in the world who did not have it in him to make of any act a facile thing or to make a travesty out of human beings—even, in spite of temptation at a time like this moment, of himself as one human being. (How the Fairchilds did talk on about their amazing shortcomings, with an irony that she could not follow at all, and never rested in perfecting caricatures, little soulless images of themselves and each other that could not be surprised or hurt or changed! That way Battle, when they were first married, had told her something like this.) Only George left the world she knew as pure—in spite of his fierce energies, even heresies—as he found it; still real, still bad, still fleeting and mysterious and hopelessly alluring to her.

She had feared for the whole family, somehow, at a time like this (being their mother, and the atmosphere heavy with the wedding and festivities hanging over their heads) when this girl, that was at first so ambiguous, and so lovely even to her all dull and tired—when she touched at their life, ran through their woods. She had not had a chance to face this fear before, for at the time she had had to cope with the runaway girl herself, who was only the age of her daughter Dabney, so she had believed. But at last she was standing quietly in the long twilight with George, bitterly glad (now it was certain: he was not happy) that he had been the one who had caught the girl, as if she had been thrown at them; for now was it not over?

Aware of his touch on her tired arm—for he was seldom, in the way the others were, demonstrative—she felt that he was, in reality, not intimate with this houseful at all, and that they did not know it—for a moment she thought she saw how it was.

All around them the lightning bugs had flashed to life. They flew slowly and near the earth—just beyond the reach now of India's hand.

"Ellen!" Battle called out, first from the window, then from the door. "Oh, Ellen, here's Troy! He's come up to supper! Ellen!"

"It's time to go in," Ellen said. "Dabney will be coming home and looking everywhere for her mother."

She knew she had provoked that smile again, in the blurred profile she looked into as they started up the garden. But she went in step with him through the dark wet grass, and breathed and sighed expectantly in the dark, as if before they reached the light and confusion of the house she could tell something promising and gentle to him.

"Look," George said.

Ranny was at their feet in the grass asleep—worn out—lying astride a stalk of sugar cane. George took him up without waking him, and carried him.

"He's gained!"

"He weighs thirty-six pounds."

Presently Ranny stirred, said something, and George set him down. Balancing and complaining like an old drunken man for a moment, he went forward on his own feet.

"What did he say?" Ellen asked.

"He said, 'Don't hold me.' "

Ranny, who always until now wanted dearly to be held, walked straight forward, and they sighed in amusement, drawing together, to see the little figure going in front of them, then beginning lightly, blindly, to trot, riding the horse of his mind in the big Delta night.

V

After Shelley had stayed her time in the room with Troy, waiting for her sister, she excused herself to dress for the Clarksdale dance. But up in her room, in her teddies, she sat down on her cedar chest and unlocked her Trip Abroad diary, lit a Fatima cigarette, and began to write. She had turned the floor fan on her back and seat, and behind her as she wrote the two ends of her little satin sash were dancing straight out.

Laura with her nightgown on stood in the door watching her.

In Shelley's room, the best front one, there were medallions on the wallpaper, each a gold frame with a face inside—which Laura had thought were grandfathers and grandmothers, probably from Port Gibson, until Shelley had told her they weren't anybody—which was much more mysterious. The wastebasket Shelley had woven in Crafts her summer at Camp. Her bureau was decorated with a tray and powder-box and jar set from her Dabney grandmother. The jars she had filled with rose leaves and clove pinks the summer before, and now and then, but not often, she still took the stoppers out and smelled their last year's perfume. The mirror, on the side arm of which her curling irons hung like a telephone, was stuck all around with snapshots taken mostly on a trip with Mary Denis Summers and some Yankees to the West, at which she had had the worst time she ever had away from home; she could not tell you why she kept their pictures, snooty faces against dim yawning streaks of the Grand Canyon, daily in view. Her silver comb and brush set had EVD on them—Aunt Ellen's—the initials intertwined with raised lilies of the valley, and the bristles worn curved as a thin shell now; luckily nobody brushed their hair any more. Her jewelry was inside a little box Aunt Shannon, before she was so mixed up, had given her; it was a present from her Great-Uncle Denis who had sent it to her the year she was born, from off in the Mexican War; it had a key with forked-tongued snakes on it. Inside were a pair of her mother's gold bracelets with chains, a silver butterfly ring from the Western trip, her Camp ring, one of Uncle George's cuff links she had found when little and had kept, her Great-Grandmother Mary Shannon's black cameos, earrings, and pin, and her seed-pearl comb, and two or three diamond rings. Shelley would not be caught dead wearing any of them. She liked a garnet brooch of her mother's to pin her middy blouse together, but now she could not find it; Shelley said Dabney had probably borrowed it, it was Dabney who lost everything, or maybe India, who could dress herself up like a savage this summer, scavenging from room to room.

In the cedar chest underneath her now lay all the underclothes she had received for graduation presents from high school and college in Virginia, some in little silk sacheted purses made to keep them in until she got married. There was one gown—Aunt Primrose had made it, of all people, Shelley said—of peach chiffon with a little peach chiffon coat that had a train, every edge picoted, and then embroidered all around with lover's knots: it was transparent. Shelley's mantel was wood and white marble, and the hearth was round and raised in a fat apron. The fireplace was now hidden by a perfectly square silk screen painted by Aunt Tempe, with a bayou floating with wild ducks at sunset; a line of the ducks was rising at a right angle from the water and went straight to the upper corner like an arrow. On her mantel shelf was a gold china slipper, a souvenir of Mary Denis Summers's wedding, holding matches, and that was all, except for an incense burner and a photograph of Shelley in a Spanish comb and a great deal of piled hair, taken the year she graduated from Fairchilds High School. Shelley hated it. On the washstand was Shelley's glass with three stolen late-blooming Cape jessamines from Miss Parnell Dortch's yard, now turned bright gold, still sweet. The bed was Aunt Ellen's from Virginia, a high square cool one with a mosquito net over it and a trundle bed underneath it. As a baby Shelley had slept on that, near her mother, and she despised having it still under her bed. There was no way on earth Shelley could get a lamp brought in to read by in bed. A long brass pole dangled from the center of the ceiling ending in two brass lilies from each of which a long, naked, but weak light bulb stuck out. "Plenty light to dress by, and you can read in the lower part of the house with your clothes on like other people," Uncle Battle said, favoring Dabney as he did and she never read, not having time. A paper kewpie doll batted about on a thread tied to the chandelier, that was all it was good for. Shelley wanted to read *The Beautiful and Damned* which was going around the Delta and to read it in bed, but she was about to give up hope. It was hard for her to even see how to write. In her closet were mostly evening dresses but enough middy blouses and pleated skirts hung at one end. All her shoes were flung in a heap on the floor, as if in despair. One green King Tut sandal was out in the middle of the room. Her peach ostrich mules were on her feet and as she wrote she from time to time lifted up her bare heels and waited a moment, tensely, before going on, like a mockingbird stretching in the grass. Momently, she put her Fatima cigarette ashes in her hair receiver.

"Go away, Laura!" said Shelley. "You aren't supposed to watch us every minute!"

Laura ran off, having the grace not to stick out her tongue as India would do.

Shelley was to go to Europe after the wedding, with Aunt Tempe—it was Aunt Tempe's graduation present; but she could not bring herself to wait that long before beginning to write in the book with the lock and key. The first entry was three weeks ago—"We all went fishing with Papa in Moon Lake, caught 103 fish, home in time, Indianola dance. Pee Wee Prentiss. Stomach ache. Dabney's favorite word is 'perfect.' " But already, so soon, she was writing long entries. Dressing a moment (they were calling her downstairs) and writing a moment, jumping up and down, she succeeded in getting the tulle dress, still hot from the iron, over her head and in filling in almost six pages of the diary. Her chest rose and fell in the little "starlight blue" dress, flat as a bathing suit against her heart.

> Tonight again D. was cruel to T. F. and is keeping him waiting and then going out to one last dance. T. does not go home—waits for just a glimpse. He is interested because he thinks she must be smart. To provoke a man like him. Dabney does not even know it. Why doesn't it dawn on T. F. that none of the Fairchilds are smart, the way he means smart? Only now and then one of us is gifted, Aunt J. A. says—I am gifted at tennis—for no reason. We never wanted to be smart, one by one, but all together we have a wall, we are self-sufficient against people that come up knocking, we are solid to the outside. Does the world suspect? that we are all very private people? I think one by one we're all more lonely than private and more lonely than self-sufficient. I think Uncle G. takes us one by one. That is love—I think. He takes us one by one but Papa takes us all together and loves us by the bunch, which makes him a more cheerful man. Maybe we come too fast for Papa. One by one, we get it from Mashula and Laura Allen and Great-Grandfather all, we can be got at, hurt, killed—loved the same way—as things get to us. All the more us poor people to be cherished. I feel we should all be cherished but not all together in a bunch—separately, but not one to go unloved for the other loved. In the world, I mean. Shellmound and the world. Mama

says shame, that we forget about Laura, and we loved her mother so much we never mention her name or we would all cry. We are all unfair people. We are such sweet people to be so spoiled. George spoils us, does not reproach us, praises us, even, for what he feels is weak in us.

Maybe I can tell him yet, that I know where Robbie is, but so far I can't. The moment of telling, I cannot bring myself to that. I thought it would be easy at the supper table, but in the middle of supper now we all look at each other, all wondering—before a thing like Dabney's wedding, not knowing just what to do. Sometimes I believe we live most privately just when things are most crowded, like in the Delta, like for a wedding. I don't know what to do about anybody in the world, because it seems like you ought to do it soon, or it will be too late. I may not put any more in my diary at all till after the wedding. I wish now it would happen, and be past, I hate days, fateful days. I heard Papa talking about me to Uncle G. without knowing I was running by the library door not to meet T. when he came in (but waiting, I did) and Papa said I was the next one to worry about, I was prissy —priggish. Uncle G. said nobody could be born that way, they had to get humiliated. Can you be humiliated without knowing it? I would know it. He said I was not priggish, I only liked to resist. So does Dabney like it—I know. So does anybody but India, and young children.

When T. proposed to D. I think it was just because she was already so spoiled, he had to do something final to make her notice, and this did. That is not the way I want it done to me. Nobody tells T. a thing yet, and maybe we will never tell him anything. But I think he never minds at all. I think T. likes to size things up. I would never love him. I think he could tell tonight that Uncle G. has something on his mind, those sweet worry-lines across his brow and eyes—drinking all Papa's Bounce—because T. is the one who is always thinking of ways in or ways out, and I think he gets the smell of someone studying, as if it were one of the animals in trouble. Trouble acts up—he puts it down. But I know, trouble is not something fresh you never saw before that is coming just the one time, but is old, and your great-aunts not old enough to die yet can remember little hurts for sixty years just like the big hurts you know now, having your sister walk into something you dread and you cannot speak to her.

T. just sits and looks at a family that cherishes its weaknesses and belittles its strength. He is from the mountains—very slow. Where is his mother? Father? He is not a born gambler of any description. He considers D. not anything he is taking a chance on but a sure thing and wants her for sure. Robbie is another person like that and wants George for sure. I can't stand her! Maybe Europe will change everything. When I see the Leaning Tower of Pisa will I like Robbie any better? I doubt it. (Aunt T. will be with me all the time!) All of us wish G. did not want her and tell him and tell him, she is not worthy to wipe his feet. But he does want her, and suffers. He goes on. I do not know and cannot think how it was when Papa and Mama wanted each other. Of course they don't now, and don't suffer by now. I cannot think of any way of loving that would not fight the world, just speak to the world. Papa and Mama do not fight the world. They have let it in. Did they ever even lock a door. So much life and confusion has got in that there is nothing to stop it running over, like the magic pudding pot. The whole Delta is in and out of this house. Life may be stronger than Papa is. He let Troy in, and look, Troy took Dabney. Life is stronger than George, but George was not surprised, only he wants Robbie Reid. Life surprises Papa and it is Papa that surprise hurts. I think G. expects things to amount to more than you bargain for—and so do I. This scares me in the middle of a dance. Uncle G. scares me a little for knowing my fright. Papa is ashamed of it but G. does not reproach me—I think he upholds it. He expects things to be more than you think, and to mean something—something— He cherishes our weaknesses because they are just other ways that things are going to come to us. I think when you are strong you can squeeze them back and hold them from you a little while but where you are weak you run to meet them.

Shelley with a sigh leaned out of her window to rest. A whippoorwill was calling down in the bayou somewhere, and the hiss of the compress came softly and regularly as the sighing breath of night. She heard voices on the lawn. Dabney in a filmy dress was telling Troy good night. Shelley listened; how well she could hear and see from here she had not before realized or tried out.

"Oh, I wish I didn't have to go to the old dance—or that you could dance, Troy!" cried Dabney. She clung to him, her voice troubled and tender. "Never mind, we'll soon be married."

"Sure," said Troy.

She clung to him more, as if she would be torn away, and looked over her shoulder at the night as if it almost startled her—indeed the soft air seemed to Shelley to be trembling with the fluctuation of starlight as with the pulsing of the compress on the river. Troy patted Dabney's shoulder.

"I hear your heart," she said right out, as if imploringly and yet to comfort him.

"I'll see you tomorrow," he said.

"Take care of yourself," she said.

"I will."

"It won't be long until I can take care of you."

There were tears in Shelley's eyes; their tenderness was almost pity as they clung together. She nearly cried with them.

"I have to go now, Troy, I have to."

She stood away. He stood with his arms hanging, and she went. Dickie Boy Featherstone put her in his open-top car.

Then Shelley heard Uncle George walk heavily over the porch and down the steps. She saw him strolling toward the gate, and smelled his pipe. "George!" He looked up and said how hot the night was. He went on. She could not say anything, she could not call it out a window. (It would seem so conceited of her, too.) She believed he went and stood on the bank of the bayou to smoke; she could see a patch of white through the Spanish daggers, though the mist drifted there now turning like foam in the luminous night. She leaned her forehead on the wall, the warm wallpaper pressed her head like a hand. . . .

The scene on the trestle was so familiar as to be almost indelible in Shelley's head, for her memory arrested the action and let her see it again and again, like a painting in a schoolroom, with colors vivid and thunderclouded, George and Maureen above locked together, and the others below with the shadow of the trestle on them. The engine with two wings of smoke above it, soft as a big bird, was upon them, coming as it would. George was no longer working at Maureen's caught foot. Their faces fixed, and in the instant alike, Maureen and Uncle George seemed to wait for the blow. Maureen's arms had spread across the path of the engine.

Shelley knew what had happened next, but the greatest pressure of uneasiness let her go after the one moment, as if the rest were a feat, a trick that would not work twice. The engine came to a stop. The tumbling denouement was what made them all laugh at the table. The apology of the engineer, old sleepy-head Mr. Doolittle that traded at the store! Shelley beat her head a time or two on the wall. And Maureen with no warning pushed with both her strong hands on George's chest, and he went over backwards to fall from the trestle, fall down in the vines to little Ranny's and old Sylvanus's wild cries. George did not even yet let her go, his hand reached for her pummeling hand and what he could not accomplish by loosening her foot or by pulling her up free, he accomplished by falling himself. Wrenched bodily, her heavy foot lifted and Maureen fell with him. And all the time the Dog had stopped, and Mr. Doolittle was looking from his little cab saying he was sorry, Mr. Fairchild! But George sat on the ground simply looking at Maureen. She had leaped up with alacrity, a taunting abandon, which seemed to hypnotize him. She leaped up and down on first one foot and then the other, strumming her lip.

There were things in that afternoon which gave Shelley an uneasiness she seemed to feel all alone, so that she hoarded the story even more closely to herself, would not tell it, and from night to night hesitated to put it down in her diary (though she looked forward to it all day). To begin with, there was the oblivious, tomboyish way she had led them all in walking too fast for Robbie in her high heels—a tomboy was only what she used to be, and wasn't now; all day Sunday, fishing and all, she had done it. Of course Robbie would wear the wrong heels, and it was right that she should be shown she dressed the wrong way, and should have to keep taking little runs to catch up, and finally be left as haughty as possible at the approach of a trestle. But then came Shelley's own shame in not being able to walk the trestle herself. No one would ever forget that about her, all their lives! She thought herself that it must have been premonition—with Uncle George along something was bound to happen, it was his recklessness that told her to hold back. Then there was the terror with which the engine filled her—that poky, familiar thing, it was sure to stop—of course she had no born terror of the Yellow Dog. Maureen's assumption that she could stop it by holding both her arms out across its path was more logical than you thought at first. But Shelley's deepest uneasiness came from Robbie's first words, "You didn't do this for *me!*" In her fury Robbie rose straight up as untouchable, foolish heels and all, away out of their hands all at once. . . . And how George had looked at her! ("Certainly he thinks nothing of danger, none of us ever has," her father had told Robbie later, when at the supper table she came to tears.) But Shelley felt that George and Robbie had hurt each other in a way so deep, so unyielding, that she was unequal to understanding it yet. She hoped to grasp it all, the worst, but fiercely feeling herself a young, unmarried, unengaged girl, she held the more triumphantly to her secret guess—that this confrontation on the trestle was itself the reason for Robbie's leaving George and for his not going after her. The guess made even his presence at Dabney's wedding take on the cast of assertion: here he was not looking for his wife. . . . But Dabney felt nothing of this, she felt no more about that black moment since she saw it was not fatal—when the engine stopped a hair's breadth from George and Maureen, she put up her elbows and did a little dance step with herself. After the train passed, Dabney and Troy had simply gone on up the railroad track and got engaged.

Was it possible that it was because of something strong *George* had felt, that the way a stroke of lightning can blaze a tree she could not forget that happening? Extravagantly responsible just as he was extravagantly reckless, what had he been prepared for—how many times before had something come very near to them and stopped?

Dabney if she knew would tell George in a minute, that Robbie was no farther away than Fairchild's Store this day, hiding from him and crying for him. But she could not enlighten him. She and Robbie had seen each other across the crowded room—a suspended cluster of long-handled popcorn poppers turned gently between them to block their vision—and both their faces, her crying one too, went fixed, the way it was in High School: they did not speak.

She could hear under her window now the faint sound of the idling motor in some boy's automobile, and downstairs the Victrola ending "By the Light of the Stars" and then the dancers catching their breaths.

"Shelley, Shelley! Are you ever coming?" called Mary Lamar Mackey.

Then Shelley put a little coat of peach silk around her and went down, where at the foot of the stairs Piggy McReddy was waiting for her, shouting up, " 'I'm the Sheik of Araby!' "

VI

Much later, in her room, Dabney opened her eyes. Perhaps she had only just gone to sleep, but the silver night woke her—the night so deep-advanced toward day that she seemed to breathe in a well, drenched with the whiteness of an hour that astonished her. It hurt her to lift her hand and touch at her forehead, for all seemed to be tenderness now, the night like herself, breathless and yet serene, unlooked-on. The daring of morning light impending would have to strike her when it reached her—not yet. The window invited her to see—her window. She got out of bed (her filmy dress like a sleeping moth clung to the chair) and the whole leafy structure of the outside seemed agitated and rustled, the shadows darted like birds. The gigantic sky radiant as water ran over the earth and around it. The old moon in the west and the planets of morning streamed their light. She wondered if she would ever know . . . the constellations. . . . The birds all slept. (The mourning dove that cried the latest must sleep the deepest of all.) What could she know now? But she could see a single leaf on a willow tree as far as the bayou's edge, such clarity as there was in everything. The cotton like the rolling breath of sleep overflowed the fields. Out into it, if she were married, she would walk now—her bare foot touch at the night's hour, firmly too, a woman's serious foot. She would walk on the clear night—angels, though, did that—tread it with love not this lonely, never this lonely, for under her foot would offer the roof, the chimney, the window of her husband, the solid house. Draw me in, she whispered, draw me in—open the window like my window, I am still only looking in where it is dark.

4

"Papa, Uncle George gave me a walking horse, red with four white socks and a star here!"

"Well, you didn't cry about that, did you?" said Battle.

"She's going to ride me!" said Ranny.

"None of this is going to do you any good that I can see, Dabney," said Battle, "across the river. I don't know whether to give you an airplane or build you a bridge."

"I know a way she could come back home from Marmion," said Ranny. "If she goes down the other side of the river to the bridge at Fairchilds and goes across and comes up this side, she could come home."

"You're too big for your breeches," said Battle, lifting him up and throwing him to the ceiling. "You think you can show Dabney the way home, do you? No, sir, Dabney's going away from us and never coming back."

Ranny burst into tears in the air, and so did Bluet out in the hall. Battle set the boy down in haste.

"Ranny!" said Shelley, looking up from her book. "Papa was joking. Papa was only joking. Dabney will come back whenever you call her, Ranny. Oh, Papa."

"Stop crying, Ranny," said Battle shortly. "Bluet can cry her eyes out if she wants to, because she's a girl, but you can't, or I'll take the switch to you promptly."

"She's never coming back," sobbed Ranny.

"Never coming back," Bluet cried after him, and hugged Ranny around the neck and cried with her forehead pressed to his. Even their little white sideburns were wet with tears. Then, without any appreciable change of their hold on each other or their noise, they were laughing.

"Good-bye, Dabney!" they shouted.

Ellen and Troy stood shyly looking at each other across the big red Heatrola where the back halls crossed. They were dismally afraid of each other, Ellen knew. She had a silver goblet in her hand she had retrieved from the sand pile.

"Troy," she said, "come help me polish these goblets. Dabney's gone to Greenwood for the groceries. You don't mind finding me busy, do you?"

"I reckon all this is bound to make you busy," said Troy. He tiptoed around the Heatrola and followed her. She felt that he lightly peeped into the back door of the library as they went by. Primrose sat in there sewing some object—George had brought the aunts up this morning. As a matter of fact, Ellen noticed, it was a bridesmaid's lace mit, and even upon a blameless garment like a mit the sweet lady could not have satisfied herself her work would go perfectly with Troy peeping in. And indeed it was not perfect, but Primrose could never have had the thought occur to her that being a lady she could not sew a seam worthy of a lady, and would have undertaken anything in the trousseau.

"Where's Jim Allen?" she called. Primrose jumped, and drew the little mit to her. "Oh—it's Ellen! She's looking at your roses, though it's the heat of the day."

"She'll find them covered with blackspot," Ellen said regretfully. She led Troy back to the kitchen. Roy and a little stray Negro child were eating cold biscuits under Roxie's foot and feeding a small terrapin on the floor, and were sent out to the back yard. Aunt Mac, ignoring Roxie, Howard stringing beans, the children, and now Ellen and the young man, was ironing a stack of something on the trestle board in the back part of the kitchen.

They sat down at the scrubbed round table in the center. A June bug flying on a thread was tied to Troy's chair. "That's Little Battle's," Ellen said as if by divination. "You don't mind June bugs, do you?"

"Oh, no'm."

"Get you another chair if you do." She collected things from the dining room and pantry. "Here's the polish, here's you a rag, and you can take half these goblets. Roxie and Vi'let and Howard and all just have so much to do, and Pinchy at this time— Be particular you get in that little ridge."

"Yes'm."

"Wait. I'll get you a bite of cooky. That cup in your hand now will be Dabney's," she said, and Troy almost let it fall. "We have so many daughters—of course you have to divide things up. One daughter couldn't have more than her share." She set a plate of cookies and a glass of buttermilk in front of him, went back and got him a cold drumstick. "Not that there's a contentious bone in any of my children's bodies.—That's Orrin's. Blessed Orrin likes silver too. He said, 'Mama, I want to have a silver cup of my own to shave out of when I'm grown,' and I told him it was surely his privilege."

"How old is Orrin now?" was all Troy could think of to reply, and Ellen could not think to save her life just then how old Orrin was.

"Here's one will be Dabney's, for you to shine. It was from the Dabneys—my family—brought over." She jumped up again and brought him a voluminous linen napkin to wipe his fingers on. "Don't leave that drumstick and let it waste. This is Dabney's cup."

Troy took it with his thumb and middle finger, sticking his forefinger well out.

"It won't say Sterling," called Aunt Mac from the ironing board. "That's because those things were made before there ever was an old Sterling, it's like B.C."

They polished in silence for a while. Troy added a little spit now and then, and held up each goblet critically but silently to see how Ellen thought it shone. His fingers were sprouted with his red hairs but they had a nice shape and they were kind, in Ellen's judgment.

"My little old mama made the prettiest quilts you ever laid your eyes on," he said, when he finally spoke. His foxy skin turned rosy with pleasure and his thick lashes growing in light-red bunches and points gave him a luxuriant, petlike look. He laid down his linen rag. "One called 'Trip around the World' and one called 'Four Doves at the Window.' 'Bouquet of Beauty,' that was one. . . ."

"And you asked your mother their names." Ellen looked at him as though he had done a commendable thing. "Where was your mother? Where was your home, Troy?" she asked softly. How she had wondered. Of course Battle would never have asked a man such a thing!

"My little mama ain't dead! No, ma'am, though she writes an infrequent letter and I take after her. Bear Creek, up Tishomingo Hills. She can crochet just as well as she can piece tops—hard to believe."

Why had Ellen wondered? She could have seen the little perched cabin in her mind any time, by just not trying. ("Howard," she said, "did you leave any strings on? Well, now, you take your hammer out under that cool fig tree and start making that altar Miss Dabney wants. Just do it your way—I can't even tell you how to start it.") She looked back at Troy. "Well, you're still Mississippi," she said, smiling.

"Though this don't seem like Mississippi to me," he said. "I mean at first. Two years back I would just as soon have been in Timbuktu as Fairchilds, not to see one hill."

"You were an only child? Like me?" she said, gently taking the goblet he had set down and putting her rag to it.

"Only boy."

Ellen could not imagine a boy not enumerating his sisters, but she nodded.

"I sure wish Dabney and myself could have one of Mammy's pretty quilts now, to lay on our bed."

"I guess your sisters ask her for them when they marry," she said rather breathlessly, and he nodded, as if to commend her. "Aunts," he said. "I had me three old-maid aunts that loved lots of cover." He cut his eye at Aunt Mac, who was by this time singing a Presbyterian hymn. "They were forever scared they'd get cold, and they had more quilts than you ever did see in your life. Lived on a mountain top. I'd go pay them a visit. They'd go to bed at sundown and I would sit up till about twelve o'clock before the fire, throwing on logs, getting the place hotter and hotter. Every time I'd throw on a log they'd throw off a quilt."

"Troy," she said, "I believe you're a tease too."

Troy straightened up, and taking a goblet as if it were unfinished business on the table between them, he attacked it with his rag, first spitting on it thinly between drawn lips. "Well, there's nothing easy about hills," he said. "And plenty like me have left them, four to my knowledge on one bend of the Tennessee River. They all come to the Delta. It sure gets you quick. By now, I can't tell a bit of difference between me and any Delta people you name. There's nothing easy about the Delta either, but it's just a matter of knowing how to handle your Negroes." He batted the June bug.

"Well, Troy, you know, if it was that at first, I believe there's more to it, and you'll be seeing there's a lot of life here yet that will take its time working out," said Ellen. She held up the goblet for him to see.

"What would it be?" Troy asked. He smiled down on her for the first time.

"The Delta's just like everywhere," she said mysteriously. "You keep taking things on, and you'll see. Things still take a little time. . . ."

Vi'let came in with a vase of wilted zinnias. "Miss Tempe's come in," she said. "Sent me out first thing to throw dead flowers out the parlor. Is it all right to throw 'em away?"

"It's all right, Vi'let, they're really dead. Go tell her Miss Ellen'll be there in a minute." She frowned over Troy's head. She was torn between her pride—presenting Troy naturally and now, to Tempe, and her conviction that she might wait just a little while about it.

"You can look for me back about sundown," Troy was saying. He stood up, put the chair up to the table again with the June bug, tired, hanging floodwards now, and took his hat off the top of the bread safe.

"Don't be late—it's supper and the rehearsal, remember. If those clothes and crooks haven't come, what'll we do?"

"Dey come," Roxie prophesied. "Ain't nothin' goin' to defeat Miss Dab, Miss Ellen."

Troy was bending in a polite bow to Aunt Mac. He started out and then stock-still asked Ellen, "Is she ironing *money*?"

"Why, that's the payroll," said Ellen. "Didn't you know Aunt Mac always washes it?"

"The payroll?" His hand started guiltily toward his money pocket.

"I get the money from the bank when I drive in, and she hates for them to give anything but new bills to a lady, the way they do nowadays. So she washes it."

"If that's what she wants to do, let her do it!" roared Battle. He was coming down the hall followed by four Negroes, all of them carrying big boxes. "Here's Dabney's doin's," he said. "All creation's coming out of Memphis. What must I do with it, throw it out the back door?"

"Take it quick, Roxie," said Ellen. "Vi'let! Howard! Aunt Mac, you'll have to soon make way at the ironing board!" she cried to the old lady's ear.

"Tempe's here along with it," said Battle. "Come on, Troy, let's get out."

Troy walked a little gingerly out of the kitchen, as if he might be offered his salary before he got out, fresh and warm from the iron, but when Ellen pulled him from Battle and led him toward the cross hall by the side door and showed him the long present table set out there, he went easier.

"Now I'm really scared for you to touch Bohemian glass till after the wedding, Troy," she said earnestly. She took up a bit of it from the tray. "From Virginia," she said. "Dabney cousins that couldn't come. They sent an outrageous number of wine glasses."

"They sure are the prettiest things yet," he said, as she turned the flower-shaped glass in the light. He watched her worn, careful, ladylike hand with the bit of fragile glass sparkling around it.

"I love the hills," she said, glancing up. "I miss them even now."

He shook his head, smiling, at the distant past.

II

India, Laura, and Ranny were sitting on the parlor floor playing cassino when Aunt Tempe arrived, their six bare feet touching. A great lot of boxes came with her, Little Uncle went by two or three times with things, and Vi'let with the whitest dress box sailed to the back. Skipping in front, Lady Clare came in all over again under the aegis of Aunt Tempe and made a face at them. She looked around for the piano (as if it had ever been moved!) and sidling through the archway sat down and began to play

"Country Gardens." Just at the door, India noticed, her father sent Aunt Tempe in with a nice, soft spank, and went off calling "Ellen! Ellen!"

Aunt Tempe, in a batik dress and a vibratingly large hat, entered (keeping time) and kissed all the jumping children. Then she straightened up from her kisses and admonitions and looked quickly around the parlor, as if to catch it before it could compose itself. Howard, who kept coming in and standing motionless, studying the spot on the floor where he had to put the altar, was caught in her gaze. "'Scuse," he said, and vanished with his hammer. The big feet of Bitsy and Bitsy's little boy, who was learning, hung inside the room; the Negroes were washing the outside of the windows behind thick white stuff, and talking to Maureen in the yard; if they knew Aunt Tempe could see their feet, they would be moving their rags.

India sat back on the floor and gazed at her aunt, admiring the way she kept her hat on, and shuffling the cassino cards gently. Aunt Tempe was about to call Vi'let—she did call Vi'let and ask her what dead zinnias were doing in front of the original Mr. George Fairchild? And where were Miss Ellen and Miss Dabney—running around frantic upstairs? And where was Mr. George? And where was just some *ice water*? Out in the back they could hear Horace, Aunt Tempe's goggly chauffeur, whistle at how hot it was at Shellmound, as opposed to Inverness.

Aunt Tempe drew a breath and sighed. She made little turns on her Baby Louis heels, and her soft plump shoulders came in view like more bosoms in the back, over her corset. India could read her mind. The table lamp provoked Aunt Tempe. The three white marble Graces holding the shade in their six arms, with dust unreachable in the folds of their draperies and the dents of their eyes, were parading the whole lack of Shellmound to Aunt Tempe—it was *outdated*—it didn't do for marrying girls off in. Of course Battle and Ellen would do the place over, the day one of the children prevailed on them hard enough—perhaps it would be quick little India—dress it up and maybe brick it over, starting with the gates. One day they would take up the floral rugs and the matting, and put in something Oriental, and they would get rid, somehow, of that Heatrola she hated to pass in the hall. They were only procrastinating about it. But here Dabney was marrying, and still the high, shabby old rooms went unchanged, for weddings or funerals, with rocking chairs in them, little knickknacks and playthings and treasures all shaken up in them together—and those switches on the mantel would probably stay right there, through the ceremony. On the table before her now a Tinker-Toy windmill was sitting up and *running*—with the wedding two days off—right next to the exquisite tumbler with the Young Pretender engraved on it, that was her wedding present to Battle and Ellen—cracked now, and carelessly stuffed with a bouquet that could have been picked and put there by nobody but Bluet—black-eyed Susans, a little chewed rose, and a four-o'clock.

Aunt Tempe closed her eyes to see Mashula's dulcimer still hanging by that thin ribbon on the wall—did she know Shelley could take it down and play "Juanita" on it? India followed her gaze; it passed fleetingly over Uncle Pinck's coin collection from around the world, that Aunt Tempe had been tired of looking at in Inverness and taking out of little Shannon's mouth—and fell sadly on the guns that stood in the corner by the door and the pistols that rested on a little gilt and marble table in the bay window. "Those firearms!" she murmured, freshly distressed at their very thought, as if in her sensitive hearing she could hear them all go off at once. That was Somebody's gun—he had killed twelve bears every Saturday with it. And Somebody's pistol in the lady's workbox; he had killed a man with it in self-defense at Cotton Gin Port, and of the deed itself he had never brought himself to say a word; he had sent the pistol ahead of him by two Indian bearers to his wife, who had put it in this box and held her peace, a lesson to girls. There (India sighed with Aunt Tempe) was Somebody's Port Gibson flintlock, and Somebody's fowling piece he left behind him when he marched off to Mexico, never to be laid eyes on again. There were the Civil War muskets Aunt Mac watched over, an old Minie rifle coming to pieces before people's eyes. Grandfather's dueling pistols, that had not saved his life at all, were on the stand in a hard velvet case, and lying loose was Grandmother Laura Allen's little pistol that she carried in her riding skirt over Marmion, with a flower scratched with a penknife along the pearl handle, and Battle's, her father's, little toothmarks in it.

"Bang bang!" said Ranny.

"No longer a baby," Aunt Tempe sighed. She sat down in a rocker, and Vi'let brought a pitcher of her lemonade—so strong it would bring tears to the eyes. "And poor Laura," she said, reaching out at her and kissing her again. To her, girls were as obvious as peony plants, and you could tell from birth if they were going to bloom or not—she said so.

"I've brought Dabney a forty-piece luncheon set for

the time being," she said, seeming to address Ranny. "I couldn't put my *mind* to anything more."

"How is Mary Denis's little new baby?" Ranny asked. "Is it still a boy?"

"Mm-hmm, and he's the image of me—except he has Titian hair," said Aunt Tempe. "That he got from Mr. Buchanan. It took wild horses to drag me away from Mary Denis at such a time, but I was prevailed on. I felt compelled to come to you."

"How is Mary Denis?" asked Ranny. "I love her!" He was sitting like a lamb at Aunt Tempe's feet, and letting her pet him.

"As well as I ever expected her to be, precious. She gets along very well considering she's married to a Yankee that wants his windows washed three times a week."

"They aren't though, are they?" cried India staunchly.

"Look, look! Aunt Tempe, look!" Dabney whirled in laughing, with flimsy boxes and tissue paper and chiffon ruffles flying.

"I should say they're not!" Aunt Tempe opened her arms and kissed Dabney three times under her big hat. (In the back, Vi'let was crying, "Miss Dab, ain't you 'shamed, you bring my dresses on back here!") "Mercy! You've always just washed your hair! Don't ever let this husband of yours, whoever he is, know you can cook, Dabney Fairchild, or you'll spend the rest of your life in the kitchen. That's the first thing I want to tell you."

"He doesn't know anything about me at all," Dabney laughed, dancing away in her mules around the wreath on the floral rug, whirling with her white wedding dress held to her. Her hair hung like a bright cloud down over her eyes and when she danced she scattered drops everywhere, except on her dress.

"Bring those affairs here to me, Ranny child," said Aunt Tempe.

"Oughtn't we to wait and let Dabney open everything that comes?"

Aunt Tempe shook out a dress and held it at an authoritative angle with her head tilted to match. "I must say I never heard of a *red wedding* before."

"American Beauty, Aunt Tempe!" cried India, teasingly whisking it from her and beginning to dance about after Dabney, holding it high.

"I stand corrected," said Aunt Tempe.

"They fade out before they get to Shelley and Dabney," Laura told her consolingly.

Maureen ran in, got Aunt Tempe's hug and kiss—and took, as if for her prize, the rosy dress slightly less bright and danced with it, nicely. The little girls went delicately though gleefully, and soundlessly on their bare feet. Laura too, with a sudden spring, had gently extracted the next dress from Aunt Tempe's fingers, and slid 1, 2, 3 into a ballroom waltz, hidden behind her pink cloud.

"Play, Lady Clare! Play till you drop," India's voice called.

Ranny leaped up and got under the wedding dress Dabney was holding, and then dancing frantically cried, "Let me out, let me out!"

"Slower, Lady Clare! Vi'let!" Aunt Tempe called, and Vi'let came and stood in the door with her hands on her hips. "If you don't press these dresses right away, you won't get a chance! They'll be worn out completely!"

"I *can't* go slower!" cried Lady Clare.

Outside, Bitsy and his little boy rubbed round peepholes in the window polish to see in, and laughed so appreciatively that they nearly fell out of the window, to India's ever-watchful delight as she pony-trotted.

"Well, of course I can't talk," said Aunt Tempe, looking fixedly at the bride dancing and the three dresses without any heads dancing around her, with Vi'let beginning to chase them. "My own daughter married a Yankee. —Naturally, I bring her to Memphis and Inverness to have her babies—*and* name them."

"It's not like Dabney was going out of the Delta," called the pale pink waltzing dress.

"Poor Mary Denis went clear to Illinois."

"Oh, Aunt Tempe, how's Mary Denis?" Dabney cried, coming to a momentary stop. "I did so want her for a bridesmaid!"

"She's thin as a rail and white as a ghost now!"

"I bet she's beautiful as ever! How much did her baby weigh?"

"Ten pounds, child: little George."

"Oh, how could you tear yourself away?" asked Dabney in a painful voice, holding a pose before the long mirror. She bent her arm and looked tenderly down over imaginary flowers. Vi'let smiled.

"I was prevailed on," said Aunt Tempe, but Dabney had run lightly out of the parlor again, snatching a flight of dresses and letting them fall over Vi'let, covering her as she giggled, with a bright cascade. Bluet, Maureen, Ranny, and Laura reeled after her, still under the spell, and Lady Clare was still playing "Country Gardens."

"The overseer," announced Aunt Tempe, nodding as if to imaginary people on both sides of the room, the tiniest smile on her face. India sat down and looked up at it.

They danced out, and Laura at the tail end would have danced her way upstairs too, dancing as if she were going to be in the wedding. The whole house was shaking like the joggling board or the compress, with dancing and "Country Gardens." Only in the hall Aunt Ellen stood leaning by the stairpost, leaning as if faint, her eyes and cheeks luminous. Just back of her, Roxie stood with a plate of coconut cake, erect and murmuring.

Uncle George, who had gone fishing before breakfast, had come in at that moment with a slam of the side door, stamping across the hall against the beat of bare feet. His face was burned and streaming, his white pants spotted with swamp mud. Behind him walked Howard's little boy, holding a string of fish—not very many and not very big.

Aunt Ellen and Uncle George, their gazes meeting, fell back while the laughing parade pushed and passed between them—Dabney gave George her passing kiss, and drops from her hair went in his eyes. Laura slowed down, and instead of going between them she waltzed from side to side; somehow she could not go between them, like the cousins. Her tingling feet were dancing but her body held her still in place, at a blind alley of desperation, as paralyzed from escape as a rabbit in sudden light.

It was the last thing she would have thought of—to pity Aunt Ellen or Uncle George at Shellmound, or to pity Maureen, just going around the turn of the stairs, dancing so sweetly today without fighting, or to pity Dabney who would always kiss just as quick as she saw. Where could she go just to hold out her arms and be taken, quickly—what other way, dark, out of sight of what was here and going by? She suddenly considered snatching Roxie's cake and running out the back. . . . She waltzed in a kind of crisis of agitation. People that she might even hate danced so sweetly just at the last minute, going around the turn, they made her despair. She felt she could never be able to hate anybody that hurt her in secret and in confidence, and that she was Maureen's secret the way Maureen was hers. Maureen! Dabney! Aunt Ellen! Uncle George! She almost called them, all—pleading. There was too much secrecy, too much pity at the stairs, she could not get by.

Uncle George suddenly shouted at the top of his voice, "That's enough!"

There was silence everywhere at Shellmound, prompt as India's gasps of half-distress, half-delight; then only Lady Clare's wistful complaint, "I don't know how to *ever* end it!" Wide-eyed, Roxie suddenly reached for Howard's little boy's hand, and he yielding George the fish they bolted. Where the clamor had been, Uncle George's two words shot out like one bird, then beat about the walls, struck in the rooms upstairs. Could Dabney bear it? Laura, who could not stop even then shuffling her foot, moved helplessly up and down in one place, wondering if Uncle George would kill her. Poor Aunt Primrose, who would not hurt anything on earth, appeared blinking at the library door, holding her little lace mit, nearly finished, before her breast.

Presently Dabney's light, excited laugh floated back at them from above, and then her face, bright and mischievous under the sparkling hair, looked smiling down over the rail, as if disembodied. Aunt Ellen looked up at her a minute and then said, "Dabney, you're supposed to be in Greenwood getting the groceries, dear," and walked serenely toward the parlor. Uncle George, his burned face still shining, came past Laura and she felt that she would turn to stone, but his fishy, tobacco-y hand came down ever so gently over her hair, and she stopped dancing.

Aunt Tempe's voice rose. "Why, bless your heart! George Fairchild! Come here and kiss your sister!"

Uncle George ran from her and from poor Aunt Primrose who looked after him without words. (The Fairchild men would just run from you sometimes.) He went to the back, holding out his fish. "Give them to the Negroes," Laura heard him tell somebody. Then Aunt Mac's voice: "Georgie, you look like Sin on Earth, wash your face at the kitchen sink!"

But I'm a poor little motherless girl, she thought, and sat down on the bottom step and cried a tear into the hem of her skirt, for herself. Before long she thought she'd go back to the kitchen and see what Aunt Mac would say to her.

"Ho hum," said India. She fell back on the floor and set a glass of lemonade on her diaphragm. "Aunt Tempe, I bet you don't know something you wish you did."

"What, child?" asked Aunt Tempe sharply.

"I bet you didn't know Aunt Robbie ran away from Uncle George and never is coming back."

"Hush your mouth, child."

"Yes, she did!"

"The nerve!" Aunt Tempe suddenly reached up and took off her hat. Her fine hair with the Memphis permanent wave sprang to life about her temples, like kitten ears.

India was not ever quite sure whose nerve Aunt Tempe spoke of—perhaps now her mother (she heard her coming) for not writing the news. Aunt Tempe carried the notion that her mother was snooty—the only one of her father's sisters who did; because her mother didn't write. "Rate," her mother said, in her Virginia accent, "I never rate." It was her Virginia snootiness that she would never "rate" anything, Aunt Tempe thought—people had to drop everything and come to Shellmound to find out.

"Ah! What has he done?" Aunt Tempe said, with her sisterly face alive to brotherly mischief. Then, "Oh, the mortification! Who told you, baby? And when?"

"I'm nine," said India. "No-*body* told me, but I *knew* way back this morning."

"You knew what?" called Ellen warningly from the hall. "You did get here!" she said to Aunt Tempe in that warm, marveling voice with which she always welcomed people, no matter how late she was doing it, as if some planet had mysteriously entered a fresh orbit and appeared at Shellmound. She kissed Aunt Tempe's cheek—the softest cheek of the Fairchilds, which Aunt Tempe offered in a temporary manner like a very expensive possession. After all (India could read her mind as Aunt Tempe kissed back), she had been invited over long-distance telephone, and she had been only barely able to make out what *one* bolt from the blue was, that Dabney was engaged—and then it was very unsatisfactory information; they had let Bluet tell her the wedding day.

"Aunt Primrose and Aunt Jim Allen still don't know you know what," India said, putting her arm soothingly around Aunt Tempe's neck. "They don't even dream."

"Get away from me, India, you're always such a *hot* child! —*Well-madam?*"

"How's Mary Denis?" asked Ellen as if the "Well-madam?" were not Aunt Tempe's question first.

"Thin as a rail, white as a ghost. Only wild horses—The baby's my image—Has Mr. Buchanan's Titian hair, Mr. Buchanan's the same Yankee he ever was, demands the impossible. . . . Oh, the mortification of *life*, Ellen!"

"Now, Tempe, you're always further beside yourself than you need to be," Ellen said. With the hand Aunt Tempe couldn't see, she was very gently patting India's bare foot.

"Of course I am! And events come along and bear me out! But nobody tells me!" Aunt Tempe poured out another glass of lemonade and asked pitifully for a little tiny bit of sugar. "Of course I know George and Battle both try to spare me—Denis always spared me everything. It would kill me to know all poor George must have gone through, what it's driven him to!"

"India—you run out and tell Vi'let to stop whatever she's doing and come sweeten Aunt Tempe's lemonade to suit her—and take Lady Clare with you."

In the music room there was a stir as if Lady Clare roused out of some trance. "Did you hear me playing 'Country Gardens,' Aunt Ellen?" she cried, running in.

"Yes, dear, I was listening out in the hall," Ellen said. "You're a big strong girl, rounding out a little, I believe."

"I'm bigger than Laura," said Lady Clare. "I'm going out and turn around in the yard until it makes me drunk and I fall down and crack my head open."

"Now, Lady Clare—just because you're visiting!" said Aunt Tempe.

"I'm not going to tell Dabney you know what," said India as she walked out.

"That's a good girl, honey." Ellen looked at her proudly.

"She's got so many secrets from me, I'm not going to tell her mine! Maybe I'll tell her years later."

"Now! Straighten me out," Tempe said to Ellen, leaning not forward, but back.

"I can't imagine how India finds out things." Ellen was brooding. "It's just like magic."

"I don't worry about India!"

Ellen sighed. "I guess not yet. —Well, Dabney's going to marry Troy Flavin, just as we told you, and Robbie has run away from George and he won't say a word or go after her. Not connected, of course, but—"

"Two things always happen to the Fairchilds at once. Three! Have you forgotten Mary Denis having a baby at Inverness at the very moment all this was descending on you here?"

"No, I didn't forget," said Ellen. "I reckon there're enough Fairchilds for everything! But we're hoping this trouble of George's will blow over."

"Blow over! That's Battle's talk, I can hear him now. How, in the world?"

"Robbie might still come to the wedding."

"I'd like to see her! She'll get no welcome from me, flighty thing," said Tempe. "Bless George's heart! He lost his Fairchild temper." She smiled.

"Oh, Tempe, I think he's hurt," Ellen said. "You know George and Battle and all those men can't stand anybody to be ugly and cruel to them!"

"I know. And how can people hurt George?" Tempe asked. She turned up her soft face with a constricted look that was wonder, and searched Ellen's face.

"I don't know. . . . Remember Robbie's the one among us all we don't know very well," Ellen said, and then she faltered as if somehow she had conspired with Tempe's first thought, her surface of curiosity that had stopped her as she came into the room. "Vi'let, bring the sugar!" she called. "It's too late now for cake, isn't it, Tempe?"

"I don't think so. I know George's headstrong," said Tempe, piteously showing the palm of her little hand. "Nobody knows better than I do—the oldest sister! He's headstrong. Nobody has a bit of influence over him at all! But how can *she* think *she's* fit to take him down, Old Man Swanson's granddaughter? I could pull her eyes out this minute."

"I had led myself to believe they were happy," Ellen said. Vi'let was bringing the sugar on an unnecessarily big silver tray and Ellen watched her treat Tempe very specially and tell her how young and pretty she looked, not like no grandma, and she was going to bring her some of that cake. . . . "We're not telling Dabney about this until the wedding's over," she said, as Tempe sipped her lemonade.

"Pshaw! If Dabney's old enough to marry the overseer out of her father's fields, she's old enough to know what George and every other man does or is capable of doing. *I'll* tell her, the next time she dances in here."

"Tempe," said Ellen softly, "wait. Give Robbie just a little more time!"

"*Robbie?* Whose side are you on?"

"I'm on George's side! And Dabney's side . . . George is the sweetest boy in the world, but I think now it's up to Robbie—I think he's left it up to her. Tempe—we don't know—we don't know anything."

"All I know is Denis would have been in here begging my pardon half an hour ago—if *he* had yelled out 'That's enough!' like that with no warning, and my palpitations."

"Plate of cake, Miss Tempe," said Vi'let at her elbow.

"Here come me and Aunt Primrose!" India cried, singing her warning.

"Oh, Ellen—did you see how George tracked up your floor? It breaks my heart to see it. After Roxie spent the morning on her knees—now it all has to be done over. —Of course *he* don't know any better." She and Tempe kissed each other in a deprecatory, sisterly fashion. "He don't mean to. Tempe, we're getting fat. How is Mary Denis today?"

"Well, Mr. Buchanan thinks she looks 'just dandy!' " said Tempe.

"Tch!"

"He wants to raise up a lot of little Yankees in Illinois, regardless."

"Mary Denis is the prettiest thing that ever went out of the Delta."

"Have some cake, Primrose."

"It's a precious baby, too," Tempe sighed. "Looks so much like me, you'd catch your breath. (Oh, Mashula's coconut!) And you ought to see little Shannon—she's delighted. She can stamp her foot and say 'Scat!' "

"Oh, that little thing! I'd give anything if you could have brought her—the baby too!" cried Ellen.

"There is a limit on what I am able to do," Tempe said, and Ellen as if to make amends said, "Dabney will want to ask you all kinds of things, Tempe! I'm not much use to her, I'm afraid. She cried because the altar rocks—and I couldn't do a thing about it. Howard's banging on it, doing his best—I just wish somebody'd come by."

"And Battle is as helpless as a child with *machinery.* Well, everybody says Mary Denis's wedding was the most outstanding that has ever occurred in our part of the Delta. I won't say prettiest, because it was planned *al fresco* and it poured down—drenched the preacher—but it was the most outstanding once we'd moved inside."

"I remember it was," Ellen said. "Shelley and Dabney had such a good time being flower girls, scampering around. I couldn't come, being about to have—could it have been India?"

"Ha, ha," gloated India.

"Mr. Buchanan said he never saw so many cousins in his life, all scattering rose petals."

"Dabney's going to have shepherdess crooks, Aunt Tempe," said India.

"Good, *good.*"

"Have you ever heard of such a thing?" Ellen said, marveling. "They haven't come, though. They're up there in Memphis still. Dabney makes Battle phone every day, the crook people and the cake people, and bless them out, but it doesn't do a bit of good."

"Let me at the phone," said Tempe, clutching the arms of her chair as though she were held back. "I'll call Pinck immediately and have him go to Memphis and bring the cake and the crooks in his own hands when he comes. Ah, and the flowers, are you sure of those?"

"We're not sure of anything," Ellen said. "Oh, Tempe, could you? The poor child will soon be beside herself."

"I couldn't do less."

"Pinck will wear himself out! But he's so wonderfully smart about everything in Memphis."

"He ought to be." Aunt Tempe went out to the telephone.

"I've nearly finished the mit." Aunt Primrose held it up, like a little empty net.

"Primrose!"

"I think they should have mits to carry those crooks," she said.

"I believe we're getting somewhere in spite of ourselves." Ellen took a breath. "Everything's done except get Howard's altar up and put the lace cloth over it to hide it good—and put your smilax and the candelabra around and wash all the punch cups from everywhere, got them in baskets—and get the flowers and the cake and the ice cream—Dabney wanted it in shapes, you know—and the crooks! George's champagne came, enough to kill us all. Now I'm thinking about the chicken salad—we've made two or three tubs and got it covered on ice—and do you think frozen tomato salad turned in the freezer would be a reproach on us for the rehearsal supper?"

"Mary Denis demanded a cold lobster aspic involving moving the world," Tempe said, coming in. "Of course we moved it. Pinck said he would be delighted! I had to spell shepherdess—didn't you hear me calling you?"

"Dabney will be so thankful. Better wash a little faster on the windows, Bitsy and Floyd," Ellen called. "The rehearsal's tonight, there's not much time."

"Croesus, Mama!" cried Shelley, who was passing in the hall. "It's tomorrow night! Aunt Tempe, don't let her make it any sooner than it is."

"Have I got my times mixed up again!" Ellen put her hand to her forehead. "I told Troy it was tonight, and he didn't any more correct me than a spook. I was hoping we'd get somebody in the family could keep track of time."

"He just didn't want to be correcting you quite yet," said Tempe, with a brave smile. "I really think the house looks pretty well, Ellen!"

"Oh, do you think it looks all right?" Ellen looked around anxiously and yet in a kind of relief. "There was so little time to do much more than get the curtains washed and starched and the rugs beat."

"Child! They'll grind down so much chicken salad in everything it'll all have to be done over anyway," said Tempe in a dark voice.

"I thought in the long run, Primrose thought of it, we could just cover everything mostly with Southern smilax."

"Of course that will suffer with the dancing," said Primrose timidly.

"I consider our responsibility ceases with the cutting of the cake," Tempe declared. "Primrose, what are you putting your eyes out on now? Have you any idea how many bridesmaids there are in this wedding?"

"I set myself to finish this mit before I take a bite of dinner, and I will." Primrose accepted a little crumb of cake from Ellen. "It's my joy."

"I do hope," Tempe was saying, "you won't have the sliding doors open there in full view of Jim Allen's cornet. Jim Allen is forty-four years old in October and I can't think she would appreciate it."

"Oh, she wouldn't mind, Tempe," said Primrose. "Jim Allen's *beyond* all that."

"We have to have the doors open, so Mary Lamar can be heard perfectly playing for the wedding," Ellen said. "Or it would break Dabney's heart."

"It's a living shame these children don't take music," said Tempe. "India, now, *needs* to have music lessons: look at her." India was lying on the floor with her legs straight up in the air, listening.

"Well, there's nobody in Fairchilds giving lessons now," Ellen said, "since Miss Winona Deerfield married that traveling man that came through. If Sue Ellen would just get up from her bed and come back to these children, they'd be kept out of a lot." She suddenly smiled: Roy had come in, washed and combed, and silently opened *Quo Vadis?*

"You used to teach the early ones," said Tempe. "Don't deny it."

"Oh, I tried on Shelley. But I couldn't play pea-turkey now. Dabney's best friend Mary Lamar Mackey from over at Lookback plays if we want music—listen!" In the music room Mary Lamar, restored to the bench, softly began a Schubert song.

"Yes, but she takes it seriously," Aunt Tempe said, lifting a warning finger. "And Laura"—for Laura came in, trailing Roy—"it would be such a consolation to her when she's older."

"I'm not going to be in the wedding, Aunt Tempe," said Laura, veering to her.

"No, poor little girl, you."

"I went to tell Aunt Jim Allen but she was asleep in the dining room on the settee."

"Well, poor thing! She worked too hard counting cut-glass punch cups."

"She said 'Scat!' in her sleep when I looked at her."

"I'm glad it's cats and not rats she's dreaming about," Primrose said. "Oh, Ellen, she knows they're at the

Grove—though I smile and don't let on I hear them." Primrose smiled now, a constricted little smile, as she talked. "You remember how rats madden poor Jim Allen, Tempe. If she thought we heard a rat she would be rushing screaming from the house now—maybe be killing us all, I don't know." She looked with her nervous smile toward Ellen. "That's one thing I want to talk over with George—rats. I want to ask him what to do about the rats in the Grove. It's George's house and he ought to know."

"Oh, but I'd wait till after the wedding, Primrose! Wait till—"

"*I know,*" whispered Primrose, behind the little mit. "And Jim Allen—what she's been doing is hiding her tears—not wanting George and Battle to see her red eyes." When the music climbed again she whispered, "Spare Tempe!"

"Tempe knows—but Dabney doesn't. . . ." Ellen leaned over her, and walked to the window. Then she gave a cry. "Oh, who on earth can that be coming? Oh—it's Troy. Here comes Dabney's sweetheart, you all!" They peeped behind her. "Don't let him see us!"

"I believe to my soul *he's* got red hair!" cried Tempe.

"Let's us not move." India put her eye on Laura and Roy, but Roy was reading and heard nothing.

"I think he's a very steady, good boy," said Ellen. "And he's going to *learn*."

"That's a bad sign if I ever heard one," Tempe cried instantly. "My, he's in a hurry about it too. Flavin is a peculiar name."

"He doesn't usually come that fast, does he?" Primrose whispered, as Troy leaped over little Ranny's stick-horse in the drive and hurried toward the steps. "He's bringing something. My, it looks like Aunt Studney's sack, but of course it isn't."

"Let's still don't get up and look," muttered India, lying flat.

"I wouldn't have known him!" said Primrose. "But I always think of him as part horse—you know, the way he's grown to that black Isabelle in the fields."

"It's bigger than Aunt Studney's sack! Is old Aunt Studney dead yet?" asked Tempe, her fine brows meeting as she peered.

"No, indeed," Ellen said. "She still ain't studyin' us, either. She told Battle so yesterday, asking him for a setting of eggs. He's at the door."

"Here's Troy!" cried Dabney's voice. She was rushing down the stairs and letting him in.

Aunt Mac came through the parlor and by their sashes pulled the three ladies neatly away from the window, and went out again.

"You didn't kiss me!" cried Dabney.

But Troy was pushing his way into the parlor, intent. "Look," he said, "everybody look. Did you ever think your *mother* could make something like this? My mammy made these, I've seen her do it. A thousand stitches! Look—these are for us, Dabney."

"Quilts!" Dabney took his arm. "Shelley! Come in and look. Troy, come speak to Aunt Tempe—she's come for the wedding, Papa's sister from Inverness." But he flung her off and held up a quilt of jumpy green and blue. " 'Delectable Mountains,' " he said. "Pleased to meet you, ma'am. I swear that's the 'Delectable Mountains.' Do you see how any lady no higher'n a grasshopper ever sewed all those little pieces together? Look, 'Dove in the Window.' Where's everybody?"

They all came forward and watched Troy spread out the quilts, snatch them together, spread them out again. "Wedding presents." "They're lovely!" "Get up off the floor, India, or you'll get a quilt over you!"

"She sent so many," said Shelley, backing away a little each time she came forward.

"It gets cold in Tishomingo," said Troy gravely.

"Couldn't your mother come to the wedding, Troy?" asked Ellen gently. "We could send for her." Even if his mother wrote to him, she had not been sure he wrote to his mother.

"Not just to a wedding." He thoughtfully shook his head.

"What's the name of this quilt?" asked Dabney, arms on her hips.

"Let's see. I think it's 'Tirzah's Treasure,' but it might be 'Hearts and Gizzards.' I've spent time under both."

"Didn't you know either about George's predicament?" Aunt Tempe said to Aunt Primrose across the room. "I'm glad somebody else didn't know."

"He told me when I came in. Bless his heart! *She'll* come back," Aunt Primrose said, looking around Troy's arm.

"Ma pieced that top of a snowy winter," said Troy gravely staring, his eyes far away.

"I wish I could make something like that," said Aunt Primrose gallantly.

"Not everybody can," said Troy. "But 'Delectable Mountains,' that's the one I aim for Dabney and me to sleep under most generally, warm *and* pretty."

Aunt Tempe gave Ellen a long look.

"I think they are beautiful, useful wedding presents," said Ellen. "Dabney will treasure them, I know. Dabney, you must write and thank Troy's mother tonight."

"Let her wait till she tries them out, Mrs. Fairchild," said Troy. "That's what will count with Mammy. She might come if we have a baby, sure enough."

Aunt Primrose darted her little hand out, as if the quilt were hot and getting hotter, and Ellen and Dabney and Troy pulled it out taut in the air. The pattern shone and the ladies and Dabney all fluttered their eyelids as if the simple thing revolved while they held it.

"Look," said Ellen. "Troy, there's a paper pinned to this corner."

"Oh, that's Ma's wish," said Troy. "I noticed it."

"She says here, 'A pretty bride. To Miss Dabney Fairchild. The disappointment not to be sending a dozen or make a bride's quilt in the haste. But send you mine. A long life. Manly sons, loving daughters, God willing.' "

"That's Ma. She'll freeze all winter."

"Your pretty bride," said Dabney, going around. "How did she know I was pretty?"

"I don't know," said Troy. "I didn't give her much of a notion." He bent to her disbelieving kiss. "I guess you'd better get these off the floor and fold them nice, Dabney. And lay them on a long table with that other conglomeration for folks to come see."

The dinner bell rang. Battle and the boys came in rosy and slicked, playing with the barking dogs. Orrin had on his pompadour cap. George came down with Ranny riding him, knees on his shoulders. Ranny had the family telescope up to his eye, and turned it with both hands about the room, exclaiming.

"Who do you see in this room?" George was asking him quietly. "Do you see Mama having secrets with Aunt Primrose and Aunt Tempe and Aunt Jim Allen?" They went toward them.

"Yes, sir!"

"I always thought Robbie was a very *strenuous* girl," said Aunt Primrose hesitantly, looking up at George.

"She's *direct*," said Ellen.

"She has her cheek," Tempe snapped, while Jim Allen was still asking pleadingly, "Who, who?"

"She has the nerve of a brass monkey," said George, and Ranny crowed from his head. George's forehead, nose, and cheeks still fiery from the sun, he seemed to be beaming now at the sight of his sisters all gathered, with a midday fragrance of stuffed green peppers and something else floating over them like a spicy cloud.

They're both as direct as two blows on the head of a nail, George and Robbie, Ellen was thinking with surprise. George was so tender-hearted, his directness was something you forgot; when he was far away, in Memphis, she thought of him—as she always thought of the man or the woman—as at Robbie's *mercy*. Robbie, anywhere, was being direct.

"I've racked my brains to think of something we can tell the Delta," Tempe declared, with Ranny's telescope turned on her. "Mary Denis named her *baby* for you, George, and you yell and run off like a maniac when I try to inform you."

"How's Mary Denis?" said George. "Tell the Delta about what?"

"About Robbie Reid, your wife," said Tempe. "You have to tell the Delta something when your wife flies off and you start losing your Fairchild temper. Right at the point of another wedding! You should have thought of it when you married her, woke up the night. Ranny, is that the manners your Uncle George teaches you? That's staring."

"I don't see Robbie," Ranny said, turning George with his digging knees. He looked through the front window, out at the glare. "I just see Maureen chasing a bird, and Laura turning round and round in the yard."

"Call them in," growled Battle.

"Tell the Delta to go to Guinea," said Ellen stoutly.

Aunt Mac came up the hall, her strong voice singing, belligerently sad, " 'O where hae ye been, Lord Randall my son? . . . O mother, mother, mak my bed soon. . . .' "

"Of course Mary Denis is thin as a rail. Mercy," Tempe said to Lady Clare, who appeared too and circled round her, ecstatically walking on her knees and drinking something green. "Don't you drink that in here—ink? Take it on out, I can't watch you."

"Well, is everything all pretty near ready now?" Troy's voice was asking.

"I see Dabney kissing Troy," Ranny announced.

"Oh, Troy, the altar rocks!" Dabney cried.

"Put a hammer in my hand, I'll knock it into shape before we sit down to dinner!"

"I see Lady Clare drinking Shelley's ink," said Ranny dreamily.

"Lady Clare, you know what happens when you show off," Aunt Primrose said, putting her finished bridesmaid's mit to her lips and biting the thread.

"She doesn't care," said Ranny, smiling, at the telescope. "She doesn't care."

"I seem to hear the dinner bell," said Aunt Jim Allen.

"Roy, close your book." Ellen kissed the top of his head, and he looked up with sucked-in breath.

"Laura and Maureen," said Battle, with the condensed roar in his fatherly voice carrying out the window, "will you obey me and come to the table before I skin you alive and shake your bones up together and throw the sack in the bayou? And Mary Lamar Mackey," he said, to the other direction, "will your ditty wait?"

"Oh, Papa, you're so *hot*," said Shelley. She pulled at his starched coat sleeve and tried to kiss him, and he spanked her ahead of him to the table.

"Miss Priss! Do you love your papa, not forget him?"

"Naturally," said Aunt Tempe, when Roy with his eyes bright told what George did, about the Yellow Dog on the trestle, "he did it for Denis."

She smiled and fanned with the Chinese fan she brought from Inverness, nodding at them. Dabney, who loved her father and adored George, knew beyond question when Aunt Tempe came and stated it like a fact of the weather, that it was Denis and always would be Denis that they gave the family honor to. She held Troy's hand under the table and accepted it with a feeling not far from luxuriousness: Denis was the one that looked like a Greek god, Denis who squandered away his life loving people too much, was too kind to his family, was torn to pieces by other people's misfortune, married beneath him, threw himself away in drink, got himself killed in the war. It was Denis who gambled the highest, who fell the hardest when thrown by the most dangerous horse, who was the most delirious in his fevers, who went the farthest on his travels, who was the most beset. It was Denis who had read everything in the world and had the prodigious memory—not a word ever left him. Denis knew law, and could have told you the way Mississippi could be made the fairest place on earth to live, all of it like the Delta. It was Denis that was ahead of his time and it was Denis that was out of the pages of a book too. Denis could have planted the world, and made it grow. Denis knew what to do about high water, could have told you everything about the Mississippi River from one end to the other. Denis could have been anything and done everything, but he was cut off before his time.

He could have one day married some beautiful girl worthy of him (Mary Lamar Mackey would have grown up to him), leaving Virgie Lee (Denis's choice was baffling, not to be too much brooded on) to somebody she would better have tried to live with; he would have had a beautiful child—a son—a second Denis, though not his father's equal. It was a shame on earth that Maureen, though George would naturally risk his life for her, was the only remnant of his body; she bore no more breath of resemblance to him than she did to, as Aunt Jim Allen always remarked, the King of Siam; if anything, she took after her mother, though her hair was light. It would be wrong to see in her dancing up and down any bit of Denis's tender mischief or marvelous cavorting.

"These fields and woods are still full of Denis, full of Denis," Tempe said firmly. "If I were to set foot out there by myself, though catch me!—I'd meet the spirit of Denis Fairchild first thing, I know it."

She looked pleased, Dabney thought, as if she were mollified that Denis was dead if his spirit haunted just where she knew. Not at large, not in transit any more, as in life, but fixed—tied to a tree. She pressed Troy's hand, and he pressed back. Poor Denis! she thought all at once, while Maureen, eyeing her, stuck out her tongue through her smiling and fruit-filled mouth.

5

It was morning, the day of the rehearsal. Roy ran out of the house and scattered some crumbs to the birds. Ellen saw him from her window—his face tender-eyed under the blocky, serious forehead and the light slept-on hair pushed to the side, with a darker shadow the size of a guinea egg under the crest. Alone in the yard, he said something to a bird. This was her last day with her daughter Dabney before she married. How she loved her sons though!

"This is Dabney's wedding rehearsal day," Ellen said, turning to the old great-aunts, with Roxie by her offering them a second cup of black coffee while breakfast was getting ready.

"Gordon, dear, I'm hot," said Aunt Shannon fretfully. She lay back with her soft black Mary Jane slippers crossed, on Aunt Mac's chaise longue, frowning slightly at the mounted blue butterflies on the wall.

"She thinks none of the rest of us know it's September," growled Aunt Mac. She snapped her watch onto her bosom. "Nobody but Brother Gordon killed in the Battle of Shiloh. Foot!"

The two old sisters were not too congenial, had never been except for a little while when Battle's generation were growing up and absorbing their time, and in recent years the belief on Aunt Shannon's part that she was conversing with people whom Aunt Mac knew well to be dead seemed a freer development of the schism. Far back in Civil War days, Ellen had been told or had gathered, some ineradicable coolness had come between them—it seemed to have sprung from a jealousy between the sisters over which one agonized the more or the more abandonedly, over the fighting brothers and husbands. With the brothers and husbands every man killed in the end, the jealousy did not seem canceled by death, but extended by it; memory of fear and the keeping up of loyalty had its rivalries too—made them endless and now wholly desperate, for no good was ever to come of anguish any more and so it never had when anguish was fresh.

Aunt Shannon now, with her access to their soldier brothers Battle, George, and Gordon, as well as to James killed only thirty-three years ago in the duel, to her husband Lucian Miles and even to Aunt Mac's husband Duncan Laws, was dwelling without shame in happiness and superiority over her sister. Poor Aunt Mac did indeed seem to think less of her husband now, in spite of herself (she made little flung-off remarks about his family, "Columbus new-comers") when Aunt Shannon spoke casually to "Duncan, dearie," and bent her head, as if he had come up behind her while she was knitting to give her a little kiss on the back of the neck, as indeed he had done often long ago.

"The wedding's right here. Are we ready, Aunt Mac?"

"Duncan, dearie, there's a scrap of nuisance around here ought to be shot," said Aunt Shannon, glancing sideways without stirring. "You'll see him. Pinck Summers, he calls himself. Coming courting here."

"Duncan Laws will shoot who I tell him, thank you," said Aunt Mac. "Shannon, be ashamed of yourself for getting your time so mixed up. Vainest of the Fairchilds! —Well, then, Ellen, go on to Dabney! Wake her up!"

But Dabney had ridden out on her red filly before any of them were awake, out through the early fields. Vi'let had not yet swept the night cobwebs from the doors, and she had dashed through shuddering, with fighting hands, and pushed open the back gate into the early eastern light which already felt warm and lapping against her face and arms. In her stall the little filly looked at her as if she were waiting for her early, there was a tremor to go in her neck and side. Howard's little boy was sitting in the hay and he saddled the filly and put Dabney on and held the gate. She rode out looking back with her finger to her lips—Howard's boy put finger to lips too, and jumped over the ditch watching her go. She thought she would ride out by herself one time. She had even come out without her breakfast, having eaten only what was in the kitchen, milk and biscuits and a bit of ham and a chicken wing, and a row of plums sitting in the window.

Flocks of birds flew up from the fields, the little filly went delightedly through the wet paths, breasting and breaking the dewy nets of spider webs. Opening morning-glories were turned like eyes on her pretty feet. The occasional fences smelled sweet, their darkened wood swollen with night dew like sap, and following her progress the bayou rustled within, ticked and cried. The sky was softly blue all over, the last rim of sunrise cloud melting into it like the foam on fresh milk.

With her whip lifted Dabney passed Troy's house, and passed through Mound Field and Far Field, through the Deadening, and on toward the trees, where the Yazoo was. Turning and going along up here, looking through the trees and across the river, you could see Marmion. Around the bend in the early light that was still night-quiet in the cypressy place, the little filly went confidently and fastidiously as ever.

Dabney bent her head to the low boughs, and then saw the house reflected in the Yazoo River—an undulant tower with white wings at each side, like a hypnotized swamp butterfly, spread and dreaming where it alights. Then the house itself reared delicate and vast, with a strict tower, up from its reflection, and Dabney gazed at it counting its rooms.

Marmion had been empty since the same year it was completed, 1890—when its owner and builder, her grandfather James Fairchild, was killed in the duel he fought with Old Ronald McBane, and his wife Laura Allen died broken-hearted very soon, leaving two poor Civil War–widowed sisters to bring up the eight children. They went back, though it crowded them, to the Grove, Marmion was too heart-breaking. Honor, honor, honor, the aunts drummed into their ears, little Denis and Battle and George, Tempe and Annie Laurie, Rowena, Jim Allen and Primrose. To give up your life because you thought that much of your *cotton*—where was love, even, in that? *Other* people's cotton. Fine glory! Dabney would not have done it.

The eagerness with which she was now going to Marmion, entering her real life there with Troy, told her enough—all the cotton in the world was not worth one moment of life! It made her know that nothing could ever defy her enough to make her leave it. How sweet life was, and how well she could hold it, pluck it, eat it, lay her cheek to it—oh, no one else knew. The juice of life and the hot, delighting taste and the fragrance and warmth to the cheek, the mouth. She hated the duel for her grandfather, actively, while the little filly trembled with impatience under her hand and hated being kept standing still. Everybody in the family had nearly forgotten the old duel by now (it was "bad about Marmion," they "abandoned the place") except Dabney, whom it had lately come to horrify. She would not leave Marmion, having once come to it, if there were duels for any cause. What was the reason death could be part of a question about the crops, for instance?

Yes, honor—she had been told when she asked questions as a little girl, Marmion was empty out in the woods because Old Ronald McBane at Old Argyle had not protected his landing where some of the people's cotton for miles around was shipped from his gin; Grandfather, who had a gin too, had accused him of it, had been challenged, called out to pistols on the river bank, had been killed instantly. But both gins went on the same. Dabney had always resisted and pouted at the story when any of the boys told it—when they said "Bang bang!" she covered up her ears and wept, until they comforted her and gave her something for having made her cry.

She knew, though—even the surrender of life was the privilege of fieriness in the blood. She felt it in herself, but would anything ever make her tell, ever find it out? Not while she could resist and lament the fact that dear life would surrender itself for anything.

The sun lifted over the trees and struck the face of Marmion; all the tints of cypress began to shine on it, the brightness of age like newness. Her house! And somehow the river always seemed swift here, though it was the same river that passed through Fairchilds under the bridge where the cotton wagons went over as noisily as a child beating a tin pan, and passed the Grove where the aunts sat on the porch and cried for a breeze from it. As a child she would run off here and throw sticks in, just at this spot, convinced that they would tear around the curve where the river looked fast, only to see them gently waltz and drift here and there. . . . She threw a stick in again, and once more it went slowly. The river was low now. In the spring it would be up over where she was now. The little filly turned with Dabney, willfully, and took the path back toward Shellmound.

"I will never give up anything!" Dabney thought, bending forward and laying her head against the soft neck. "Never! Never! For I am happy, and to give up nothing will prove it. I will never give up anything, never give up Troy—or *to* Troy!" She thought smilingly of Troy, coming slowly, this was the last day, slowly plodding and figuring, sprung all over with red-gold hairs.

Shelley couldn't stand him because he had hair in his ears. She called him Hairy Ears—Dabney smiled biting her lip at that small torment. The truth was, slowness made any Fairchild frantic, and Dabney delighted now again in Troy's slowness like a kind of alarm. "Papa never gave up anything," she was thinking. "I am the first thing Papa has ever given up. Oh, he hates it!" He would not tell her how he really felt about her going to Troy—nobody would. Nobody had ever told her anything—not anything very true or very bad in life.

Proud and outraged together for the pampering ways of the Fairchilds, she put the little switch to her filly where she had kissed her. The rehearsal was tonight. If they didn't say anything to her now, or try to stop her, it was their last chance.

And let them try! Just now, while they never guessed, she had seen Marmion—the magnificent temple-like, castle-like house, with the pillars springing naked from the ground, and the lookout tower, and twenty-five rooms, and inside, the wonderful free-standing stair—the chandelier, chaliced, golden in light, like the stamen in the lily down-hanging. The garden—the playhouse—the maze—they had all been before her eyes when she was all by herself, even her own boat landing!

Then after she got in and was living there married, she wanted it to rain, rain—sound on the roof like fall, like spring, bend the trees and the lightning to glare and show them trembling, lifted, bent, come-alive, the way trees looked from windows during storms at night. She wanted this to be outside, and inside herself, sitting in dignity with her cheek on her hand.

She rode by the thick woods where the whirlpool lay, and something made her get off her horse and creep to the bank and look in—she almost never did, it was so creepy and scary. This was a last chance to look before her wedding. She parted the thonged vines of the wild grapes, thick as legs, and looked in. There it was. She gazed feasting her fear on the dark, vaguely stirring water.

There were more eyes than hers here—frog eyes—snake eyes? She listened to the silence and then heard it stir, churn, churning in the early morning. She saw how the snakes were turning and moving in the water, passing across each other just below the surface, and now and then a head horridly sticking up. The vines and the cypress roots twisted and grew together on the shore and in the water more thickly than any roots should grow, gray and red, and some roots too moved and floated like hair. On the other side, a turtle on a root opened its mouth and put its tongue out. And the whirlpool itself—could you doubt it? Doubt all the stories since childhood of people white and black who had been drowned there, people that were dared to swim in this place, and of boats that would venture to the center of the pool and begin to go around and everybody fall out and go to the bottom, the boat to disappear? A beginning of vertigo seized her, until she felt herself leaning, leaning toward the whirlpool.

But she was never as frightened of it as the boys were. She looked in while she counted to a hundred, and then ran. Behind her the little filly had been stamping her foot. She climbed on her and kissed her neck, and galloped back into the fields, the Deadening, Far Field, Mound Field, back to Shellmound. When she went under Troy's window she drew the reins a moment and cried out rapidly, tauntingly, all run together like one word,

Wake up, Jacob, day is breaking!
Pea's in the pod and the hoe-cake's baking!
Mary, get your ash-cake done, my love—!

Was he awake? Did he hear? She rode flying home, and began calling "Mama! Roxie! Roxie! Papa!" How hungry she was!

II

"Shelley!" Ellen called at the foot of the stairs.

"Ma'am?" came Shelley's ladylike voice from around several corners in the upper regions. Where on earth was she?

"She's painting her name on her trunk to go to Europe," India said at her mother's feet. She kept her informed about what everybody was doing at all times, which she knew though she herself, as now, might be cutting paper dolls out of the *Delineator* on the hall floor with Laura and Roxie's little Sudie; she seemed truly the only one who knew.

"I want you to go to the store for me and get me a spool of strong string, for Howard's altar!" called Ellen in a patiently high voice. "The pony cart's out front now, while it's still a little cool! And go to Brunswick-town and take Partheny a cup of that broth Roxie's pouring off and tell her if she's over being mindless to come up without fail to help in the kitchen! What else? Oh, my old garnet pin, Shelley! Tell Partheny Miss Ellen wonders if she could think what happened to it—you might try her memory a little! She came up and cooked for your papa's birthday and I had it on my dress. But tell her to be here tomorrow morning with the birds!—You can take Laura and India with you," she added in her normal voice. "Where's Lady Clare?"

"On the joggling board, joggling," said India.

"Yes'm, Mama! In a minute," called Shelley. "I'm all covered with black!"

"Oh, gracious," called Ellen perfunctorily. "Mind you invite Partheny to the wedding! She *loves Dabney*!"

Tempe was coming in the side door, they had heard her exclaiming in the yard. ("Poor Tempe, if there's a flower, she wants it!" Primrose always sighed.)

"Did the mosquitoes get you, Tempe?"

"I'm peppered!"

"We can go see Partheny without Shelley," said India, her face close to Laura's. She poked her scissors at Laura's heart. "We'll go with each other."

"Let me at the phone," said Aunt Tempe. "Pinck's going to have to get me some little fluted-paper salted-nut holders! It occurred to me in the garden—twelve silver ones won't go anywhere. I'll catch him at the Peabody!"

Nothing tired Ellen herself more than the spectacle of marital bullying, but it was the breath of life to Tempe, spectacle and all. She sailed among the children to the telephone, while little India smiled in the wake of her pleasure in demanding one more little old thing from Pinck.

"Oh, Mama," cried Shelley, running down the stairs into her mother's arms, as though something dreadful had that moment happened. "It's the only pin you ever really had. I don't count your sunburst! Oh, Mama, and it's lost!"

"Tragedy," remarked Tempe, turning from Pinck's

voice at the receiver, "I'm surprised more things aren't lost around here than there are."

"Why, Shelley," Ellen said in surprise. "You mustn't start taking things that hard."

"Maybe *I* lost it!" said Shelley.

"Straighten your shoulders, dear. Just ask Partheny—she won't know anything, very likely. It's only a pin. Don't forget the string. Don't let the children go off without you. Oh, and bring Ranny back! Battle set his heart on getting Ranny's hair cut to show a little of his ears, so they won't think he's a girl at the wedding, and nobody with him but Tippy."

"Let's sneak off from Shelley," said India to Laura. They threw down their scissors and paper dolls and trailed toward the door.

George walked through, and the children all swept around him. Tempe took hold of him. Caught in their momentum, he looked out at Ellen perfectly still, as if from a train window.

"No, I'm going to the Grove and have dinner with Jim Allen and Primrose," he was saying.

"*Today*?" Tempe exclaimed.

"Has the wedding anything to do with today? That's tomorrow." He teased Tempe, but went out the front door. Through the side lights Ellen saw him stretch out in the porch hammock and lie prone as if asleep when Troy rode Isabelle up in the yard and called "Hi, George!" with his arm raised in that rather triumphant way. She waited a moment watching him, feeling that there was something radical in George, or that some devastating inner picture of their unnecessary ado would flash before his vision now and then. There was a kind of ascetic streak in him, even, she felt timidly. Left to himself, he might not ask for anything of any of them —not necessarily. . . . No, she could not think that for more than a moment. He was too *good.* He would not wish them any way but the way they were. But she, herself, wished they could all be a little different on occasion, more aware of one another when they were all so close. They should know of one another's rebellions, *consider* them. Why, children and all rebelled!

Laura and India were hunching down the steps like dwarfs together under the big black umbrella that completely obliterated their shadows down to their trotting feet.

"Wait-wait-wait!" cried Shelley. She ran flying out the door lacing her fresh middy, and tying it with the impatient knot of a tomboy. Her hair from under her tight headband blew straight back in the wind. Her cheeks were both smudged with shiny black lacquer. She pretended not to see Uncle George, for she did not beg him to come or tell him good-bye.

"I had to finish my name," she said to India and Laura. "Looks like you all could wait that long."

"She wants her name in *black*. When will it be ready?" cried India.

"It won't be dry until eleven o'clock tonight," said Shelley. "Do I smell?"

"Uh-huh."

She dipped between them and took the umbrella up to her height and tilted it stylishly. Three pairs of leg shadows jiggled on the grass. Above them, Roy was sitting on the roof and singing, " 'My name is Samuel Hall and I hate you one and all, damn your eyes!' "

"Just don't look at him and he'll come down," said Shelley. "Now you can come with me, but don't touch me." They sat in the pony cart and Shelley drove Tiny down the road. India and Laura carefully held the umbrella over her and made faces behind her back. "I'm still full of breakfast," Laura ventured to say.

No one on the street of Fairchilds spoke any way but beautifully-mannered to Shelley, all the men promptly swept off their hats. No one told her her face was dirty, and India was waiting until they got home to make her look in the glass. They drove up and down the street three times and had Coca Colas, speaking to people over and over, with all the men's hats going up and down. India cried joyously, "Hi, Miss Thracia! Hi, Miss Mayo! —Oh, I'm so lonesome at Shellmound!" she sighed to Laura. "Miss Mayo has an oil painting that winks its eye."

Laura remembered Fairchilds—the notice nailed to the post-office wall warning people not to be defrauded by the Spanish swindle, the blind man standing up singing with his face to the Yazoo River, the sign, "Utmost Solitude," in Gothic letters over the door of a lady dying with T. B., who would not let Dr. Murdoch in. When they went in the post office, she saw the notice still there—and so the swindle was still going on—and recognized the cabinet photographs of the postmistress's family sitting around her ledge, and the framed one hanging over the window. At the barber shop they stopped and laughed. All wrapped up, Ranny was getting his hair cut, biting his lip. Sue Ellen's little girl Tippy was holding his hand, and swinging her foot. They threw him an encouraging kiss.

They passed the store by.

"Later," said Shelley.

She turned the pony into a short sunny road behind the compress that seemed to dip down, although it was level like everywhere, into the abrupt shade of chinaberry trees and fig trees.

Brunswick-town lay all around them, dead quiet except for the long, unsettled cries of hens walking around, and the whirr of pigeons now and then overhead. Only the old women were home. The little houses were many and alike, all whitewashed with a green door, with stovepipes crooked like elbows of hips behind, okra, princess-feathers, and false dragonhead growing around them, and China trees over them like umbrellas, with chickens beneath sitting with shut eyes in dust holes. It was shady like a creek bed. The smell of scalding water, feathers, and iron pots mixed with the smells of darkness. Here, where no grass was let grow on the flat earth that was bare like their feet, the old women had it shady, secret, lazy, and cool. A devious, invisible vine of talk seemed to grow from shady porch to shady porch, though all the old women were hidden. The alleys went like tunnels under the chinaberry branches, and the pony cart rocked over their black roots. Wood smoke drifted and hung in the trees like a low and fragrant sky. In front of Partheny's house, close up to her porch, was an extra protection, a screen the same size as the house, of thick butter-bean vines, so nobody could see who might be home. The door looked around one side, like a single eye around a veil.

The girls climbed out of the pony cart and Shelley led the way up the two steps and knocked three times on the closed door.

In good time Partheny came out and stood on the porch above them. She was exactly as she had always looked, taller than a man, flat, and narrow, the color of midnight-blue ink, and wore a midnight-blue dress reaching to and just showing her shrimp-pink toes. She did not appear mindless this morning, for she had put a tight little white cap on her head, sharp-peaked with a frilly top and points around like a crown.

"Parthenia," said Shelley, speaking very politely, as she excelled in doing, "we wanted to invite you to Miss Dabney's wedding."

"Wouldn't miss it!" Partheny said, rolling her protruding eyes and looking somber.

"Mama says for you to come up with the birds in the morning."

"Thank you, ma'am."

"And Partheny," Shelley said, "Mama is so sad, she missed her garnet pin. It was Papa's present."

"Mr. Battle's present!" Partheny said dramatically.

"Yes, and, Partheny, Mama wondered if maybe while you were cooking for Papa's birthday barbecue, if maybe you might have just seen it floating around somewhere —if maybe you could send word to her where you think it might be. Where to look."

"Oh-oh," said Partheny regretfully. She shook her white crown. "I surely don't know what best to direct your mother, Miss Shell, where she could look. Hush while I think."

"Mama thinks now it's been lost all summer, and she just noticed it was gone," said Shelley.

"Now ain't that a shame before God?"

"Yes, indeed, it is," said Shelley. "Papa gave that pin

to Mama before they were married." She was all at once carried away, and fell silent.

"What kind of hat is that?" asked India, passionately springing forward.

"Oh, Miss India Bright-Eyes! It's a drawer-leg," said Partheny, giggling up very high. "Miss Shell, don't you go back tellin' your Mama you caught me with no drawer-leg on my old head!" Then she took a serious step at them.

"Well."

"I like it," said India.

"Yes, it's real pretty, Partheny," said Shelley in a kind of coaxing voice.

"How is your mama—not speaking of garnet present?" asked Partheny.

"She's fine. She's not going out, right now."

Partheny gave them a bright look, like a bird. All of a sudden she gave a little cackle, bent down, and said, "Step inside—don't set your heels down, I've been mindless four and a half days. But let me just look around in parts of the house. Don't suppose that pin could have flown down *here* anywhere, do you?"

They went inside, Partheny shaking her head somberly, India dragging them forward. Partheny looked, patting the bed quilt and tapping the fireplace, and then disappearing into the other room where they could hear her making little sympathetic, sorrowful noises, and a noise like looking under the dishpan.

The three girls sat on one of the old Shellmound wicker settees, in a row. Laura's mouth was a little open; she was surprised to learn, this way, that Aunt Ellen had ever had such a fine present given to her. Uncle Battle himself had given it to her, she had lost it, and now Partheny was back there playing-like looking for it.

"What don't happen to presents!" Partheny cried out from the other room, in genial outrage.

Laura stole a glance at Shelley. She was sitting caught here in a boxy, vine-shadowed little room decorated with chicken feathers and valentines, with a ceiling that made her almost bump her head and a closeness that did make her droop a little. Now was a good time to ask Shelley something. Just as she opened her mouth, India threw herself abruptly to the floor. She caught a guinea pig.

"Put him down," whispered Shelley.

"You make me," said India, and sat holding the squirming guinea pig and kissing its wrinkled forehead.

Laura put her weight on Shelley's arm. "Can I give Uncle George a wedding present?" she whispered.

"Uncle George? You don't have to give him anything. India, put him down," whispered Shelley. She did not turn her head, but fussed at both of them looking straight in front of her. . . . This was a lowly kind of errand, a dark place to visit, old Partheny was tricky as the devil. Only—suddenly the thought of her mother's loss swept over Shelley with such regret, indignation, pity as she was not in the least prepared for, and she almost lost her breath.

"I want to give Uncle George a present, and to not give Dabney a present. I chose between them, which was the most precious."

"That was ugly," Shelley whispered, as if she had never heard of such a thing.

"Precious, precious guinea pig," India whispered on Shelley's other side.

Laura tugged her arm.

"Give him a kiss," whispered Shelley. "India, put him down before he bites you good."

India kissed the guinea pig passionately, and Laura said, "No, I want to give him not a kiss but a present—something he can keep. Forever."

"All right! When we go by the store, you can *find* something to give him, if you have to."

"Will that be my present, all mine?"

"Yes, all yours," whispered Shelley. "You do try people, Laura, I declare!"

"Precious, heavenly guinea pig! I bite thee," said India.

"Just don't you all touch me," said Shelley, and at that moment Partheny appeared in the room again, coming silently on her long bare feet. There was no sign of the guinea pig in India's arms, only a streak on the floor as it ran under Partheny's skirt. The little girl was leaning on her hand, dreamy-eyed.

This time Partheny brought something, which her long hands went around and hid like a rail fence. "Ain't no garnet present anywhere around," she said. She was smoking her pipe as she talked. "I ransacked even de chicken house—felt under de hens, tell your mama. Nary garnet present, Miss Shell. I don't know what could have become of Miss Ellen's pretty li'l garnet present, and her comin' down agin, cravin' it, who knows. Sorry as I can be for her."

"But what have you got?" cried India, jumping up and trying to see.

"But! Got a little somep'm for you to tote back," Partheny said, suddenly leaning forward and giving them all a look of malignity, pride, authority—the way the old nurse looked a hundred times intensified, it seemed.

"Little patticake. Old Partheny know when somep'm happ'm at de big house—never fool yo'se'f. You take dis little patticake to Mr. George Fairchild, was at dis knee at de Grove, and tell him mind he eat it tonight at midnight, by himse'f, and go to bed. Got a little white dove blood in it, dove heart, blood of a snake—things. I just tell you enough in it so you trus' dis patticake."

"What will happen when he eats it?" cried India, joining her hands.

"Mr. George got to eat his patticake all alone, go to bed by himse'f, and his love won't have no res' till her come back to him. Wouldn't do it for ever'body, Partheny wouldn't. I goin' bring Miss Dab heart-shape patticake of her own—come de time."

"How did you know *she'd* ever gone, Partheny?" Shelley whispered, so India and Laura couldn't hear her any more than they could help.

"Ways, ways."

"Thank you, Partheny, but you keep the patticake."

"No! I bid to carry it! I'll make him eat it!" cried India. "Uncle George will have to swallow every crumb—goody! Oh, look how black it is! How heavy!"

India ran out before Shelley could catch her, the cake in both hands up over her flying hair.

"Then take it!" cried Shelley after her.

"I'm still taking Uncle George *my* present," Laura said doggedly.

Partheny followed them out to the porch. "Tell Miss Dab I'm comin'. Surely hopes she be happy wid dat high-ridin' low-born Mr. Troy. *You* all looks pretty." She watched them down the steps and out the gate. As they put up the umbrella she considered them gone, for she nodded over to a hidden neighbor and drawled out, "Got a compliment on my drawer-leg."

"Are we going to the store now?" asked Laura.

"Look. Do you want to go by the cemetery and see your mother's grave?" asked Shelley in a practical voice. "We're near it now."

"Not me," said India, and jumped out of the pony cart with Partheny's cake, when Shelley drew the reins.

"All right," said Laura. "But I want my present for Uncle George before dinner."

The cemetery, an irregular shape of ground, four-sided but narrowing almost to a triangle, with the Confederate graves all running to a point in the direction of the depot, was surrounded by a dense high wall of honeysuckle, which shut out the sight of the cotton wagons streaming by on two sides, where the roads converged to the railroad tracks, the river, the street, and the gin. The school, where the Fairchild children all went, was across one road, and the Methodist Church, with a dooryard bell in a sort of derrick, was across the other. The spire, the derrick, and the flag pole rose over the hedge walls, but nothing else of Fairchilds could be seen, and only its sound could be heard—the gin running, the compress sighing, the rackety iron bridge being crossed, and the creak of wagon and harness just on the other side of the leaves.

A smell of men's sweat seemed to permeate the summer air of Fairchilds until you got inside the cemetery. Here sweet dusty honeysuckle—for the vines were pinkish-white with dust, like icing decorations on a cake, each leaf and tendril burdened—perfumed a gentler air, along with the smell of cut-flower stems that had been in glass jars since some Sunday, and the old-summer smell of the big cedars. Mockingbirds sang brightly in the branches, and Fred, a big bird dog, trotted through on the path, taking the short cut to the icehouse where he belonged. Rosebushes thick and solid as little Indian mounds were set here and there with their perennial, worn little birdnests like a kind of bloom. The gravestones, except for the familiar peak in the Fairchild lot of Grandfather James Fairchild's great pointed shaft, seemed part of the streaky light and shadow in here, either pale or dark with time, and ordinary. Only one new narrow stone seemed to pierce the air like a high note; it was Laura's mother's grave.

All around here were the ones Laura knew—Laura Allen, Aunt Rowena, Duncan Laws, Great-Great-Grandfather George, with Port Gibson under his name in tall letters, the slab with the little scroll on it saying Mary Shannon Fairchild. A little baby's grave, son of Ellen and Battle. Overhead, the enormous crape-myrtle tree, with its clusters of golden seed, was the same.

"Annie Laurie," said Shelley softly, still in that practical voice that made Laura wonder. It always seemed to Laura that when she wanted to think of her mother, they would prevent her, and when she was not thinking of her, then they would say her name. She stood looking at the mound, green now, and Aunt Ellen or Uncle Battle or somebody had put a vase of Maréchal Niel roses here no longer ago than yesterday, thinking of her for themselves. . . . It was late in January, the funeral. But all Laura remembered about that time was a big fire—great heaps of cottonstalks on fire in the fields and thousands of rabbits jumping out with the Negroes chasing after them. . . . "Have you seen my letter?" was all she could say, as Shelley took her hand.

"What letter?" asked Shelley, letting go and looking down at her frowning.

Laura had got a letter from her father which, as usual, somebody else opened first by mistake, and which she then passed around and lost. She nearly cried now, for she could not remember all it said. She suffered from the homesickness of having almost forgotten home. She scarcely ever thought, there wasn't time, of the house in Jackson, of her father, who had every single morning now gone to the office and come home, through the New Capitol which was the coolest way, walked down the hill so that only his legs could be seen under the branches of trees, reading the *Jackson Daily News* so that only his straw hat could be seen above it, seen from a spot on their front walk where nobody watched for him now.

Why couldn't she think of the death of her mother? When the Fairchilds spoke so easily of Annie Laurie, it shattered her thoughts like a stone in the bayou. How could this be? When people were at Shellmound it was as if they had never been anywhere else. It must be that she herself was the only one to struggle against this.

She tried to see her father coming home from the office, first his body hidden by leaves, then his face hidden behind his paper. If she could not think of that, she was doomed; and she was doomed, for the memory was only a flicker, gone now. Shelley and Dabney never spoke of school and the wintertime. Uncle George never spoke of Memphis or his wife (Aunt Robbie, where was she?), about being a lawyer or an aeronaut in the war. Aunt Ellen never talked about Virginia or when she was a little girl or a lady without children. The most she ever said was, "Of course, I married young." Uncle Battle did talk about high water of some year, but was that the worst thing he remembered?

And it was as if they had considered her mother all the time as belonging, in her life and in her death (for they took Laura and *let* her see the grave), as belonging here; they considered Shellmound the important part of life and death too. All they remembered and told her about was likely to be before Laura was born, and they could say so easily, "Before—or after—Annie Laurie died. . . ," to count the time of a dress being made or a fruit tree planted.

At that moment a tall man with a bouquet of Memphis roses and fern in green paper strode by. He tipped his hat to Shelley, and then puckering his handsome, pale lips, looked down at the Fairchild graves. "How many more of you are there?" he said suddenly.

"More of us? Seven—eight—no—I forgot—I forgot the old people—" Shelley gripped Laura's hand again. "Dr. Murdoch, this is my cousin—"

"You'll have to consider your own progeny too," said Dr. Murdoch, rubbing his chin with a delicate touch of his thumb. "Look. Dabney and that fellow she's marrying will have three or four at the least. That will give them room, over against the Hunters—have to take up your rose bush." He wheeled about. "Primrose and Jim Allen naturally go here, in line with Rowena and What's-his-name that was killed, and his wife. An easy two here. George and the Reid girl probably won't have children—he doesn't strike me as a family man."

"He is so!" flashed Shelley.

"Nope, no more than Denis. I grew up with Denis

and knew him like a book, and George's a second edition. Of course, grant you, he's got that spirited little filly the Reid girl trotting with him. You—what are you going to do, let your little sisters get ahead of you? You ought to get married and stop that God-forsaken mooning. Who is it, Dickie Boy Featherstone? I don't like the white of your eye," and all at once he was pulling down Shelley's lower eyelid with his delicate thumb. "You're mooning. All of you stay up too late, dancing and what not, you all eat enough rich food to kill a regiment, but I won't try to stop the unpreventable."

He turned abruptly and stepped off a number of steps. "You'll marry in a year and probably start a houseful like your mother. Got the bones, though. Tell your mother to call a halt. She'll go here, and Battle here, that's all right—pretty crowded, though. You and your outfit can go here below Dabney and hers. I know how it could be done. How many more of you are there? I've lost track. Who's this?" and he stopped his stepping off in front of Laura and glared down at her.

"Aunt Annie Laurie's daughter," said Shelley and with a trembling finger pointed at the new shaft.

"Ah!" He made a wry face as if he would prefer they hadn't mentioned Annie Laurie. "Jackson's a very unhealthy place, she talked herself into marrying a business man, moving to Jackson. Danced too much as a girl to start with, danced away every chance she had of dying an old lady, and I told her so, though she *looked* good. It's God's wonder she ever had *you*, and kept you *alive*!" He gave Laura a slight push on the shoulder. "Of course you were born *here*. I brought you into this world and slapped you to ticking, Buster." He flicked her collarbone with his knuckle. "Stay away from Jackson. Hills and valleys collect moisture, that's my dogma and creed."

"We have to go now, Dr. Murdoch, we're so busy at our house. We've got all the company in the world," said Shelley.

"What are you going to do about Virgie Lee, let her in? She'd go in. Be a good thing if Maureen would up and die—that aunt of yours, too, Aunt Shannon—both of 'em, Mac's a thousand years old."

"Will you excuse us, Dr. Murdoch?"

"But—can't do a thing about Delta people," said Dr. Murdoch. "They're the worst of all. One myself, can't do a thing about myself."

He glared at them and swung off.

Shelley stood where she was and rubbed her eye tenderly, like a bruise.

"When are you going to get married, Shelley?" asked Laura faintly.

"Never," said Shelley.

"Me neither," said Laura.

After Dr. Murdoch, how beautiful the store looked!

Any member of the Fairchild family in its widest sense, who wanted to, could go into the store, walk behind the counter, reach in and take anything on earth, without having to pay or even specify exactly what he took. It was like the pantry at Shellmound. Anything was all right, since they were all kin.

And no matter what any of them could possibly want, it would be sure to be in the store somewhere; the only requirement was that it must be looked for. There was almost absolute surety of finding it. One day on the ledge with the hunting caps, India found a perfect china doll head to fit the doll she had dropped the minute before.

At the moment nobody seemed to be keeping the store at all, except little Ranny, whom Tippy must have set down in here to wait; smelling of violets, he was bouncing a ball in a cleared space, his soft voice going, "—Twenty-three, twenty-four—last night, or the night before, twenty-four robbers at my back door—" There were some old fellows ninety years old sitting there around the cold stove, still as sleeping flies, resting over a few stalks of sugar cane.

Laura, who loved all kinds of boxes and bottles, all objects that could keep and hold things, went gazing her fill through the store, and touching where she would. At first she thought she could find anything she wanted for a wedding present for her uncle George.

Along the tops of the counters were square glass jars with gold-topped stoppers—they held the kernels and flakes of seed—and just as likely, crusted-over wine-balls, licorice sticks, or pink-covered gingerbread stage-planks. All around, at many levels, fishing boxes all packed, china pots with dusty little lids, cake stands with the weightiest of glass covers, buckets marked like a mackerel sky, dippers, churns, bins, hampers, baby baskets, popcorn poppers, cooky jars, butter molds, money safes, hair receivers, mouse traps, all these things held the purest enchantment for her; once, last year, she threw her arms around the pickle barrel, and seemed to feel then a heavy, briny response in its nature, unbudging though it was. The pickle barrel was the heart of the store in summer, as in winter it was the stove that stood on a square stage in the back, with a gold spittoon on each corner. The name of the stove was "Kankakee," written in raised iron writing across its breast which was decorated with summer-cold iron flowers.

The air was a kind of radiant haze, which disappeared into a dim blue among hanging boots above—a fragrant store dust that looked like gold dust in the light from the screen door. Cracker dust and flour dust and brown-sugar particles seemed to spangle the air the minute you stepped inside. (And she thought, in the Delta, all the air everywhere is filled with things—it's the shining dust that makes it look so bright.) All was warm and fragrant here. The cats smelled like ginger when you rubbed their blond foreheads and clasped their fat yellow sides. Every counter smelled different, from the ladylike smell of the dry-goods counter with its fussy revolving ball of string, to the manlike smell of coffee where it was ground in the back. There were areas of banana smell, medicine smell, rope and rubber and nail smell, bread smell, peppermint-oil smell, smells of feed, shot, cheese, tobacco, and chicory, and the smells of the old cane chairs creaking where the old fellows slept.

Objects stood in the aisle as high as the waist, so that you waded when you walked or twisted like a cat. Other things hung from the rafters, to be touched and to swing at the hand when you gave a jump. Once Laura's hand went out decisively and she almost chose something—a gold net of blue agates—for Uncle George. But she said, sighing, to Ranny running by, "I don't see a present for Uncle George. Nothing you have is good enough!"

"Nine, ten, a big fat hen!" Ranny cried at her, with a radiant, spitting smile.

But Shelley had stiffened the moment she entered the store. Sure enough, she could hear somebody crying, deep in the back. She went to look, her heart pounding.

Robbie was sitting on the cashier's stool, filling the store with angry and shameless tears, under a festoon of rubber boots.

Shelley stood beside her, not speaking, but waiting—it was almost as if she had made Robbie cry and was standing there to see that she kept on crying. Her heart pounded on. Robbie's tears shocked her for being unhesitant—for being plain, assertive weeping for a man—weeping out loud in the heart of Fairchilds, in the wide-open store that was more public than the middle of the road. Nothing covered up the sound, except the skipping of Laura up and down, the little kissing sound of Ranny's bouncing ball, and the snore of an old man. Shelley stood listening to that conceited fervor, and then Robbie raised her head and looked at her with the tears running down, and then made an even worse face, deliberately—an awful face. Shelley fell back and flew out with the children. An old mother bird dog lay right in the aisle, her worn teats flapping up and down as she panted—that was how public it was.

III

Robbie bared her little white teeth after Shelley Fairchild and whatever other Fairchilds she had with her. The flat in Memphis had heavy face-brick pillars and poured-cement ornamental fern boxes across a red tile porch. It was right in town! The furniture was all bought in Memphis, shiny mahogany and rich velvet upholstery, blue with gold stripes, up and down which she would run her fingers, as she would in the bright water in a boat with George. There were soft pillows with golden tassels, and she would bite the tassels! Two of the chairs were rockers to match the davenport and there were two tables—matching. The lamps matched, being of turned mahogany, and there were two tall ones and two short ones, all with shades of mauve gorgette over rose China silk. On the mantel, which was large and handsome made of red brick, was a mahogany clock, very expensive and ticking very slowly. The candles in heavy wrought-iron holders on each side had gilt trimming and were too pretty to be lighted. There were several Chinese ash trays about. (Oh, George's pipe!) The rugs were both very fine, and he and she went barefooted. The black wrought-iron fire-screen, andirons, and poker set were the finest in Memphis. Every door was a French door, the floors were hardwood, highly waxed, and yellow.

His books had never a speck of dust on them, such as the Shellmound books were covered with if you touched them. His law books weighed a lot and she carried them in her arms one by one when she moved them from table to chair to see all was perfect, all dusted. She was a perfect housekeeper with only one Negro, and one more to wash. How fresh her curtains were! Even in the dirtiest place in the world: Memphis.

Only the bedroom was still not the way she wanted it. She really wanted a Moorish couch such as Agnes Ayres had lain on in the picture show, but a mahogany bed would come in a set with matching things and she knew that would please George, new and shiny and expensive. Just yet they had an old iron bed with a lot of thin rods head and foot, and she had painted it. There were unnoticeable places where the paint had run down those hard rods, that had never quite got dry, and when George went away on a case or was late coming home she would lie there indenting these little rivers of paint with her thumbnail very gently, to kill time, the way she would once hold rose petals on her tongue and gently bite them, waiting here in the store, the days when he courted.

They lived on the second floor of a nice, two-story flat, and nobody bothered them. The living room faced the river with two windows. In front of those she had the couch so they could lie there listening to the busy river life and watching the lighted boats on summer nights. As long as they stayed without going to bed they could hear colored bands playing from here and there, never far away. The little hairs on her arm would rise, to think where she was. Then they would dance barefooted and drink champagne, and sometimes in the middle of the day they would meet by appointment in the New Peabody by the indoor fountain with live, pure Mallard ducks in it!

"Are you waiting on people?" asked a slow-talking man in front of her. It was Troy Flavin, the Fairchild overseer, his red hair on end.

"I'm not waiting on people, I'm just waiting. Looking for somebody," she said, opening her own eyes wide, expecting him to see who she was.

"Oh, I beg your pardon." Suddenly he swept his straw hat upwards from his side and fanned her face with it, vigorously. When she bent away he held her straight on the stool and fanned her as firmly as if he were giving her medicine. "Is it the heat? Who're you looking for?" He did not recognize her at all—maybe the heat had him.

"None of your business! Well, all right, stop fanning and I'll tell you. For George Fairchild."

He looked down and put his head on one side as if he talked to some knee-high child. "Why didn't you ask me somebody hard, from the way you're about to cry about it?"

"I'm not! Where is he?"

"Could put my finger on George Fairchild this minute, I'm marrying *into* that family, come eight o'clock tomorrow night."

"Not Shelley! Oh—Dabney!"

She began to laugh, and he said, "You look familiar."

"Don't you know me? I'm Robbie Fairchild. I'm George's wife."

Miss Thracia Leeds came into the store and fingered over the ribbon counter, like a pianist over trills. "Why, hello, Robbie, are you back at the store?"

"Well, George's right there at Shellmound in the porch hammock, if you want him," said Troy. "His wife? You look like you've been to Jericho and back, so dusty."

"I've been leaving him—that's what I've been doing. If anybody wondered!"

"In the porch hammock, he *was*," said Troy, with some reserve in his voice. Then he added politely, "Dabney's who I'm carrying—you know, Mr. Battle's girl, not the oldest—the prettiest. High-strung sometimes, though!"

"High-strung!" said Miss Thracia with much sarcasm.

"But they're all high-strung. All ready to jump out of their skins if you don't mind out how you step. 'Course, it would be worse for a *girl*, marrying into them."

"I didn't *marry into* them! I married George!" And she beat his hat away, for he started that again—as though he had brought some insufferably old argument into her face.

"Well, it's a close family," Troy said laconically, catching his hat. "Too close, could be."

"A family *can't* be too close, young man," said a new voice. Miss Mayo Tucker had come in.

Robbie rocked gently on her stool, and like a courtesy Troy put his hand over her flushed forehead as if trying to feel there how dangerously close the Fairchilds were. Miss Maggie Kinkaid stood behind Miss Mayo and asked Robbie, if she had come back to work, if she would make good a nest egg, since the other one broke.

"I might have known! I might have known he wouldn't hunt for me—I could kill him! Right back at Shellmound in a hammock," Robbie cried. "I thought he might drag the river, even."

"Drag which river? Why, Dabney wanted George here, is why he's here," Troy said, looking down at her in concern. "*Dabney* sent for him. He's my what-you-call-it—best man. They didn't care for Buster Daggett, for that friend of mine over at the ice and coal."

"Buster Daggett, I don't wonder," remarked Miss Mayo. "Robbie, did I hear you'd run away, and George Fairchild used to beat you unmercifully in Memphis? Cut me off a yard of black sateen, child, you're right at it."

Robbie laughed and brushed at her eyes. "Dabney's marrying—marrying you? You're the overseer out there."

"Sure I am. How'd you know?"

"We've *met*," said Robbie with energy. "Don't you remember me on the trestle—that day? I remember you. All you did was keep looking up at the sky and saying, 'Why don't she storm?' "

"And she didn't?" Troy smiled in delight after a moment. "That day! I don't remember but one thing. I got engaged up yonder!"

"You got engaged, and George Fairchild missed by a hair letting the Yellow Dog run over him for the sake of a little old crazy! Never thinking of me!"

To her surprise, Troy Flavin became more dignified than before. "Yes, your husband'll make you worry-like," he said. "It'll come up."

Robbie with furious neatness cut off a yard of sateen, tied it up, and rang up thirty cents on the cash register.

"You're Robbie, George's wife. People've been norating about you, sure!" said Troy, watching her speed. "Well, you're just in time."

"I bet it's a big wedding and all. Did Miss Tempe make herself come? How's Mary Denis?" asked Miss Thracia.

"They've come from far and near, Fairchilds," said Troy. "You *could* have been too late." He momently reversed the fanning hat and fanned himself. "But now you'll see the wedding."

"Me! Who's going to invite me?"

"I invite you," said Troy. "Now I've invited me somebody." He stared at her appreciatively. Then he put his hat, carefully, over her head to make her laugh, and spread a big hand sprinkled with red hair over each of her shoulders.

"Which way is this? Set me straight, did you run off and leave George, or did he run off and leave you? I believe those Fairchild men are great consorters," said Miss Mayo. "Does he make any money in the law business? It's bad luck for a girl to put a man's hat on."

"It would be fun to walk in *during* it, and make George and everybody jump," Robbie said, looking up at Troy and smiling for the first time, under the yellow brim.

"What! Not during the wedding!"

"Oh, look at me forget about *you* being there."

"It would cause a stir," he said, and balanced a pencil on his finger. "Furthermore, I'd be scared of Aunt Mac. Why don't you go walk in now? What's keeping you, if you're going in the end? like I say to myself."

"Do you mean to say, Robbie Reid, you had gone off and *left* George Fairchild and now you're just *coming back*?" said Miss Thracia. "I know what he ought to do to you."

"Must I go now, and push him out of the hammock?" said Robbie softly. Her eyelids fell, as if she were being lulled to sleep. She thought Troy was very kind, and clever. Tears ran down her face.

"That sounds better than the other," said Troy. She jumped off the stool. "And considering we're next thing to kin,—go wash your face."

She gave him back his hat and he stood holding it politely.

"And to tell you the truth," he said when she came in from the little back porch with a clean face, "I feel without doubt you ought to be getting somewhere near your husband, not sitting here baking by yourself in this hot store."

Robbie went out, past Miss Thracia, Miss Maggie, and Miss Mayo, fluffing her hair. "See if you think she's going to have a baby," said Miss Maggie. "I wonder if it will be a boy or girl and how they'll divide up the land in that case."

"She's not," said Miss Mayo definitely.

With a start Troy went to the door and looked up and

down the street. "I forgot to wonder how she'd get there," he said.

India was walking up the sidewalk eating ice, with her eyes shut. She opened her eyes and saw Troy.

"Troy Flavin! I've got something for you," she said, her face alight. She put something in his hands. "A cake! Dabney baked it with her own hands, just for you."

"Well, it surprises me," Troy told her, accepting it. "I didn't know she could even make light bread."

India turned a handspring and looked back over her shoulder at him—it was a look so much like Dabney's that he started again, and he called after her, "Much obliged!" But she too had got out of sight.

IV

Robbie saw it would be a long hot walk in the boiling sun. But Troy Flavin had been right, though high-handed, for somebody that came from "away"—anything was better than that oven of a store. She couldn't stand it any longer. And, oh, George must have known he could come and get her, Shelley must have tattletaled, and when she had come as far as Fairchilds, as far even as the store—! She passed the shade of the cemetery and took the road. Off there was the bayou, but if she was going back to George in the hot sun, then she was going in the hot sun. She glanced through the distant trees; the whirlpool was about there. She and George had once or twice gone swimming in that, once at night, playing at drowning, first he and then she sinking down with a hand up. There were people she would like to see go down in that, and a snake look good at them.

She was in the road through the Fairchild Deadening. What a wide field! All this was where the old Fairchilds had started, deadened off the trees to take the land a hundred years ago. She could hardly see across. The white field in the heat darted light like a prism edge. She put a hand over her eyes, but the light came red through her fingers. She knew she was a small figure here, and went along with a little switch of elderberry under the straight-up sun.

Caught in marriage you were then supposed to fling about, to cry out and ask for something—to expect something—what was the look in all unmarried girls' eyes but the challenging look of knowing what? But Robbie—who was greatly in love and so would freely admit everything—did not know what. It was not this!

In the depths of her soul she had at first looked for one of two blows, or magic touches, to fall—unnerving change or beautiful transformation; she had been practical enough to expect alternate eventualities. But even now—unless the old bugaboo of pregnancy counted—there was no eventuality. Here she was—Robbie, making her way, stamping her feet in the pink Fairchild dust, at a very foolish time of day to be out unprotected. There was not one soul to know she was desperate and angry.

The Fairchild women asked a great deal of their men—competitively. Miss Tempe in particular was a bully, or would have been, without the passive, sweet Miss Primrose and Miss Jim Allen to compete with another way. Naturally, the Fairchild women knew what to ask, because in their kind of people, the Fairchild kind, the women always ruled the roost; Robbie believed in her soul that men should rule the roost. (George, showing how simple and difficult he was in a Fairchild man's way, did not betray it that there *were* two kinds of people.) It was notoriously the women of the Fairchilds who since the Civil War, or—who knew?—since the Indian times, ran the household and had everything at their fingertips—not the men. The women it was who inherited the place—or their brothers, guiltily, handed it over.

In the Delta the land belonged to the women—they only let the men have it, and sometimes they tried to take it back and give it to someone else. The Grove had been left to Miss Tempe and she married Mr. Pinckney Summers (a terrible drinker) and moved to Inverness, presenting it to George—and George had told his unmarried sisters, Primrose and Jim Allen, that they could live there. Marmion belonged by rights to that little Maureen, for whom Miss Annie Laurie Fairchild had felt that wild concern some ladies feel for little idiot children, even the wicked ones—though if she knew, she would be sorry now, with her own child cheated. She had given Marmion to Denis when she married and went out of the Delta, and now of the two children would it in all strictness be Maureen's? A joke on the Fairchilds. And Shellmound—Miss Rowena, the quiet one, the quiet old maid, had let Mr. Battle have it before she ever lived in it herself; no one could ever be grateful enough to Rowena! Not then, not now, when she was dead and triumphantly beyond gratitude, but Robbie would tell anybody that Miss Rowena was *forgotten*, if a Fairchild could be. She let all her brothers take from her so, she *let* them! Robbie shivered for Miss Rowena. All the men lived here on a kind of sufferance!

She had never thought it strange in her life before, having no land or possessions herself—Reids and Swansons had never become planters—but now she did. It was as if the women had exacted the place, the land, for something—for something they had had to give. Then, so as to be all gracious and noble, they had let it out of their hands—with a play of the reins—to the men. . . .

She remembered all at once a picture of some old-time Fairchild lady down at the Grove. On a picnic, playing, Robbie had got wet in the river and Miss Jim Allen had not been able to rush her into the house fast enough, to get the river off her—she had put her in a little parlor to sit on a plaid while she readied a bedroom that couldn't have helped but look as perfect as possible already—and looking down at Robbie was the old-time Fairchild lady with the look on her face. It was obviously turned upon her husband, upon a Fairchild, and it was condemning. Robbie had been caught staring up at it (she still knew the outside of the Fairchild houses better than the inside) when Miss Jim Allen ran back in. "That's Mary Shannon," Miss Jim Allen had said, as though she told her the name of a star, like Venus, so generally known that only poor little visitors come up from holes in the river bank would need to be told. "That's Mary Shannon when she came to the wilderness."

And of course those women knew what to ask of their men. Adoration, first—but least. Then, small sacrifice by small sacrifice, the little pieces of the whole body! Robbie, with the sun on her head, could scream to see the thousand little polite expectations in their very smiles of welcome. "He would do anything for me!" they would say, airily and warningly, of a brother, an uncle, a cousin. "Dabney thinks George hung the moon," with a soft glance at George, and so, George, get Dabney the moon! Robbie was not that kind of woman. Maybe she was just as scandalous, but she was born another kind. She did want to ask George for something indeed, but not for the moon—not even for a child; she did not want to, but she had to ask him for something—life waited for it. (Here he lay in a hammock, just waiting for her to walk this whole distance!) What do you ask for when you love? If it was urgent to seek after something, so much did she love George, that that much the less did she know the right answer.

Then, at the head of a railroad trestle, in high heels, fuming and wondering then if she had a child inside her, complaining to him that she worshiped his life, she had tried and been reproved, denied and laughed at, teased. When she jumped up for him to look back at and heed, not knowing how love, anything, might have transformed her, it was in terror that she had held the Fairchilds' own mask in front of her. She cried out for him to come back from his danger as a favor to her. And in his forthright risk of his life for that crazy child, she had seen him thrust it, the *working* of the Fairchild mask, from him, on his face was an elation of throwing it back at her. He reached out for Maureen that demanded not knowing any better. . . .

In Robbie's eyes all the Fairchild women indeed wore a mask. The mask was a pleading mask, a kind more false than a mask of giving and generosity, for they had already got it all—everything that could be given—all solicitude and manly care. Unless—unless nothing was ever enough—and they knew. Unless pleading must go on forever in life, and was no mask, but real, for longer than all other things, for longer than winning and having.

She shaded her eyes and turned looking for one tree. She was so little she could take refuge in an inch of shade. Finally she saw a cotton shed that looked not too far to get to before she dropped in the heat. She had had the foresight to bring a sack of pickles and a box of cakes.

But when she stepped into the abrupt dark, she jumped. There was a Negro girl there, a young one panting just inside the door. She must have been out of the field, for sweat hung on her forehead and cheeks in pearly chains in the gloom, her eyes were glassy.

"Girl, I'm going to rest inside, you rest outside," said Robbie.

Like somebody startled in sleep, the girl moved out a step, from inside to outside, to the strip of shade under the doorway, and clung there. Her eyes were wild but held a motionless gaze on the white fields and white glaring sky and the dancing, distant black rim of the river trees.

Robbie ate the cool wet pickle and the little cakes. She had run off from her sister Rebel now, who would about this time begin to wonder where she was. She stretched her bare feet, for her high heels had made them tired. It was nice in here. She felt as if she were in a shell, floating in that sea of light, looking out its mouth with good creature comfort.

The moment she had thought over with the most ruin to her pride was the one after the train had actually stopped. George was safe, and the engineer had leaned out. George had suddenly leaped up from where he had fallen on the swampy earth, to greet him. "Oh, it's Mr. Doolittle!" he had said.

The engineer had raised his stripey elbow, saluted George, and said, "Excuse *me*." "You nearly got a whole mess of Fairchilds that time! Where do you think you're taking that thing?" George had shouted. "Taking it to Memphis, ever heard of it?" Mr. Doolittle had said—what absurd conversation men could indulge in with each other, at the most awful moments! Oh, Robbie could have killed them both. "It was somebody I knew!" George scoffed, right in bed, groaning for sleep. "Mr. Doolittle wasn't going to hit me!" When she knew all the time that George was sure Mr. Doolittle *was*. Until she couldn't stand it any longer. He would not say anything more; he wasn't used to saying anything more to women.

Robbie sat still, cross-legged, on the floor of the cotton house, with a forgotten motion fanning herself with her skirt. Across her vision the Negro clung and darted just outside, fitful as a black butterfly, perhaps crazy with the heat, and beyond her the light danced. Was this half-way? Her eyes fastened hypnotically on the black figure that seemed to dangle as if suspended in the light, as she would watch a little light that twinkled in the black, far out on the river at night, from her window, waiting.

The pure, animal way of love she longed for, when she watched, listened, came out, stretched, slept content. Where he lay naked and unconscious she knew the heat of his heavy arm, the drag of his night beard over her. She knew what he cried out in his sleep, she was outside herself as a cup those three drops fell in. She breathed the night in beside him, away off from dreams and time and her own thoughts awake—the companion of his weight and warmth. Then she was glad there was nothing at all, no existence in the world, beyond George asleep, this real and forgetful and exacting body. She slept by him as if in the shadow of a mountain of being. Any moon and stars there were could rise and set over his enfolding, unemanating length. The sun could lean over his backside and wake her.

She heard the Fairchilds' plantation bell ring in the dense still noon. Dinner. She drew her breath in fiercely as always when the fond, teasing, wistful play of the family love for George hung and threatened near. Nothing was worthy of him but the pure gold, a love that could be simply beside him—her love. Only she could hold him against that grasp, that separating thrust of Fairchild love that would go on and on persuading him, comparing him, begging him, crowing over him, slighting him, proving to him, sparing him, comforting him, deceiving him, confessing and yielding to him, tormenting him . . . those smiling and not really mysterious ways of the Fairchilds. In those ways they eluded whatever they feared, sometimes the very thing they really desired. . . .

Robbie desired veracity—more than she could even quite fathom, as if she had been denied it, like an education at Sunflower Junior College; from a kind of poverty's ambition she desired it—as hard and immediate a veracity as the impact of George's body. It meant coming to touch the real, undeceiving world within the fairy Shellmound world to love George—from all she had spent her life hearing Fairchild, Fairchild, Fairchild, and working for Fairchilds and taking from Fairchilds, with gratitude for Shelley's dresses, then to go straight through like parting a shiny curtain and to George. He was abrupt and understandable to her as the here and now—and now had become a figure strangely dark, alone as the boogie-man, back of them all, and seemed waiting with his set mouth open like a drunkard's or as if he were hungry. She, plain hard-head who never dreamed, dreamed every night now she saw him like that, until the image had become matter-of-fact as some glimpse of him on a daylight street corner in Memphis watching her coming. It was a nightmare, Rebel would shake her till she woke up in terror. Where are you? the cry would be in her throat. What if it was she who had run away? It was he who was lost, without her, a Fairchild man, lost at Shellmound.

Robbie drew up sharply; she heard a horse. The next minute she heard Troy Flavin's voice call out, "Go on, Pinchy! Go on! I get tired of seeing you everywhere!"

Robbie looked out the door. Troy laughed at her. "I wondered how far you'd get," he said. "Jump up in front of me and ride."

"No, sir," said Robbie. Then because she always told everything, she said, "I want it to be real hard, like this, to make him feel worse."

Troy put his thumb knuckle in his mouth and bit it gently. Then he got off his horse meditatively, telling her to wait. He came holding out a little round cake affair with one big bite gone, for Robbie to see.

"You're a married woman," he said. "Taste this," and watched her take a bite.

"It tastes like castor oil," said Robbie.

"Dabney made it for me. But myself, I don't think

that positively requires me to eat it all." He clapped his hands at Pinchy, hovering.

"Oh-oh," said Robbie. "It tastes plenty awful. I do pride myself I could cook better than that when I was a bride."

"Well, I think myself something spilled in it. Such a big kitchen to try to cook anything in. I'll just tell her plainly, try again."

"She might pull your eyes out, on her wedding day," Robbie said darkly.

"Here, Pinchy—here's a cake, Pinchy," said Troy. "Eat it or give it to the other Negroes. Now scat!" He clapped his hands at her skirt.

Pinchy, with the cake, moved on stiffly, out into the light, like a matchstick in the glare, and was swallowed up in it.

"Hate to ride off and leave a lady," said Troy, "but surprise your husband if that's the way you want. A wet leaf on the head prevents the sunstroke."

He galloped toward Shellmound.

"My nose itches," said Troy in the parlor. "Company's coming."

"I'll tell you how to make the best mousse in the world," said Aunt Tempe.

"How?" cried India.

"Take a pair of Pinckney's old drawers." Aunt Tempe began to describe how she made gelatin. The boys were coming in one by one, with wet hair and glowing fiery cheeks, and grabbing up their books. Lady Clare swayed in, in a lady's dress and Dabney's pink satin shoes.

Shelley, pulling Laura, flew in out of breath.

"I'm a wreck! Partheny's got something of yours, Mama, but she wouldn't give it to me for fear she didn't know what a garnet was, and India bit a guinea pig and ran away."

"Not for good, I'm afraid," said Battle. "She beat you home."

"Wait! *Then*, we saw old Dr. Murdoch in the cemetery taking flowers to his wife's grave and he poked me in the eye and hit Laura after her mother died, and he said there wasn't enough room in our lot for all of us," Shelley said furiously.

"Where is he? I'm going to kill the man yet," Battle cried, jumping to his feet.

"I forgot the string for Howard's altar," Shelley said tremulously, and ran to the door in tears and cried pausing there against the wall. Bluet ran in and hid her face in her skirt.

"Shut up if you want me to kill him!" cried Battle.

"Remember, dear, he's the smartest man in the Delta," Ellen said, and he sat down again truculently.

"He is not!" Shelley sobbed.

"Don't cry! He's any old fool," Troy exclaimed suddenly. His face was glowing-red and concerned; could it be that he had never seen Shelley cry before? There was a feeling in the room, too, that this was the first time he had ever addressed Shelley directly.

"He's a fool, a fool, a fool!" Laura cried in triumph, hopping forward.

Ellen felt a stab of pain to see her. It seemed to her that being left motherless had made little Laura feel *privileged*. Laura was almost dancing around Troy.

Shelley, with a fresh burst of tears, ran out of the parlor.

"Troy," Aunt Tempe said, leaning her cheek on her forefinger, "you are speaking of one of our closest friends, a noble Delta doctor that has brought virtually every Fairchild in this room into the world."

"Laura McRaven," Battle was saying rapidly, "go directly and wash your mouth out with soap. You know better than call anybody a fool. Your mother told you that."

"Old Dr. Murdoch, I despise him," said Laura, preening for one more moment.

"Who doesn't?" said Aunt Shannon, with lucid eyes.

"You could have cussed him out if you wanted to, and we'd all listened. But you call him a fool, or anybody in the Yazoo-Mississippi Delta a fool, and I'll blister your behind good for you. Switch for that right in this room. Now march in the kitchen and tell Roxie to wash your mouth out with soap. And tell her to hurry and get something on the table. You contradicted your aunt, too."

"Yes, sir. He stood on my mother's grave!" said Laura, and opened her mouth and cried. That was not quite true, but at the moment she thought she could go out crying if Shelley could.

She waited for Uncle Battle to clap his hands together and shoo her. But it was Troy's words that hung in the parlor air, not hers. Aunt Tempe, it was easy to see, had made up her mind about him. Troy, who stood with his feet apart on the hearth rug, with his eyes a little cast up, was capable of calling the Fairchilds some name or other too, without much trouble, the way he spoke up. Laura had to go get her mouth washed out with soap for *Troy*.

"Well," said Ellen. "We'd better eat, if we're so righteous. I'm *certain* Dabney's back with the groceries. Don't I hear Roxie's bell?"

Sure enough, as if in answer, the dinner bell rang.

"Here I am!" cried Dabney, rushing in radiant in a fresh blue dress, closing her little blue ruffled parasol as she came.

"You all can come to some old crumbs and scraps," said Roxie in the door. She looked hardest at Dabney and said, "Lucky for you we can wring a chicken and had a *ham* left."

"I forgot the groceries," Dabney whispered to Troy as she kissed him.

There was a new commotion in the hall. It was Pinck.

"Uncle Pinck!"

"Did you get the shepherdess crooks?" asked Aunt Tempe forthrightly from across the room.

"Tempe, I didn't," said Uncle Pinck. "I tried, God knows—couldn't even *find* the place. However, Dabney, look in front of the house."

Dabney ran to the window. "A Pierce-Arrow? Oh, Uncle Pinck, you shouldn't!"

"Well, I couldn't get the damn crooks," said Uncle Pinck.

"I thought Uncle Pinck was a man of influence," said India anxiously.

They laughed affectionately at Aunt Tempe. That was what she thought.

"But, oh, I'd so much rather have my shepherdess crooks!" Dabney cried at the window.

"Well! All I can say is, Pinck Summers didn't give his own baby grandson a Pierce-Arrow," Aunt Tempe said.

Uncle Pinck was going around kissing everybody, his

prematurely white hair bobbing, bending down with his handsome lips and his sober breath.

"No matter what anybody omits or commits in September, good people," he said, and kissed Aunt Tempe loudly, "it's because: it's hot as fluzions."

Aunt Tempe hit him with the Chinese fan from Inverness.

V

At first Robbie thought wildly that they were making a to-do over her return. From the porch she smelled the floors just waxed, and at the windows saw the curtains standing out stiff-starched, and flowers even in the umbrella stand. Then she remembered once more—Dabney was getting married.

Of course George was not in the hammock! There was no sign of him or of any Fairchild. There was not even a sound, except the tinkle of chandelier prisms in the hall breeze. They were probably back there eating—they always were. She reached inside and tapped with the knocker on the open door—an absurdly tiny sound to get into that big house. Nobody answered the door at all. They were all back there in oblivion, eating.

Immediately, from within the house, a burst of unmistakable dinner-table laughter rose and went round its circle. The Fairchilds! She would make them hear. She beat on the screen door and on the thick side lights with her small fist, in which were wrinkled up together a wet handkerchief and a pinch of verbena she had taken from the front gate.

Little Uncle came toward the door, and then backed up and called Roxie through the back porch. Miss Robbie, the one Mr. George threw himself away on, stood knocking. Roxie came and let her in, and for a moment Robbie nearly wavered. Everybody would be hard to confront at noon dinner. Suppose she just fainted? That would scare George. Roxie, her hands out like baby wings, turned and tiptoed, absurdly, down into the dining room. Robbie could hear what was said.

"Miss Ellen, surprise. Miss Robbie cryin' at de do'."

"Well! Good evening." That was Miss Tempe, all right, in the austere voice she admitted surprise with.

"Well, tell her quickly to come on back in the dining room and have dessert with us, Roxie," said Ellen. Of course as if nothing had happened! No shout from George, no sign.

Robbie came through the dining-room archway a little blindly—she had collided with Vi'let carrying an armload of fresh-pressed evening dresses up the hall. But George was not in here. "Where's George?" she asked.

"Say! Where's George?" asked Troy suddenly, looking up and down the table.

"At the Grove eating Aunt Primrose's guinea fowl," said India or somebody.

"He's left out for the Grove," Troy said, squinting up at Robbie, as if his eyes flinched.

"That booger! Did he know you were coming?" asked Battle, glancing up at her with bright eyes above the napkin he put to his lips.

She tried to shake her head, while Little Battle was dragging a chair up to the table for her, and Mr. Battle and Mr. Pinck and the boys were getting to their feet.

"Won't you have some dinner? You must have some dinner," Ellen said anxiously, but "No, thanks," Robbie said. They all insisted on getting her kiss, passing and turning her from one to the other around the table. "Oh, Aunt Robbie, I love you, you're so pretty," said Ranny. Then Roxie was clearing off. They had been eating chicken and ham and dressing and gravy, and good, black snap beans, greens, butter beans, okra, corn on the cob, all kinds of relish, and watermelon-rind preserves, and that good bread—their plates were loaded with corncobs and little piles of bones, and their glasses drained down to blackened leaves of mint, and the silver bread baskets lined with crumbs.

"Won't you change your mind?" Ellen begged earnestly. But Robbie said, "No, thank you, ma'am."

Then Roxie was putting a large plate of whole peaches in syrup and a slice of coconut cake in front of her—she was seated between Shelley and Dabney—and bringing more tea in, and Mr. Battle was going on in a loud, sibilant voice which he used for reciting "Denis's poetry."

"*You shun me, Chloe, wild and shy,*
As some stray fawn that seeks its mother
Through trackless woods. If spring winds sigh
It vainly strives its fears to smother.

"*The trembling knees assail each other*
When lizards stir the brambles dry;—
You shun me, Chloe, wild and shy,—"

"Where have you been, Aunt Robbie?" asked Laura.

"*As some stray fawn that seeks its mother.*

And yet no Libyan lion I—"

"Battle," said Ellen.

"*—No ravening thing to rend another!*
Lay by your tears, your tremors dry . . ."

"Try your nice peach—you look so hot," Ellen whispered, pointing.

Then a silence fell, like the one after a flock of fall birds has gone over. Uncle Pinck Summers, who had passed Robbie at forty miles an hour in the road and covered her with a cloud of his dust, stared at her as if in clever recognition. Robbie had worn a dust-colored pongee dress, bought in Memphis, with a red silk fringed sash, and on the side of her hair a white wool tam-o'shanter—but what could get as many wrinkles just from sitting down in some little hot place, as pongee? She felt wrinkled in her soul. And she trembled at the mention of lizards; they ran up your skirt.

"Well, my dear, I suppose wherever you were, your invitation to the wedding reached you," Miss Tempe said. "And you made up your mind to accept!"

"I'm afraid you just missed George," Ellen said, all afresh, and added in haste, "He happened to go to eat dinner with his sisters at the Grove—but he'll be back. He always takes a nap here—where it's quiet."

"He must have gone another way, then. I saw every inch of the road," Robbie said aloud, without meaning to.

"We didn't quite expect you," Battle said heavily, again over the folds of his napkin.

The family were having just a pieced dessert, without George to fix something special for—some of Primrose's put-up peaches and the crumbs of the coconut cake; Ellen was sorry Robbie had picked just this time. "Wouldn't you *try* a little dinner? Let me *still* send for a plate for you. You don't like the peaches!"

"No, thank you, Mrs. Fairchild."

"There's plenty more food! Enough for a regiment if they walked in!" Dabney was saying with a new, over-bright smile she had—was it her married smile, that she would practice like that?

"I'm not to say hungry," Robbie said. She bent over her plate and tried to take a spoonful of her whole peach while they all looked at her, or looked at Ellen.

This child was so unguarded—in an almost determined way. She would come, not timidly at all, into Shellmound at a time like this! Shelley sat actually cringing, while Dabney was giving her mother a conspirator's look, as if they should have expected this. Aunt Tempe's elevated brows signaled to Ellen. As if she would ever truly run away and leave him! Ellen could have asked Tempe: she never would. She would say she would, to have them thinking of explanations, racking their brains, at a time like this, and then run back and show herself to make fools of them all.

Aunt Shannon gazed out the window, at a hummingbird in the abelias, but Aunt Mac sat up stiffly; it would show the upstart a thing or two if they ceased being polite and got anything like a scene over with at once.

Only Mary Lamar had excused herself, some moment or other, and beyond call again in her music was playing a nocturne—like the dropping of rain or the calling of a bird the notes came from another room, effortless and endless, isolated from them, yet near, and sweet like the guessed existence of mystery. It made the house like a nameless forest, wherein many little lives lived privately, each to its lyric pursuit and its shy protection. . . .

Ellen saw Shelley look at the girl failing at her peach and say nothing to her. And Robbie was scarcely listening to anything that was being said (Orrin was politely telling her about the longest snake he had ever seen). She would only look down and try to eat her peach. She was suffering. Her eyelids fell and opened tiredly over her just-dried eyes. The intensity of her face affected Ellen like a grimace.

When Ellen was nine years old, in Mitchem Corners, Virginia, her mother had run away to England with a man and stayed three years before she came back. She took up her old life and everything in the household went on as before. Like an act of God, passion went unexplained and undenied—just a phenomenon. "Mitchem allows one mistake." That was the saying old ladies had at Mitchem Corners—a literal business, too. Ellen had grown up not especially trusting appearances, not soon enough suspecting, either, that other people's presence and absence were still the least complicated elements of what went on underneath. Not her young life with her serene mother, with Battle, but her middle life—knowing all Fairchilds better and seeing George single himself from them—had shown her how deep were the complexities of the everyday, of the family, what caves were in the mountains, what blocked chambers, and what crystal rivers that had not yet seen light.

Ellen sighed, giving up trying to make Robbie eat; but she felt that perhaps that near-calamity on the trestle was nearer than she had realized to the heart of much that had happened in her family lately—as the sheet lightning of summer plays in the whole heaven but presently you observe that each time it concentrates in one place, throbbing like a nerve in the sky.

"Roxie, bring us just a *little* more iced tea," she called, as if she asked a boon.

Then a little jumpily they all drank tea while Robbie turned her peach over and over in the plate.

"Do you start to school next year, Little Battle?" Lady Clare broke the silence in a peremptory conversational voice nearly like Aunt Tempe's.

"Yes, but I *hate* to start!" cried Little Battle.

"Well—why don't you cut your stomach out?"

"I'm going to take you out of here," said Aunt Tempe, motionless.

"Oh, Troy," India said, leaning forward so that she could watch Shelley, Dabney, and Laura, all three, "did you eat the cake Dabney sent you? How did it taste?"

"This isn't the time to speak of the cake," Troy said, and stared back at India. She giggled, and cutting her eye at Shelley said contritely, "Oh, me."

But suddenly Lady Clare, her fiery Buchanan hair spangling her Fairchild forehead, put out her tongue straight at Robbie and pulled down red eyelids. "This is the way *you* look!"

"You almost ruined my wedding!" cried Dabney, and then as if in haste she had said the wrong thing she put her hand comically to her lips. "I couldn't get married right if George wasn't as happy as I am!" she said, leaning intensely toward Robbie, as if to appeal to her underlying chivalry.

"*Why* have you treated George Fairchild the way you have?" said Tempe across from her. "Except for Denis Fairchild, the sweetest man ever born in the Delta?"

"How could you?" Shelley suddenly gushed forth tears, and Orrin had to get his dry handkerchief out for her and run around the table with it.

Robbie drew in her shoulders, to give Shelley room, and looked with burning eyes at the slick yellow peach she had not made a dent in. What vanity was here! How vain and how tenacious to vanity, as to a safety, Shelley and Dabney and all were! What they felt was *second*. They had something else in them first, themselves, that core she knew well enough, why not?—it was like a burning string in a candle, and *then* they felt. But it was a second thing—not all one thing! The Fairchilds! The way that Dabney rode her horse, when she thought herself unseen!

Robbie was not afraid of them. She felt first—or perhaps she was all one thing, not divided that way—and let them kill her, with her wrinkled dress, and with never an acre of land among the Reids, and with a bad grief because of them, but she felt. She had never stopped for words to feelings—she felt only—with no words. But their smile had said more plainly than words, Bow down, you love our George, enter on your knees and we will pull you up and pet and laugh at you fondly for it—we can! We will bestow your marriage on you, little Robbie, that we sent to high school!

"Do you like butter?" asked a soft voice.

"Yes," said Robbie, looking around the table, not quite sure from which direction that had come.

"Then go sit in the gutter," said Ranny.

"Excuse yourself and leave the table, Ranny," said Battle.

"Oh, let him stay, Papa, he was trying to be *nice*," said Orrin and Roy together.

"Now you think up one," said Ranny to Robbie.

"I can think up one," growled Battle. "Why isn't George here where he belongs? What are we all going to do, sit here crying and asking riddles? Excuse me! That boy's *never* here, come any conceivable hell or high water!"

How unfair! Why, it's the exact opposite of the truth! Robbie looked up at Battle furiously. That's always when George is here—holding it off for you, she thought. If *he* were here and I came in he would make everything fine—so fine I couldn't even say a word . . . and never tell them what I think of them . . .

All at once Vi'let came calling out in a lilting voice down the stairs and appeared in the doorway with both arms raised. "Bird in de house! Miss Rob' come in lettin' bird in de house!"

"Bird in de house mean death!" called Roxie instantly from the kitchen. She ran in from the other door, and the Negroes simultaneously threw their white aprons over their heads.

"It does mean that," said Troy thoughtfully. He pushed back his chair and slowly removed his coat and pushed a sleeve up. "A bird in the house is a sign of death—my mammy said so, proved it. We better catch her and get her out."

The Fairchilds jumped up buoyantly from their chairs. Orrin was the first out of the room, with the men next, and the children next, then Dabney and Shelley. Ellen looked after them. It was not anything but pure distaste that made them run; there was real trouble in Robbie's face, and the Fairchilds simply shied away from trouble as children would do. The beating of wings could be heard. Frantically the girls ran somewhere, their hands pressed to their hair. The chase moved down the hall—seemingly up the back stairs. . . . "Get it out! Get it out!" Shelley called, and Little Battle called after her, "Get it! Get it!"

"*I* shall go to the kitchen and make a practice cornucopia for tomorrow," said Aunt Tempe rather grandly. "I am too short of breath to chase birds, neither am I as superstitious as my brother, or my nephews and nieces. Will you excuse me, Ellen?"

And only Aunt Mac and Ellen were left to attend to Robbie now. No, Aunt Shannon did rock on in her corner; George had brought her, when he came (stopping to remember her always!), something fresh to embroider on.

Robbie did not seem to know whether she had let the bird in or not; she did not know what she had done. Running out, the children wore smiles in their excitement and even took a moment to look expectantly at Robbie, who stood up. They left their mother in the dining room with the little figure of wretchedness, who stood up staunch as the Bad Fairy, and cried, "I won't fool a minute longer with that round peach!"

Aunt Mac moved into a comfortable rocker and even eyed the peony-flowered bag that held her Armenian knitting. Stone-deaf as she was, she probably neither divined nor cared that there was a bird in the house, but she knew enough not to knit. She gave a positive nod, a little cock, of her topknotted head and made her curls bounce.

Ellen looked sighing from Aunt Mac to Robbie. Mr. Judge Reid, a Justice of the Peace, was her father; he was dead now—Dr. Murdoch threw up his hands on the case, in public, years before he died, he had some hopeless thing. "I don't see why you don't shoot yourself," he said. Mr. Judge had married Irene Swanson, the daughter of Old Man Swanson; she was trying to be a schoolteacher. Old Man Swanson was an old fellow at the compress, who stuttered. Every little boy in this part of the Delta proverbially cut up by talking and walking like Old Man Swanson. They could all hobble, the way his back hurt, into the store and ask for some s-s-s-s-sweet s-s-s-s-s-spirits o' niter. And mock him, little boys and their little boys, eventually to his own granddaughter working there; Robbie tried to be a schoolteacher too (the lower grades), but her sister Rebel had run off with that drunkard, and of course the board had thrown her out. George, who had not seemed to mind courting over the counter, as Battle called it, must have had to listen to that deathless joke of poor Old Man Swanson's stutter a thousand times, right through his kisses.

"Don't clear off now—little while yet," Aunt Mac called toward the Negro-deserted kitchen. "Of course you only married George for his money," she continued without a break, in that comfortable sort of voice in which this statement is always made.

Robbie answered, lifting her voice politely to the deaf, "No, ma'am. I married him because he begged me!" Then she sat down, in the dining-room chair with its carved basket of blunt roses that always prodded the shoulder blades at emphatic moments.

To be begged to give love was something that she could not have conceived of by herself, and she assumed no one else could conceive of it. Now for a moment it struck Robbie and also Ellen humbly to earth, for it implied a magnitude, a bounty, that could leave people helpless. Robbie knew that now, still, George in getting her back would start all over with her love, as if she were shy. It was his way—as if he took long trips away from her which she did not know about, and then came back to her as to a little spring where he had somehow cherished only the hope for the refreshment that all the time flowed boundlessly enough. As if in his abounding, laughing life, he had not really expected much to his lips! Well, she was always the same, the way a little picnic spot would remain the same from one summer to the next, under its south-riding moon, and he was the different and new, the picnicker, the night was the different night.

Luckily Aunt Mac did not hear Robbie's answer, or suppose there could be one; she was an old lady. But the Fairchilds half-worshiped alarm, and Ellen knew just how they would act if they could hear Robbie say "He begged me"—as well as if they had never left the room. It was a burden of responsibility, the awareness that had come to supply her with the Fairchild accompaniment and answer to everything happening, just as if they all were present, that unpredictable crowd; the same as, thinking in the night, she referred to Battle's violent and intricate opinions when his sleeping body lay snoring beside her.

Now when Robbie said "He begged me," and sat down, Ellen could see in a mental tableau the family one and all fasten an unflinching look upon George. . . . It was a look near to reproach, though George, exactly like little Ranny, would sit innocent or ignorant in the matter of reproach, blind to the look, but listening with great care for what would come next. The most rambunctious of the Fairchild men could all be extremely affected by nervous changes around them, things they could not see, and put on a touching protective serenity at those times, a kind of scapegoat grace, which only reminded Ellen of pain—as when Dr. Murdoch, a rough man, set Orrin's broken arm and Orrin quite visibly filled himself with blissful trust to meet the pain he thought was coming. . . . The family of course had always acknowledged by an exaggerated and charming mood of capitulation toward George that George was mightily importunate—yet they had to reproach him, something made them or let them, and they would reproach him surely that they had never been granted the sight of him begging a thing on earth. Quite the contrary! Surely he took for granted! So he begged love—George? Love that he had more of than the rest of them put together? He begged love from Robbie! They would disbelieve.

"Then he risked his life for—for—and you all let him! *Dabney* knew the train was coming!"

"Now, listen here, Robbie, we all love Georgie, no matter how we act or he acts," said Ellen. "And isn't that all there is to it?" All of a sudden, she felt tired. She was never surer that all loving Georgie was not the end of it; but to hold back hurt and trouble, shouldn't it just now be enough? She had said so, anyway—as if she were sure.

But she sighed. There was a tramping upstairs and around corners, a sudden whistle of flight in the stair well, the tripping cries of her daughters in laughter or flight, and then vaguely to Ellen's ears it all mingled with the further and echoing sounds of a worse alarm. Dimly there seemed to be again in her life a bell clanging trouble, starting at the Grove, then at their place, the dogs beginning to clamor, the Negroes storming the back door crying, and the great rush out of this room, like the time there was a fire at the gin.

"Get it out! Get it out!" It was one cry, long lasting, half delight, half distress, all challenge.

"He won't be pulled to pieces over something he did, and so he ran away," said Robbie, her voice suddenly full. "Sure I came here to fight the Fairchilds—but he wasn't even here when I came. *Shelley* warned him. All the Fairchilds run away."

"Where have you been, Robbie Reid?" asked Aunt Mac.

"You've got a piece of cotton or a feather, one, in your hair." Aunt Shannon with rising voice hummed a girlhood ballad.

"There is a fight and it's come between us, Robbie," said Ellen, her voice calm and a little automatic. "But it's not over George, we won't have it. And how that would hurt him, and shame him, to think it was, he's so gentle. It's not right to make him be pulled to pieces, and over something he did, and very honorably did. There's a fight *in* us, already, I believe—*in* people on this earth, not between us, and there is a fight in Georgie too. It's part of being alive, though you may think he cannot be pulled to pieces."

Another near flutter of wings, a beating on walls, was in the air; but the throbbing softly insinuated in a strange yet familiar manner the sound of the plantation bells being struck and the school bell and the Methodist Church bell ringing, and cries from the scene of the fire they all ran to, cries somehow more joyous than commiserating, though it threatened their ruin.

Robbie stood up again. Her poor wrinkled dress clung to her, and her face was pale as she said, "If there's a fight in George, I think when he loves me he really hates you—hates the Fairchilds that he's one of!"

"But the fight in you's over things, not over people," said Ellen gently. "Things like the truth, and what you owe people. —Yes, maybe he hates some thing in us, I think you're right—right."

But Aunt Mac was answering Robbie too, knocking her folded fan on the arm of her chair. "You'll just have to go on back if you're going to use ugly words in here," she was saying. "You're in Shellmound now, Miss Robbie, but I know where you were brought up and who your pa and your ma were, and anything you say don't amount to a row of pins."

"Aunt Mac Fairchild!" said Robbie, lifting her voice again, and turning to the old lady her intense face. "Mrs. Laws! You're all a spoiled, stuck-up family that thinks nobody else is really in the world! But they are! You're just one plantation. With a little crazy girl in the family, and listen at Miss Shannon. You're not even rich! You're just medium. Only four gates to get here, and your house needs a coat of paint! You don't even have one of those little painted wooden niggers to hitch horses to!"

"Get yourself a drink of water, child," said Aunt Mac, through her words. "You'll strangle yourself. And talk louder. Nobody's going to make me wear that hot earphone, not in September!"

"Of course not, dear heart!" Aunt Shannon remarked.

Robbie sank into her chair and leaned, with her little square nails white on her small brown fingers, against the side of the table. "My sister Rebel is right. You're either born spoiled in the world or you're born not spoiled. And people keep you that way until you die. *The people you love* keep you the way you are."

"Why, Robbie," said Ellen. "If you weren't born spoiled, George has certainly spoiled you, I can *see* he has. And I've been thinking you were happy, surely happy."

"But he went to the Grove for dinner, when Miss Primrose had guinea for him, he couldn't stay for me! *Troy* knew I was coming!"

"If George knew you were coming, it was his deepest secret," said Ellen. "He just went to his dinner, he had a royal meal waiting for him at the Grove, and he went and ate it like any man, a sensible human being."

"He always goes to you. He always goes when you call him," said Robbie. "If *Bluet* would call him!" Her small fingers, with one of Mashula's rings, curled into fists in the cake crumbs over the cloth, and then opened out and waited as Ellen spoke.

"But George loves us! Of course he comes. George loves a great many people, just about everybody in the Delta, if you would count them. Don't you know that's the mark of a fine man, Robbie? Battle's like that. Denis was even more, even more well-loved. Why, George loves countless people."

"No, he doesn't!" Robbie looked at her frantically, as if Ellen had told her just what she feared. "I'm going to l-leave out of here," she said, with a sob like a little stutter in her words. "Mr. Doolittle. He loves him," she said seemingly to herself, to mystify herself.

"Well. You love George," Ellen told her, as if there were no mystery there. There was a faint little scream from a bedroom, ending in laughter—Dabney's.

Robbie looked around the room fatalistically—was she too imagining all the Fairchilds' rapt faces? "Maybe he didn't run away from me," she said. "But he let me run away from him. That's just as bad! Oh, I wish I was dead." Her brown eyes went wide.

A boy's gleeful cry rose from upstairs, from Ellen's and Battle's room. "Don't," Ellen whispered, not to Robbie. Then she could hear—from where, now, it did not matter—the most natural and yet the most terrible thing possible to hear just now—laughter, laughter filled with the undeniable music of relief.

Robbie flinched—at her own words, perhaps.

"Don't you die. You love George," Ellen told her. "He's such a splendid boy, and we have all of us always honored him so." She leaned back.

"It's funny," Robbie said then, her voice gentle, almost confiding. "Once I tried to be like the Fairchilds. I thought I knew how." When there was no answer from Ellen, she went on eagerly and yet sadly, "Don't any other people in the world feel like me? I wish I knew. Don't any people somewhere love other people so much that they want to be—not like—but the same? I wanted to turn into a Fairchild. It wasn't that I thought you were so wonderful. And I had a living room for him just like Miss Tempe's. But that isn't what I mean.

"But you all—you don't ever turn into anybody. I think you are already the same as what you love. So you couldn't understand. You've just loving yourselves in each other—yourselves over and over again!" She flung the small brown hand at the paintings of melons and grapes that had been trembling on the wall from the commotion in the house, forgetting that they were not portraits of Fairchilds in this room, and with a circle of her arm including the two live old ladies too. "You still love *them*, and they still love you! No matter what you've all done to each other! You don't need to know how to love anybody else. Why, you couldn't love *me!*"

She gave a daring little laugh, and let out a sigh that was a kind of appeal after it. Ellen sat up straight with an effort. In the room's stillness, in Aunt Mac's stare and Aunt Shannon's sweet song, the absence of the Fairchilds and the quiet seemed almost demure, almost perverse. There was a festive little clatter from Tempe in the pantry, laughter coming downstairs.

Then there was George in the door, staring in.

Ellen got up and took hold of the back of her chair, for she felt weak. She held herself up straight, for she felt ready to deliver some important message to George, since he had come back. She was moved from her lethargy, from hearing things, a fluttering in the house like a bodily failing, by a quality of violation she felt quivering alive in Robbie, and looking at George she grew courageous in his implied strength. Yet in the same moment, for her eyes, he stood with his shirt torn back and his shoulders as bare (she thought in a cliché of her girlhood) as a Greek god's, his hair on his forehead as if he were intoxicated, unconscious of the leaf caught there, looking joyous. "Is it out? Is the fire out?" she asked. Her hand held tightly to little Laura McRaven's blue hair ribbon that lay caught over the chair back, flung behind her. Then, "Georgie," she said, "don't let them forgive you, for anything, good or bad. Georgie, you've made this child suffer."

The Yellow Dog had not run down George and Maureen; Robbie had not stayed away too long; Battle had not driven Troy out of the Delta; no one realized Aunt

Shannon was out of her mind; even Laura had not cried yet for her mother. For a little while it was a charmed life. . . . And after giving George an imploring look in which she seemed to commit herself even further to him and even more deeply by wishing worse predicaments, darker passion, upon all their lives, Ellen fell to the floor.

VI

Primrose and Jim Allen came in through the archway behind George, wearing their Sunday hats, and both gave little screams—first the little screams of mild surprise or greeting with which they always entered Shellmound, and then second screams of dismay. "Oh, Primrose," said Jim Allen, and stopping still they shook their flowered heads at each other as if there were no more to be done.

Tempe, coming that instant into the room with a pastry cornucopia on a napkin, shrieked to hear her sisters and then to see Ellen being lifted in George's arms. Then she said calmly, "Fainted. I have these spells myself, semi-occasionally. They are nothing to what I used to have as a girl. —I bet the bird came in here!" She shuddered.

The new screams in the dining room brought in a roomful of Fairchilds with amazing quickness. Robbie backed against the china closet. Orrin was carrying a stunned or dead bird in his cupped hands. The girls, fingers still darting reminiscently to their hair, all fell kneeling, in a stair-steps, around the settee. George was taking off their mother's shoes. Ellen lay with her eyes closed, and with her childlike feet propped shallowly on the inclining end under the fern.

George pushed the children a little. He rushed from Ellen's side to fill a glass from a decanter on the sideboard, and as he went back to her with it, he leaned out and brushed Robbie's wrist with his free hand. Next time he went by, for water, he bent and kissed her rapidly, and asked in pure curiosity that gave her a fierce feeling of joy, "Why did you throw the pans and dishes out the window?" Then he was touching Ellen's lips with various little glasses of stuff, frowning with concentration.

"I thought I saw Battle go by with a wild look, did you?" said Tempe. "Battle! You can come in, she's not dying!"

Battle came in and roamed up and down the room and now and then gave a touch or shake to Ellen's shoulder. Bluet climbed up beside her mother and sang to her softly and leisurely, "Polly Wolly Doodle All the Day," crowding her a little where she was stretched out. It was taking some time to revive her, she was too clumsy now for other people to make easy. There was a tight ring of Fairchilds around her. Maureen every now and then went around the table, arms pumping, long yellow hair flying.

Roxie pressed her forefinger under her nose. Poor Miss Ellen just wasn't strong enough *any longer* for such a trial. She wasn't strong enough for Miss Dabney and Miss Robbie and everything *right now*. One time before, Miss Ellen fainted away when everybody went off and left her—it was when the gin caught fire—and she had lost that little baby, that came between Mr. Little Battle and Ranny. Wasn't it pitiful to see her so white? Poor Miss Ellen at *this time*.

Robbie caught glimpses of the white face from her distance outside the ring.

"Rub her wrists, George," pleaded Battle.

It was Mrs. Fairchild's tenth pregnancy. But oh, why had she waited to faint just at this moment? Why couldn't Battle bring his own wife to? For the same reason the bird had got in the house when she came in, Robbie thought; for the reason Aunt Primrose killed her guinea fowl today for George: the way of the Fairchilds, the way of the world.

Ellen opened her eyes, then closed them again.

"I saw her peep," said Roxie. "Now then. Git to work, Vi'let, Little Uncle!"

"Half an hour," Tempe announced to Ellen, as if that would gratify a lady who had fainted.

"Oh, Mama!" cried Dabney. "Shelley, bring a pillow to prop her up."

"We caught the bird, Mama," said Ranny clearly. "It was a brown thrush. It was the female."

"It could have flown around our house all day and night with a thousand windows and never found the way out," said Little Battle. "I didn't think we was going to catch it, but Orrin caught it with Papa's hat and batted it to the wall."

Ellen opened her eyes. Orrin held out the still bird. "*Veni, vidi, vici!*" he said.

Dabney was leaning over her mother accusingly. "Mama! What happened? I know! You were upset about me."

"I'm all right," said Ellen, lifting one arm and pulling Dabney's hair low over her forehead the way she thought it looked nicer.

"Mama! Oh, Mama!"

Shelley, wordless beside Dabney, knelt on as if in a dream.

"I have the same thing, every now and then," said Aunt Tempe. "I nearly died when Mary Denis married—could scarcely be revived."

"Mama! Do you *want* me to get married?"

"Certainly she doesn't," said Tempe with surprise.

"Oh, she does too," said Primrose.

"I think about your happiness," said Ellen, in the thoughtful, slow voice of people coming out of faints.

"Oh, then!" Dabney jumped up, whirled, and with a scatter of tissue-paper and ribbons she flung wide her newest present, which somebody had put on the table ("A Point Valenciennes banquet cloth!" exclaimed Tempe. "Who from?") and pulled it to her with it spreading behind her like a peacock tail, and pranced around. Then she spread it out before her with her arms wide and smiled tenderly over it at her mother, as if from a balcony. "Don't you see you don't need to worry?" she asked, showing how wide, how fine, how much in her possession she had everything, all for her mother to see.

Shelley, getting up to look, turned on her heel, to go write in her diary. Then she turned back; belatedly, the dining room's one forlorn figure had printed itself on her mind.

"Don't you want to take a bath, Robbie?" she asked meditatively. "Where'd Little Uncle put your suitcase?"

"It got lost when I turned George's car over in a ditch and wrecked it," Robbie said, rocking gently on her high heels from one to the other.

"What?" cried George across the room, with his finger on Ellen's pulse.

"Right out of Memphis, and the day I left," Robbie said with some satisfaction.

"You haven't a stitch but what's on your back?" cried Tempe. "Fathers alive, what a state to come to a wedding in!"

George looked at Robbie intently, without smiling, across the still prancing Dabney, who marched between them.

Battle let out a generous laugh and ambled over to give Robbie a spank. "I'm going to get you a horse to ride for the next time you run away—no, a safe old mule with a bell around the neck. Hear, George?"

"Do you feel stronger? —How'd you get here?" George patted Ellen's hand. His voice for both women had an intolerant sound that made him seem trapped. Tempe made her way toward him and with a smile of mischief popped a pastry into his mouth.

"Do you know that she walked from Fairchilds?" said Ellen, turning her face toward the room. "And nobody's even offered her a bath till Shelley just now, or a place to lie down? Robbie, you lie down *here*."

George glared across the room. "What? You fought the mosquitoes clear from Fairchilds? I ought to whip you all the way home."

"By yourself? You could easily have met a mad dog," said Aunt Jim Allen, who had been able to hear all this.

"Don't chide her, Georgie," said Aunt Primrose. "She won't do it again, will you, Robbie?"

Robbie was basking a little, and fanned her face with the back of her hand.

"Well!" said Troy. "Now then. I've got to get back to East Field before dark." He picked up Aunt Tempe's cornucopia which went to bits under his thumb. "Oh-oh. Something you made me, Dabney?"

Dabney was still prancing—she seemed to see nobody in the room, and was smiling with her lower lip caught under her pretty teeth. "Dabney can't cook!" Tempe and several more cried together.

"She evermore can't," said Troy.

"I'm awfully sorry *I* can," said Aunt Tempe severely.

" 'Fare thee well,' " sang Bluet, patting her mother with soft raps like drum beats, her eyes gazing blissfully at Dabney in the glittering train. " 'Fare thee well, fare thee well, my fairy fay . . .' "

"The right place for a tablecloth is on a table, though," said somebody—Troy. He gazed at Dabney, side-stepped her path, and left the room.

VII

"Want to get out?" asked Roy, just outside the dining-room arch. He and Laura both stood there, chins ducked. "Come on, Laura." He had seen a lady's hand reach out and pull his father in.

"All right." She loved Roy—his scars, bites, scabs and bandages, and intricate vaccination—his light eyes and his sunburn, little berry-colored nipples. The minute he was out of the dining room he was with a visible flash naked to the waist, flat and neat as a hinge in his short pants with the heavy leather belt that was too big around for him, so that he seemed to walk stepping in a tub.

Roy was eight. He still shivered to hear the hounds in the night. He was giving her an intent, sizing-up look.

"You'll have to tote my turtle," he said. "The whole time, and keep him right side up and not set him down anywhere, if you come with me."

"Oh, I will," Laura promised, shuddering.

"You'll have to wait till I find him, so you can carry him."

India skipped out, her heavy straight hair swinging behind like a rope; she carried a stack of crackers in her mouth and skipped from side to side, going off to eat by herself.

"Do you want to come, India?" asked Roy, running up with his turtle.

"No," said India, who could talk plainly with anything in her mouth. "Do you want Maureen to come?"

"O—nay, I—day on't-day."

"Let's all the girls go sit in the chinaberry tree and see who is the one can make their crackers last the longest," said Lady Clare, coming out; she seemed tired—company always was.

"You have to chunk at Maureen, or she'll come." India picked up a stone and threw it.

"Don't hit her," said Laura.

"You *can't* hit her," said India scornfully.

"India, let us take Bluet!" said Roy crazily.

"Take me," said Bluet, clasping Roy around the knees and kissing them fervently.

"Not this time, Roy. I need her here." They all skipped off except Maureen, who did not go away but did not come either, this time. She only threatened, taking stamping steps forward with one foot.

They ran down to the bayou, the turtle in Laura's hands bouncing against her diaphragm. Roy went between two close Spanish daggers and she went after him. The bayou had a warm breath, like a person.

"Is that your boat?" cried Laura.

"It's as much mine as anybody's. I'll take you for a row if you get in," said Roy, stepping in himself.

The boat was in a willow shadow, floating parallel to the bank—dark, unpainted, the color of the water. She would have to step deep. A fishing bucket was in it, and also one oar where a dark line of water went like a snake along the bottom.

"Here's the other oar," she said; it was resting on a dogwood tree. She stepped down in, and he instructed her to sit at the other end of the boat and be quiet. "I know how," said Laura. On her lap the turtle looked out. Roy pushed off, his old tennis shoes splashed water which ran under her sandals, and he sat down and looked nowhere, frowning in the sun. The boat was cut loose but almost still, for as a current urges a boat on, the lack of current seems to pull it back, not let go. Laura could not see beyond a willow branch that hung in her face. Then with a gruff noise the oars went into the water, with the unwilling-looking, casual movement of Roy's arm. The water was quieter than the land anywhere.

"Let me row," said Laura.

"Be quiet," said Roy. He took his tennis shoes slowly off and put them on the little seat between them. He hooked his toes. At the stroke of his oars a shudder would interrupt the smoothness of their motion.

The bayou was narrow and low and soon the water's edge was full of cypress trees. They went in heavy shade.

There were now and then muscadines hanging in the air like little juicy balls strung over the trees beside the water, and they rode staring up, Roy with his mouth open, hoping that grapes might fall. Then leaves cut out like stars and the early red color of pomegranates lay all over the water, and imperceptibly they came out into the river. The water looked like the floor of the woods that could be walked on.

"Are we going down the river?" asked Laura.

"Sure. And the Yazoo River runs into the Mississippi River."

"And it runs into the sea," said Laura, but he would say no more.

As they went down the Yazoo, a long flight of ducks went over, going the way they were going, the V very high in the sky, very long and thin like a ribbon drawn by a finger through the air, but neither child said anything, and after a long time the ducks were a little wrinkle deep down in the sky and then out of sight.

On the other side of the river from where they had come, facing them, Laura saw what they were getting to, a wonderful house in the woods. It was twice as big as Shellmound. It was all quiet, and unlived in, surely; the dark water was going in front of it, not a road.

"Look," she said.

Roy glanced over his shoulder and nodded.

"Let's go in!"

There was a dark waterlogged landing, and Roy got the boat to it neatly and ran the chain around a post. He jumped out of the boat and Laura climbed out after him. "Bring my turtle, remember," he said. She brought it, like a hot covered dish. They were in a wood level with the water, dark cedar trees planted in some pattern, some of them white with clematis. It looked like moonlight.

"Why, here's Aunt Studney, way over here!" cried Roy. "Hi, Aunt Studney!"

Laura remembered Aunt Studney, coal-black, old as the hills, with her foot always in the road; on her back she carried a big sack that nearly weighted her down. There at a little distance, near the house, she was walking along, laboring and saying something.

"Ain't studyin' you."

"That's what she says to everybody—even Papa," said Roy. "Nobody knows what she's got in the sack."

"Nobody in the world?"

"I said nobody."

"Where does she live?" asked Laura a little fearfully.

"Oh, back on our place somewhere. Back of the Deadening. You'll see her walking the railroad track anywhere between Greenwood and Clarksdale, Aunt Studney and her sack."

"Are you scared of Aunt Studney?" asked Laura.

"No. Yes, I am."

"I despise Aunt Studney, don't you?"

"Papa's scared of her too. Me, I think that's where Mama gets all her babies."

"Aunt Studney's sack?"

"Sure."

"Do you think *Ranny* came out of that sack?"

"Sure. . . . I don't know if *I* came out of it, though." Roy gave her a hard glance, and looked as if he might put his fist to her nose.

"I wonder if she'd let *me* look in—Aunt Studney," said Laura demurely.

"Of course not! If she won't let any of *us* look in, even Papa, you know she won't let *you* walk up and look in."

"Do you dare me to ask her?"

"All right, I dare you."

"Double-dog-dare me."

"I just dare you."

"Aunt Studney, let me look in your sack!" screamed Laura, taking one step in front of Roy and waiting with open mouth.

"Ain't studyin' you," said Aunt Studney instantly. She stamped on, like an old wasp over the rough, waggling her burden.

"Look! She's going in Dabney's house!" cried Roy.

"Is this Dabney's house?" cried Laura.

"Cousin Laura, you don't know anything."

"All right: maybe she's gone in to open her sack."

"If she does, we'll run off with what's in it!"

"Oh, Roy. That would be perfect."

"Be quiet," said Roy. "How do you know?"

"All right: you go in front."

They went up an old drive, made of cinders, shaded by cedar and crape-myrtle trees which the clematis and the honeysuckle had taken. There were iron posts with open mouths in their heads, where a chain fence used to run. Taking the posts was a hedge that went up from the landing, higher than anybody's head, with tiny leaves nobody could count—boxwood; it was bitter-green to smell, the strong fearless fragrance of things nobody has been to see.

When they came to the house, there was a dead mockingbird on the steps. They jumped over it, Laura not looking back—dead birds lay on their sides, like people. Roy reached down and touched the bird to see how dead it was; he said it was hot. The porch was covered with leaves, like the river, and there were loose, joggling boards in it. The door was open.

Roy and Laura, Laura with the turtle against her, held in the crook of her arm now like a book, went in a vast room, the inside of a tower. Their heads fell back. Up there the roof, if there was one, seemed to fade into the light. Before them rose two stairs, wooden spirals that went up barely touching at wavery rims, little galleries on two levels, and winding into the depths of light—for Laura had a moment of dizziness and felt as if she looked into a well.

There was an accusing, panting breathing, and the thud of a big weight planted in the floor. "Look," said Laura. Aunt Studney, whom she had forgotten about, was in the middle of the room, which was quite empty of the furnishings of a house, standing over her sack and muttering.

"I know," said Roy impatiently. He was regarding the chandelier, his hands on his hips—probably wishing it would fall. Laura all at once saw what a thing it was too; it was as prominent as the stairs and came down between them. Out of the tower's round light at the top, down by a chain that looked the size of a spider's thread, hung the chandelier with its flower-shaped head covered with clusters of soft and burned-down candles, as though a great thing had sometime happened here. The whole seemed to sway, to almost start in the sight, like anything head downward, like a pendulum that would swing in a clock but no one starts it.

"Run up the stairs!" cried Roy, starting forward.

"Aunt Studney," whispered Laura.

"Well, I know!" cried Roy, as if Aunt Studney were always here on his many trips to this house.

"Did you say this was *Dabney*'s house?" asked Laura. There were closed doors in the walls all around, and leading off the galleries—but not even an acorn tea-set anywhere.

"Sure," said Roy. "Make yourself at home. Run up the stairs. (What's in your bag, Aunt Studney?)"

Aunt Studney stood holding her sack on the floor between her feet with her hands knotted together over its mouth, and peeping at them under an old hat of Mr. Battle's. Then she threw her hands up balefully. Laura flung out and ran around the room, around and around the round room. Roy did just what she did—surprising!—and so it was a chase. Aunt Studney did not move at all except to turn herself in place around and around, arms bent and hovering, like an old bird over her one egg.

"Is it still the Delta in here?" Laura cried, panting.

"Croesus, Laura!" said Roy, "sure it is!" And with a jump he mounted the stair and began to run up.

Laura probably would have followed him, but could not leave, after all, for a little piano had been placed at the foot of the stair, looking small as a fairy instrument. It was open. In gold it said "McClarty." How beautiful. She set the turtle down. She touched a white key, and it would hardly sink in at the pressure of her finger—as in dreams the easiest thing turns out to be the hard—but the note sounded after a pause, coming back like an answer—a little far-off sound. The key was warm. There was a shaft of sun here. The sun was on her now, warm, for—she looked up—the top of the tower was a skylight, and around it ran a third little balcony on which—she drew back her finger from the key she had touched—Roy was walking. And all at once Aunt Studney sounded too—a cry high and threatening like the first note of a song at a ceremony, a wedding or a funeral, and like the bark of a dog too, somehow.

"Roy, come down!" Laura called, with her hands cupped to her mouth.

But he called back, pleasure in his voice, "I see Troy riding Isabelle in Mound Field!"

"You do not!"

All at once a bee flew out at her—out of the piano? Out of Aunt Studney's sack? Everywhere! Why, there were bees inside everything, inside the piano, inside the walls. The place was alive. She wanted to cry out herself. She heard a hum everywhere, in everything. She stood electrified—and indignant.

"Troy! Troy! Look where I am!" Roy was crying from the top of the house. "I see Troy! I see the Grove—I see Aunt Primrose, back in her flowers! I see *Papa*! I see the whole creation. Look, look at me, Papa!"

"If he saw you he'd skin you alive!" Laura called to him. The bees, Aunt Studney's sack, the turtle—where was he?—and Roy running around going to fall—all at once she could not stand Dabney's house any longer.

But Roy looked down (she knew he was smiling) from the top, peering over a shaky little rail. "Aunt Studney! Why have you let bees in my house?" he called. The echoes went flying around the walls and down the stairs like something thrown down. It so delighted Roy that he cried again, "Why have you let bees in my house? Why have you let bees in my house?" and his laughter would come breaking down over them again.

But Aunt Studney only said, as if it were for the first

time, "Ain't studyin' you," and held the mouth of her sack. It occurred to Laura that Aunt Studney was not on the lookout for things to put in, but was watching to keep things from getting out.

"Come back, Roy!" she called.

"Not ready!"

But at last he came down, his face rosy. "What'll you give me for coming back?" he smiled. "Aunt Studney! What's in your sack?"

Aunt Studney watched him swagger out, both hands squeezing on her sack; she saw them out of the house.

Outdoors it was silent, a green rank world instead of a play-house.

"I'm stung," said Roy calmly. With an almost girlish bending of his neck he showed the bee sting at the nape, the still tender line of his hair. A submissive yet arrogant pleasure seemed to radiate from him, having for its source the angry little bump. Now Laura wished she had one. When they went through the deep cindery grass of the drive she saw the name Marmion cut into the stone of the carriage block.

Suddenly they cried out in one breath, "Look."

"A treasure," said Roy, calmly still. Catching the high sun in the deep grass, like a penny in the well, was a jewel. It might have been there a hundred years or a day. They looked at each other and with one accord dropped down together into the grass. Laura picked it up, for Roy, unaccountably, held back, and she washed it with spit.

Then suddenly, "Give it here," and Roy held out his hand for it. "You can't have that, it's Mama's. I'll take it back to her."

Laura gazed at it. It was a pin that looked like a rose.

She knew it would be worn here—putting her forefinger to her small, bony chest. "We're where we're not supposed to be looking for anything," she said, as if something inspired her and made her clever, turning around and around with it as Roy tried to take it, holding it away and hiding it from Aunt Studney's fastening look for Aunt Studney with her sack was suddenly hovering again. "You can't have it, you can't have it, you can't have it."

Roy chased her at first, and then seemed to consider. He looked at Laura, and the pin, at Marmion, Aunt Studney, even the position of the sun. He looked back at the river and the boat he had rowed here.

"All right," he said serenely.

They walked down and got back in the boat. They moved slowly over the water, Roy working silently against the current. Yet he seemed almost to be falling asleep rowing—he could sleep anywhere. His gaze rested a thousand miles away, and now and then, pausing, he delicately touched his bee sting. Presently he rocked the boat. He never asked even a word about his turtle.

"The only place I've ever been in the water is in the Pythian Castle in Jackson with water wings," said Laura. "Tar drops on you, from the roof."

"*What?*"

Roy dragged in the oars, got on his feet, and threw Laura in the river as if it were all one motion.

As though Aunt Studney's sack had opened after all, like a whale's mouth, Laura opening her eyes head down saw its insides all around her—dark water and fearful fishes. A face flanked by receding arms looked at her under water—Roy's, a face strangely indignant and withdrawing. Then Roy's legs drove about her—she saw Roy's tied-up toe, knew his foot, and seized hold. He kicked her, then his unfamiliar face again met hers, wide-eyed and small-mouthed and its hair streaming upwards, and his hands took her by her hair and pulled her up like a turnip. On top of the water he looked at her intently, his eyelashes thorny and dripping at her. Then he pulled her out, arm by arm and leg by leg, and set her up in the boat.

"Well, you've been in the Yazoo River now," he said. He helped her wring out her skirt, and then rowed on, while she sat biting her lip. "I *think* that's where Aunt Studney lives," he said politely once, pointing out for her through the screen of trees a dot of cabin; it was exactly like the rest, away out in a field, where there was a solitary sunflower against the sky, many-branched and taller than a chimney, all going to seed, like an old Christmas tree in the yard. Then, "I couldn't believe you wouldn't come right up," said Roy suddenly. "I thought girls floated."

"You sure don't know much. But I never have been in the water anywhere except in the Pythian Castle in Jackson with water wings," she said all over again.

They went from the river back into the bayou. Roy, asking her pardon, wrung out his pockets. At the right place, willow branches came to meet them overhead and touched their foreheads where they sat transfixed in their two ends of the boat. The boat knocked against the shore. They jumped out and ran separately forward. Laura paused and lifted up her hair, and turned on her heels in the leaves, sighing. But Roy ran up the bank, shaking the yucca bells, and disappeared in a cloud of dust.

India walked down to meet Laura and they walked up through the pecan grove toward the shady back road, with arms entwined. India was more startling than she because she was covered with transfer pictures; on her arms and legs were flags, sunsets, and baskets of red roses.

Dabney was at the gate.

"Where have you been?" asked Dabney, frowning into the sunset, in a beautiful floating dress.

"Where have *you* been?" said India. They passed in.

"It's nearly time for rehearsal. She's waiting for Troy," India said, as if her sister could not hear. On the gatepost itself sat Maureen, all dressed in another new dress (she had the most!) but already barefoot, and looking down at all of them, her fists gripped around her two big toes.

"I'm dripping wet," Laura murmured. They walked on twined together into the house. "Do you want to know why?" Mary Lamar was playing the wedding song. Laura's hand stole down to her pocket where the garnet pin had lain. For a moment she ached to her bones—it was indeed gone. It was in the Yazoo River now. How fleetingly she had held to her treasure. It seemed to her that the flight of the ducks going over had lasted longer than the time she kept the pin.

Roxie with a cry of sorrow had fallen on her knees behind Laura to take up the water that ran from her heels.

"Shelley did this," India remarked contentedly to the bent black head, and pulled up her skirt and stuck out her stomach, where the word Constantinople was stamped in curlicue letters.

"Lord God," said Roxie. "Whatever you reads it's a scandal to the jaybirds."

India, softly smiling, swayed to Laura and embraced and kissed her.

"Hold still both of you," said Battle over their heads. "No explanations either one of you." He switched them equally, his white sleeve giving out a starch smell as strong as daisies, and went up and down their four dancing legs. "A man's daughters!" He told them to go wash their separate disgraces off and be back dressed for decent company before he had to wring both their necks at one time.

"Laura!" India cried ecstatically in the middle of it. "Lady Clare's got chicken pox!"

Then she won't be the flower girl! and I can! Laura thought, and never felt the pain now, though it was renewed.

VIII

"Your flower girl," Aunt Tempe announced a little later at the door of the parlor, where the family were gathering for the rehearsal supper party—the clock was striking one, which meant seven—"has the chicken pox—unmistakably. She is confined to my room." She turned on her heel and marched off, but came right back again.

"Lady Clare's brought it from Memphis!" Ellen

gasped. She reclined, partly, there on the horsehair love seat. Battle had told her to deck herself out and *lie* there, move at her peril.

"I have to take her to Memphis to get those Buchanan teeth straightened," Tempe said shortly. "All life is a risk, as far as that goes."

"Look out for the bridesmaids!" warned Roxie. "Miss Dab, look out for your bridesmaids and fellas!" She giggled and ran out, ducking her head with her arm comically raised before Mr. Battle. It was the children that stalked in at the door, fancily bearing down on all the canes and umbrellas in the house, Ranny at the front, Bluet at the back, with India and Laura in starchy "insertion" skirts and satin sashes falling in at the last minute.

"We're the wedding!" said Ranny. "I'm Troy! Oof, oof!" He bent over like an old man. "Shepherd crooks have come!" cried Little Battle, hooking Maureen with Aunt Mac's Sunday cane.

"Stop, Ranny, you're going to get the chicken pox," said his mother.

"Papa!" cried Dabney.

There were further cries in the yard and in the back of the house.

"Hallelujah! Hallelujah! Pinchy's come through!"

Roxie rushed in a second time, but seriously now, bringing Vi'let and embracing her, with some little black children following and appearing and disappearing in the folds of their skirts, and Little Uncle marched in with his snowiest coat standing out, and stood there remote and ordained-looking.

"Hallelujah," he said.

"Well, hallelujah," said Aunt Tempe, rather pointedly. George smiled.

Some open muffler roared in the yard.

"Dabney!" cried a chorus of voices, and the real bridesmaids ran in, in a company, all in evening dresses ready to go to the Winona dance afterwards. The boys ran in, some in blazers, and started playing with the children, lifting Ranny to the ceiling, kissing Aunt Tempe, spanking Bluet, and pulling Laura's hair.

"Oh, you all, the crooks haven't come! I'm a wreck," said Dabney in their midst.

"They'll be here tomorrow, precious," said Aunt Tempe. "They won't disappoint you, ever in this world."

"Shoo, shoo! All children git out!" shouted Battle. "We've got to rehearse this wedding in a minute, shoo!" But the children all laughed.

"Who's that?" Dickie Boy Featherstone was asking.

"Oh, Robbie," said Dabney, "this is Nan-Earl Delaney, Gypsy Randall, Deltah and Dagmar Wiggins, Charlsie McLeoud, Bitsy Carmichael," and she pulled all the bridesmaids forward with a fitful movement like flicking things out of a bureau drawer, "and then, there's Pokey Calloway, Dickie Boy Featherstone, and Hugh V. McLeoud and Shine Young and Pee Wee Kuykendall and Red Boyne. They're in the wedding. She's my aunt-in-law—isn't that it, Mama?"

"Aunt?" said Red Boyne. "Aren't you going to the dance?"

"And you already know the best man, Robbie," said Dabney, nervously smiling. "It's George."

"Aunt Ellen," said Laura, kneeling at the love seat. "I've already had chicken pox."

"All right, dear," said her aunt. But it did not seem to occur to her that now Laura might be slipped into the wedding in the place of Lady Clare. And Laura, staring at her, suddenly wondered where, truly where, the rosy pin was. She got to her feet and backed away from her aunt slowly—she wanted to know in what wave. Now it would be in the Yazoo River, then it would be carried down to the Mississippi, then . . .

"When's that dish-faced preacher of yours coming, Ellen? Did you remind him?" said Battle, sprawling gently on a mere edge of the love seat, as if to show them all he would not take up too much room.

"This is his *business*, dear," said Ellen.

"Where's *Troy*?" cried some bridesmaid.

"We could have a little wine now," Ellen said to Shelley. "With that excitement in the kitchen, there's no telling how or when or in what state our supper will get to us, when the rehearsing's done. Take my keys."

"Mama, they're the heaviest and most keys in the world."

"I know it! Some of them are to things I'll never be able to think of or never will see again," said Ellen.

One of those inexplicable pauses fell over the room, a moment during which Aunt Shannon's voice could be heard in another part of the house, singing "Oft in the Stilly Night." Then Ellen pulled out a key. "This one's to your father's wine, though—to the best of my knowledge. Do you know that little door?"

Robbie sat in the middle of the whirl. Where was George now—she thought she had heard his voice. . . . Something in her had taken note of every dress on Vi'let's arm even when she came storming through the door of Shellmound, and now she saw that Mary Lamar Mackey wore the Nile-green tulle that had the silver sash, and Aunt Tempe had on the Chinese coat of yellow velvet with roses and violets printed on it, the most dazzling bright spot in the room. Shelley wore the tea-rose silk dress with the gathered side panels, and Dabney the white net with the gold kid gardenia on the chest. Robbie herself had on a dress of Dabney's—a black chiffon one that felt no different from a nightgown. Mary Lamar Mackey was playing "Constantinople." The bridesmaids and groomsmen were dancing in the music room around the piano and across the hall and around the table in the dining room to cup up nuts in their hands.

"Dabney, don't you ever drag Troy over the country to the dances with you?" asked Uncle Pinck, with Aunt Tempe pinning a Maréchal Niel bud in his lapel.

"Troy wouldn't get up on the floor with me, Uncle Pinck, if it was the last thing he did on earth!" cried Dabney. She was dancing with Red Boyne. "I tell him I think he's just too big and clumsy to *learn.*" It was a reason for loving him, but Uncle Pinck did not seem to understand this at once, from the bemused look that came on his face. Very daintily he took a little glass of wine—Shelley and Roy were passing it.

"You can't drink wine and not eat cake!" said Battle. "Look here. What kind of house is this?"

"It will spoil your supper afterwards, dear," said Ellen. "The rehearsal supper."

"I say let's have cake!" said Battle rambunctiously.

"Well . . . somebody will have to get it then, it looks like," said Ellen with an uncertain movement, which Battle stopped. "Roxie! Howard! Somebody!" he shouted.

George moved through the room and Ellen called, "Just bring that one in the glass stand, and a sharp knife—bring more plates, those little Dabney plates."

"Are those the best?" asked Battle, falling back, and she said, "Well, they're from the Dabneys: yes."

"I'm holding back my cornucopias," said Tempe flatly. "You needn't think you'll gobble those up till the proper moment."

Mr. Rondo arrived, and not being able to make himself heard at the door, rapped on the windowpane, causing the bridesmaids to scream at that black sight through the wavery glass. Aunt Tempe insisted on his taking her chair and a little wine and even changed her mind about the cornucopias. She said she would go back and fill them with cherries.

"I'm especially pleased to see you, Mrs. Fairchild," Mr. Rondo told Robbie. "I was inquiring about you earlier in the week," and she fluffed her hair a little and faint color came in her cheeks.

"Now where's Troy?" asked Uncle Pinck. "Still, Primrose and Jim Allen haven't got here. Has anybody ever got here from the Grove less than an hour or two late?"

"Here's Troy," said Little Battle, prancing up. "I'm Troy!"

"Be Troy, Little Battle," said Battle. "Listen, Pinck. Ask him where he's from."

"Where are you from, Troy?" asked Uncle Pinck, drawling his words and bobbing his distinguished white head.

"Up near the Tennessee line," said Little Battle, in the voice of Troy. "Mighty good people up there. Have good sweet water up there, everlasting wells. Cool nights, can tolerate a sheet in summer. The land ain't what you'd call good.

"Little Battle, Little Battle," said Ellen anxiously.

"Isn't it lonesome, Troy?" prompted Battle.

"Lonesome? Not now. One of my sisters married a supervisor. Now we enjoy a mail and ice route going by two miles from the porch. Just reach down the mountain."

"Papa!" cried Shelley. "George!"

"And the road's got a bridge in, and a little sprinkle of gravel on it now. And my mammy's health is good, got a letter from her in my pocket. I'll read it to you—Dear Troy, be a good boy. I would write more but must plead company. Have called in passing to mail this for me. Your ma."

"The letter's too much!" cried Ellen, extremely upset, and addressing herself to Mr. Rondo.

But Dabney leaned on the mantelpiece, her cheek in her hand, and smiled at them all a moment; all their eyes were on her. Aunt Tempe, who had laughed till she cried, brought her the first cornucopia on the tray. "Here, dear heart." Dabney could see Troy's eyes open wide at the sight of Aunt Tempe tonight. Troy did venerate women—he thought Aunt Tempe should be home like his mammy, making a quilt or meditating words of wisdom, as he said his mother sat doing instead of getting lonesome. Dabney smiled at Aunt Tempe, who had been going to Delta dances for thirty years.

She had never put on her grown-up mind, Dabney thought fondly—as if her grown-up mind were a common old house dress Aunt Tempe would never want to be caught in. She did not want to be venerated . . . Dabney ran after her and kissed her soft, warm cheek.

You never had to grow up if you were spoiled enough. It *was* comforting, if things turned out not to be what you thought. . . .

Dabney looked around the room, the big parlor where they all sat now, eating and waiting, with the western sun level with the windows now, and a hummingbird just outside drinking and suspending herself among the tall unpruned topknots of the abelias. Somewhere the dogs were barking fitfully at the guineas or the birds that had begun to fly over. . . . Her mother in a dress with a bertha was dutifully holding a tiny glass of cordial, sitting on the love seat beside her father who was leaning behind her, his brows contorted but unwavering, as though he had forgotten his expression. Maureen sat on the floor meekly bending her head to have her shining hair patted, and her mother's hand patted there. George came and stood in front of the mantelpiece, and looked out beside her. And the bridesmaids were only there to fill up the room . . . "You're a genius, Tempe," said Battle, after he let her put a cornucopia in his mouth.

Dabney gazed at them thinking, I always wondered what they would do if I married somebody they didn't want me to. Poor Papa is the only one really suffering. All her brothers would try to hold her and not let her go, though, when the time came actually to leave the house. Her mother had fainted—but Dabney had not believed too well that the fainting counted as a genuine protest—her mother did not have "ways." "Your mother *lacks ways*," Aunt Tempe always said to the girls, darkly.

"Another new dress, Tempe?" asked her father, who admired Tempe very much while he ran from her voice.

Aunt Tempe hit him with her fan. "This old thing? I had it before Annie Laurie died. . . ."

Battle, catching Dabney's eye, looked poutingly across the room. "He didn't do it for you, eh, Robbie?" he said teasingly. Dabney looked at George, where he stood there at the middle of the mantel, looking out, and she moved away, to take a bite of a bridesmaid's cake.

It seemed to Ellen at moments that George regarded them, and regarded things—just things, in the outside world—with a passion which held him so still that it resembled indifference. Perhaps it *was* indifference—as though they, having given him this astonishing feeling, might for a time float away and he not care. It was not love or passion itself that stirred him, necessarily, she felt—for instance, Dabney's marriage seemed not to have affected him greatly, or Robbie's anguish. But little Ranny, a flower, a horse running, a color, a terrible story listened to in the store in Fairchilds, or a common song, and yes, shock, physical danger, as Robbie had discovered, roused something in him that was immense contemplation, motionless pity, indifference. . . . Then, he would come forward all smiles as if in greeting—come out of his intensity and give some child a spank or a present. Ellen had always felt this in George and now there was something of surprising kinship in the feeling; perhaps she had fainted in the way he was driven to detachment. In the midst of the room's commotion he stood by the mantel as if at rest.

Robbie looking at him from across the room smiled faintly. "You were so sure of yourself, so conceited! You were so sure the engine would stop," she murmured, like a refrain, like one last refrain—they had had no time alone; here nobody had. So she spoke as though no one else but George were in the room. It was something not a one of them had ever thought of. . . . Battle groaned, then raised up on his elbow to hear more.

George stood drinking his home-made wine by the summer-closed fireplace. A tinge of joyousness pervaded him still, for Ellen, he had a rampant, presiding sort of attitude. The others had all thrown themselves down, in the soft flowered chairs, or else they danced at the room's edges, in and out the door.

"The Dog didn't hit us," George said, speaking with no mistake about it straight across them all, tenderly and undisturbedly, to Robbie. "I don't think it matters what *happens* to a person, or what comes."

"You didn't think it mattered what happened to Maureen?" Robbie lowered her eyelids. His words had hurt her. Under Ellen's hand Maureen began to chug. "Choo—choo—"

George was still a moment, then crossed the room and pressed Robbie's arms, pinned them to her side so that he seemed to hurt her more.

"To *me!* I speak for myself," he said matter-of-factly. Battle made a rude sound. "Something is always coming, you know that." For a moment George moved his gaze over the bobbing and shuttling bridesmaids to Ellen. "I don't think it matters so much in the world what. Only," he bent over Robbie with his look gone relentless—he was about to kiss her, "I'm damned if I wasn't going to stand on that track if I wanted to! Or will again."

Perhaps he is "conceited," thought Ellen tiredly.

"Ah! Doesn't that sound like his brother Denis's very words and voice?" cried Tempe, passing by with her little silver dish. "He would murder me if I contradicted him, and he loved me better than anybody in the world."

George did kiss Robbie.

"But you're everything on earth to me," Robbie said plainly. Mr. Rondo put his fingertips to his brow. With an extremely conscious, an almost brazen, power of explicitness that seemed to match George's, Robbie was leaving out every other thing in the world with the thing she said. The *vulgar* thing she said! Aunt Tempe cast her eyes simply up, not even at anybody.

For Tempe, her young brother George, who pulled Ranny out of the path of mad dogs, was simply less equal to pulling Dabney out of the way of Troy Flavin, Mary Denis out of the way of Mr. Buchanan, or himself out of the way of Robbie Reid, much less of trains turned loose on the railroad tracks. Deliver her from any of them, she didn't care what mercifully got her out of their path. Of course if anything ever did bear down on her, Pinckney would be in Memphis, she knew that much. Nobody could really do anything about her ever except Denis. How idle other men were! It was laziness on men's part, the difficulties that came up in this world. A paradise, in which men, sweating under their hats like field hands, chopped out difficulties like the green grass and made room for the ladies to flower out and flourish like cotton, floated vaguely in Tempe's mind, and she gave her head a toss.

Ellen leaned back against Battle's long bulk, sipping her cordial, and under her gaze her family, as they had a trick of doing, seemed to separate one from another like islands being created out of a land in the sea that had sprawled conglomerate too long. Under her caressing hand was Maureen. The Dog had stopped in time not to kill her. Here in the long run so like them all, the mindless child could not, as they would not, understand a miracle. How could Maureen, poor child, see the purity and dullness of *fact*, of the outside-world fact? Of something happening? Which was miracle. Robbie saw the miracle. Out of fear and possession, perhaps out of vulgarity itself, she saw. Not by George's side, but tagging behind, in the clarity of wifely ferocity, she had seen the true vision, and suspected it.

For Robbie, a miracle in the outer world reflected the worse on her husband—for her it made him that much more of a challenger, a proud defier that she had to protect. For her his danger was the epitome of the false position the Fairchilds put him in. Ellen saw clearly enough that George was not a challenging man at all; was he "conceited"—Robbie's funny little high-school world? He was magnificently disrespectful—that was what Ellen would have called him. For of course he saw death on its way, if they did not.

No, the family would forever see the stopping of the Yellow Dog entirely after the fact—as a preposterous diversion of their walk, resulting in lovers' complications, for with the fatal chance removed the serious went with it forever, and only the romantic and absurd abided. They would have nothing of the heroic, or the tragic now, thought Ellen, as though now she yielded up a heart's treasure.

Here they sat—all dreamily now, each with a piece of cake to spoil his supper—their truest selves, like their truest aberrations and truest virtues, not tampered with. Here in the closest intimacy the greatest anonymity lay, and a kind of basking, a kind of special pleasure, was in it. She heard Jim Allen and Primrose coming in that old electric car, that they had a colored preacher to drive . . .

Georgie had not borne it well that she called him heroic, as she did one day for something; but this, she saw now, was not for the reason that the heroism was not true, but that it too was after the fact—a quality of his heart's intensity and his mind's, too intimate for her to have looked into. That wild detachment was more intimate than desire. There was something unfair about that. Would Robbie's unseeing, fighting anger suit him better, then, than too close a divination? Well, that depended not on how Robbie loved him but on how he loved Robbie, and on other things that she, being mostly mother, and being now tired, did not know. Just now they kissed, with India coming up close on her toes to see if she could tell yet what there was about a kiss.

The whole family watched them "make up." And how did George himself think of this thing? They saw him let Robbie go, then kiss her one more time, and Battle laughed out from the pillows.

George wished it might yet be intensified. Inextinguishable, the little adventure, like anything else, burned on.

In the music room Mary Lamar resumed playing "Constantinople" and the bridesmaids, rising a little blankly as if from sleep or rest, took the groomsmen and began to dance here in the room, and around George and Robbie there in the center. Aunt Tempe too, with her finger drawing little circles, kept time. While George was kissing Robbie, Bluet had him around his knees and kissed him down there, with such fervor that she sat down, sighing. Then George and Robbie were dancing too—how amazingly together they went. In and out wove little Ranny, waving a pretended shepherd crook, shouting "I'm the wedding!" and stamping the floral wreath in the rug.

"Oh, Aunt Ellen," said Laura once more, coming forward. "Could I be in the wedding instead of Lady Clare? Because . . ."

"Why, yes, dear," said Ellen, "of course."

Then Bluet wandered by, dead on her feet, dragging Mashula's dulcimer, which she had asked for and someone had given her.

"Bluet, aren't you asleep? Bluet!" she cried, suddenly realizing the hour.

"Nobody put me to sleep," whispered Bluet. Ellen caught hold of her and kissed her—her seriousness sweeter than Ranny's delight now.

"Where do you think you're going now, Ellen?" said Battle.

He held her down a minute and she thought tenderly, there's no reason in the world why he should have been cowed in his life by Denis and George. . . .

"I'm going to put my baby to bed. You can't hold me down from that." She left them carrying Bluet in her arms, giving Robbie a soft, open look as she went out.

Tempe sighed. Ellen simply didn't know how to treat Robbie Reid—she should have just let *her* at her! But then Ellen was a very innocent woman, Tempe knew that. There were things you simply could not tell her. Not that Ellen hadn't changed in recent years. That shy, big-eyed little thing Battle had brought back with him from school dying laughing at her persistence in her own reticent ways . . . Ellen had come far, had yielded to much, for a Virginian, but still now a crowd, a roomful of people, was not her natural habitat, a plantation was not her true home.

"I'm the wedding!" Ranny was still calling, running by and twirling Tempe round. "I'm the wedding!" He carried a little green switch now for a stick, with peach leaves on it. In that moment Tempe, laughing, experienced not a thought exactly but a truer thing, a suspicion, that what she loved was not gone with Denis, but was, perhaps, perennial.

"Oh, there's always so much—so *much* happening here!" she cried contentedly to one of the bridesmaids, the McLeoud girl.

Robbie put her hand up to her head a minute as she danced, against the whirl. Dabney was dancing before her, by herself, eyes shining on them all. . . . Indeed the Fairchilds took you in circles, whirling delightedly about, she thought, stirring up confusions, hopefully working themselves up. But they did not really want anything they got—and nothing really, nothing really so very much, happened! But the next moment Miss Primrose and Miss Jim Allen arrived with so much authority and ado that she almost had to believe in them.

"This is our third trip between the Grove and Shellmound today," said Miss Jim Allen, almost falling against Battle in the door. "Nobody let us in!"

"Pinchy's come through."

"Of course."

"It's a wonder poor Primrose is not dead from carrying those Japanese lanterns in all by herself!"

"Why didn't you holler?" said George, still dancing.

Primrose and Jim Allen looked in at the room, playfully holding up their little unlighted paper lanterns.

"Oh, George, George, I'm *still* ashamed that guinea hen was tough!" Primrose cried.

"Why, it was deliciously tender," said George, over Robbie's shoulder.

"George! Was it?"

Robbie knew he smiled, with his chin in her hair. Well, the comfort they took in him—all the family—and that he held dear, was a far cry from *knowing* him. (They did a trick step.) The Fairchilds were always seeing him by a gusty lamp—exaggerating, then blinding—by the lamp of their own indulgence. While she saw him lighted up by his own fire—no one else but himself was there, a solid man, going through the world, a husband. It was by his being so full of himself that she felt the anger, the love, pride, and rest of marriage.

But oh, when all the golden persuasions of the Fairchilds focused upon him, he would vaunt himself again, if she did not watch him. He would drive her to vaunt herself too. After the Yellow Dog went by, he had turned on her a look that *she* would call the look of having been on a debauch. She could not follow. Sometimes she thought when he was so out of reach, so far away in his mind, that she could blame everything on some old story. . . . For he evidently felt that old stories, family stories, Mississippi stories, were the same as very holy or very passionate, if stories could be those things. He looked out at the world, at her, sometimes, with that essence of the remote, proud, over-innocent Fairchild look that she suspected, as if an old story had taken hold of him—entered his flesh. And she did not know the story.

She beat her hand softly, in time to "Constantinople," on George's hard back, for whatever threatened to waste his life, to lead him away, *even if he liked it*, she was going to go up against if it killed her. He laughed, and she bit him through his sleeve. Shelley saw her.

"I wonder where Troy went, Mr. Rondo," said India.

It was a little before then that Laura started up and raced out of the parlor. She met Aunt Ellen carrying Bluet and pressed thin as a switch against the stair banister as she hurried, to let them by. It was out of love and the logic of love, and the thrill of loss she had, that she had seen a vision of Uncle George's own pipe as a present for him.

She slid still flatly and on tiptoe into the dining room. Nobody was there. Only the stack of plates for the supper and the flowers in the vases were there to see. On the chair under the lamp lay Uncle George's pipe, where by her memory he had left it. She took the pipe up and holding it gently, its stem to her nose, she started away.

All at once Aunt Shannon's voice spoke. She was sitting in the rocker she sat in all the time, only Laura had not noticed her. She was sewing on a little piece of embroidery.

"Denis," she was saying pleasantly, in an afterthought tone of voice, "I meant to tell you, little Annie Laurie's here. Set her heart on being in your wedding."

Anxious as she was to get away with the pipe, Laura had to wait to hear what Aunt Shannon said about her mother.

"Has a little malaria, I'm sure," murmured Aunt Shannon. "But looks a hundred times better already, now that she's here with *us*. —Gals are growing too fast.

That's all." Aunt Shannon rocked a little and then bit off her thread, and that was all she ever told Denis about Laura's mother.

Uncle George's pipe was perceptibly warm. It smelled stronger than Laura had guessed—it smelled violently. But she bore that, and crept out with it and edged up the stairs, meeting nobody. She knew where to hide the pipe—in her hat, which lay up in the wardrobe not to be touched till the day she put it on for the Yellow Dog to go home. The hat was a grand hiding place for her present for Uncle George, and the pipe was the thing he would want.

"Do you realize, dear hearts, that we have been waiting all this time on His Honor the Bridegroom?" said Aunt Tempe.

"Ah! What time is it?" inquired Mr. Rondo, but nobody answered. The piano was playing something soft and "classical," and George was passing cake among the fast-breathing, fallen bridesmaids all around the room.

"Not a *soul* to send for him."

Shelley did not want to stay, did not want to go and look for Troy. She saw Maureen grow overjoyed at the sight of the cake. "I take-la all your cake-la," she said, taking two big handfuls.

"Not for me, not for me," she murmured, stunned at the sight of George at that moment offering the loaded plate to her. It seemed to Shelley all at once as if the whole room should protest, as if alarm and protest should be the nature of the body. Life was too easy—too easily holy, too easily not. It could change in a moment. Life was not ever inviolate. Dabney, poor sister and bride, shed tears this morning (though belatedly) because she had broken the Fairchild night light the aunts had given her; it seemed so unavoidable to Dabney, that was why she cried, as if she had felt it was part of her being married that this cherished little bit of other people's lives should be shattered now. Dabney at the moment cutting a lemon for the aunts' tea brought the tears to Shelley's eyes; could the lemon feel the knife? Perhaps it suffered; not that vague vegetable pain lost in the generality of the pain of the world, but the pain of the very moment. Yet in the room no one said "Stop." They all lay back in flowered chairs and ate busily, and with a greedy delight anticipated what was ahead for Dabney. . . . All except Shelley, who stared at George as he held the cake plate before her. She realized he was looking at her inquiringly. "Aren't you famished?" It occurred to her that he suffered no grievance against the hiding and protesting that went on, the secrecy of life. What was dark and what shone fair—neither would stop him. She had to love him as she loved the darling Ranny. For who was going to look after men and boys like that, who would offer up everything? She took his cake.

"Shelley, *you* go," said Dabney, smiling. "You go to the office and get Troy. Tell him we're all mad and we'll break his neck if he's not here in a minute."

IX

Shelley ran out, down the steps, and across the grass in her satin slippers. The air was blue. She heard the falling waves of the locusts' song, as if the last resistance of the day were being overcome and the languor of night would be soon now. She could see the lightning bugs plainly even between flashes of their lights—flying nearly upright through the blueness, tails swinging, like mermaids playing beneath a sea. She went along the bayou, by the startling towers of the yuccas, and heard only faintly the sounds of the house behind her.

Theirs was a house where, in some room at least, the human voice was never still. Laughing and crying went rushing through the halls, and assuagement waylaid them both. In contrast, the bayou, in its silence, could seem like a lagoon in a foreign world, and a solitary person could walk beside it with inward, uncomforted thoughts. The house was charged with life, the fields were charged with life, endlessly exploited, but the bayou was filled with its summer trance or its winter trance of sleep, its uncaught fishes. And the river, that went by the Grove. "Yazoo means River of Death." India was fond of parading the thing they learned in the fourth grade, and of parading morbidity before Shelley anyway, but Shelley looked back at her unmoved at the word. "Snooty, that's what you are," said India.

"River of Death" to Shelley meant not the ultimate flow of doom, but the more personal vision of the moment's chatter ceasing, the feelings of the day disencumbered, floating now into recognition, like a little boat come into sight; and tenderness and love, sadness and pleasure, being let alone to stretch in the shade. She thought this because of the way the Yazoo looked, its daily appearance. River of the death of the day the Yazoo was to Shelley, and their bayou went in and out of it like the curved arm of the sleeper, whose elbow was in their garden.

Then Shelley ran along the bayou. Oh, to be beyond all this! To have tonight, tomorrow, over! The office, one of the houses none of the girls ever paid any attention to, was down near their bridge, on the other side. She felt the breath of air from the bayou as she ran over, and heard the clothes-like rustle of the fig trees that shaded the other bank. It was not yet dark—it would never get dark. The pervading heat and light of day lasted over even into night—in the pale sky, the warm fields, the wide-awakeness of every mockingbird, still this late in the year. They could mate another time before it was cold.

Yes, there was a light in the office. And Troy was keeping them all waiting! To show him what she thought of him, and rather shocking herself, she walked in with the briefest of knocks.

The green-shaded light fell over the desk. It shone on that bright-red head. Troy was sitting there—bathed and dressed in a stiff white suit, but having trouble with some of the hands. Shelley walked into the point of a knife.

Root M'Hook, a field Negro, held the knife drawn; it was not actually a knife, it was an ice pick. Juju and another Negro stood behind, with slashed cheeks, and open-mouthed; still another, talking to himself, stood his turn apart.

Shelley ran to Troy, first behind him and then to his side. Wordlessly, he pushed her behind him again. She saw he had the gun out of the drawer.

"You start to throw at me, I'll shoot you," Troy said.

Root vibrated his arm, aiming, Troy shot the finger of his hand, and Root fell back, crying out and waving at him.

"Get the nigger out of here. I don't want to lay eyes on him."

"Pinchy cause *trouble* comin' through," said Juju to

the other boy as they lifted Root and pulled him through the doorway.

"All right, who're you now?" Troy said, before he spoke to Shelley.

"I's Big Baby, de one dey all calls."

"All right, stop making that commotion and tell me what's got hold of you. Alligator bite your tail?"

"Mr. Troy, *I* got my seat full of buck-shot," said the Negro, in confessional tones.

Troy groaned with him, but laughed between his drawn lips.

"Find me that ice pick. Pull down your clothes, Big Baby, and get over my knee. Shelley, did you come in to watch me?"

"I can't get past—there's blood on the door," said Shelley, her voice like ice.

"Then you'll have to jump over it, my darlin'," said Troy, sing-song.

Shelley halfway smiled, with the sensation that she had only seen a man drunk. The next moment she felt a sharp, panicky triumph. As though the sky had opened and shown her, she could see the reason why Dabney's wedding should be prevented. Nobody could marry a man with blood on his door. . . . But even as she saw the reason, Shelley knew it would not avail. She would jump as Troy told her, and never tell anybody, for what was going to happen was going to happen.

"Mr. Rondo's waiting," she said. "We're all ready, when you are. You have to practice coming into the parlor."

"I'll be there in due time, Shelley," said Troy evenly. He held the ice pick in a hand bright with red hairs, and red hairs sprang even from his ears.

Shelley jumped over the doorsill.

Running back along the bayou, faster than she had come, Shelley could only think in her anger of the convincing performance Troy had given as an overseer born and bred. Suppose a real Deltan, a planter, were no more real than that. Suppose a real Deltan only imitated another Deltan. Suppose the behavior of all *men* were actually no more than this—imitation of other men. But it had previously occurred to her that Troy was trying to imitate her father. (Suppose her *father* imitated . . . oh, not he!) Then all men could not know any too well what they were doing. Everybody always said George was a second Denis.

She felt again, but differently, that men were no better than little children. She ran across the grass toward the house. Women, she was glad to think, did know a *little* better—though everything they knew they would have to keep to themselves . . . oh, forever!

After, at last, the rehearsal, and the supper, and the Winona dance, Shelley, in a cool nightgown, opened her diary.

What could she put down? . . . "First, the wrong person has eaten Partheny's cake," she wrote, "like in Shakespeare . . ."

There was a whirr and a clawing at the window screen back of the light. A big beetle, a horned one, was trying to get in. All at once Shelley was sickeningly afraid of life, life itself, afraid *for* life. . . . She turned out the light, fell on her bed, and the beating and scratching ceased.

6

Next morning Pinchy was setting the table and Aunt Mac was at the china closet loudly counting the glasses of each kind. Horace was hosing down the Summers's car and in a mystifiyingly high falsetto he was singing "Why?" Howard, with Maureen running about the foot of his ladder, was with almost imperceptible motions hanging paper lanterns in the trees, gradually moving across the yard like the movement of shade under the climbing sun. In the soft early air—Ellen stood at her window, with Battle asleep—in which there was a touch, today perhaps the first touch, of fall, the sounds of the busy fields came traveling up to the yard, the beat and sashay of a horse's feet. Though by another hour the fields would seem to jump in the sight with heat, now there was over them—and would be later when evening would come—the distance and clarity of fall, out of which came a breath of cool. Ellen took it, the breath, and turned to wake Battle.

"When does Primrose Fairchild think she can make that ton of chicken salad, if she doesn't come on?" cried Tempe aloud in the kitchen as the clock was striking the dot of something. Some of the roast turkeys and the ham were lined up in the middle of the kitchen table, and the oven gave off waves of fire and fragrance. Roxie was cooking breakfast over a crowded little unused stove in another part of the kitchen, followed by Ranny begging sticks of bacon, and stamping her foot at some kittens that ran about over there. "I bet Jim Allen is trying to make mints. That can keep you running crazy all day, and with a wedding waiting on you. Roxie, where are the Memphis mints?"

"Great big pasteboard box yonder in de pantry, Miss Tempe," called Roxie. "Have to untie you de ribbon to git you a taste. But you ought to see dem Memphis ice slippers! Green!"

Tempe went from the pantry to the back-porch icebox. "And hard as rocks—*I* know," she said. "And slippery—! People'll lose them off their plates and they'll slide across the floor from here to yonder, oh me. It's an old story, Roxie, weddings to me." She slammed the icebox door, after taking out a little piece of celery.

"Yes, ma'am, sure is. Old story."

"Who's going to make the beaten biscuit, Roxie? I have to have the kitchen to myself when the cornucopias are made! I'll kill anybody making beaten biscuit around me."

"Miss Tempe, you sure will. Miss Ellen say she make one or two ovens of biscuit while you all be taking your napses."

"Good idea. *Everything* would be done more satisfactorily if you could do it with most people asleep. I don't think that's even remotely near the number of pickled peaches it will take for going around the hams and turkeys!" She started counting on her fingers. Ranny offered her a bite of bacon and she bent and took it.

The Memphis flowers had come down just right, on the Yellow Dog that morning, and Miss Thelma had sent them up on horseback, the boxes tied over Sammie McNair's saddle, with Sammie holding Miss Thelma's umbrella over them.

"Oh, mercy—the bride's bouquet! We ought to look at it," Tempe said darkly, as Sammie got off to have breakfast with them.

"Why?" asked India, appearing in her nightgown.

"Just to be sure."

India in a moment had the bouquet out, and held it up at arm's length over her head. "Are you sure, Aunt Tempe?"

"We'll have to doctor it a little, just as I thought," Aunt Tempe said, "take out those common snapdragons. Vi'let! You can take Miss Dabney's bouquet and all these flower boxes to the spring-house, Vi'let, but keep their paper around them so not even your breath touches them."

"Ain't they pretty?" Vi'let cried. "Oh. Oh!"

"There's a ladybug on Dabney's," said Bluet, gazing up. She had come out in her nightgown too.

"I bid it!" India went off with the ladybug on the back of her hand, Bluet following hopefully, asking the ladybug if the trip from Memphis wasn't simply *smothering*.

In a little while here came bumping a wagon. "It's the cake!" said Tempe clairvoyantly. It was the cake, in the tallest box yet from Memphis.

"Now the cake will have to be lifted out by everybody, on the cutting board—there's no two ways about that, if you don't want a ruined toppling thing," said Aunt Mac with spirit.

"One strong, sure-footed man might be the best," said Tempe, "*I* would think."

"Go to grass," said Aunt Mac. Vi'let ran for the old cutting board in the attic, big as the head of a bed, and she, Howard, and Little Uncle began to get the cake on it and so down from the wagon. Old Man Treat, a passer-by who had driven the cake up specially for Miss Thelma at the post office, was not allowed to put in a word or move.

"Mercy! Open it first!" cried Tempe. "So it won't rub off on the box! So we can see it!" They opened the box and stripped it back, like the petals of a flower. Mr. Treat looked over his shoulder. There it was, the tall white thing, shining before God in the light of day. It was a real fantasy! Only God knew if it was digestible.

Ellen already held the door, and some of the girls in their nightgowns and kimonos came out watching.

"It's leaning! It's leaning!" cried India, laughing and joining her hands.

"It looks like the Leaning Tower of Pisa," said Shelley critically.

"Well, it cost your father thirty-five dollars," Ellen told her. "It's no wonder it looks like something or other—do you think, Mr. Treat?" she threw in, for she remembered he was a distant cousin of the Reids.

"Talk about spun sugar!" said Tempe. She gave a little smack. In her arms, forgotten, were the early-cut flowers from the yard. "I think they did real well, considering it was all done by telephone. Now did they forget the ring and thimble and all inside?"

"That's something we won't know till the cake's cut and eaten," said Ellen. "That's too late to tell Memphis about."

"I'm going to cut the ring!" sang India.

"Who're you going to marry, child?" asked Aunt Tempe.

"Dickie Boy Featherstone! No, Red Boyne."

"Red hair!" cried Aunt Tempe exasperated. "What has happened to this clan? Don't you dare do it, India."

"All my children will be ugly like Lady Clare."

"And she upstairs with the chicken pox, shame," said Ellen. "Stand here by me, India."

"There will be no holding Lady Clare when they're all in their dresses, I'm afraid," said Aunt Tempe, flinching now as she watched the cake actually being lifted down. "I'm not saying she won't fight her way to the wedding after all—you watch that cake, Howard! Do you know what'll happen to you if you drop that?"

"Yes, ma'am. *Dis* cake not goin' drop—no'm."

"That's what you *say*. You have to *carry* it straight up, too."

"Little Uncle, you kind of go *under*—like that. Spread your arms out like a bird—now. That's grand, Little Uncle."

"I'm a wreck," said Shelley. "I'm glad Dabney's not here watching. Oh, Croesus, I wish old Troy Flavin would just *quit wanting* to marry Dabney!"

"Don't frown like that, you'll hurt your looks, Shelley. A fine time now, for Troy Flavin to do a thing like that," said Aunt Tempe. "You all set the cake where it's going to *go*, on the middle of the dining-room table. We'll just have to eat like scaries all day and not do any shaking or stamping."

"Can you all tell the middle of the table?" asked Ellen anxiously as the cake went in the door. "You run in, India, and show them with your finger, right in the center of that lace rose that's the middle of Mashula's cloth. This was certainly nice of you, Mr. Treat. Run lightly, India, don't shake the house, from now on."

George, coming downstairs, held still with his eye on the cake—it was crossing the hall. Howard, Vi'let, and Little Uncle with the cake coming in were meeting Bitsy and some of the field Negroes, Juju and Zell, carrying a long side-table out.

"No collisions, I tell you!" cried Tempe, at the heels of the cake party.

"You've got to find a level place in the yard to set that down now, Bitsy," said Ellen, in the voice of one who is not sure there are any level places in the Delta.

"Yes, ma'am! Dis table goin' to go down in a *level* place."

"Where's Robbie, Georgie?"

"She's still asleep," said George, running down and kissing them. "All of you look beside yourselves!"

"I think Robbie's going to sleep the day away! Like Dabney."

"That's *all right*, she was good and tired," said Ellen.

"Well! It looks like she could show some interest. After all, there's a wedding in the house!" Tempe said.

George grinned and snapping off a Michaelmas daisy from her armful handed it to her.

"Where's my pipe, girls?" he said.

Bluet went in and woke up Dabney, carrying her coffee, with her sisters watching in the door. "Wake up, Dabney, it's your wedding day," she said carefully.

"Oh!" Dabney sat bolt upright. She seized the cup and drank off the coffee. Then she fell back, pulling Bluet up in the bed with her. She pressed the little girl to her.

"Precious! Precious!"

They all laughed and came in, and saw that she got up. They brought her down to the table and made her eat her breakfast. They all sat down around her wedding cake.

"It didn't break?" smiled Dabney, giving it a bright glance as she ate a plum. She and Shelley looked at each other, their kimono sleeves, pink and blue, fluttering together in the morning wind.

"Oh!" exclaimed Tempe, rising from her breakfast and running to the window. "Lady Clare's out there talking to a mad dog!" She turned to George—and time was when he would have dashed out of the house to hear that, but not now. He smiled absently and ate a bite of his mackerel. Pattering out the door, Tempe sighed. She ran through the sun as she would run through a pounding rain, and took hold of Lady Clare, who was in her nightgown and all spots.

"Don't you know strange dogs may be mad dogs?" she said, running in with her. "Probably *are* mad dogs.

I fully expected something to happen to you, Lady Clare. A time like this and a house like this—!"

The strange dog—mad or not, Lady Clare would never know—looked after their retreat and trotted off to the bayou bank.

"How do I look, Aunt Ellen?" cried Laura, running into the parlor, where Ellen was getting the smilax hung. Mary Lamar, in a yellow kimono, was kneeling over the stool running her hands over the piano keys. Laura had on Lady Clare's flower-girl dress, without the petticoat. "Shelley's trying it on!"

"Mercy, I see your knees. But Primrose can let out the hem for you in two shakes of a lamb's tail when she ever gets here."

"Do I look like the flower girl?" asked Laura. "Shelley wants to know."

"Mama, will she do?" called Shelley's voice from the upper regions. This was the callingest house! thought Laura anxiously.

"You couldn't look *more* like one," Ellen said, and held her tight. "You'll have to put a little of Dabney's or Shelley's face powder over those old bites—where have you been?—and let somebody turn your hair over their finger, and you'll be splendid. Run back and tell Shelley to get the dress off you quick now. Would you like your hair up on old rags all day?"

"Oh, Aunt Ellen!"

"All right, I'll tie you up myself. I wish you'd prevail on India to wear curls just for tonight. She won't let anybody touch her."

"Mama used to curl my hair in curls," said Laura

shyly. "Mary Lamar—what are you playing?" and she walked near the music, spreading her dress.

"It's not always anything," said Mary Lamar in a soft voice. "I'm improvising."

Up close, beautiful Mary Lamar's arm showed great covering freckles below the chiffon sleeve, her arms were leopard-like!

"Well, Pinchy," said Dabney, frowning.

There stood Pinchy in the dining room, swatting an old September fly. For a few days a creature of mystery, now that she had come through she was gawking and giggling like the rest.

"You swat every fly, Pinchy. That's what you're for, now, this whole day," she said sternly.

"I'll git 'em," said Pinchy.

On the back porch, surrounded by fireless-cooker pots and cake pans of cut flowers, Shelley and Dabney were making shiny bows. Battle wandered out.

"What are those made of, now?"

"Material," said Dabney.

Nobody else seemed to be around, except Ranny, who sat on the back steps motionless, looking at his father over a bright beard of what seemed also to be material.

"Well, Dabney, little girl, I wanted to confer my blessing, my paternal blessing," Battle said rather heartily.

"Two princess baskets of pink and white Maman Cochet roses, Miss Tessie at the icehouse sent up, Dabney," said Ellen, carrying them onto the porch. "She sent them over by *twins*."

"Then it was every one she had," called Tempe's voice

from within. Her brother looked in the direction of her voice as if in a moment he would comprehend Tempe.

"Who sent these real late Cape jessamines—Miss Parnell Dortch?" Shelley leaned over and buried her face in them while Vi'let held them out.

"Yes, Miss Parnell." Ellen whispered, "I don't know what we'll do with old Roxie's nasturtiums—little bitty short stems, look, they don't even peep over that shoe box. But it was every nasturtium Roxie had—she *loves Dabney.*"

"We can float them in an old card tray. She'll be looking for them at the wedding," Shelley said.

"She used to let me pick them, nasty-turtiums," said Dabney idly. "I'd pick them and eat them all the way from the stems up, when I was little."

"Then you can eat these," said Ellen with a little laugh. She leaned on the door.

"Come here and let me kiss you, puddin'," Battle said.

But, "Look at Miss Bonnie Hitchcock's *fern,*" groaned Shelley.

Four little colored boys holding a tub balanced on the handle of a broom staggered up the back path. Tub, boys, and all were in the shade and glow of an enormous fern that tilted its weight over them and fluttered its fronds in every direction like a tree in a gale.

"Mama! She sent that up for Aunt Annie Laurie's funeral!" Dabney said in an awe-struck voice.

"We almost never got it back to her after *that,*" Shelley said doubtfully. "Or did we?"

"I don't want it where it was before," said Dabney.

"Dabney!" Battle said. "Come kiss me."

"It can go behind Jim Allen and India serving punch," said Ellen. "It will go fine there. It won't do anything but hide the china closet. If we could put it by the outdoor table! But that would hurt Miss Bonnie's feelings—it will have to come in the house."

"Mama, I think it's so tacky the way Troy comes in from the side door," said Shelley all at once. "It's like somebody just walks in the house from the fields and marries Dabney."

"You're sure you wouldn't rather have a trip to Europe than get married?" Battle remarked into the air off the porch. "Ranny, will you take off that beard, or stop looking at me?"

Dabney ran to her father, the shiny material in hand, and laughed as his whispering lips tickled the nape of her neck. "Or go back to college?" he said.

"Horrors, Papa," she said.

"You don't have but one silver champagne bucket, I know that," said Tempe, stepping out dramatically from the kitchen. "Why didn't I think to bring you mine? It would have been no trouble in the world. Mercy!" she spoke to the fern, which was at the door.

"It's grown, Mama!" said Dabney, leaning back as the fern went by, vibrating and seemingly under its own power, up the steps and across the back porch. Battle pinned her backwards against him and kissed the crown of her head.

"Well, one thing," said Tempe in a low voice to Shelley, looking after the fern with a sigh of finality, "when people marry beneath them, it's the woman that determines what comes. It's the woman that coarsens the man. The man doesn't really do much to the woman, I've observed."

"You mean Troy's not as bad for us as Robbie," whispered Shelley intently.

"Exactly!"

"Don't stop, don't stop! This way!" Ellen hurried ahead of the fern and led it into the house.

"The crooks have come, the crooks have come!" cried Orrin, racing in. "Dabney, I brought your crooks! Watch!" He reached in Little Uncle's arms as Little Uncle ran up with yellow sticks everywhere, and began throwing them in the air like a juggler. All the children ran picking them up—each got one.

"Orrin!"

"I was watching for the Dog! I saw them take everything off, and I wanted to bring you the crooks ahead of everything, Dabney! Only I went in swimming a minute—I was on Junie—"

"Oh, Orrin! Oh, I hate to go off and leave you and everybody!" Dabney kissed his smiling lips, and he untied her sash behind her.

"Give me one," she said, looking at the running children. "Ranny, I want that one."

"What's that old Bojo brought on the mule?" asked Ellen.

"Aunt Primrose's cheese straws," said Shelley, rushing to lift the lid of the corset box. "From the secret recipe!"

"I just have to have *one*," said Aunt Tempe, putting in her hand. "Excuse me, you all."

Dabney took the box, laughing, and ran to the kitchen.

Aunt Studney was in the kitchen taking a little coffee. Howard's little boy, Pleas, who was on the back porch twisting smilax on the altar, came stealing in behind Roxie and tried to look in Aunt Studney's sack. But Aunt Studney was up with a kettle off the stove and like lightning poured it over him, making him yell and run off as if the devil had him.

"Why, Aunt Studney," said Dabney. "I wanted to invite you to my wedding!"

"Ain't studyin' you," said Aunt Studney. She lifted her coffee cup in her quick, horny hand that was bright pink inside, and drank. Then she was gone with her sack.

Primrose and Jim Allen came up to Shellmound only in time to sit down to dinner, to Battle's teasing. And as it turned out, Primrose was making the chicken salad (which Roxie had luckily cut up for her), Ellen baking the beaten biscuit with Robbie (swallowed in a Fairchild apron) watching the pans, Tempe rolling out her cornucopias, and Roxie and Pinchy squeezing the fruit for the punch all in the kitchen together. Jim Allen had spent the morning making green and white mints, which they all declared were better than the Memphis mints, so she lay down and dozed a little on a bed.

"Mr. Horace," Vi'let said, coming through the shade in the yard with more napkins dry enough to iron, "you standin' up pretty good." All Horace had to do was wash cars and shine them, and get his flashlight ready for tonight, make sure it would burn. Preacher, the Grove chauffeur, who thought yesterday he had better not try to carry so much as a paper lantern in his old age, never do anything except drive an electric automobile, felt younger today and said he would be glad to fish seeds out of cook's juice, give him a spoon. Some wagons loaded with planks came up in the yard and Howard was told to fix a dancing place as he saw fit, but hurry! out of an old landing Mr. Battle was sending up from the river. "Mr. Battle sure love doin' things at las' minute, don't he, Miss Ellen?" laughed Howard from the top of his ladder, making it sound attractive, even irresistible of Mr. Battle.

"Don't you fall off that ladder, Howard, before you come down and nail those planks! Dancing on the platform's what the lanterns are *for.*"

"No'm, I ain't goin' fall off *dis* ladder. Dance, yes, ma'am!"

Laura heard behind the bathroom door sounds of great splashing, and in between the splashes Dabney's voice, talking to Bluet.

"Now, Bluet, you mustn't ever brag."

"What's brag?"

Splash, splash.

"And, Bluet, you mustn't ever tell a lie."

"What's tell a lie?"

Splash, splash.

Laura banged on the door. "Let me in! I have to get ready too!"

They let her in. There were all the girls—tall Shelley too, naked and splashing. And they had Ranny, so little and sweet still. There was water everywhere, even dotting the fireplace like beads on a forehead. Bluet was in the center of the big pedestaled bathtub and they were squeezing washrags over her and putting soap on her hands, which she stuck forward for them. Bluet, her long hair pinned up in a topknot, was very serious today, at the same time slithering like a fish.

"And, Bluet," said Laura comfortably, "you mustn't ever steal."

"Don't *you* tell me," said Bluet gently, "just Dabney," and they all dashed her with water.

Finally, people began to come out in the halls or downstairs dressed. "Orrin! You look like a man!" cried Ellen. "Oh, the idea!"

"Mr. Ranny growin' up too, in case nobody know it," said Roxie. "Miss Ellen, did you know? That little booger every mornin' befo' six o'clock holler out de window fo' me. 'Roxie! I need my coffee!' and make me come right up."

"The idea!" said Ellen.

When the clock struck for seven, Laura in the flower-girl dress brought the pipe out of the hat and stood in the decorated hall with it until she saw George come through there. She followed him and confronted him at the water cooler on the back porch. Lizards were frolicking and scratching on the wire outside, being gazed at from inside by the old cat Beverley. Nobody else was around.

Bringing it slowly from behind her sash, she gave the pipe to him very slowly, inching it out to him to make the giving longer. At first he did not seem even to understand that he could take it, for she was so ceremonious.

"I wanted to give you a present you really wanted to get, so I kept it away from you a while," explained Laura. He bent his handsome head. He listened to her closely—that was the way Uncle George always listened, as if everyone might tell him something like this. "I wanted to surprise you," she said.

"Yes, honey." He kissed her right between the eyes. He took the pipe. "Thank you," he said. "You're growing up to be a real little Fairchild before you know it."

She was filled with happiness. "Is there any other thing I could give you after this, for a present?" she asked finally.

Instead of saying "No" he said gently, "Thanks, I'll let you know, Laura."

More happiness struck her like a shower of rain. She looked at him dazzled. "Tonight?"

"It might be later," he said. He pulled her hair a little then, her curls. When she waited shyly, he put the pipe in his mouth, lighted it, puffed out a strong cloud, and nodded his head at her to show her the pipe was nice to get back.

Then they both had a drink of water out of the spigot, he drinking from the tarnishy cup, she from the ridgy glass.

"Why is smoke coming out of the hall chimney?" asked India, walking in at the side door. She had been trying out her shepherdess crook.

"Smoke?"

In the hall Roy in his everyday clothes lay on the floor painting with Laura Allen's watercolors. Six or eight pictures—he finished them rapidly—were laid around the stove where his fire dried them as quickly as possible, though the heat did curl the older ones up tight.

"Roy!" cried Dabney in tears. "I'm going to get married in this house in fifteen minutes. Everybody will perish from the heat!"

"It was already as hot as it could be," said Roy. "This fire feels cool to me."

"Do you want your papa to stop Dabney's wedding to give you a switching?" asked Ellen. "I thought you were all in your white suit."

"I'll be there when you look for me," said Roy agreeably.

"Then run!"

"I thought you loved me," said Dabney. She and Shelley and Mary Lamar were all three in tears.

"Shelley, hush crying, who'll be next?" said Ellen, and Bluet came up and cried loudly.

"My God, girls!" shouted Battle, taking a step sideways. "Stop your tears! Can't raise you, can't even marry you, without the shillelagh all over the place."

"What is the picture of, Roy?" asked India in practical tones.

"Lady Clare being hanged by the pirates. That's her tongue sticking out."

"Well, now, it's through, then," said Ellen. "Run! Make Orrin part your hair. It's the first time he's ever wanted to use the paints, as far as I know, Battle."

II

The bridesmaids came all of a company and flew upstairs to Shelley's room to get into their bridesmaid dresses, with Vi'let and Pinchy to put them over their heads, hot from the iron. "Ever'body git a crook," said Little Uncle, mincing it over and over, where they gathered in the upstairs hall. "Got you a crook, missy? Here a pretty one for you," as if shepherdess crooks were the logical overflow from Fairchild bounty. Old Partheny had come up just at the time she pleased, the time for Dabney to be putting on her wedding dress and be ready to stamp her foot at the way it did, and now appeared at the head of the back stairs clothed from top to bottom in purple. She went straight and speaking to nobody to Dabney's closed door and flung it open. "Git yourself here to me, child. Who dressin' you? Git out, Nothin'," and Roxie, Shelley, and Aunt Primrose all came backing out. The door slammed.

Downstairs, with all the boys in white suits gallantly running about, the family gathering in the parlor around Ellen and Battle greeted the arriving families of the wedding party and too-early arrivers for the reception from the more distant plantations. Aunt Mac and Aunt Shannon came in on Orrin's arm, one at a time. Aunt Mac wore her corsage of red roses and ferns on the shoulder opposite the side with her watch, so she could keep up with things. Aunt Shannon proceeded uncertainly and yet with pride, her little feet in their comfort slippers planted wide apart, as a year-old child walks, her hot little hand digging into Orrin's arm. White sweet peas were what Aunt Shannon wore, and she liked them.

"It's time we were sitting down, now, as many as can," said Ellen, and all at once sank, herself, into one of the straight chairs before the altar.

All the windows were full of black faces, but the family servants stood in a ring inside the parlor walls. Pinchy stole in, all in white, and she looked wild and subdued together now in that snowiness with her blue-black. Maureen went up to her and gave her a red rose from her basket, not being, as a flower girl, able to wait. Partheny stood at the front of all the Negroes, where the circle had its joining, making the circle a heart. Her head was high and purple, she was thistlelike there, and perhaps considered herself of all the Negroes the head and fount. Man-Son, Sylvanus, Juju, more than that were all in the hall, spellbound and shushing one another. Aunt Studney, wherever she was, was keeping out of sight.

Uncle Pinck, who was laughing at something, hushed suddenly, Mr. Rondo had taken his place, and music began. The groomsmen entered, and then people leaned backwards from the doorway, so that everybody could see what came down the stairs. In twos the bridesmaids began coming, they entered and arranged themselves in front of the boys, fanning out from Howard's altar, deep to pale, dark to light in their pairs, fading out to Shelley, who entered trembling and with excruciating slowness, her sleeves aquiver. Their crooks they held seriously in front of them in their right hands, each crook crowned with Memphis flowers tied on with streamers. India came in, throwing petals, and Maureen, then Laura came in down the little path between people where she was supposed to walk; at last she was out before everybody, one of the wedding party, dressed up like the rest in an identical flower-girl dress, and she scattered rose petals just as quickly as India, just as far as Maureen. Did it show, that her mother had died only in January? Mary Lamar, in place at the piano, played in that soft, almost surreptitious fashion of players of wedding music.

It was Shelley that Ellen was watching anxiously. Ever since Dabney had announced that she would marry Troy, Shelley had been practicing, rather consciously, a kind of ragamuffinism. Or else she drew up, like an old maid. What could be so wrong in everything, to her sensitive and delicate mind? There was something not quite *warm* about Shelley, her first child. Could it have been in some way her fault? Ellen watched her anxiously, almost tensely, as if she might not get through the wedding very well. Primrose was whispering in Ellen's ear. Shelley would not hold her shepherdess crook right—it should be straight in line with all the other girls' crooks—look how her bouquet leaned over. Like a sleepy head, Ellen thought rather dreamily in her anxiety.

"Crook like the others, dear," whispered Primrose from her front chair. She made a quick coaxing motion with her little lacy mits (she had indulged herself with a pair just like the bridesmaids').

Shelley, with a face of contrition, held her shepherdess crook like the others. Aunt Primrose had such an abundance of small, hopeful anxieties—the mere little ferns and flowers of the forest she had never guessed could be! Shelley was glad to hold her crook right.

Troy came in from the side door, indeed like somebody walking in from the fields to marry Dabney. His hair flamed. Had no one thought that American Beauty would clash with that carrot hair? Had no one thought of that? Jim Allen blinked her sensitive eyes.

Robbie looked up at George, who had entered with Troy and stood up beside him, listening and agaze at his family. In the confusion she had been seated a little toward the back. There was no one looking at him—except a bridesmaid to primp for a moment, push at a curl, or long-legged Laura that smiled—there was no one seeing him but herself. George was not the one they all looked at, she thought in that moment, as he was always declared to be, but the eye that saw them, from right in their midst. He was sensitive to all they asked of life itself. Long ago they had seized on that. He was to be all in one their lover and protector and dreaming, forgetful conscience. From Aunt Shannon on down, he was to be always looking through them as well as to the left and right of them, before them and behind them, watching out for and loving their weaknesses. If anything tried to happen to them, let it happen to him! He took that part, but it was the way he was made, too, to be like that.

But there was something a little further, that no one could know except her. There was enough sweetness in him to make him cherish the whole world, but in himself there had been no forfeiture. Not yet. He had not yielded up to that family what they really wanted! Or they would not keep after him. But where she herself had expected light, all was still dark too.

He wanted her so blindly—just to hold. Often Robbie was back at the time where she had first held out her arms, back when he came in the store, home from the war, a lonely man that noticed wildflowers. She could not see why he needed to be so desperate! She loved him.

But he turned his head a little now and glanced at her with that suddenness—curiosity, not quite hope—that tore her heart, like a stranger inside some house where he wanted to make sure that she too had come, had really come.

It was all right with her, she wanted him to look at her and see that. She was rising a little on her chair as if she would stand up, while the music swelled—looking over Aunt Tempe's hothouse corsage and meeting the dark look. Somehow it was all right, every minute that they were in the one place.

There was a groan from upstairs, as at a signal given perhaps by Mary Lamar's rising music, and Battle, his skin, too, fiery red against his white clothes, brought Dabney down and entered with her on his arm.

In the early morning, climbing out of bed, Dabney had looked out her windows, walked around her room; at her door she had looked out and down the sleeping hall, out through the little balcony under its ancient awning. There were soft beats in the air, which she dreamily identified as her father's sleeping snorts. The sun, a red ball down East Field, sat on the horizon. Faint bands of mist, in the fading colors of the bridesmaids' dresses, rose to the dome of clear sky. And that's me, she had thought, pleased—that little white cloud. She had got back in bed and gone back to sleep. And she felt she had not yet waked up. Though Partheny had just come up to her and seemed to shake at everybody and everything in her room, wild old nurse—the way a big spider can shake a web to get a little straw out, seeming to summon up all the anger in the world to keep the lure of the web intact.

"Never more beautiful!" whispered Primrose.

That is what will always be said about a bride, thought Tempe, suddenly agitating her fan. And they all look dead, to my very observant eye, or like rag dolls—poor things! Dabney is no more herself than any of them.

Ellen looked at Battle as he sat down beside her, and took his hand.

Ranny in his white satin walked in on some kind of

artificial momentum, bearing the ring on the pillow, never looking behind him though everyone was murmuring "Sweet!"

Then the women put their handkerchiefs to their eyes. Mr. Rondo married Dabney and Troy.

III

"Nobody from Virginia came, eh, Ellen?" asked somebody—Dr. Murdoch.

"Not this time," said Ellen, blushing somewhat. A piece of the family sat about in the dining room, more guests had poured in and been greeted and now stood eating food or carrying it out, or danced all over the downstairs, or sat in every chair in the house and halfway up the stair steps. Little Uncle, with a retinue, carried the tray that was bigger than he was, taking champagne around. The fans blew the candles. The children ran outdoors, chasing each other around the house, those that should be in bed wild with the rest.

"Tell about when your mama came!" Was that Orrin or Battle?

"The idea!"

She saw Mr. Rondo seat himself in their little group—and it was so hot for a preacher, too, poor man; he looked so resigned, yet cheerful.

"Mama!" said Ellen softly. "I've been thinking of her tonight. —Well, I was fixing to have Shelley, and Mama was alive. Mama came down from Virginia to stay with me. We were living at the Grove. So Mama was up when I called her, it was before day, and sent and got Dr.

Murdoch. The Fairchilds turned out to be late getting there, or couldn't come—Aunt Mac was sick and Aunt Shannon, who was the busiest woman in the world then, had to be waiting on her hand and foot, and Primrose and Jim Allen were still out at a dance."

"But already it wasn't doing them a smidgen of good, Tempe had cut them out," Battle said, tweaking Tempe's little diamond-set ear. He loved her absurdity and would fish it out of any story even if she wasn't in it.

"Dr. Murdoch," said Ellen, her voice a little livelier as she went, "was a young man starting out and he brought a brand-new gas machine with him in his buggy and had a little Negro specially to carry it in the house and then wait for it on the doorstep. As soon as he got here he just sneered at me, the way he would now, and said fiddle, I had all the time in the world and he was going to go and we could call him when I was good and ready. But Mama thought that was so ugly of him, and it was, Dr. Murdoch!—and she said, 'Don't you fret, Ellen, I'll cook him such a fine breakfast he wouldn't dare go.'

"Mama was from Virginia, so sure enough, she cooked him everything in the creation from batter bread on. She might even have had shad roe except I don't know where she would have found it. Dr. Murdoch sat down and ate like a king, all right, but he, or Mama one, forgot how early in the morning it was for all that. Poor Dr. Murdoch got the worst off he ever got in his life, I imagine, on that Virginia breakfast, and then of course he had to lie down and groan and feel sorry for himself, and the only bed he could get to with Mama helping him was mine, downstairs—Mama couldn't drag him all the way upstairs by his feet! She put him down by me. So I began to poke his side presently, to attract his attention.

"I poked his side and he just groaned. Finally he popped his eyes open and looked at me from the other pillow and said, 'Madam,' meaning Mama, 'will you please do such and such and kindly stoop over the gas machine and see if it is in order.' And Mama did what he said and took one breath and fell down in a heap.

"So Dr. Murdoch used some profane words, he thought Mama was snooty anyway toward the Delta, and he got up—he could have done it in the first place. He pulled Mama up and he put her on my bed. She opened her eyes and said, 'Is my baby born yet?'—like you were hers, Shelley.

"So Dr. Murdoch went over and he fiddled with the gas machine and he bent over and took a testing breath and he fell over. Mama just was not able to pick him up a second time, so we just let him alone, and I asked Mama to leave the room, I was shy before her, and I had the baby by myself—the cook came and she knew everything necessary—Partheny it was."

"Papa, where were you?" asked India, leaning on Mr. Rondo.

"Greenwood! And you hush, you weren't born yet."

"Aunt Shannon got there and was deviling Dr. Murdoch—oh, her positive manner then!—for being nothing but a green Delta doctor that couldn't even tend himself, and Mama was snooting Aunt Shannon—snooting things clear back to Port Gibson—!"

They laughed till the tears stood in their eyes at the foolishness, the long-vanquished pain, the absurd prostrations, the birth that wouldn't wait, and the flouting of all in the end. All so handsomely ridiculed by the delightful now! They especially loved the way it made a fool of Dr. Murdoch, who was right there, and Ellen, her eyes bright from the story, felt a pleasure in that shameless enough to make her catch her breath. Dr. Murdoch looked straight back at her as always, as if he counted her bones. She laughed again, pressing Battle's hand.

"Mama, don't tell how much I weighed," Shelley begged, darting in and darting out of their circle.

"You weighed ten pounds," said Ellen helplessly, for that was the end of the story.

The laughter focused on Shelley, and she fled from the room, almost upsetting the aunts.

"One little glass of champagne and I don't know bee from bumble!" cried Aunt Primrose. "And neither do you, Jim Allen!" India sprang up between them and joining hands swung the ladies off. Dr. Murdoch, smiling handsomely, merged with the champagne drinkers over in the fern corner, where Uncle Pinck welcomed him by raising his glass.

"Well—it's over, the wedding's over. . . . Did you hear how old Rondo threw in his prayer, 'Lord, I know not many people in the Delta love thee'?" Battle said, stretching himself up and then slapping Mr. Rondo's back as if he were congratulating him.

"Cut the cake! Cut the cake! Cut the cake!" cried Ranny, running through.

"I'm tired of the cake! All day long in front of us!" glowered Roy. "Cut it and get it over."

Dabney was brought in and given the knife, and she

cut the first slice. Then the bridesmaids and all rushed to cut after her. "I'm cutting the ring!" India cried, and sure enough, she did. "I'm the next!"

"Here comes the picture taker, Aunt Tempe!" For Tempe had said she had taken the liberty of giving permission to the Memphis paper to send down. Now she said "Mercy!" and clutched her hair. "Oh, we're all flying loose."

Battle wanted the photograph taken of the whole family, not of simply the bride and groom. Taking absolute charge he grouped his sons and daughters around him the way he wanted them. "Get in here, Ellen!" he roared through the room.

They posed, generally smiling. "Say cheese," Aunt Primrose reminded them, and said it herself.

"Now we're all still!" cried Battle. "I'm still!"

"Domesticated." People still pointed at Battle Fairchild after twenty years of married life, as if he were a new wonder. Ellen stood modestly beside him, holding some slightly wilted bridesmaids' flowers in front of her skirt. She herself, it occurred to Ellen as she stood frowning at the hooded man with his gadget, was an anomaly too, though no one would point at a lady for the things that made her one—for providing the tremendous meals she had no talent for, being herself indifferent to food, and had had to learn with burned hands to give the household orders about—or for living on a plantation when she was in her original heart, she believed, a town-loving, book-loving young lady of Mitchem Corners. She had belonged to a little choral society of unmarried girls there that she loved. Mendelssohn floated for a moment through the confused air like a veil upborne, and she could have sung it, "I Would that My Love . . ."

The flashlight went off. Just as it did, Ranny saluted.

"You all moved," announced the photographer, looking out from his black hood. "Try again! You know what's in my satchel?" He patted it until they all attended. "Train victim. I got a girl killed on the I.C. railroad. My train did it. Ladies, she was flung off in the blackberry bushes. Looked to me like she was walking up the track to Memphis and met Number 3."

"Change the subject," commanded Aunt Tempe, who was the right-end figure of the group.

"Yes, ma'am. Another picture of the same pose, except the little gentleman that saluted. Everybody looking at the bride and groom."

"I'm holding it!" Battle cried, and the light flashed for the picture.

Ellen looked at the bride and groom, but if the first picture showed her a Mitchem Corners choral singer, then the second showed her seeing a vision of fate; surely it was the young girl of the bayou woods that was the victim this man had seen. Then Battle was giving her a kiss. George and Robbie danced off, the group broke, and more and more people were arriving at the house. They had better be standing at the door.

Everybody for miles around came to the reception. Troy said he did not know there could be so many people in the whole Delta; it *looked* like it was cotton all the way. The mayor of Fairchilds and his wife were driven up with the lights on inside their car, and they could be seen lighted up inside reading the Memphis paper (which never quite unrolled when you read it); in the bud vases on the little walls beside them were real red roses, vibrating, and the chauffeur's silk cap filled with air like a balloon when they drove over the cattle guard. Shelley's heart pounded as she smiled; indeed this was a grand occasion for everybody, their wedding was really eventful. . . . Lady Clare came down once—pitiful indeed, her spots all painted over with something, and for some reason clad in a nightgown with a long tear. "I'm exposing you! I'm exposing you all!" cried Lady Clare fiercely, but was rushed back upstairs. More champagne was opened, buffet was carried out, and all started being served under the trees.

Then Dabney changed from her wedding gown to a going-away dress and the new Pierce-Arrow was brought up to the door. Dabney began kissing the family and the bridesmaids all around; she ran up and kissed Lady Clare. When she kissed Aunt Shannon, the old lady said, "Now who do you think you are?"

A brown thrush in a tree still singing could be heard through all the wild commotion, as Dabney and Troy drove away, scattering the little shells of the road. Ellen waved her handkerchief, and all the aunts lifted theirs and waved. Shelley began to cry, and Ranny ran down the road after the car and followed it as long as it was in hearing, like a little puppy. Unlike the mayor's car that had come up alight like a boat in the night, it went away dark. The full moon had risen.

IV

Then the party nearly all moved outdoors, where the lanterns burned in the trees. "I hear the music coming," said Laura, coming up and taking Ellen around the knees for a moment. The band came playing—"Who?" coming out over the dark and brightening fields above the sound of their rackety car—a little river band, all very black Negroes in white coats, who were banjo, guitar, bass fiddle, trumpet, and drum—and of course saxophone, that was the owner. Horace flagged them down with his flashlight. Howard showed them their chairs which he had fixed by the dance platform like a place for a select audience to come and watch a performance of glory. The dancing began.

At midnight, Shelley came in by herself for a drink of cool water. On the back porch the moths spread upon the screens, the hard beetles knocked upon the radius of light like an adamant door. She drank still swaying a little to the distant music. "Whispering" turned into "Linger Awhile."

Only that morning, working at the wedding flowers with Dabney, she had thought to herself, hypnotically, as though she read it in her diary, Why do you look out thinking nothing will happen any more? Why are you thinking your line of trees the indelible thing in the world? There's the long journey you're going on, with Aunt Tempe, leading out . . . and you can't see it now. Even closing your eyes, you see only the line of trees at Shellmound. Is it the world? If Shellmound were a little bigger, it would be the same as the world entirely. . . . Perhaps that was the real truth. But she had been dancing with George, with his firm, though (she was certain) reeling body so gaily leading her, so solicitously whirling her round. "Bridesmaid," he called her. "Bridesmaid, will you dance?" She felt it in his cavorting body—though she danced seriously, always moved seriously—that he went even among the dancers with some vision of choice. Life lay ahead, he might do anything. . . . She followed, she herself had a vision of choice, or its premonition, for she was much like George. They played "Sleepy Time Gal," turning it into "Whispering." Only the things had not happened to her yet. They would happen. Indeed, she might not be happy either, wholly, and she would live in waiting, sometimes in terror. But Dabney's marriage, ceasing to shock, was like a door closing to her now. Entering into a life with Troy Flavin seemed to avow a remote, an unreal world—it came nearest to being real for Shelley only in the shock, the challenge to pride. It shut a door in their faces. Behind the closed door, what? Shelley's desire fled, or danced seriously, to an open place—not from one room to another room with its door, but to an opening wood, with weather—with change, beauty . . .

There was a scratch at the back door, and Shelley unlatched it. Her old cat, Beverley of Graustark, came in. He had been hunting; he brought in a mole and laid it at her feet.

In the music room, with some of the lingering guests there, Tempe and Primrose sang two-part songs of their girlhood, arch, full of questions and answers—and Tempe was in tears of merriment at the foolishness she had lived down. Primrose with each song remembered the gestures—of astonishment, cajolery—and Tempe could remember them the next instant. The sisters sang beckoning and withdrawing like two little fat mandarins, their soft voices in gentle, yielding harmony still. But soon Tempe, who had only come inside looking for her fan, was back where the dancing was.

Ellen strolled under the trees, with Battle somewhere

near, looking among the dancers for her daughters. The lanterns did not so much shine on the dancers as light up the mistletoe in the trees. She peered ahead with a kind of vertigo. It was the year—wasn't it every year?—when they all looked alike, all dancers alike smooth and shorn, all faces painted to look like one another. It was too the season of changeless weather, of the changeless world, in a land without hill or valley. How could she ever know anything of her own daughters, how find them, like this? Then in a turn of her little daughter India's skirt as she ran partnerless through the crowd—so late!—as if a bar of light had broken a glass into a rainbow she saw the dancers become the McLeoud bridesmaid, Mary Lamar Mackey (freed from her piano and whirling the widest of all), become Robbie, and her own daughter Shelley, each different face bright and burning as sparks of fire to her now, more different and further apart than the stars.

She saw George among the dancers, walking through, looking for somebody too. Suddenly she wished that she might talk to George. It was the wrong time—she never actually had time to sit down and fill her eyes with people and hear what they said, in any civilized way. Now he was dancing, even a little drunk, she believed—this was a time for celebration, or regret, not for talk, not ever for talk.

As he looked in her direction, all at once she saw into his mind as if he had come dancing out of it leaving it unlocked, laughingly inviting her to the unexpected intimacy. She saw his mind—as if it too were inversely lighted up by the failing paper lanterns—lucid and tortuous: so that any act on his part might be startling, isolated in its very subtlety from the action of all those around him, springing from long, dark, previous, abstract thought and direct apprehension, instead of explainable, Fairchild impulse. It was *inevitable* that George, with this mind, should stand on the trestle—on the track where people could indeed be killed, thrown with their beauty disfigured before strangers into the blackberry bushes. He was capable—taking no more prerogative than a kind of grace, no more than an ordinary responsibility—of meeting a fate whose dealing out to him he would not contest; even when to people he loved his act was "conceited," if not absurd, if not just a little story in the family. And she saw how it followed, the darker instinct of a woman was satisfied that he was capable of the same kind of love. Indeed, there danced Robbie, the proof of this. To all their eyes shallow, unworthy, she was his love; it was her ordinary face that was looking at him through the lovely and magic veil, little Robbie Reid's from the store.

George made his way through the dancers now, sometimes caught up by one, sometimes not. She thought that everything he did meant something. Not that it was symbolic—with all her young-girl's love of symbols she could scorn them for their meagerness and her fallible grasp—everything he did meant something to him, it had weight. That seemed very rare! Everything he lost meant something. . . . Of course . . . She did not need to know each little thing about him any more—to be a mother to him any more. She recognized him as far from kin to her, scarcely tolerant of her understanding, never dependent on hers or anyone's, or on compassion (how merciless that could be!). He appeared, as he made his way alone now and smiling through the dancing couples, infinitely simple and infinitely complex, stretching the opposite ways the self stretches and the selves of the ones we love (except our children) may stretch; but at the same time he appeared very finite in that he was wholly singular and dear, and not promisingly married, tired of being a lawyer, a smiling, intoxicated, tender, weather-worn, late-tired, beard-showing being. He came forward through a crowd and anybody's hand might beckon or reach after him. He had, and he gave, the golden acquiescence which Dabney the bride had in the present moment—which Ranny had. "Are you happy, Dabney?" Battle had kept asking her over and over. How strange! Passionate, sensitive, to the point of strain and secrecy, their legend was *happiness*. "The Fairchilds are the happiest people!" They themselves repeated it to each other. She could hear the words best in Primrose's gentle, persuading voice, talking to Battle or George or one of her little boys.

"Will you dance this with me, Ellen?" George asked.

"Don't you dare, Ellen," said Battle. "Do you want to kill yourself?"

Clumsily, with care, she put up her arms and took hold of his. She pressed his arms tenderly a moment, as if she could express it, that he had not been harmed after all and had been ready for anything all the time. She loved what was pure at its heart, better than what was understood, or even misjudged, or afterwards forgiven; this was the dearest thing.

"I would always dance with you as quick as anything," she told him. She felt lucky—cherished, and somehow *pretty* (which she knew she never was). There were some people who lived a lifetime without finding the one who relieved the heart's overflow. She bore a little heavily on George's arm. She would not know in her life, or ask, whether he had found the one. She was his friend and loved him. But starting new, she thought as the waltz played and they moved by a tree where a golden lantern hung, and without one regret for her life with Battle, she might have been the one. There was the mistletoe in the tree. It was like a tree, too—a tree within a tree.

"You're tired," he said.

"No, not tired, I haven't danced in a long time, I guess, and when now again?"

They danced, the music progressed, changed, and slowed. It was "Should Auld Acquaintance Be Forgot"—it was good night.

7

Then they were waiting for Dabney and Troy to come back, and for George and Robbie to go, for Laura to go—three days.

The first morning, they were all beating their aching heads, Battle and George groaning out pitifully, waked up by Ranny and Bluet with the birds. Mary Denis telephoned from Inverness that Baby George had gained an ounce, and asked, did Dabney get off? Mary Lamar was driven home, the house was more or less silent, and Uncle Pinck sat meditating out all alone by the sundial.

Ellen in the morning cool walked in the yard in her old dress, her scissors on a ribbon around her neck, and one of the children's school gloves on in case she wanted to poke around or pull much.

"Howard! Start the water running out here. Let it run from the open hose, soak everything." She reached down and pulled up, light as down, a great scraggly petunia bush turned white every inch. In those few days, when she had forgotten to ask a soul to water things, how everything had given up, or hung its head. And that little old vine, that always wanted to take everything, had taken everything—she pulled at a long thread of it and unwound it from the pomegranate tree.

The camellia bushes had all set their buds, choosing the driest and busiest time, and if they did not get water they would surely drop them, temperamental as they were. The grass all silver now showed its white roots underfoot, and was laced with ant beds up and down and across. And in just those few days, she must warn Battle, some caterpillar nets had appeared on the pecan trees down in the grove—he would have to get those burnt out or they would take his trees. Toward the gate the little dogwoods she had had brought in out of the woods or saved, hung every heart-shaped leaf, she knew the little turrety buds were going brown, but they were beyond help that far from the house, they would have to get along the best they could waiting for rain; that was something she had learned. Dabney loved them, too.

A bumblebee with dragging polleny legs went smotheringly over the abelia bells, making a snoring sound. The old crape myrtle with its tiny late old bloom right at the top of the tree was already beginning to shed all its bark, its branches glowed silver-brown and amber, brighter than its green. Well, the cypresses in the bayou were touched with flame in their leaves, early to meet fall as they were early to meet spring and with the same wild color. The locust shells clung to the tree trunks, the birds were flying over every day now, and Roy said he heard them calling in the night.

And there was that same wonderful butterfly, yellow with black markings, that she had seen here yesterday. It was spending its whole life on this one abelia.

The elaeagnus had overnight, it seemed, put out shoots as long as a man. "Howard, bring your shears, too! Did this look this way for the wedding? It's a wonder Tempe didn't get after us for that."

The robins fed like chickens in the radius of the hose. A whole tree was suddenly full of warblers—strange small greedy birds from far away, that would be gone tomorrow. The Shellmound blue jays fussed at them furiously. Old Beverley opened his eyes, closed them again. A Dainty Bess that wanted to climb held a cluster of five blooms in the air. "I can't reach," Ellen remarked firmly. She needed to take up some things that would go in the pit for winter, she wanted to flower some bulbs too. When, when? And the spider lilies were taking everything.

Her chrysanthemums looked silver and ragged, their few flowers tarnished and all their lower leaves hanging down black, like scraggly pullets, and Howard would have to tie them up again too. "Howard, remind me to ask Mr. Battle for three or four loads of fertilizer *to-morrow.*" The dead iris foliage curled and floated wraith-like over everything. "Howard, you get the dead leaves away from here and be careful, if I let you put your hands any further in than the violets, do you hear?"—"*I* ain't goin' pull up anything you don't want me pullin' up, *no'm*. Not *this* time." She looked at the tall grass in her beds, as if it knew she could no longer bend over and reach it. What would happen to everything if she were not here to watch it, she thought, not for the first time when a child was coming. Of all the things she would leave undone, she hated leaving the garden untended—sometimes as much as leaving Bluet, or Battle.

"Now those dahlias can just come up out of there," she said, pausing again. "They have no reason for being in there at all, that I can see . . ." She wanted to separate the bulbs again too, and spread the Roman hyacinths out a little under the trees—they grew so thick now they could hardly bloom last spring. "Howard, don't you think breath-of-spring leans over too much to look pretty?"

"Yes, *ma'am.*"

"Howard, look at my roses! Oh, what all you'll have to do to them."

"I wish there wasn't no such thing as roses," said Howard. "If I had my way, wouldn't be a rose in de world. Catch your shirt and stick you and prick you and grab you. Got thorns."

"Why, Howard. You hush!" Ellen looked back over her shoulder at him for a minute, indignant. "You don't want any roses in the world?"

"Wish dey was out of de world, Miss Ellen," said Howard persistently.

"Well, just hush, then."

She cut the few flowers, Etoiles and Lady Hillingtons (to her astonishment she was trembling at Howard's absurd, meek statement, as at some impudence), and called the children to run take them in the house. Bluet and Ranny and Howard's little boy had three straws down a doodlebug hole and were all calling the doodlebug, each using a separate and ardent persuasion.

In the house she could hear India and Roxie laughing in a wild duet, Roxie turning the ice cream freezer, and at an upper window Aunt Shannon singing. Poor Lady Clare was calling that she was going to drop her comb and brush out the window if nobody came to make her look pretty and sweet. Shelley had taken Maureen and Laura with her to Greenwood for the groceries—they were out of everything. (Should she keep Laura? Billie McRaven was solid and devoted, but he had *no imagination*—should she take Laura and keep her at Shellmound?) Aunt Mac, driven by Little Uncle, had set off to Fairchilds for the payroll, as she had decided to iron it this morning—too much had happened, said Aunt Mac, and it seemed a little cool. Ellen had no idea where Roy and Little Battle had gone, racing out by themselves, she hoped and prayed they were all right and on the place. But Dabney. If only she could see Dabney, if Dabney would be home soon. Time, that she had wanted to stand still in the garden, waiting for her to catch up, if only it would fly and bring Dabney home. Memphis for three days even *sounded* like Forever.

She might go see what the men wanted for dinner. They were gone, except for poor Pinck, but she would go stand at the empty icebox and see if something would come to her. Battle, after having the bell beat on, had addressed a back yard full of Negroes that morning, all sleepy and holding their heads. "This many of you all are going over to Marmion today, right now—start in on it. Men clear off and clear out, women do sweeping—and so forth. Want you all to climb over the whole thing and see what has to be done—I imagine the roof's not worth a thing. Don't you go falling through, and skittering down the stairs, haven't got the time to fool with any broken necks, Miss Dabney wants Marmion *now*. Take your wagons, shovels, axes, everything—

now shoo. Orrin, you go stand over this. —I believe we can do it in three days," he said to Ellen.

"Three days!"

"Sure. I could get it done in one day, if I could spare that many Negroes—all but the fine touches!"

"It *is* hard on you," she had said, watching him sink groaningly into his hammock.

"The weather's liable to change any day now," he agreed, shutting his eyes. "Then the rains."

George had wanted to plunge straight into fishing again, set off for Drowning Lake down the railroad track, and wanted Robbie to go with him—the minute he was out of bed. George—men—expected a resilience in women that exasperated Ellen while she wanted to laugh. Robbie had reached up and rapped him over the head—he stood in his pyjamas in the kitchen casually taking a bacon bone from Roxie's fingers. Robbie made him take her to Greenwood after breakfast, to buy her a little dress and some kind of little hat, saying that then they might fish somewhere, if he had to fish, and it wasn't too late. He would tolerate exactly that treatment, that was what he wanted, and they went off cheerfully together, in Tempe's car.

Pinchy, passing by, looked at Ellen stupidly. When Pinchy was coming through, she had not looked at her at all, but simply turned up her face, dark-purple like a pansy, that no more saw her nor knew her than a pansy. Now, speaking primly, back in her relationship on the place, she was without any mystery to move her. She was all dressed up in her glittering white.

"Pinchy! Where are you going, Pinchy?"

"To *church*, Miss Ellen," said Pinchy, with a soft, lush smile. "*This* is *Sunday*!"

Sunday! What has come over Aunt Mac? Ellen wondered, stricken. She'll never forgive herself, when she gets to the bank. Or us! We have every one lost track of the day of the week.

Laura liked to go along for the groceries, because in the Delta all grocery keepers seemed to be Chinese gentlemen. The car moved rapidly through the white fields toward Greenwood. A buzzard hung up in the deeps of sky, as if on a planted fish pole. Not another living creature was in sight.

"Is it still Shellmound?" she asked, but nobody answered her. Shelley must be thinking. Laura looked with speculation at the pure profile, the flying hair bound at the temples. She had thought Shelley perhaps knew more than anybody in the family, until Dabney's wedding night came, and Shelley was scorned a little, out in the hall—she had heard it.

She and India had gone to bed in an opened-out cot outside their room, because Dickie Boy Featherstone and Red Boyne had been put in their bed. One of the McLeouds had the place downstairs on the settee, and she thought Uncle Pinck might have stayed where last she saw him, in the hammock out under the stars.

Shelley had come down the hall barefooted, with her hair down, in her white nightgown. "Oh, Papa," she had said, standing in the door. "How could you keep getting Mama in this predicament?"

"How's that?" Uncle Battle asked drowsily.

"You'll catch cold, Shelley, come in out of that hall draft," Aunt Ellen said.

"I said how could you keep getting Mama in this predicament—again and again?"

"A predicament?"

"Like you do."

"I told you we were going to have another little girl, or boy. It won't be till Christmas," Aunt Ellen said sleepily in the voice she used to India, and Shelley hearing it said, "I'm not India!"

"Mama, we don't *need* any more." Shelley gave a reason: "We're perfect the way we are. I couldn't love any more of us."

"I've heard that before," said Aunt Ellen. "And what would you do without Bluet now?"

"What do you mean—a predicament?" said Uncle Battle once more.

"I thought that was what people call it," Shelley faltered. "I think in Virginia—"

"Maybe they do. And maybe they're right! But it's damn well none of your concern tonight, girlie," said Uncle Battle. "Waking up the house that's just getting to sleep."

But Shelley hung there as if she had nowhere to go. Robbie and George were sleeping in her room, its door pulled to, and one of Robbie's shoes had been dropped in the hall, as though George had picked her up and carried her in barefooted. This was Dabney's wedding night and the clock was striking. "The gas machine," Shelley tried to say, through the noise. "I'm so *sorry*, Mama—"

"Get in out of the draft, Shelley," said Aunt Ellen. "Even on a still night like tonight there's always a draft in that hall. Come in or go out."

"I'm going," said Shelley.

"Skedaddle," said her father. "Come kiss me."

"Yes, sir."

"You've got a bed."

"I can see you shivering right through your nightgown—standing with your back to the moon," said Aunt Ellen reproachfully, and Shelley folded her arms across herself and ran out on tiptoe.

"I hear people!" called Bluet from the sleeping porch. "I hear fairies and elves and gnomes! I hear pretty little babies fixing to dance!"

"Lie back down, Bluet!" yelled her father from his bed. "Go back to sleep or I'm coming to break your neck!"

"Are they going to dance by the light of the moon?" Bluet softly called a very subdued question.

"Yes, they *are*," Ranny could be heard answering her in an aerial voice.

"I'm going to move to a raft on the river where I can sleep!" shouted Orrin—though it sounded a bit like Little Battle too.

Then there was only the murmur of the night, the gin. There was once the cry of a hound far off, and Laura thought, Roy heard that too, and shivered in his bed. She would tell him that there was no mention of Aunt Studney's sack, and another baby was coming; that would stop him as he flitted by.

When Shelley got the groceries from a nice Chinese man who immediately unlocked the store for her (for it was Sunday) she saw Mr. Rondo forlorn on a corner and invited him to ride back to Fairchilds; something or other had delayed him, they could not follow other people's profuse talk, and he wanted by all means to get to church. He insisted that Maureen was the very one he wanted to sit by, though she did not want him to pat her, it was plain to see. He even drove her to try to steal Laura's doll.

"Give my darling back to me!"

Laura lay back in the whizzing car, her head gently rolling against the soft seat and Shelley's arm, and brought Marmion, her stocking doll, up to her cheek. She held him there, though he was hot—hotter than she was—and smelled his face which became, quite gently, fragrant of a certain day to her; his breath was the wind and rain of her street in Jackson.

It was a day they—her mother, father, and herself—were home from the summer's trip. With the opening of the front door which swung back with an uncustomary shiver, a sudden excitement made Laura run in first, pushing ahead of her father who had turned the key. She ran pounding up the stairs, striking the carpet flowers with the flat of her hands. The house was so close, so airless, that it gave out its own breath as she stirred it to life, the scents of carpet and matting and the oily smell of the clock and the smell of the starch in the curtains. It was morning, just before a rain. Through the window on the landing, the street was in the shadow of a cloud as close as a wing, fanning their tree and rolling sycamore balls over the roof of the porch.

Her mother, delighting in the threat of storm, went about opening the windows and on the landing leaning out on her hand as though she were all alone or nothing distracted her from the world outside. Her father was at the hall clock, standing with his driving cap and his goggles still on, reaching up to wind it. "I always like to know what time it is." She listened for her mother's familiar laugh at these words, and could imagine even without looking around at her how she flickered her eyelids as she smiled, so her father would not appear too bragging of his virtues or herself too unappreciative. The loud ticks and the hours striking to catch up responded to him and rose to the upper floor, accompanying Laura as she ran from room to room, in and out, flinging up shades, passing and looking in the mirrors.

Before the storm broke, before they were barely settled or had more than their faces washed, Laura cried, "Mother, make me a doll—I want a doll!"

What made this different from any other time? Her father for some reason did not ask "Why another?" or remind her of how many dolls she had or of when she last said she was tired of dolls and never wanted to play with one again. And this time was the most inconvenient that she could have chosen. Her mother, though, simply smiled—as if she shared the same excitement. As though Laura had made a perfectly logical request, her mother said, "Would you like a stocking doll?" And she began to turn things out of her basket, a shower of all kinds of colorful things, saved as if for the sheer pleasure of looking through.

Laura gazed at her mother, who laughed as she pulled the colored bits out and flung them on the floor. She was wearing a blue dress—"too light for traveling"—her hair was flying from the wind of riding and the breath of outside, fair long hair with the bone hairpins slipping loose. She was excited, smiling, young—as the cousins were always, but as she was not always—for the air at Shellmound was pleasure and excitement, pleasure that did not need to be explained, tears that could go a nice long time unsilenced, and the air of Jackson was different.

It was like a race between the creation of the doll and

the bursting of the storm. In its summer location on the sleeping porch, the sewing machine whirred as if it spoke to the whirring outside. "Oh, Mother, hurry!"

"Just enough to stuff him!" She put every scrap in—every bright bit she had, all in one doll.

Now she was sewing on the head with her needle in her fingers. Then with the laundry ink she was drawing a face on the white stocking front. Laura leaned on her mother's long, soft knee, with her chin in her palm, entirely charmed by the drawing of the face. She could draw better than her mother could and the inferiority of the drawing, the slowly produced wildness of the unlevel eyes, the nose like a ditto mark, and the straight-line mouth with its slow, final additions of curves at the end, bringing at maddening delay a kind of smile, were like magic to watch.

Her mother was done. The first drop of rain had not fallen.

"What's his name?" Laura cried.

"Oh—he can be Marmion," said her mother casually. Had she been, after all, tired? Had she wanted to do something else, first thing on getting home—something of her own? She spoke almost grudgingly, as if everything, everything in that whole day's fund of life had gone into the making of the doll and it was too much to be asked for a name too.

Laura snatched Marmion from her mother and ran out. She did not say "Thank you." She flew down the stairs and out the front door.

The stormy air was dark and fresh, like a mint leaf. It smelled of coming rain and leaves sailed in companies through the middle air. Jackson to come back to was filled with a pulse of storm and she stood still and felt it, the forgotten heartbeat, for of course it had not rained on them visiting. The ground shook to some thunder not too far to hear, or of which only one note could be heard, like the stroke of a drum as far as Smith Park on band-concert nights. She ran to the corner, which was down a hill, down a brick sidewalk, and at the corner house she called Lucy Bell O'Malley. Sometimes it is needful to show our dearest possessions to a comparative stranger. Lucy Bell was not a very good friend of Laura's, being too little. Last Christmas Laura had been taken calling on Lucy Bell by a neighbor in order that she might see something Santa Claus had brought her—a Teddy bear with electric eyes. The O'Malley parlor had had curtains and shades drawn—it was still and dark, almost as if a member of the family had died. And on the library table glittered, on and off, two emerald-green eyes. The Teddy bear lay there, on his back. But he could never be taken up from the library table and loved, for out of his stomach a cord attached him to the lamp, and Lucy Bell could only stand by and touch him. His eyes were as hot as fire.

"Lucy Bell! Look at my doll! We just came back from a car trip!" (Why, they had been to the Delta—been here! To Shellmound. And come home from it—it was under its momentum that her mother had been so quick and gay.) "His name is Marmion!"

She did not remember a thing Lucy Bell said to that. But as she cried it all out to her she knew that the reason she felt so superior was that she had gotten Marmion the minute she wished for him—it wasn't either too soon for her wish or too late. She had not even known, herself, that she wanted Marmion before that moment when she had implored her mother, "Make me a doll!"

She turned around and ran back in the winglike dark, holding Marmion high, so that Lucy Bell's eyes could follow. She got home and watched it storm, she and her mother standing quietly at the windows.

Now she held Marmion close, looking out across his crooked flat eye at the flying cotton, the same white after white, the fire-bright morning. She could kiss his fragrant face and know, Never more would she have this, the instant answer to a wish, for her mother was dead.

"Ah," said Mr. Rondo from the back seat. "The Yellow Dog!" as if he knew that subject interested the Fairchilds.

The track ran beside them on its levee through the fields and swamps, with now and then some little road, like the Shellmound road, climbing over the track to go off into the deep of the other side. Laura and Maureen waved at the Dog as it came down going back to Yazoo City. The engineer looked out of his window. "Mr. Doolittle," said Mr. Rondo.

"Mit-la Doo-littla can-na get-la by!" called Maureen.

Laura looked up at Shelley, her head with the band around it, as if she thought so much that she had to tie her brain in, like Faithful John and his heart and the iron band. It was good that Shelley had not that kind of heart too.

At that moment, with no warning, Shelley took one of the little crossing roads and drove the car up over the track, in front of the Yellow Dog, and down the other side.

"If you tell what I did, Laura," Shelley said calmly, after she let out her breath, "I'll cut you to pieces and hang you up for the buzzards. Are you going to tell?"

"No," said Laura, before she was through. Shelley's desperate qualities, out of the whole family, were those in which she unreservedly believed.

"I hope you won't speak of this, Mr. Rondo."

"Oh, no, no . . . !"

"Or Papa'd break my bones," Shelley said deprecatingly.

With her chin high, she drove along this side of the tracks where no road followed, taking the ruts, while the wildflowers knocked up at the under side of the car. It had struck her all at once as so fine to drive without pondering a moment onto disaster's edge—she would not always jump away! Now she was wrathful with herself, she despised what she had done, as if she had caught herself *contriving*. She flung up her head and looked for the Dog.

"Run home, Miss Shelley Fairchild!" called Old Man Doolittle.

Oh, horrors, he had stopped the Dog again! There it waited on the track, before the crossing, as if politely! How patronizing—coming to a stop for them a second time. Who on earth did Old Man Doolittle think he was, that he could even speak to a Fairchild out of that little window! The Yellow Dog started up again and came on by, inching by, its engine, with Mr. Doolittle *saluting*, and four cars, freight, white, colored, and caboose, its smoke like a poodle tail curled overhead, an inexcusable sight.

"Damn the Yellow Dog!" cried Shelley. "Excuse me, Mr. Rondo."

"Quite understand," said that foolish little man; even Laura knew he would have been the last person knowingly to let prudence, and respect for the spoiled young ladies of Shellmound, be damned, and on a Sunday morning.

They rode, one way or another, into Fairchilds. "Is that Aunt Virgie Lee?" cried Laura.

Shelley slowed the car down and spoke to Virgie Lee. Usually she would have tried to pass without seeming to notice—the wild way Virgie Lee looked in the face, her cheeks painted red as if she were going to meet somebody, and in the back, with her hair tied up in a common rope.

Virgie Lee Fairchild, shaking her hair, going along in the ripply shade under the corrugated iron awning over the walk, rustled a green switch in their faces. As a matter of fact, she was going toward the church, fighting off the dogs—the Baptist Church.

"Go away! Go away! Don't tamper with me! Go home to your weddings and palaver," she said throatily. In her other hand she carried a purse by its strap (the way no lady would), a battered contraption like a shrunken-up suitcase. She might never end up in church, at all. When she swung the purse and danced the leafy branch, her long hair seemed to move all over in itself, like a waterfall.

Maureen leaned out over the side of the car and laughed aloud at her mother.

The sight and sound of that so terrified Laura that she flung herself over the back of the seat and threw her arms around Maureen as if to pull her back from fire, and held her, calling her as if she were deaf, "Maureen, Maureen!"

Virgie Lee, who had never stopped for them, emerged in the naked sun of the road and went on, her black hair seeming if possible to spread in the morning light, growing under eyes that hardly believed it, like a stain.

"You see! She'll have none of us!" said Shelley, in her light voice that had the catch in it.

Mr. Rondo, probably remembering he had already been asked not to mention one thing, looked polite, taking the shortest glance at Virgie Lee. If he seemed to recognize her at all, it was as a Baptist. Shelley whirled off up the street and across the bridge, and they put Mr. Rondo down at the Methodist stile, where he thanked them and took out his watch, which, Laura told Shelley, seemed to have stopped.

"Poor Ellen," said Tempe, clasping her softly, her delicate, fragrant face large and serious as it pressed Ellen's close. "This has nearly killed you. I know! But, child, it's what mothers are for." They embraced in the kitchen, with Ranny pulling his mother's skirt—only a baby still.

"Tempe, I couldn't have done it without you." It was true, and she held Tempe the longer for being tired, from everything, from waiting—from mentally taking out shrubbery, from trying to make Howard love roses, from trying to make Bluet not want chicken pox or anything else because Lady Clare had it, from letting Aunt Mac get clear to the bank on a Sunday morning . . . Look at me, am I sorry for myself? she thought, shaken, seeing a mist in Tempe's eye.

Aunt Mac as a matter of fact had long since returned from her trip, without announcing whether it was successful or not. She came sitting as straight as she sat going out, in the pony cart under its wide flounced umbrella, and alighted at the carriage block without the slightest remark or notice of the world. She made her way into the house, Roy running up from somewhere like a flash, with a cut on his foot bleeding (he was the most *courteous* of her boys!), and escorting her, holding her elbow on the flat of his hand like a fine tray. No word would ever be said to *her* about money! Sunday money or any other kind.

Battle woke up and called for her, Jim Allen and Primrose were driven home, and the boys left over from the dance last night ate breakfast and departed, Red Boyne leaving Shelley a wild note which India read out loud. George and Robbie—who had gone off hours ago to buy a little dress and hat—came back in two cars, with the joke between them that it was Sunday. "We bought a car, though!" said Robbie. "The man opened up everything for George, and sold him a Hudson Super-Six." Shelley and the children came in starved from Greenwood, but bringing groceries from some charitable man, thank goodness.

Then Ellen was saying, catching the little girl in the hall, "Laura, there's something to tell you. We want you to stay, to live with us at Shellmound. Until you go to Marmion, perhaps. . . . Would you be happy? Your papa would listen to reason, he hopes you'd be happy too. India would be glad . . . Something's got all the curl out of your poor hair!"

The visit, the round-trip ticket on the Dog, had been just a premonition—now they told her what would really be. Shellmound! The real thing might always dawn upon her slowly, Laura felt, hanging her head while Aunt Ellen sadly stretched a straight strand of her hair out on her finger. That feeling that came over her—it was of having been cheated a little, not told at once. And so she answered overly soon, overly brightly, "Oh, I want to! I want to stay!" Then she cried, "But I don't want to go to Marmion!"

"Marmion'll be yours, you know, when you want it. I reckon! Someday you'll live there like your Aunt Ellen here, with all your chillen," said Uncle Battle, looking around Aunt Ellen and stepping out from behind her.

"I will?" said Laura. "It's big—isn't it?"

"Now, Battle, that's all too complicated to think of now, here in the hall," said Aunt Tempe, passing by. "You let Dabney have Marmion now, she wants it!"

"Besides—do you ever trust Virgie Lee not to flare up?" Aunt Ellen seemed to brood for a moment, her fingers went still in Laura's hair. "She'll have none of us now, but . . ."

"Did you have a dream about Virgie Lee?" Uncle Battle laughed.

Laura felt that in the end she would go—go from all this, go back to her father. She would hold that secret, and kiss Uncle Battle now.

Uncle Battle laughed and gave her a little dressing on her skirt. "Big? You'll grow, Skeeta," he said. "But no need to hurry."

And there was Aunt Shannon.

"Aunt Shannon," said Battle gruffly, sent in. His softened voice was always hoarse; India listened, as she passed with her doll. "There's a plenty of everything. There's a plenty all around you. All in the world to eat, no need at all hiding bread crusts in your room. And nobody is dreaming they could get you or harm you. I'm here. See me?"

She nodded her head, gently and then sharply, and regarded him; India leaned in the door. "My little old boy," she said, and patted him. "Oh, you have a great deal to learn. Oh, Denis, I wish you wouldn't go out in the world unshielded and unprotected as you are. I have a feeling, I have a feeling, something will happen to you. . . ."

"If it isn't the Reconstruction, it's things just as full of trouble to you, isn't it?" Battle said softly, letting her pat her little hand on his great weight, holding still. He changed the level of his voice. "I'll stay, Aunt Shannon. I'll stay. I'm here. Here I am."

"Good-bye, my darling," she said.

II

It was the first night Dabney and Troy were back, and George's and Robbie's last night at the place. They would have a little family picnic.

"I don't see a bit of use trying to sit down to a big supper tonight, after all we've been eating, wedding food, company food . . . We'll just have a little picnic," said Ellen at the dinner table.

"Come to the Grove!" cried Primrose. The aunts were on hand at Shellmound for the welcomes and good-byes, of course.

"Marmion!" said Battle. "By God, it's not too hot for a barbecue. Not if we keep good and away from the fire."

"Troy loves barbecue," said Dabney gravely. It was Tuesday. They had just been away three days, on account of the picking.

But it was too hot for a barbecue, as could be seen by four o'clock, and they took a cold supper.

"Let's try out your new car, Dabney," said Orrin. "See how it takes the ruts. I'll drive."

"Oh, you will? Child, no. Robbie, you have a new car too." She turned an earnest look on Robbie.

"We just got it in Greenwood, on Sunday," smiled Robbie.

But they went in buggies and wagons when the time came, prevailed on for the sake of the tangles and brambles across the river.

"You know, old Rondo's quite a fellow," said Battle. "Let's invite him on the picnic!"

"No, then we'd have to go to church some Sunday," Ellen pointed out. She said she had better stay home and keep Aunt Mac and Aunt Shannon company, and poor Lady Clare, who would know something was going on, but Battle and George would not hear to that. Ranny and Bluet went nicely to sleep at dark (Bluet still wearing her wedding shoes in bed part of the night) never knowing about any of it, though Lady Clare tore some of her red hair as she watched them go, pulled it out by the roots to see a picnic start off without her, and screamed that she would tell her papa.

It was a starry night—truly a little cool; that was hard to believe! Laura and India, in the back of the buggy with the food, rode at the head, Little Uncle, invisible, driving. A little black horse mule was pulling them. They dangled their feet over the track, looking at the rest of the procession. With them rode a freezer of ice cream, the huddled napkins of chicken, turkey, and sandwiches, the covered plates with surprises, the boxes with the caramel and the coconut cakes and Aunt Tempe's lemon chiffon pie. The jug of iced tea was somewhere—they could hear it shake and splash.

It was a beautiful night. "Still powder-dry!" called Battle, out into it. "How much longer?" They were taking the plantation road into Fairchilds, to cross the river and follow the old track to Marmion. Cotton was everywhere, as far as the sky—the soft and level fields. Here and there little cabins nestled, far away, and dark as hen roosts. In some of the wagons they were singing "Some Sweet Day." Laura was sleepy, very sleepy. By night the Delta looked just like a big bed, the whiteness in the luminous dark. It was like the clouds that spread around the east for the moon, that the horses walked through and the buggies rolled over.

"The bayou ghost didn't cry once at Dabney's wedding," said Shelley's voice as they went by trees. "Did you notice her not crying, anybody?"

"If she held back, us Fairchilds consider that as lucky as you'd want." That was George.

"Listen—is that the crying now?"

But it was some night bird.

Dabney kept telling of how they went to New Orleans, not Memphis, and fooled everybody.

"We watched the river . . . the sea gulls . . ."

"It's the same river, Memphis and New Orleans," said Laura, opening her eyes and speaking from the back of their leading buggy. "My papa has taken me on trips—I know about geography . . ." But in the great confines of Shellmound, no one listened.

The night insects all over the Delta were noisy; a kind of audible twinkling, like a lowly starlight, pervaded the night with a gregarious radiance.

Ellen at Battle's side rode looking ahead, they were comfortable and silent, both, with their great weight, breathing a little heavily in a rhythm that brought them sometimes together. The repeating fields, the repeating cycles of season and her own life—there was something in the monotony itself that was beautiful, rewarding—perhaps to what was womanly within her. No, she had never had time—much time at all, to contemplate . . . but she knew. Well, one moment told you the great things, one moment was enough for you to know the greatest thing.

They rolled on and on. It was endless. The wheels rolled, but nothing changed. Only the heartbeat played its little drum, skipped a beat, played again.

"Is all of this Shellmound?" called little Laura McRaven.

"Remains to be seen!" called Battle gaily back.

From the last wagon came a chorus that started at Dabney's high pitch and changed in the middle—

"Ye flowery banks o' bonnie Doon,
How can ye bloom sae fair!"

They were crossing the river, rolling across the bridge, which groaned only lightly under their buggy wheels and the hoofs of the little horse mule.

"Wi' lightsome heart I pu'd a rose
Upon a morn in June,
And sae I flourished on the morn,
And sae was pu'd or' noon."

They went through the tangles and brambles, singing, and India took Laura around the waist, they held each other in.

"My secret is," India said in her ear, "I'm going to

have another little brother before very long, and his name shall be Denis Fairchild."

Another wagon began its soft singing.

"Oh, you'll take the high road and I'll take the low road,
And I'll be in Scotland afore ye."

"My secret is," Laura murmured, "I've been in Marmion afore ye. I've seen it all afore. It's all happened afore." They leaned their heads together.

"But me and my true love will never meet again . . ."

They're singing to Uncle George that his wife has left him, Laura thought sleepily but open-eyed. And to Dabney that she and Troy will never meet again. It was a picnic night. All secrets were being canceled out, sung out.

Uncle George's wagon came in view. Robbie and Maureen and George made a jolted but steady triangle, with little black boys hanging on and spilling off and catching up behind. And George was left still the adored one for the picnic, loved by the whole long procession with a love going further than the love for Dabney though she was the girl and the bride. The picnic was to tell Dabney hello but George good-bye. She gazed back at him, a figure in white clothes, face and throat dark by the starlight and in the brambly road—looking up at that moment, as if something wonderful might happen to him tonight, where he was going in the wagon. Maureen, now in all contrariness tame as a pigeon, squatted at his knee. She was *mostly* gentle,

Laura dreamily realized. It was only now and then that she showed what she could do, just like most people. And Uncle George was singing—not "Loch Lomond," or "Some Sweet Day," but something . . . He was not really singing any song that she knew. It was something different and playful. He could not carry the tune—or he was improvising. It was that. She listened to it.

That picnic night she felt part of her cousins' life—part of it all. She was familiar at last with that wonderful, special anticipation that belonged to the Fairchilds, only to the Fairchilds in the whole world. A kind of wild, cousinly happiness surged through her and went out again, leaving her on India's shoulder.

She heard Uncle George's soft tune climb and fall, learned it—and then he changed to a whistle, just like a bird.

Marmion's grove rose up ahead, but Laura was asleep.

They had eaten everything they could, everything there was, and lay back groaning on the plaids and rugs. Battle had indeed cleared all the brambles away, it was a picnic place now by the riverside. There was a smell of cut green wood. And a smell of smoke—Howard was wafting it gently over them from a distant fire, aided by six or eight. George lighted his pipe to drive away the mosquitoes Tempe could tell were still after her. The dogs had the bones, those good for them and not, and worked contentedly by the water, now and then lifting up, listening . . . Overhead, showing it was the first cool night on the Delta, the Milky Way came out and wound like a bright river among the stars.

Troy handed a muscadine to his wife, like a present,

and she gave him a weak tap and lay still with it in her teeth. Troy wore a new seersucker suit whose stripes in the house had seemed vibrant as if lightning were playing around him, but out here he looked like any other man in an old costume. Somebody sighed deeply. Once somebody said, "Too bad Pinck had to go to Memphis *today*." Little Battle was asleep, his cheek on his fist. Roy sat wordless, his gaze passing with the pure contact of starlight over all around. Orrin wandered off, first one way, then another, whistling like a whippoorwill.

"Did you all know Rowena wanted to be buried over here?" Jim Allen said once, out into the night. "Well, she did. But she wasn't."

"Wake up, Laura!"

"Oh, let her sleep."

"George," said Battle from where he lay on Ellen's blanket, "did I ever hear you say what you'd do if you came back and took possession of the Grove again?"

"Sure—I'd change things."

The silence drifted.

"Why, George," Tempe remarked, she alone sitting erect, and wielding her own little fan, "that's where Primmy and Jim Allen Fairchild are counting on living. If you came back, would you run your sisters away?"

There were little sounds never far away—the river and the woods. Their picnic had scared up the peafowls and peacocks, very fierce, long since gone to the wild, and now and then they ran in the viny ways to the river. The tower of Marmion was there over the trees.

"Let's go in," said Shelley, rising up. "Who wants to go in Marmion?"

"Nobody!" said Battle. "You can't go in, I've had that door locked for just such as you."

"Oh, if I took over, they could stay with us as long as they enjoy it," George said. "Or I could build them their own house near by. Or they could move in Shellmound—Dabney'll be here, and Orrin soon off to school—old Shelley'll not be long with us, I imagine," and he gave her ribbon a touch and it came off.

"I think you'd be *right* to, George," said Primrose, trying to make her voice carry. "And it's been such a responsibility!"

"Further than cotton, I might try fruit trees, might try some horses, even cattle," said George, smiling in the starlight.

"You're crazy, man," Battle roared delightedly.

"Who knows, I might try a garden. Vegetables!"

"Vegetables!" They all cried out together. "What would the Delta think?" Tempe demanded.

"And melons where all that sand was deposited on the bottom there."

"Is it what Robbie wants?" asked Shelley.

"Robbie wouldn't want it at all, I'm afraid," George said. "Robbie's our city girl born."

"I'd probably hate it," said Robbie dreamily. She laughed softly where she lay on her back beside him, looking up at the sky. The lady moon, with a side of her hair gone, was rising.

"George," said Primrose, her voice shaking a little. "I forgot to tell you until now—there are rats at the Grove."

George laughed out. "Afraid to tell me!" He got up from Robbie's side and walked over to where Primrose sat on her little stool to keep "the damp" from her. "Primmy. Yes, I know, it has rats, and a lot of things—a ghost to keep you awake, and also it's the place Denis was going to come back to and enjoy a long, voracious old age and raise a houseful of healthy offspring. Now what if I want in, and others out, even you, Primmy?" He spoke softly.

"Georgie!"

"George said, What if he took the Grove?" Tempe called to Jim Allen.

The Grove? Robbie was thinking. Well, for her, it would be that once more they would laugh and chase by the river. Once more she and Mary Shannon, well-known as that star Venus, would be looking at each other in that house. Things almost never happened, almost never could be, for one time only! They went back again . . . started over . . .

"Robbie," said India. "Are you going to have a baby?"

"India!" said Ellen, shocked. "What do you know about babies?"

"I won't tell you," said Robbie in a clear voice, still lying on her back, one arm flung out, looking up at the sky.

Battle laughed uproariously.

"Excuse my back, please, ma'am," said Troy to Tempe. He pivoted around and kissed Dabney. "Do we have to kiss in front of your whole family from now on, Dabney, now that we're married?" He set her up straight again like something he had knocked over and was putting back so no one would tell the difference.

"Yes!" She looked on him beaming, maternally—to tease him.

How quickly she had known she loved Troy! Only she had not known how she could reach the love she felt already in her knowledge. In catching sight of love she had seen both banks of a river and the river rushing between—she saw everything but the way down. Even now, lying in Troy's bared arm like a drowned girl, she was timid of the element itself. Troy set her up again, and she smiled, looking at him all over and around him, up at the two rising horns of his parted hair. They had fooled everybody successfully about their honeymoon, because instead of going to the Peabody in Memphis they had gone to the St. Charles in New Orleans. Walking through the two afternoons down streets narrow as hallways, they had had to press back against the curb, against uncertain dark-green doors, to let the streetcars get through. The streetcars made an extraordinary clangor at such close quarters, as they did in the quiet of night, and some of them had "Desire" across the top. Could that have been the name of a street? She had not asked then; she did not much wonder now.

"Old Georgie. If you took possession of the Grove, you'd change it, eh?" said Battle. Ellen was leaning against him, she rubbed his arm tenderly. "Well—Shellmound's open, Prim, bear it in mind."

"Uncle Denis would never do this," said India dramatically.

"India," said Ellen, "you don't even remember your Uncle Denis, and why are you so wide awake? Laura's asleep."

"No, I'm not!"

"Well, Denis wouldn't," said Tempe. "Selfish, selfish! Spoiling the picnic. I don't understand George, he was always supposed to be so unselfish, unspoiled, never do anything but kind things. Now listen, he's as spoiled as any of us!"

"Oh, foot, Tempe," said Primrose. "Can't you listen

to man talk without getting upset? Can't you listen to George and Battle talking?"

"What would Jim Allen think?" Battle said, yawning.

"She hates rats." Primrose laughed breathlessly. "We're two old maids, all right!"

"Well, *take* it then!" said Jim Allen all at once.

Ellen sighed. Poor deaf sister, she could not listen to herself, hear how grudging she sounded.

"I'd let George build Jim Allen and me a little house quick as anything," said Primrose. "And furniture, there's enough beds and all in the attic for a world of houses here."

"Your night light will be gone," said India. "Dabney broke it for good, carrying it away."

There was another silence, but gentler, more restful.

"Come back, George," said Robbie.

"Bless your hearts, Primrose," said George. He kissed her and Jim Allen.

"It's got *rats*!" said Jim Allen, and she sank back, restfully, as if there were comforts, after all, in a little spitefulness.

"But I don't understand George at all," Tempe began again, as if George himself were not there, and he kissed her too. "You just want to provoke your sisters, you're just teasing."

"It's his house," said Ellen. (Had she started interfering with the Fairchilds again—this far along? She sounded to herself for a moment like herself as a bride.)

"But I didn't dream he wanted it," Battle said. " 'Here, take the Grove,' he said to the girls, when they wanted to fool with a house. Did that sound like he wanted it?"

"Why not?" said Primrose proudly. "Anyway—he only said tonight 'If—then maybe.' "

"Oh, my." Dabney yawned in luxury. "I'm glad he doesn't want to take Marmion away from me."

"Shame on you, pussy," said Troy sharply, and she was quiet.

"Watermelons and greens!" Tempe still fumed softly. "Sisters out in the cold. George, sometimes I don't think you show the most perfect judgment." Then they both laughed gently at each other.

> *"Oft in the stilly night,*
> *Ere Slumber's chain has bound me . . ."*

They began to sing, softly, wanderingly, each his way. But Jim Allen, whose voice rose strongest, stretched tilted on her small plump elbow on the grassy blanket, was looking at Robbie Reid as if she were for the first time quite aware that her brother was married—not hopelessly, like the dead Denis, but problematically, not promisingly!

> *"Oft in the stilly night—"*

"I like your idea, George," Troy said with deliberation through the song. "Growing greens and getting some cows around. I love a little Jersey, more than anything."

George, with his left-handed throw, put pebbles in the Yazoo. "We'll keep in touch. . . ."

One great golden star went through the night falling.

"Oh!" cried Laura aloud. "Oh, it was beautiful, that star!"

"I saw it, I saw it!" cried India.

Dabney reached over and put her arm around her, drew her to her. "Yes. Beautiful!" India smiled faintly, leaning on Dabney's beating heart, the softness of her breast.

Then, "Oh, India, you still look so tacky!" cried Dabney breathlessly. "I thought you'd be changed, some! Oh, *Mama*, look at her!"

"Stand still, India," said Ellen.

But India darted off and ran to look in the river. She stood showily, hands on hips, as if she saw some certain thing, neither marvelous nor terrible, but simply certain, come by in the Yazoo River.

Laura lifted on her knees and took her Aunt Ellen around the neck. She held her till they swayed together. Would Aunt Ellen remember it against her, that she had run away from her when she fainted? Of course Aunt Ellen would never find out about the rosy pin. Should she tell her, and suffer? Yes. No. She touched Aunt Ellen's cheek with three anxious, repaying kisses.

"Oh, beautiful!" Another star fell in the sky.

Laura let go and ran forward a step. "I saw that one too."

"Did you?" said somebody—Uncle George.

"I saw where it fell," said Laura, bragging and in reassurance.

She turned again to them, both arms held out to the radiant night.

Books by Eudora Welty
available in Harvest paperback editions
from Harcourt Brace & Company

The Bride of the Innisfallen and Other Stories
The Collected Stories of Eudora Welty
A Curtain of Green and Other Stories
Delta Wedding
The Golden Apples
The Ponder Heart
The Robber Bridegroom
Thirteen Stories
The Wide Net and Other Stories